Dog Walker Mystery Series

Begging for Trouble

"McCoy is as adept at creating colorful, compelling characters, two-legged and four-legged, and writing sharply humorous prose as she is at crafting a cleverly constructed plot."
—*Booklist*

"Charming and funny."
—*New York Times* bestselling author MaryJanice Davidson

Death in Show

"Author Judi McCoy has once again gone to the dogs, in a very good way! Not only does she present an intriguing mystery with lots of action and a healthy dose of romance; McCoy also gives a very accurate and realistic accounting of the competitive world of dog shows. Dog fanciers and mystery lovers will adore this new addition to McCoy's canine tales."
—Fresh Fiction

"A hilarious, fun-filled story full of eclectic characters and bits of romance.... This venue will keep you in stitches as you can picture in your head the different voices dogs would use to communicate.... If you are a pet lover, this is a must read."
—The Romance Readers Connection

"McCoy deserves a blue ribbon herself for coming up with such an entertaining paranormal-spiced mystery and then perfectly seasoning the plot with just the right dash of romance."
—*Booklist*

continued...

"There is nobody quite like professional dog walker Ellie Engleman as she talks to her canines and hears what her four-legged friends have to say. . . . Readers will enjoy the latest escapades of the heroine . . . while her dog, Rudy, and her canine clients add amusing antics to the mix."
—Midwest Book Review

"Ellie is wonderful [and] insightful, and her special way of communicating with her charges makes the reader laugh out loud."
—Romantic Times

Heir of the Dog

"What a clever, clever series. Rudy is a small dog with a big attitude. . . . Judi McCoy has done an excellent job with her narrative and the story threads, sewing everything together nicely."
—Fresh Fiction

"The second book in former romance writer McCoy's captivating mystery series is a wickedly entertaining mix of terrific characters, an intriguing plot, sexy romance, and a touch of the paranormal."
—Booklist

"Humorous and suspenseful . . . a lighthearted yet intriguing cozy mystery."
—Romance Junkies

"McCoy brings back professional dog walker Ellie Engleman and her reincarnated pooch with a witty and fast-paced mystery set on New York's fashionable East Side. McCoy has a simmering plan of vengeance, peppered with humor, that readers will love."
—Romantic Times

Hounding the Pavement

"McCoy fills this delightful story with humor, quirky characters, and delicious hints of romance."

—*Publishers Weekly* (starred review)

"The crisp writing, humorous dialogue, and delightful characters, both human and canine, all make this book a winner."

—*Romantic Times*

"Judi McCoy writes with heart and humor. Anyone who loves dogs or books will have a howling good time."

—Lois Greiman

"A delightful dog's-eye-view romp through the streets of New York. If you've ever talked to your dog and wished that he would answer back, this is the book for you. Four paws up!"

—Laurien Berenson, author of
Doggie Day Care Murder

"Engaging characters and a cute premise kick off this delightful series. This canine caper will have you begging for more!"

—Nancy J. Cohen, author of the
Bad Hair Day mystery series

"*Hounding the Pavement*, the first book in the Dog Walker Mystery series, is a treat for everyone, whether a dog lover or not. . . . Ms. McCoy has written a cozy mystery sure to please."

—Fresh Fiction

Also in the
Dog Walker Mystery Series

Begging for Trouble
Death in Show
Heir of the Dog
Hounding the Pavement

Till Death Do Us Bark

A DOG WALKER MYSTERY

JUDI MCCOY

OBSIDIAN
Published by the Penguin Group
Penguin Group (USA) Inc., 375 Hudson Street,
New York, New York 10014, USA

USA | Canada | UK | Ireland | Australia | New Zealand | India | South Africa | China

Penguin Books Ltd., Registered Offices: 80 Strand, London WC2R 0RL, England
For more information about the Penguin Group visit penguin.com.

First published by Obsidian, an imprint of New American Library,
a division of Penguin Group (USA) Inc.

First Printing, August 2011
First Printing (Read Humane Edition), May 2013

READ HUMANE EDITION ISBN 978-0-451-24024-8

Printed in the United States of America
10 9 8 7 6 5 4 3 2 1

This book is dedicated to Barbara Noyes, a brave and brilliant woman and an exceptional writer. Thank you, Barb, for all the "Spanglish" translations, especially because you made certain the Mexican influence was correct. You are my rock.

To the real Arlene Millman, who earned the first character part in one of my books because she showed proof of her sizable donation to Best Friends. She also contributed Ellie's astrological chart, which I edited slightly for the epilogue of this story. Arlene doesn't own an African gray, but she does have three adorable Boston Terriers named Corey, Isabelle, and Darby-Doll.

To Best Friends, the largest no-kill shelter in the U.S. The work they do to save God's creatures is mind-boggling. If you haven't yet seen *Dogtown*, their show on the National Geographic Channel, find it and watch it. You will be amazed.

Chapter 1

"The man in the next lane just flipped you off." Ellie clenched the car's safety strap in her right hand and clutched the seat belt in her left. "I think you're crowding him."

It was the middle of July, and she and her best friend, Vivian, were on their way to Viv's sister's wedding in the Hamptons. They'd spent the morning at an upscale car rental company, where Viv had demanded a vehicle that screamed "expensive, fast, and flashy," whether or not she knew how to drive it.

"Yeah, well, he can chill. I'm doing the best I can." It was the same response she'd given after Ellie's last three warnings, and though she'd spent the past half hour trying to tame the six-speed BMW M6, Viv's driving skills hadn't improved one iota.

"I still say we should have rented our transportation through Zipcar. Their cars are small and they get good gas mileage. We could have gotten a decent sedan for a tenth of what you're paying for this behemoth."

"Are you crazy?" Viv hit the horn and veered around a stopped bus. "I'd be humiliated if I showed up at my sister's house in the Hamptons and my family saw me with one of those dinky budget rentals."

"We could have taken a helicopter or limo. Navigating this hellacious traffic is like trying to wade through quicksand," Ellie told her as they jerked up to a traffic light.

Since Viv had gotten them out of the parking garage of Royal Luxury Automobile Rentals and onto Fortieth, going east, the bright red BMW had crawled along like a turtle with the hiccups, crowding the far right lane and terrorizing automobiles and pedestrians alike.

"A helicopter is just too Billy Joel," Viv answered, peering over the dashboard. "And taking a limo means we'd be at the mercy of the Hamptons' Jitney."

"Couldn't we borrow one of your sister's cars? An automatic, maybe?"

"I want the McCreadys to know I have a successful career, and this baby is the way to show them." She shifted into first, ground into second, and followed the signs for the Queens Midtown Tunnel. "Besides, I took all the insurance coverage the company offered. We won't be liable for a penny if we have an accident . . . or something."

"But you've never driven a manual transmission before, let alone a six-speed," Ellie said for the tenth time that morning. "Please be more careful."

Viv's driving expertise seemed to dry up once she jammed the car into third gear. After that, she'd screech to a stop and slam on the brakes and the clutch to avoid the ass end of a bus. Then she'd start all over again, grinding from first to second to third, braking to a stop, and receiving dirty looks from everyone on the street.

And forget about double-parked delivery vans or the valiant bicycle messengers. The side-view mirror on Ellie's door had already whacked the mirror on a stretch limo and a cab, and they'd gotten so close to a bike rider, Ellie swore she'd seen his molars when he yelled out a threat.

"Watch out! That taxi's stopping for a pickup," she shouted, her voice hoarse from the warnings. If only Viv had taken her suggestion and rented a small and sensible automatic, they might actually arrive in the Hamptons in one piece. "And please depress the clutch *before* you hit the brake."

"Leave my girl alone and let her do her thing," warned Mr. T from the backseat. *"She just needs a little practice."*

Vivian needs a "little" lobotomy, thought Ellie, holding her tongue. Their dogs, as well as all the canines belonging to the guests invited to the wedding, had been encouraged to attend. And since her boyfriend, Dr. Dave, had to speak at a conference in San Diego, Viv had named Ellie her "plus one" and given her the opportunity to take her first real vacation in ten years.

"Okay. There's the sign pointing to the tunnel entrance. Just a few more blocks," Viv announced, shifting the BMW into jackrabbit mode. "The rental agent said this car was forgiving." She hit the gas and eased ahead. "I guess we're putting it to the test."

Ellie had paid close attention to the five-minute clutch-shift-accelerate lesson they'd been given in the parking garage, but the high-powered BMW still scared the pants off her. She silently thanked the powers-that-be that they were almost out of Manhattan, where it was a direct shot to the farthest eastern city on Long Island.

After that, the drive would be a piece of cake.

"How about a quick stop on a nice grassy patch of lawn, Triple E?" asked Rudy from the backseat.

"Yeah. My back teeth are floatin'," Mr. T joined in.

"I think we should take a break once we get to a rest stop," said Ellie. They were due in Montauk for a six p.m. prewedding dinner celebration, and it was just after noon. "The boys probably need an out, and I'm starving."

"Fine. We forgot water, so we can pick up a couple of bottles," was Viv's answer. "We should be through the worst of this traffic soon."

Ellie blew out a breath as they drove into the tunnel and followed the lead car at a respectful distance. She didn't mean to rain on her friend's parade. Viv had received a promotion and a healthy raise a few months back, and she was determined to impress her difficult family. According to Viv, her parents, especially her father, were snobs, and her middle sister was a spoiled brat. If that wasn't enough, she claimed the bride, the oldest of the three sisters, was an astrologer and a bit on the oddball side, sort of a younger version of Shirley MacLaine.

Viv had no idea how many guests were scheduled to attend the event, but she'd assured Ellie it would be, if not a blast, a very interesting week.

Several hours later, Ellie was still enthralled with the scenery as they traveled Route 27 east to Montauk. The traffic had been worse than Manhattan at rush hour, so they'd stopped in a half dozen small towns for short breaks. Each city had a water view and quaint shops and eateries, as well as a soupçon more of an elitist attitude than she found on the Upper East Side.

Now, on the final leg of their journey, they veered onto Old Montauk Highway and began reading house numbers, but she found it difficult to stay focused on mailboxes when the homes, more like mini-mansions, took her breath away.

When Viv downshifted and turned into a secluded driveway, Ellie gasped as she gazed at the enormous two-story weathered cedar-shingle building that sat on at least two acres of rolling lawn. Besides the circular drive holding two hardtop Mercedeses, a Mercedes convertible, a Jaguar, and a Rolls-Royce, there was still a four-car attached garage on the right and a two-story wing on the left. Beyond the house, and closer to the ocean, looked to be the charming double-decker guest cottage Viv had mentioned, with its own parking area filled with more cars.

"Wow," Ellie muttered as they jerked to a stop. "This is some summer house."

"It is when you compare it to the house next door. That one belonged to Bernie Madoff until it was seized by the government to help reimburse his bamboozled customers. My sister's house is comfortable inside, and a tiny bit offbeat, just like Arlene. It was already spectacular when she moved here with Myron, but she added a few touches to make it her own. Myron was a nice old guy, a lot like Judge Stanley, only way more wealthy."

Ellie swallowed hard. More wealthy than her stepfather? It boggled the mind. "How many times did you meet Myron?"

"Two, maybe three times. The last was about five

years ago, when Mom and Dad held a New Year's party, and his funeral, of course." She gave a huge sigh. "God, I'm glad we're here. I'll need a day to recuperate before I get behind the wheel again."

"Me, too," Rudy yipped from the backseat. *"Can we take a helicopter home?"*

"That goes ditto for me," said Mr. T. *"I love Vivie, but I've changed my opinion of her drivin'. I'd rather be a thousand feet in the air with a pilot than in anything she's steering."*

Ellie knew how the boys felt. Happy to be back on solid ground, she climbed out of the car and opened the back door to retrieve the dogs.

"Oh, Vivian! I can't believe you're here."

She turned at the sound of a cheerful voice and saw a short woman with a sleek black bob running down the front porch steps. Arlene wore a huge grin as she raced to the car on stilettoed sandals, her bright red halter dress flying in the breeze.

"Vivie! It's been too long," Arlene cried, hugging her baby sister. After a set of air kisses, she gave Viv another hug. "I'm thrilled you're here for the celebration." Spinning in place, she continued to grin. "And you must be Ellie, Vivie's plus one, and her dearest friend." They shook hands. "I hear you're a dog person, too, so we're going to get along great."

"I hope so. It's nice to—"

"Ooh, look at these doll babies." Arlene stooped and grabbed Mr. T's muzzle. "Hello, Twink. Do you remember me? I'm your auntie Arlene."

"It's Mr. T to you, Auntie Nut Job."

"And you can call me Auntie Arlene, too." She clasped Rudy to her ample chest. "Oh, you're a cuddly one, aren't you?"

"Aargghhh! I can't breathe," Rudy yelped as she continued to snuggle him to her bosom.

Still smiling, Arlene stood. "They are so adorable. I know they'll have fun with my babies and the rest of the pack. There are about six dogs in the fenced area I set up in the backyard, but I'm expecting more. You can take them there as soon as you're settled." She sidestepped to the trunk, where Viv was wrestling with the bags. "Now, Vivie, I have someone who can do that for you." She cupped her hands around her mouth. "Julio! Julio, where are you?"

Ellie held on to the dogs' leashes, exhausted by Arlene's frenetic chatter. The bubbly woman was either experiencing an adrenaline rush from seeing her youngest sister for the first time in months, or panicked about hosting her weekend wedding.

Arlene gazed into the trunk and grabbed the smallest bag. "Oh, this is lovely. Louis Vuitton does such a beautiful job."

Viv just shook her head and let Arlene continue.

"Julio? Julio! Where is that man?" After stomping her Ferragamos, Arlene scrunched her face. "We have to get out of this sun. I can't afford any more wrinkles. Just carry what you need and leave the trunk open. Julio will bring everything inside and up to your room."

"Where're Mom and Dad and the rest of the family?" Viv asked before Arlene could leave.

She waved a manicured hand toward the cottage. "In the guesthouse with Adrianne. They decided to throw a little afternoon get-together to keep whoever is staying here busy while I took care of things in the house."

"And Dr. Kent?"

"He's still seeing patients. The man is so busy, I have

to remind him we're getting married tomorrow." Arlene stared at the main house. "Julio! I need you!"

"What about the rest of the guests?" asked Ellie, hoping to calm down the bride-to-be. She was dying to find out how many people had been invited and what kind of dogs they owned.

"I booked a floor at the Montauk Manor. They're dog-friendly, and it's just down the road. The group is scheduled for a round of golf or spa treatments for today, and the hotel van will bring those who didn't drive over tonight, and again tomorrow afternoon." She heaved a breath. "I just don't know how I'm going to get everything done."

"But I thought you hired a wedding planner," said Viv.

"I did, but she was a disaster. Ran out on me yesterday without a word. Thank God Rosa's daughters have pitched in or I don't know where I'd be."

"And the caterer?"

"Mario and his men will be here in an hour. Rosa's in charge of the terrace and they're taking care of the backyard. Wait until you see the tent they erected. It's beautiful."

"Can't Mother and Adrianne help with the details?"

"Those sticks-in-the-mud? Absolutely not." Arlene headed for the front door. "Julio! Julio! Where is that—"

"I'm tired just watching her," Ellie said as Arlene stalked off, talking to the air.

"She's always been a ditz, but it appears this weekend has her running in circles. I can't believe the wedding planner quit just like that."

After watching Viv's sister, Ellie was on the planner's side, but she kept the comment to herself. She'd only been in Arlene's presence for ten minutes and she felt as if she'd run a marathon.

Viv hoisted her shoulder bag and walked toward the front porch. "You coming?"

"Let me take the dogs for a quick trip outside first," Ellie called, leading the boys to the street.

"That woman has a couple of screws loose," said Rudy, lifting his leg against the base of the mailbox.

"No kiddin'," grumped T. *"I can't believe we're related."*

"Related?" Ellie hid a smile.

"Auntie Arlene?" Rudy muttered. *"I don't want an auntie anybody."*

"Me, neither," T agreed.

After the dogs did their business, she pulled her scoop bags from her tote. It wouldn't hurt to be a concerned pet owner, even if this neighborhood didn't have a cleanup law.

Just then, her cell phone rang. When she checked caller ID, she grinned. Sam had asked her to call him as soon as they arrived. His ESP was working at full throttle. "Hi. Are you through with your afternoon in court?"

"Yes, and I'm happy to add that my testimony put the mope and his attorney on the run," said Sam, a trace of swagger in his voice. "Right after the defense attorney questioned me, he asked for a continuance. Seems he didn't like what I had to say about his boy."

"Then congratulations are in order. We can celebrate when I get home." Things had been going well since stalwart Detective Sam Ryder had moved into her place two months ago. "We're here, by the way, and it's beautiful."

"Glad to hear you arrived in one piece. So tell me, did Viv blow the clutch on that big-deal BMW?"

Ellie bit out a laugh. "It was slow going for a while, but once we made it to the highway, she got the hang of it."

"Just be careful tooling around out there. I hear the cops 'out east' are tough on the speeding laws."

"Like I said, I don't intend to do any 'tooling around.' Vivie wanted that car, so she's going to drive it. All Rudy and I want is peace and quiet, time on the beach, and a bit of sightseeing. Maybe some shopping, and we'll be set." She cleared her throat. She didn't want to sound like his mother, but . . . "Any plans for tonight?"

"I'm going home and eating in. I'll be thinking about you, babe. You'll call if you need me, right?"

The longing in his voice made her heart melt. Her big brave NYPD homicide detective rarely said the words, but he told her he loved her in a lot of little ways. "I'll call. And, Sam?"

"I'm still here."

"I'll be thinking of you, too." She snapped the phone closed and tucked it away in her bag. Knowing that Sam would miss her was sweet, because she was going to—

"All right already. Enough with the mushy stuff. Get us inside," ordered Rudy, pulling at his lead alongside Mr. T.

She dug in her heels to stop being dragged up the driveway. "Hang on a second. Remember those rules we talked about?"

"Yeah, yeah, yeah. Be good, no fighting, no whining, and no begging at the table."

"And be polite."

"Polite is my middle name," her boy announced, prancing into the house.

"Me, too," said T. *"Unless some fool starts actin' stupid. Then all bets are off."*

Inside, they were met by a short, middle-aged Hispanic man wearing a white jacket and black pants. "Welcome. I am Julio Suarez, Rosa's *esposo*."

"Hello. I'm a friend of Vivian, the bride's sister."

"I get your bags and bring them to your room. Miss Arlene, she say you go right at the top of the stairs and find her."

He went out the door and Ellie led the dogs to the sweeping curved staircase, where she stopped to gaze at a lovely distressed oak table butted against a sky blue wall. Even though New York was a harbor town, and she'd visited the seaport and been to the beaches when she was younger, she'd never collected finds from the ocean. This week was her chance.

"Are we just gonna stand here, or are you gonna move it along?" said a voice.

She gazed down at her questioning canine. When she'd gone to pick out a dog from a local shelter after the demise of her marriage, she had gotten the surprise of her life to realize that she could communicate with the yorkiepoo. He was the reincarnation of the dog she'd been devastated to lose ten years earlier. "I thought I'd bring you and T to the dog area, so you could meet the resident Boston Terriers and get a drink of water."

"Water sounds good, but if any of them black-and-white bug-eyed geeks try to get chummy, I'm gonna do some damage."

"Now, T, from what I've read, Boston Terriers are friendly and intelligent. I thought you had a change of heart and decided to be nice to your fellow canines."

"Nice? Yes. Chummy? Not in this lifetime."

Julio took that moment to enter the house loaded down with Viv's Louis Vuitton luggage and Ellie's single large black wheeler. "Why you no go up?" he asked, dropping the bags on the tile.

"I think it's better if I get the dogs settled first."

The houseman grinned. "Ah, *sí*, *sí*. The pen is through there." He pointed to the dining room. "Find my Rosa. She will show you the way." He slung a travel bag over his shoulder, tucked a smaller case under his arm, lifted the two largest pieces, one in each hand, and headed up the stairs.

Impressed by the man's strength, Ellie smiled. According to Viv, Julio, Rosa, and their girls were Arlene's friends as well as her housekeepers. She'd even gone to the trouble of hiring extra help for the big day so they wouldn't be overtaxed by the guests.

She headed into the dining room to find Rosa. If everyone actually brought a dog, the weekend could erupt into canine chaos. She only hoped that when people discovered her profession, they wouldn't expect her to take control of any badly behaved dogs.

This was her vacation.

A few hours later, armed with a glass of white wine, Ellie sat people-watching in a far corner of the enormous terrace. Viv had introduced her parents, Evan and Vanessa McCready, and Adrianne, the middle sister, a short while ago, and Viv was now making the rounds greeting family. Ellie, on the other hand, enjoyed hanging back and observing her fellow man. And with this group, there was a lot to observe.

First off, unless she counted her mother's over-the-top Sunday brunches, she'd never been in the presence of so much Armani, Versace, or Elie Saab. Even Vivian had been impressed, and happy she'd had the good sense to arrive with the entire Ralph Lauren summer collection.

Unless she let Viv take her in hand to shop, Ellie wore regular clothes from regular stores, and didn't care a whit if anyone thought her out of fashion. Thanks to her mom's and Viv's lectures, she recognized many of the "in" designers, and she was smart enough to know that bell-bottoms, button-down oxford shirts, and Crocs were passé. Wearing comfortable clothes that complemented her curvy figure was all that mattered.

Viv hadn't let Ellie down. She'd been her usual honest and sharp-witted self throughout the evening, including making a joke out of the McCready clan's perpetual name-dropping and flaunting of wealth. As for Arlene, instead of posturing, she'd been acting more like a bumblebee on speed. Wearing a yellow ruffled top à la Donna Karan, tight black leggings, and a pair of Kadreyas, one of the newest Christian Louboutin summer styles, with four-inch heels, she'd flitted from group to group, giving air kisses, shouting to Julio and Rosa, and running herd on the hired help. She'd even gushed over her three Boston Terriers, the only dogs allowed on the terrace for the party.

Arlene referred to this part of the night as the "family hour," which meant the twelve or so guests present were those staying on the property. The real party was supposed to start with the arrival of the several dozen friends housed at Montauk Manor, but that wouldn't happen for another half hour.

Looking for Vivian, Ellie scanned the crowd. She'd

met Scott and Miriam, Viv's aunt and uncle, and their adult children, Christian and Faith, a cousin Denise from somewhere on the family tree, and a group of four, each of whose first name started with the letter R, from Evan's side of the family. No way could she keep them straight.

She'd only met two people who claimed to be personal friends of the soon-to-be-groom. One was a tall, rawboned woman named Sabrina Bordowski. She was attractive, in a frigid sort of way, and she insisted on being called Dr. B. Her companion was a heavyset older man resembling a bulldog in both size and temperament, who'd been introduced as Martin Kent's uncle Mickey.

Still searching, she spotted a good-looking guy standing in the opposite corner of the terrace. She had yet to meet him, but he was alone, just like her, and he seemed to be people-watching as well. *Strange*, she thought, *he's too attractive to be here alone*. Who was he and why hadn't Viv filled her in?

When their eyes met, the mystery man smiled and raised his glass, and heat inched from Ellie's chest to her cheeks. Great, he probably thought she was interested in him, but she wasn't, at least not in *that* way. The living arrangement she and Sam shared was working out fine, thank you very much, and Sam had high marks in the hunk department, too. Still, something about this guy set off warning bells in her brain.

She finally located Vivian talking with two older women, and focused on them instead of the stranger. A moment later, Viv was leading the ladies toward her.

"You are not going to believe this," said Viv when she arrived with the women. "These are my aunts, Elsie and Connie." She cocked her head. "Well, they're sort of my aunts. Elsie was married to my father's stepbrother, who died about ten years ago, and Connie is her sister, so we're related somehow . . . and maybe removed a few times? They're in a room down the hall from us."

Ellie smiled at the beaming ladies. "I'm Ellie Engleman. It's nice to meet you."

"I'm Elsie Hogarth." The shorter, dark-haired woman spoke first. "Went back to my maiden name after I lost the mister. I had no idea I'd get to meet you here."

Ellie searched her brain. She'd heard the name before, but not from Viv. So where?

They shook hands and Elsie continued. "I'm caretaker for a tiny white Poodle named Coco, and the two of us live in the Davenport with my sister, Connie, and her Jack-a-Bee, Greta."

Coco? The Davenport? Ah, now she remembered.

"I think Randall mentioned you last summer. Your Coco received a bundle in a will, correct?"

"That's right. I guess Viv didn't think to mention me." Elsie gave her "almost" niece a pointed look. "We sort of lost touch over the past few years."

Vivian locked gazes with Ellie. "Mother never told me about Elsie's position as Coco's guardian," she said, pleading her case. "If I'd known I would have introduced you last summer when Rudy got his inheritance." After taking a sip of her merlot, she grinned at the women. "Now that I know how close you both are, I'll drop in to see you whenever you want company."

"I'm Connie Whipple," the other sister broke in, shaking Ellie's hand. "Just moved here from North Carolina. When I lost my husband, Elsie was kind enough to offer Greta and me a home. We heard you were a dog walker."

"I've been meaning to ask Randall about you," added Elsie. "Now that there are two dogs in the apartment, Connie and I could use a professional walker."

Getting good vibes from both women, Ellie decided not to give the I'm-on-vacation excuse she had planned to use if anyone asked her to look after their dog. "How about if I stop in to see you after I return home? We can talk about my rate and the time I'm scheduled to do runs at your building then."

"We'd love it," said Connie, a smile crinkling her face. "Greta's a Jack Russell–Beagle mix, and she's only three, so she's full of energy, and sometimes . . . well, you'll see."

"Don't worry," Ellie assured her. "Vivian has a Jack Russell, and he's a bit on the wild side, too. My dog and I get along with him just fine."

Arlene took that moment to join them. After giving the aunts a nod, she clutched Viv's hand. "You've got to help me. I've looked everywhere, and I can't find Martin."

When Arlene mentioned her fiancé, Vivian set her empty wineglass on a passing waiter's tray and put her free hand on a hip. "I'd be happy to help, Arlene, but you're forgetting something. I have yet to meet the man. I thought you'd been hiding him somewhere for a big unveiling."

"Hiding him? Of course not. He's been with patients all afternoon. He gets so involved in caring for them he sometimes forgets to come up for dinner. I sent Julio to get him at least twenty minutes ago." She huffed out a breath. "And where did Mickey go? If that man went to the cottage and corralled him into talking about business, I'm going to pitch a fit." She scanned the terrace. "And Dr. B? Where the hell is everyone?"

Ellie gazed over the crowd and saw why Arlene might

be concerned. The bulldoggish Mickey appeared to be missing, and it sounded as if he was a business acquaintance—not a real uncle. But who in the heck was Dr. B, that Arlene thought she was so important?

Arlene stomped her foot. "This is crazy. It's our night to celebrate, and he's supposed to be here." She heaved another sigh. "And his so-called close friends, too."

"Maybe he got cold feet after he met some of your family," teased Viv. "Just remember, you can't blame me."

Arlene missed the humor in her baby sister's statement. "Something must have happened to him, but I can't imagine what." Spinning in a circle, she broke out in a full-fledged dither. "Julio! Julio! Oh, where is that man?"

"Awwwk! Julio! Awwwk! Where is that man! Awwwk!"

Mimicking Arlene's voice to a T, a large parrot who'd been tucked in a corner near Ellie burst into the fray by flapping his wings and wagging his head. Ellie had noticed him earlier. She'd watched his beady eyes follow folks as they passed, and kept to herself. Birds were not high on her list of animal favorites, and she hadn't wanted to rouse his curiosity, so she'd kept her fingers to herself and ignored him.

The guests laughed, but Arlene began to wring her hands and pace. "I'm going to send a few of the catering staff out to look for the four of them. How can we have a prewedding celebration when the groom, the best man, and the head of the hired help are missing?"

"Awwwk! Missing. There's money missing, Marty, and I want my share. Awwwk! Or I'm gonna! Awwwk! Julio! Awwwk!"

"Oh, hush, Myron," Arlene admonished. Flapping her arms much like the parrot, she tottered off on her stilettos talking to anyone in her path.

"I don't know how Arlene lives with that crazy bird imitating everything she says." Viv gave the parrot the evil eye.

"I was meaning to ask," Ellie began. "What's up with him?"

"Myron is an African gray that Arlene rescued from a pet store that was closing after the first Myron died. She said he kept her company while she grieved, but I don't understand how. All the idiot does is imitate whatever he overhears."

"Sounds kind of spooky, if you ask me," said Ellie. "Whose voice was that just now asking for his share?"

"Beats me, but the parrot's been living in the doctor's office while the interior of the house was being painted. She probably should have left him in there until this whole affair was over." Viv shook her head. "I'm starving. I hope the other guests arrive soon so we can eat. And Dr. Kent, too. I can't imagine where he's been hiding."

Ellie had snacked on a dozen delicious canapés, so she was fine in the food department, but it did appear the other guests were getting restless. When she glanced across the terrace and no longer saw "hunky guy," she thought to take her friend's mind off eating by questioning her about the stranger.

"I've met just about everyone, but what's up with the tall, dark-haired man who was standing alone in the opposite corner a while ago? No one introduced us."

"I wish I knew, but I have no idea who he is, either," said Viv. "I thought he might belong to Dr. Kent's family, since he's not a part of mine, but Arlene's already told us who's here from Dr. Kent's side."

"I'm sure we'll find out before the weekend is over." Ellie gave her wineglass to another waiter. "I'm going to check on Rudy for a minute. You want to come to the pen and see Mr. T?"

"Okay, sure. Lead the way."

They took the stairs down to the lawn and searched for Rosa's teenage daughter, Maria, who was supposed to be supervising the canines, but she was nowhere to be found. Ellie opened the gate, walked to her boy, and stooped to ruffle his ears. "Hey, how are things going?"

"Boring, boring, boring," Rudy gruffed. *"That Yorkie is a pain in the behind, and so is some Jack-a-Bee named Greta. T and those Boston Terriers do not get along, so it's a good thing nutty Arlene brought them upstairs. It's been quiet since they left."*

Ellie looked to her right, where Viv was giving Twink a belly rub. "He looks fine now."

"So, when can we come up and mingle?"

"I'm not sure, but I'll find out. Right now our hostess is in distress. Seems she can't find her fiancé."

"I'd be in distress, too, if I had those pointy things she calls shoes on my paws. Arlene acts like she's had one too—"

A round of shouts, not Arlene's or Myron's, broke out and Ellie stood. Glancing across the yard, she saw a man wearing a catering jacket running toward the house from the guest cottage.

"El doctor está muerto! Help! *El está muerto!"*

Chapter 2

Ellie took off running before she could think. She flew past Vivian, pushed through the gate, and met the shuddering, pale-faced man.

"El doctor—el—doctor—" he gasped.

The caterer's horrified expression told the story, but she had to ask. "What happened to Dr. Kent?"

"No sé." He gasped again. *"Es muerto."*

Viv reached them, her breath a rasp. "Oh, my God. Is he saying what I think he's saying?"

"Sounds like," said Ellie. "How's your Spanish?"

"Negligible. What are you going to do?"

Ellie checked the terrace, where people in the crowd were staring, while a few of the male guests were coming down the stairs. She grabbed the caterer's arm. "Go. Tell someone to call nine one one. Ask for an ambulance . . . and the police . . . *policía*. Okay?"

"Ah, *sí, sí, señorita*."

He took off and Ellie started toward the guesthouse.

"Where are you going?" Viv raced along beside her.

"To wherever Dr. Kent is. The catering guy might be wrong. Maybe all he needs is CPR."

"Can you do CPR?" Viv asked as they followed the raised brick path over the sand and salt grass and around to the rear of the cottage. Even though the sun hadn't set, the outside motion sensors worked and the walkway was clearly in view.

"Uh, not exactly, but I could try." They circled the house and stopped in their tracks when they saw a body lying with its head crooked at an awkward angle against the raised bricks edging the sidewalk.

"Don't come any closer." A man stepped out from the cottage wall and stood in front of them. "Is someone calling the police?"

Ellie stumbled to a stop and Viv ran into her from behind. Righting herself, she gazed up at the hunky guy from the terrace. "What are you doing here?"

"Yeah, who is this bozo?"

Rudy? It figured the little stinker would squirm his way out of the pen and follow her. She bent and picked up her boy. "No snooping and stay close," she ordered, then set her yorkiepoo back on the walkway.

"I hope that mutt understands you, because the last thing the cops need is dog hair muddling the scene." Hunky Guy frowned. "And to answer your question, I was taking a walk and heard the caterer's shouts, so I came to see if I could help."

"Is the body really Dr. Kent?" asked Vivian, peeking over Ellie's shoulder. "And he's dead?"

The body was dressed in a dark suit and tie; its features were chalky white, and its eyes were open wide, as if in shock. "Since neither of us has met him, I'm going to take a wild guess and say, yes, that would be the missing Martin Kent." Ellie sighed.

"Oh, Lord, what am I supposed to say to Arlene?" asked Viv. "She's going to fall apart."

Voices came from behind them and the hunky guy clasped Viv's elbow. "How about you meet whoever's coming and tell them to return to the terrace? This is a possible crime scene. Make sure someone's called nine one one and the local authorities. Then find your sister. She's going to need you."

Viv locked gazes with Ellie. "Should I do what he says?"

"It's a good idea. If it's really a crime scene, the less people tromping through here, the better." She nudged Rudy with her toe. "Maybe you'd like to go with Viv."

"Ahh, no."

Viv took off and Ellie set her eyes on the stranger. "Who are you that you know so much about handling possible crime scenes?"

He shrugged. "I've had some experience. The name's Bond, by the way. James Bond."

"Oh, brother."

Ellie rolled her eyes, and he cracked a wry smile. "I know. Blame it on my parents, especially my mother. She loves Sean Connery."

"Poor you," said Ellie. She nodded toward the victim. "What do you think happened?"

"I didn't get close, but it looks like he fell backward and smacked his head on the brick edging. There's a lot of blood. It's—"

"Gory?"

"That's a good way to put it." He crossed his arms over his impressive chest. "And you are . . ."

"Ellie Engleman. I'm a friend of the woman who just

left—one of the bride's sisters." She took a step of retreat. James Bond was as tall as Sam, with dark curly hair. Square-jawed, with deep-set eyes and a blade of a nose, he was also a tad . . . imposing. "And this is my dog, Rudy."

"I'm her main man, so don't get any ideas."

Ignoring the canine's comments, she bit her bottom lip and waited, but Mr. Bond didn't explain his relationship to anyone in the group. "You're positive he's dead?" she asked him.

"He's gone, all right. I'd say the TOD was within the last sixty minutes or so."

TOD! Ellie had heard enough police talk to know this man was more than a casual observer. "You still haven't said. Why are you here?"

"I'm renting a summer house a couple of doors down. Arlene asked me to attend the party just yesterday, and I arrived a little early, so I tried to stay out of the way of family." He used air quotes for the last word, and his pearly whites gleamed in the floodlights. "So, you're not a member of the immediate family, either, huh? Guess that makes us connected somehow."

"Not in this lifetime, pal."

Sirens wailed in the distance and Ellie heaved a sigh of relief. She was absolutely not connected to this guy, and she didn't want to be. Once the cops got here, she and Viv, and Rudy and Mr. T, could retreat and watch the action. It was tragic that Arlene had lost her future husband, but this was one crime scene investigation she was not going to be a part of.

"Lord, what a mess," muttered Viv, plopping her bottom next to Ellie on the sofa. "When are the cops going to leave?"

Ellie rolled her shoulders and leaned back into the cushions of the couch centered in the house's spacious living room. She and the rest of the guests and their dogs had been hanging around waiting to be questioned for the past two hours, while Vivian had been upstairs with her sister. "I have no idea, but I'm sure they're doing the best they can."

"You're the one with experience in this kind of thing. Can't you give me a guess on what they're planning to do?"

Ellie cocked her head. "The way I understand it, jurisdiction is handled differently out here. When someone calls nine one one, they phone the EMTs and the local police, who are first on the scene. The cops inspect the site and decide if the death is suspicious. Then they cordon off the area and call the medical examiner and Suffolk County Homicide. The ME gives a preliminary cause of death, and if they say it might be murder, the homicide detectives take over the investigation, which means—"

"Hang on. Who gave you all this information?" asked Viv.

"I heard a couple of the cops talking. Since the next string of investigators has already arrived, I assume the death was considered suspicious, which is why every guest is being questioned. I imagine there's already a forensics team at the cottage and a pair of detectives who are taking down the info needed to start the case rolling."

Viv raised a hand, her way of begging for things to stop. "TMI, Ellie. Twink and I are tired. We just want to go to bed, not sit through this ridiculous cross-examination."

"That goes ditto for me," quipped Rudy, who'd been

asleep at Ellie's feet since they'd done as the first officers on the scene had asked, and taken a seat in the house.

"Just be glad the police stopped those vans from Montauk Manor before they unloaded their passengers, or this place would be a real zoo." Ellie scanned the room and saw Elsie Hogarth being led to one of the questioning areas. "With a suspicious death, every person here has to be grilled."

"Can't you call Sam and ask him to stick his nose in this mess? His opinion has to count for something."

"Not here, it doesn't."

Ellie poked a toe in Rudy's bottom. "A Manhattan detective's opinion counts for squat here. The way I heard it, the crime is investigated down the line, with a procedure already in place."

"Whatever happened to that guy we met at the cottage?" Viv glanced out over the room. "And who did he say he was?"

"I'd like the answer to those questions myself. If you ask me, James Bond should be a suspect."

Viv's eyes opened wide. "A what?"

"You heard me. He was on the terrace. Then he disappeared. And wasn't it funny how he turned up right as we hit the scene? It was a little too convenient, if you ask me."

"So this is how it starts," said Vivian, cracking a smile.

"How what starts?"

"You're already working on this death, just like you've done all the other murders you solved, and—"

"For God's sake keep your voice down," Ellie said, throwing her a look. "The last thing I want is for people to know I've played amateur sleuth. I promised Sam I'd turn over a new leaf and stay out of stuff that didn't concern me, and I meant it."

"All right, I'll keep it buttoned," Viv answered, her lower lip thrust out in a pout. "But really, this does concern you—because it concerns me. And I'm your best friend. That means something in my book. You might even be able to figure this out faster than the real cops."

"I forgot to ask. How is Arlene?" Ellie said, changing the subject.

"I don't know what a normal reaction would be for a person who finds out she just lost a loved one through a violent death, but if you ask me, her actions were a little strange. At first she flew in six different directions—crying, shouting, stomping. I wasn't sure if it was the shock or grief that had her going." Viv heaved a sigh. "Then my mom took over and Arlene broke down again. Adrianne checked out her medicine cabinet and found something to calm her down. Arlene took one of the tablets and she was more in control after a while. Mom said she needed to sleep, so we left."

"Sounds as if your mom and dad are in charge now."

"I guess. Mother is good at planning and arranging, and Dad loves to boss people around, so this might be just the ticket for them." Viv looked around again. "She said they'd been ordered by the cops to move out of the guesthouse, but they weren't going to do it tonight."

"Your father told me the police put him in charge of the guests. The caterers are clearing the tents and tables from the backyard, and Rosa is cleaning the kitchen and terrace. Since you and I sort of found the body—"

"We'll be up soon? Lord, I hope so."

Ellie rested her head on the cushions. "I hope so, too. Elsie just left for one of the rooms, but she should be out soon because you and I are probably her and Connie's alibi."

"I know they've already spoken with Scott and Miriam, Faith and Christian, and the rest. Have you seen the R relatives?"

Ellie blew out a breath. "That's one group I can't keep straight. Robert, Roberta, Rachel, Reba . . . what other women's names begin with the letter R?"

"Try Roseanne and Rita for the last two, and you're right. They're cousins from my mother's side. Until today, I'd only seen them when she hosted a party."

"I never knew you had this much family," said Ellie. She had no living relatives on her mother's or her father's side, so Viv was her sister-in-heart. "You could have told me."

"Ha! Why? They're all a bunch of blowhard Mensa members, too smart for their own good, if you ask me. They're completely wrapped up in themselves. Even Adrianne, who lives with mommy and daddy because she says she isn't able to ground herself in her painting any longer. Claims her nerves are shot and her inspiration has taken a hike."

"I didn't see her for most of the night."

"Mother says Adrianne went back to the cottage for a 'lie-down' sometime before Dr. Kent's body was found."

"Really? Then she might have been in the guest cottage when he died." Ellie worked to phrase her next sentence so Viv wouldn't renew her lecture on detecting skills. "I wonder if Adrianne saw anything . . . or heard something odd from outside when the doctor fell and cracked his head."

Vivian crossed her arms. "Don't take this the wrong way, but you're doing it again."

"No, I'm not. I'm just—"

Their conversation was interrupted by Arlene stumbling into the living room from the foyer. "I just remembered. Has anyone thought about Myron? He can't stay out all night. Someone has to take care of him. He's—he's—"

"He's in his cage in the kitchen, Arlene," said Evan McCready, appearing from the dining room. "I just brought him in. Does he need special care for overnight?"

Arlene spun around and practically tripped into her father's arms. "He needs his cage covered—and—and a slice of apple for a bedtime snack—and—fresh water—and—and—" She began to sob. "Oh, Daddy, what am I going to do?"

"I thought you said Adrianne gave her medication to quiet her down." Ellie kept her tone low as Arlene wailed in her father's arms. "She sounds more revved than ever."

"I have no idea what Adrianne gave her, so I don't know what's going on," whispered Viv.

Evan McCready drew his oldest daughter back into the foyer. "We'll take care of everything, honey. You go to bed and try to sleep."

"Ms. Engleman? Ms. McCready?" said a voice from the rear of the living room.

Viv shot to her feet. "I'm Ms. McCready," she told the cop.

"And you're Engleman?"

Ellie knew the drill. "Yes, sir."

"Follow me."

"Just a second." She grasped Viv's elbow. "Viv, listen."

"What?"

"When they ask you a question, don't joke around. Answer honestly and quickly, and whatever you do, don't lie."

Viv rolled her eyes. "Oh, God, I'm not sure I can do this."

"You can. Just stay focused and do what I said."

"Ladies?" The frowning officer waved a hand. "You're wasting department time." He headed back into the hall. "Move it along."

They followed him, and reached Viv's room first, where the officer opened the door and nodded. "Ms. McCready. You'll be seeing Detective Levy."

After Viv entered, he shut the door and proceeded to the next room. Ellie had no idea how this part of the huge house lined up with the rest, but the hallway was filled with a warm, dark blue color and the walls were decorated with stars. The artist had even outlined the constellations and written their names in flowing script beneath them.

They reached the next room and her escort nodded at the open door. "Detective Wheeling is ready for you."

Ellie slouched forward in her chair. Rudy was curled around her feet, and he was not happy. It was past his bedtime—hers, too—and they both wanted sleep.

"Ask this dick how much longer, will ya? I was done for the day hours ago."

She tapped Rudy with the toe of her sandal and smiled at Detective Wheeling, who seemed an easygoing man with a ton of patience. So far, all of his questions had been short and to the point. And though many were identical, each had been asked in a slightly different manner.

She'd learned over the past year that repetitive questions were normal for the cops. Their goal? To confuse the person they were grilling, hoping his story might change. Once that happened, the detective could accuse him of lying. And if the person lied, there was a good chance he was hiding something, which meant he might be guilty or know a fact about the crime. It was the cops' standard way to corner a criminal, a trap into which Ellie never wanted to fall.

"Is that all, Detective?"

He flipped his palm-sized spiral notepad (*really, here in the Hamptons, too?*) and found what he was looking for. "I'm still not quite sure why you thought it necessary to rush to the aid of a dead man, Ms. Engleman, since, according to you, you didn't even know Dr. Kent."

Ellie heaved a sigh. She wanted to begin her next sentence with "for the fifth time, Detective," but let the snarky comment slide. "As I've already said, it was a simple knee-jerk reaction. I heard the words 'doctor' and 'dead' and my feet just took off running." She crossed mental fingers. "The catering guy was panicked, so I wondered if maybe CPR would do the trick."

"And you're trained in CPR?"

He'd asked her this twice before, so she couldn't lie. "Not really."

"So you were planning to do . . . what?"

"Whatever I could. Clear an airway? Start that pumping thing on his chest?"

"And you were willing to do this 'pumping thing' to someone you'd never met."

"I know it sounds odd, but it's the truth. I heard there was trouble, and I wanted to help."

"And you're sure about Ms. McCready? She'd never met the man her older sister was going to marry, either?"

Ellie figured the two detectives had already decided to ask her and Viv many of the same questions, so giving a short answer was best. "To my knowledge, no."

"Blah, blah, blah!" came a voice from below.

"And besides the caterer and Mr. Bond, you don't have any idea if someone had come and gone from the scene before you arrived?"

Aha! This was the perfect time to pose a question that had been itching at her brain for hours. "Now that you mention him, what about Mr. Bond? I thought it was weird to find him standing there the way we did. And he's just a neighbor, not family, so if anyone shouldn't have been at the scene it was him." She sat at attention. "Have you asked him about it?"

"Ms. Engleman." Wheeling grimaced as if he needed a double dose of Maalox. "Someone here mentioned that you'd been involved in a couple of murder investigations in Manhattan."

Ellie closed her eyes. Who had ratted on her, and how could she get out of it without lying? "Mind telling me who gave you that information?"

"It doesn't matter who, and I don't want to get into it with you now. All I have to say is stay out of my investigation. Don't inspect the crime scene, don't harass the guests, and don't annoy the police or any other official in the performance of their duty. In short, don't do anything. Is that clear?"

"I am on vacation. All I want to do is rest and relax with Rudy. We're going to lie on the sand and take it easy."

Wheeling checked his notebook. "Rudy?"

She gazed at her feet. "My dog."

"Oh, yeah. I heard this place was loaded with 'em. We put fencing around the rear of the guesthouse, just in case they get curious. The last thing we need is canines contaminating the crime scene."

"I carry cleanup bags, so you'd never find anything from my boy," said Ellie. "Now, about Mr. Bond—"

"He's no concern of yours, so you're not to bother him. You got that?"

"Okay, fine," she answered through tight lips. As her boy liked to say, the detective's statement smelled rotten.

She wouldn't bother the faux 007, but she did plan on finding out why Wheeling had evaded every question she asked about him. She'd watched the guests coming and going from the two screening rooms all evening, and hadn't once seen the mysterious stranger. Who the heck was he, and why had he been excused from the questioning process?

Wheeling said something she didn't quite hear, then, "I think we're through for now."

"For now?"

"I understand you and Ms. McCready are here for the week. We've released all the guests staying at Montauk Manor and given them the okay to come in and out through the front door if they plan to pay a condolence call tomorrow. We also ask that those staying here keep behind the crime scene tape until it's removed. Until we determine if the death was foul play, we ask that you remain accessible."

Ellie bit her lower lip. "I don't mean to sound unsympathetic to Ms. Millman's plight, but will Ms. McCready and I be allowed to visit the local towns?"

Wheeling ran a hand over his jaw. "Yeah, sure, why not? Just do me a favor and don't tell anyone you're staying here, especially if you get wind of rumors or read about it in *Dan's Papers*. This is a small community and we rely on income from the summer tourist trade. If this is a murder, I'd hate for word to get around that we have a killer running free."

"Then the ME is certain the death was suspicious?"

"We won't know until she's finished her job."

Her job? "Are you using Dr. Emily Bridges?"

"Dr. Jordan Kingsgate. You heard of her?"

Ellie sucked in a breath. She'd met the young ME-in-training at the site of a murder last February, but that wasn't any of Detective Wheeling's business. "Ah, no."

"Good. Let's keep it that way." He stood, stuffed the notebook in his jacket pocket, and headed around the desk. "I'm going to check on the CSU crew, but I expect they'll have to come back tomorrow since it's dark." He nodded. "You can go."

Ellie followed him out the door and down the hall, glancing into the now empty room where Viv had been questioned. She was probably in bed, too tired to talk about all that had happened. The house had grown quiet, which meant everyone was trying to get a good night's sleep.

"I don't know about you, but I need a trip to the little dog's room," said Rudy. *"Mind if I go out back?"*

"Okay by me," she whispered, lagging behind as Wheeling plowed ahead. When she heard the kitchen door slam, she followed the dim lights leading the way to the breakfast area and onto the terrace. "Remember what the detective said. Don't go far or we'll be in trouble before you know it."

"I just gotta water some weeds," he pronounced, going down the steps.

While waiting, Ellie inspected the rear of the property. Before all the fuss, the sky had been clear, the terrace shaded from the setting sun, and decorated for a party. Now everything had been cleaned and straightened. The moon was bright, the sky dotted with stars, the walkway sensors leading to the guesthouse snapping on as Detective Wheeling strode past.

The cottage had a single light burning in the upper floor, where Viv's mother, father, and sister were staying, while down below, every light in the doctor's office glowed. When they began to blink out one by one, she figured Wheeling was walking through the rooms, telling the forensics team to go home and return tomorrow.

Rudy came back to her and plopped at her feet. *"What'cha watchin'?"*

"Nothing, really. I guess they moved the investigation inside once the sun set, and our detective is shutting things down." Car doors slammed; then the cruisers headed up the long drive with their roof lights blazing. "I hope this is over soon. Arlene's had a rough time of it."

"Rough time? Are you kidding? With all the meds she's on, I doubt she felt a thing."

"Meds? What are you talking about?"

"You mean you couldn't tell? The woman is on something, maybe a couple of somethings, but don't ask me what."

"How do you know?"

"What I know is you're a babe in the woods. I can't believe you didn't notice. She's been actin' like a few of those wealthy pill poppers we meet walkin' Fifth Avenue.

Besides, I can smell it. A dog knows drugs when his sniffer locks on to 'em."

She'd heard about drug-searching canines, but hadn't read of one that could pick up the scent from a person's body. Of course, Arlene had been acting wonky all day, but Ellie had blamed it on the pressure of the wedding, a house full of guests, and then losing her fiancé. She hadn't dealt with many addicts in her lifetime, but maybe Rudy was right.

"I'll ask Viv tomorrow. She did say her sister Adrianne had found a calming drug in Arlene's medicine cabinet. She might know more."

"Seems to me Vivie's as innocent as you are when it comes to swallowing happy pills. Neither of you even take an aspirin unless you're dyin'."

"And we like it that way. Viv doesn't believe in wasting her money on anything but designer clothes, and me, well, even if I had the cash I wouldn't like to feel out of control. When I was in college, almost everyone smoked weed or tried the latest designer cocktail, while I just read a good book or studied. The one time I tried marijuana, I threw up. That was it for me and drugs. Pretty boring, when I think about it."

"Pretty smart, if you ask me." He gave a full-body shake. *"You ready to hit the sack?"*

"You bet, and be quiet going upstairs. I don't want to wake anyone after tonight's trying ordeal."

Chapter 3

Ellie blinked open one eye. Morning sun streamed through the windows and French doors that led to a large deck facing the ocean. Rolling over, she found her bedmate nestled on a pillow next to her. "Hey, it's time to get up."

When Rudy didn't answer, she looked across the room at Viv. "You awake?" she whispered.

Viv moaned. "No."

"I'm not," the yorkiepoo grumped.

"Me, neither," added Mr. T in a muffled voice from somewhere.

"Do you think Arlene is okay?"

Eyes closed, Viv turned to face her, and Ellie smiled. It simply wasn't fair. How in the heck could her best human friend look so good without a full night's sleep or a drop of makeup at this hour of the morning?

"I imagine she's still grieving," muttered Viv. Then she yawned. "If Rosa isn't taking care of her, Mother probably walked up from the cottage."

Ellie swung her legs over the side of the mattress, went to the French doors, and peered out the window. She'd taken a passable survey of the guesthouse last night, but it had been dark. She wanted to be sure she understood its layout. "Speaking of the cottage, how about explaining the setup to me?"

"What do you want to know?"

"For one thing, it looks huge. How big is it?"

"I don't know the square footage, but there are two floors, with a total of four bedrooms and three baths. The way I understand it, once Arlene and the doc got engaged, he took over the bottom floor. Turned the living room into a waiting area, the smaller bedroom into his office, and the other into an examining room. He kept the kitchen and bath the way they were, so he was all set."

"And the upstairs is now the guest quarters?"

"It took some remodeling, and it's smallish, but it's nice. Eat-in kitchen, living room, two bedrooms, and two baths. Both of the bedrooms have decks that look out over the ocean."

"Interesting," said Ellie. If Adrianne was in the bedroom apartment and the bedroom overlooked the rear of the house, she definitely could have heard or seen something when the doc fell. "There's even a parking area. Yesterday, it was filled with cars, while today there are only three. I see a Mercedes, a Jaguar, and a Cadillac. Who owns what?"

"The Cadillac is probably Mom and Dad's, and I imagine Adrianne came with them, so the Mercedes and Jag must belong to the doctor."

Ellie returned to the bed and sat down, her mind filled with questions. Had Dr. Kent really been seeing patients while the party was going on? Had Adrianne been asleep or was she simply bored when she went to the apartment during the party?

Viv cocked her head. "I know that look. What's going on?"

"On? Oh, I'm just trying to figure out what to wear. Are we in mourning? Because unless you count a pair of black linen walking shorts as funeral wear, I didn't bring anything appropriate for a wake."

Viv swung into a sitting position and the lump under the covers at the bottom of the mattress moved. Inch by inch, the Jack Russell crawled out, then jumped to the floor.

"Mr. T didn't get enough sleep," he complained. *"Yak, yak, yak, yak, yak."*

"Me, neither," Viv continued, almost as if she was agreeing with her boy. "But the Calvin Klein summer collection is subdued. Shades of white and beige, with a bit of color thrown in the mix." She went to the dresser, where she opened a drawer. "My guess is we should stay close for today, out of respect. I can give you a tour of the house while we hang out."

Good idea, thought Ellie. If she was looking for answers to the doctor's death—which she wasn't—a tour would be a good way to start. She faced Rudy and Mr. T, who were staring at her from the floor. "Think you two can wait to go out until after I take a quick shower?"

"Of course they can," said Viv.

"Of course we can't," muttered Twink.

Rudy just sat there grinning.

"I'll be quick," Ellie promised. "You'll watch them, right?" she asked her roommate.

"Sure, but I could find Maria. She's supposed to be in charge of the dogs."

Ellie pulled clean underwear, a pale yellow tank top, and knee-length beige shorts from the drawer. "I thought so, but she wasn't with them last night. In fact, I don't remember seeing her after the family get-together began."

Viv, busy removing the tags from her Calvins, said, "She's just a kid, so who knows where she was?" Then she raised her head. "And don't think you're fooling me by changing the subject. I'm on to what you're doing."

"Doing? What am I doing?"

"You're gathering clues, in case the doc's accident turns out to be murder. And don't deny it, because I can hear the gears turning in your head." She sat back on the bed, a pair of white cropped pants and an orange off-the-shoulder ruffled blouse in her hands. "Now I know how Sam feels when you start gunning your snoop engine."

"I am not 'gunning my snoop engine,'" Ellie pronounced, insulted. "I'm just trying to make sense of things. Who was where, doing what, when the accident happened? Stuff like that." She ducked into the bathroom and stuck out her head. "I'll be finished in a couple of minutes."

"Rudy's following you," called Viv.

Ellie inspected the beautiful bathroom, its stall shower, sand-colored marble tiles, double sinks, a rack holding piles of towels, and a private commode area. "Wow. This is three times the size of my bathroom back home."

"Think this is what it means to be stinkin' rich?"

"I guess." She started the shower and pulled a big

fluffy turquoise-colored towel off the rack. "Are you feeling lonely, or did you want to talk?"

"Both, I guess." He circled the plush turquoise rug and curved into a sit. *"Is Viv right? Are you collecting clues? Because like you've been saying, this is supposed to be our vacation."*

Stepping into the stall, she soaped up with a shower gel that turned into a luxurious lather rich with the scent of roses, and ran the washcloth over her body. "I guess, but not really. It's just getting to be a habit, trying to make things fall into place. I've never met the doctor, so I don't know anything about him. What kind of medicine did he practice? Why would someone want to kill him? That sort of thing." She rinsed, turned off the pulsing jets, and got out. "And I'm curious about the layout of this house, too. There are too many rooms and entrances to keep track of."

She hadn't washed her hair, but the steam had helped tame the frizzies, so she ran her fingers through the curls. After dressing, she added mascara, a swipe of blush, and a bit of lip gloss to her morning face. "Okay, that's it. I'm ready to deal with ditzy Arlene, Viv's family, and the rest of a crowd fresh off the death of an almost family member." She stooped and gave her boy an ear rub. "Are you going to stick close, or lounge with the other dogs in the outside pen?"

"I don't mind the pen, but I do mind that pain-in-the-butt Jack-a-Bee and her too-nosy nose. And T is gonna have a fit if those three Boston bozos are there."

"The Boston Terriers belong to Arlene," she said in a whisper. "So she might want them with her to help her through this tragedy."

"Might be the best place for 'em, especially if they're

ticking off Mr. T." He stretched from head to toe. *"Are you telling Viv the truth?"*

"About the snoop— I mean, questions?"

"Duh. Yeah."

"Kind of. But something Viv said last night got me thinking."

"Uh-oh. That sounds dangerous."

She ignored the snarky comment. "Viv said if the doctor was murdered that I'd owe her a hand in solving the crime, just as I did for my other friends who got in trouble. She means Rob and the professor and the rest, and you know how I feel about friends in need."

"I know, but Viv isn't the human in trouble here."

"Hmm. You're right, and that logic could be my way out of a sticky situation."

"You can try it, but Viv is a determined woman."

"So you think I *should* do a little investigating?"

"Sure, but Detective Wiseass won't like it."

"His name is Wheeling, not wiseass. And I won't get in his way. I just want to get the details straight in my mind, is all."

She opened the door and Viv scooted past her. "Sorry. Nature calls. Take Twink and head downstairs without me. I'll be there in a few minutes."

Ellie stood at the bottom of the stairs and surveyed her surroundings. With all that had gone down yesterday, she'd never had the time to really inspect the house. Now, here in the entry, she noted the display of shells scattered artfully across the foyer table. They varied in size, but each was polished white or pearly pink, and some were cut in half to show their amazing construction. The scent of fresh paint drifted in the air, and the tile floor sparkled, confirming Viv's admission that her sister had gone overboard to get the place ready for a wedding. The other walls, a subdued ecru, held a variety of oil and pastel paintings, with an eclectic display of shell-covered wreaths and family photos hanging alongside them.

Two baskets filled with tall, graceful dried fronds flanked the archway leading to a dining room. A large multicolored area rug in the palest of shades covered the room's sand-toned tile. On the other side of the foyer was a matching archway that led to the huge sitting area she'd waited in last night, while beyond that she spied what looked to be a spacious screened porch.

All the furniture appeared to be made of either distressed oak or high-grade rattan. She wasn't an expert, but between her mother's chatter on artwork and design, and Viv's antique hunting, she could tell these were quality pieces.

Walking through the dining room, Ellie admired the beautiful furniture. The table could easily seat twelve, the sideboard was massive, and the smaller pieces, each holding an array of pottery or sea glass, were well matched.

"Move it along, Triple E," said Mr. T. *"It's time to get where we're goin'."*

"Knock it off, T," she warned him. "No smart-mouthed pooches allowed this week."

Continuing into the kitchen, she again admired the enormous room with its wood-planked floor and vast U-shaped cooking area covered in dark speckled granite. It was there she saw Teresa, Rosa, and Julio's eldest daughter, standing at one of the two sink stations scrubbing pots. Terry, as she asked to be called, turned when she heard Ellie and the boys shuffle in.

"Help yourself to the buffet breakfast on the table. Most of the family is on the terrace, so feel free to join them or bring something up to your room."

Surprised the girl was so chipper after last night's incident, Ellie said, "Have you seen Ms. Millman?"

"Arlene? Not yet."

Arlene? Calling her employer by her first name sounded a bit too friendly, but the girl was barely twenty. "We only met for a few seconds yesterday. I'm Ellie, a friend of the bride's youngest sister."

"I remember." Terry dried her hands on a dish towel and stooped to canine level. "This is your baby Rudy, right?"

"Well, hell-ooo, dolly," Rudy said, nuzzling his snout in her hand.

Ellie tapped her boy's butt with the toe of her sandal. Terry was cute and almost elfin in stature, but she had a woman's figure and bearing. "With all the four-legged guests roaming around, you have a good memory. Yes, that's Rudy. The other dog is Mr. T. He belongs to Arlene's sister Vivian."

Terry scratched T's ears. "Hi, big man. You are such a sweetie."

"Mr. T can be sweet for you, doll face."

Holding back a *tsk* of disapproval, Ellie grinned. "Is Maria in the pen? I'd like to drop the boys there before I get breakfast."

Terry's expression grew somber. "Maria is busted up about the doc's death. I don't know when she'll be down to do her share of the chores." She returned to the sink and began to scrub. "But she's only a kid. She'll get over it."

"I'm sorry to hear that," said Ellie, wondering why

the teenager was so deeply affected by the doctor's death. "Was he treating her for something?"

"Treating her?" Terry gave a muffled snort. "Not any longer."

"Oh, well . . ." No need to ask for more. She was not on duty in this case. "I guess I'll take the dogs down. See you in a few minutes."

She nodded a good morning to Viv's mom and dad, who were sitting at the largest outdoor table, and continued to the pen, where she opened the gate and shooed in Rudy and T. "Be good. Someone will be here to look after you in a while."

Rudy ignored the Jack-a-Bee she assumed was Greta nosing his behind. *"I want a real walk, Triple E. Don't be gone long."*

"Me, too," T demanded. *"The sooner the better."*

"Let me eat first. Then I'll be back to pick you up." She climbed the steps and headed to the kitchen, where she took a helping of what could be called a breakfast burrito and a bit of fresh fruit. After adding coffee, she went to the terrace, shaded from the morning sun by a huge rollout awning. Though other guests were up and about, speaking in whispers at the smaller tables, she decided to sit with Viv's parents, Vanessa and Evan McCready.

"With all the commotion yesterday, we didn't get to talk, Ellie," said Vanessa. "Vivian speaks very highly of you, so it's nice to finally chat with you in person."

"I'm happy to meet both of you, too." She smiled at Evan, who was scooping scrambled eggs onto his toast. A thin, gray-haired, and handsome older man, he hadn't said anything since she'd sat down, which Ellie found strange, given the way he'd bossed her around the night before.

Vanessa, also thin and attractive in a sorority sister

sort of way, stirred her tea. "We're only sorry the evening turned into such a tragedy, aren't we, dear?"

Evan stopped scooping his eggs. "Damned nuisance, if you ask me. It was ridiculous for the police to get involved." His upper lip curled. "I talked to that detective by phone this morning and convinced him we didn't have to move out of the cottage. Just had to promise to stay out of the first floor and keep the downstairs door locked whenever we left the building."

"I'm glad you did," said Vanessa. "It would have been too big a chore to repack and drag everything back to the main house. Of course, we could have asked Rosa and Julio for help, but I hear they have their hands full with their son."

"Arlene pays them, doesn't she?" Evan asked, then said, "I still don't like the cops nosing around."

"I think that for Arlene's peace of mind, it's best we know what really happened, don't you?" said Ellie. *And why are you so certain the police shouldn't have been called?*

"Isn't it obvious? The man tripped and hit his head when he fell. Seems black and white to me," Evan answered.

Just then two cars pulled into the cottage lot, one a BMW, the other a late-model touring car of some kind, maybe a Bentley. The drivers got out and walked to the front door, chatted a bit, and returned to their cars. Then they pulled out with tires squealing and disappeared up the drive.

"What was that all about?" said Ellie.

"Looks like patients, if you ask me. The cops posted a sign on the front of the cottage that said the doc's office is closed. Guess it's up to them to find another physician."

"Someone should record a message on his office phone, saying his practice is closed," suggested Ellie. "I'm sure that would help Arlene and keep people from driving in at all hours."

"I imagine I'll be the one to take care of it. Arlene is a mess right now, and Adrianne is no better. Maybe Evan could—"

"Ha! Not me. I'd just start spouting that the man was inept, so clumsy he couldn't walk straight and killed himself with a trip," said Evan.

Ellie held her tongue, reluctant to point out that when someone tripped they usually fell forward, and the doctor had fallen backward, which made what happened to him odd. "I believe the police always arrive when there's a nine one one call. The EMTs must have thought something wasn't right."

When Evan glared, she decided to ignore him and concentrate on Vanessa, who seemed more approachable. "What do you think happened?"

"I have no idea. Martin is gone, so it really doesn't matter. Arlene's my worry now."

"So you didn't know the doctor very well?"

"Evan and I only met him once before. When we invited them over, Arlene always said he was busy with patients, so we had little interaction." She sighed. "Adrianne spent time with both of them while the house was being painted, so she'd have more to say on the subject, I'm sure."

"Then it was Adrianne who did the paintings of the constellations in the back hallway?"

"Yes. Aren't they beautiful? She's such a talented girl, though she's been working through some issues lately. Actually, Martin treated her while she was here."

"I don't want to pry, but what kind of medicine did the doctor practice?" asked Ellie. If he was a psychiatrist, it was possible he'd had an argument with a disturbed patient.

"I'm not exactly sure, but in the past Adrianne's had bouts of depression. She's taken some sort of martial arts lessons to help bolster her courage. She said between that and Dr. Kent, she was finally feeling better. I believe she even did a mural on his office wall as a thank-you."

Since Ellie had only met the middle sister for a quick hello early yesterday evening, she had no idea what kind of person Adrianne was. Whenever Viv talked about her, she tended to roll her eyes, which told her nothing, but at least she now had a clue to Dr. Kent's business.

"Enough about my family," said Vanessa. "Viv says you're a professional dog walker."

"Yes, and I love my job. It's not like Viv's big-time bank and trade position, but it suits me perfectly."

"Good for you. It's important to be happy in life."

Ellie turned to Evan. Maybe eating breakfast had eased his crabby quotient. "Vivian never said, Mr. McCready. What is it you did before you retired?"

He gave his wife a pointed look. "I was in the security business."

"Oh, Evan, there's no need to be so secretive," Vanessa said with a laugh. She gazed at Ellie. "He's too modest. Evan was in naval intelligence. Then he became a member of the CIA. It was back in the day when things were dicey with the Russians, so he doesn't like to talk about it."

"Really, Vanessa, that's not a stranger's business," Evan said, his voice almost a growl. "I'm sure Ms. Englewood doesn't care what I did in the past."

"It's Engleman, Mr. McCready, and it sounds like

you've lived an exciting life," said Ellie. "Maybe you should write a book of your exploits."

He didn't respond, but he did give her a grim smile. Viv took that moment to sashay to the table, her plate piled high with fruit and eggs.

"Morning, everyone." She gazed at her mother. "Where're Arlene and Adrianne?"

"Arlene is in her office, talking with the police. Adrianne went along to make sure she could handle it."

"Did the cops say if they'd heard from the medical examiner?"

Ellie was happy Viv had asked what she'd been wondering.

"I'm not sure, but we did find out where Julio was all night. It seems that besides Teresa and Maria, he and Rosa have a son named Tomas. He arrived home unexpectedly and needed help with something, so his father came to his aid." Vanessa leaned back in her chair and sipped her tea. "Very strange, if you ask me. Even Arlene found it odd that they'd never mentioned he'd be returning the night of the party."

"Is he planning to live here?" asked Ellie, figuring it was a safe question.

"I'm not sure. Maybe it's a visit. According to Arlene, Tomas has been living somewhere else since Myron died. It was just last week that he asked to come home, and Arlene said yes."

"Sounds to me as if big sis is a jinx," said Viv. "That's two men gone from the planet, and both of them were involved with her."

"Vivian Maureen McCready, I cannot believe you just said that," Vanessa scolded. "You really do need to control your mouth."

Ellie hid a grin. The irreverent comment was typical Vivian, and she knew it had been meant as a joke. "Viv tells me everyone in the family is a member of Mensa," she said, hoping to draw the older woman to another topic. "You must be proud of your family."

Vanessa locked gazes with her youngest daughter. "I'm proud of all my girls. Even those who refuse to try out for Mensa. Are you a member?"

"Uh, no. I never thought to take the test."

"Vivian tells me you're very clever. Perhaps you should sign up and see what they say."

"I said Ellie was clever, Mother, but I meant it in a more practical way," said Viv. "She's a super sleuth. Even solved a couple of homicides in the city. And she's dating an NYPD detective, too."

Ellie groaned internally. So much for her best friend's promise to keep it "buttoned." "Your daughter's exaggerating," she said, kicking Viv under the table. "I've just been lucky figuring things out."

"So that's why you're asking so many questions," said Evan. "Seems to me you should let the police do their job."

That comment cemented Ellie's opinion of Evan McCready. "I wouldn't dream of interfering in police business, but I do like things to make sense. And I'm a people person, so I enjoy learning what makes them tick." She finished her coffee and set the cup down. "But I really love dogs."

"Especially the tiny ones," added Vivian.

"Humph. If you ask me, those mini-mutts belong in a blender."

"Which is the reason we could never have a dog growing up," said Vivian, ignoring the slam against canines. "Dad just isn't an animal lover."

If Evan McCready wasn't such a grouch, Ellie might have felt sorry for him. It was obvious he had no idea how wonderful it was to have a trusting and loving animal in one's life. But with that cynical attitude, it was clear the man didn't deserve a four-legged friend. "Too bad. Dogs really do add to a person's happiness."

"Some people, maybe," he groused, pushing away from the table. "I have a ten o'clock tee time, so I'll see you all later." With that, he headed down the stairs and took the walk to the guesthouse.

"Dad's in rare form this morning," said Viv.

"He's just miffed by the police hubbub," Vanessa offered. "Once things calm down, I'm sure he'll be fine."

"So what's Arlene planning to do for a funeral? Or does Dr. Kent have family to take care of things?"

"According to the police, nothing can be done until they're finished with the investigation. I only wish they'd hurry. In the meantime, she must be making some kind of plans."

Ellie heard voices and glanced at the door leading to the kitchen. "It sounds as if Adrianne and Arlene are on their way here. Maybe they'll fill us in."

Chapter 4

Wearing bright red heeled sandals, a tight red halter top, and a pair of snug white jeans, Adrianne stepped onto the terrace with Arlene, who gave a wave and raced down the stairs.

After gazing out at the cottage, where another car had stopped, Adrianne groaned. "God, I can't stand it. People were knocking on Marty's office door at six a.m. Was the man always open for business?"

"Arlene said he kept unusual office hours, but there's a note on the door. Word will get out soon and his patients will find another doctor," said Vanessa. "Where did your sister run off to?"

"Big sis just wanted to see her babies, so she went to the pen to say hello." She sauntered to the table and glided swanlike into the chair just vacated by her father. "Thank God this mess is almost over."

It was the first time Ellie had a good chance to study the middle sister. The woman had long dark hair, the same color as Viv and Arlene, and she, too, was beautiful, but there was an air of untouchability about her, almost as if she was looking for a fight. While Arlene was on the short side, like her father, Viv and Adrianne were tall, like Vanessa. And Adrianne's arm muscles were cut, though her body was curved into a model-sized figure.

"How is your sister this morning?" asked Vanessa. "Holding up under the strain, I hope."

"I suppose, but you'll have to ask her. That detective is a pit bull when it comes to the details." Adrianne ran a hand through her straight and shiny hair. "The questions never seemed to stop."

"What did he want to know?" asked Ellie. For the time being, getting a few details secondhand was probably better than asking about things herself. Especially since she wasn't really investigating. "Did he mention an autopsy report?"

"Ugh. That's too morbid to talk about." She scanned the terrace. "Where's Rosa, by the way, or one of her girls? I could use a cup of coffee." She frowned. "Arlene really needs to do something about her help."

"You must have seen the full buffet in the kitchen," said Viv. "We're supposed to serve ourselves."

"What's the point of having servants if you have to do everything yourself?" a sullen Adrianne asked. Sounding much like her father, she scrunched her mouth into a pout, looked the terrace over again, then stood and stalked to the house. "I'll be back."

"Why, yes, thanks for asking. I'd love a coffee refill," muttered Viv. She glanced at her mother. "Adrianne seems to be in rare form this morning. In fact, she's dressed like she's ready to go clubbing instead of assisting a sibling in mourning. That drug Dr. Kent gave her must be working."

"Drug? What drug?" Vanessa asked, her expression one of total innocence.

Viv did the eye roll thing. "Come on, Mom. You must see it. She's on something. And so is Arlene, if you ask me."

Ellie leaned back in her chair, chewing the last of her fruit salad. Vivian had just backed up Rudy's observation, and she had no right to butt into the discussion. Besides, she'd probably learn more by listening.

"Yes, Dr. Kent gave her a prescription for medication, but you make it sound like she's taking one of those illegal street drugs," said Vanessa. "She's taking something for her depression. You know how she gets when the muse leaves her and she can't paint."

"Muse my ass," said Viv. "She's a spoiled brat—always has been. She fooled you and Dad completely with that 'art is my life' crapola while she was in high school and college, and she's still doing it at thirty-five. FYI, prescription drugs can be illegal, too, especially if they're not monitored."

"Vivian, enough. You're jealous of both your sisters, always have been. They're sensitive right-brainers, while you're a more practical left, and that's all there is to it."

"At least I make enough to support myself. I don't have to marry for money or live off mommy and daddy to survive."

Ellie laid a hand on Viv's knee, where no one could see the give-it-a-rest gesture. No wonder her best friend never had much to say about her family. "Maybe it's time we took that tour you promised me."

"Sure, in a minute. I want to wait for Arlene."

Before Ellie could say more, Arlene arrived at the top of the stairs. Perfectly made up, she was dressed in navy slacks and a man-styled yellow silk blouse with an upturned collar and rolled-back cuffs. Holding a sheet of paper in her hand, she seemed put together and composed.

"Sorry I rushed past you, but I had to say hello to my Bostons." Smiling, she glanced at the table and spotted the coffee cups and empty plates. "I see you found the breakfast buffet Rosa set up. I hope everything was good." She scanned the terrace. "What happened to Adrianne?"

"She's in the kitchen hoping to find a peon to boss around," said Viv. "Why don't you have a seat? I'll get you some eggs and coffee."

"Thanks, Vivie. Coffee would be great, but no food. I'm back on my diet."

"Diet?" Ellie asked without thinking. "You don't need to be on a diet."

"Oh, but I do. I have a lot of work ahead of me."

"Work? Do you have to get a job?"

"Go on, sis. Tell Ellie why you're dieting while I get you that coffee," said Viv, leaving the terrace.

Figuring it was some kind of family joke, Ellie grinned. "I can't believe how good you look after what you went through last night. And you need to eat. The next few days will probably be stressful."

"Maybe so, but I'll be back on the husband hunt by the end of summer." Arlene inspected Ellie's tank top and bare arms. "It's fine if you don't care about your figure, but I do. In my experience, it's being slim that first attracts a man."

"Now, Arlene," said Vanessa. "Ellie has a police detective for a boyfriend. He might like his women a bit big—er—more generously proportioned."

Unable to utter a word, Ellie blinked. She was used to her mother cracking sly comments about her daughter's double-digit dress size, but Vanessa and Arlene were practically strangers. She had no idea how to react to what they'd just said. It was then Viv arrived with her sister's coffee and fruit, and set everything in front of her.

Arlene pushed the fruit to the center of the table and added a blue packet of sweetener to the coffee. "How are you and Daddy doing in the cottage? The police told me I couldn't go inside the office space to collect Martin's personal belongings until they were through with the investigation. And I know they hung a notice on his door." She pointed to the sheet of paper she'd brought outside. "This is a list of everything they've gathered, which they're supposed to return to me when the investigation is over."

Vanessa straightened in her chair. "They collected scads of things, and left with their sirens blaring. Once they were gone, we had a good night."

"What about you girls?" Arlene asked her sister. "Did you get enough rest?"

"More important, did you?" said Viv.

"I managed to sleep after I took another sedative. I'm waiting to hear from Martin's brother. He's on business somewhere in Texas, and he couldn't make it to the wedding."

Still wrapped in a cocoon of surprise over the comment about her size, Ellie rested her chin in her palm. If anything happened to Sam, she'd be falling apart right about now. And if he died? She wouldn't be sitting on a terrace planning to diet so she could catch her next man.

"I don't mean to sound unsympathetic, but does that mean Dr. Kent's body disposal might be up to you?" asked Viv.

Without warning, tears welled in Arlene's eyes. "I guess. He didn't have a will, so I'll have to consult with his brother, but he did tell me he'd want to be cremated, so I'll do whatever I need to do to see that it happens. What I don't like is waiting to hear if his death was an accident or a—or a—you know." She sniffed. "It's going to be hell living alone again."

Relieved to see a bit of remorse from her hostess, Ellie patted her hand. "Vivian and I will be here all week, if your offer for us to stay still holds. You can depend on us to help you through everything."

"How about a muffin?" asked Viv, still trying to force-feed her sister. "Rosa did a wonderful job with the buffet, and I think you need some food in your stomach."

She rose and aimed for the kitchen just as Adrianne walked through the door with a coffee cup in her right hand and a muffin in her left.

"Here you go," said Viv, snatching the treat. "Just what the doc—er—your youngest sibling ordered." She brought the muffin to the table and placed it in front of Arlene. "Eat this while we talk."

Adrianne muttered a halfhearted "Nice going, Viv," spun on her heel, and headed back to the house.

"Don't mind Miss Bossy Boots. Just take a bite," Viv coerced, smiling when Arlene broke off a piece of the crust and nibbled. "You need to keep up your strength."

"Awwwk! You're a doll! Kiss me, sweetie. Awwwk! Do it to me. Yeah, just like that. Awwwk!"

Adrianne carried Myron in on his perch while the

bird announced his arrival. "Here you go. Myron ought to cheer you up." She set the parrot in the same corner he'd occupied the night before. "I even brought a couple of M&Ms to keep him happy."

She returned to the kitchen, and Viv put her head in her hands. "Now I'm positive the brat's on some kind of happy pill. M&Ms?"

"They're Myron's favorite treat," said Arlene. She walked to the parrot and gave him a blue candy. "Here you go, darling. Now, not another bad word."

"Awwwk! The bird, the bird. The bird is the word. Awwwk!"

Ellie stifled a smile. She didn't recognize the voice, but figured it was Dr. Kent's, which might upset Arlene further. "If it's too painful to hear Martin's voice, I can bring him back to the foyer," she offered.

"Awwwk! I've been waiting, baby. Where have you been? Awwwk!"

"No, no. He's fine," said Arlene, giving a tepid smile. "He'll be a reminder of happier times."

"So, that is Dr. Kent's voice?" asked Ellie.

"Yes. African grays have a unique ability to imitate a sound or a voice perfectly. Martin used to sing oldies and get Myron to repeat them. Once in a while, when Myron and I are in the house alone, I'll hear a cat meow or a lion roar, and I'll know it's him. He loves to watch *Animal Planet.*" She shrugged. "The problem is, you just never know what he'll say or when. Sometimes, he comes out with the strangest things."

"Awwwk! Ah, ah, ahh, yes, Marty, yes, ahhhh! Awwwk!"

Ellie gauged the tone, certain it was a woman in the throes of an orgasm. She wasn't sure if she should laugh or not, because Arlene's face was wreathed in confusion.

"It sounds like you and the doc had him in your bedroom one time too many," said Viv.

Arlene said nothing, but her expression grew grim as she returned to her chair. Ellie thought her not responding was strange, but the woman had just been dropped into a tragedy, so who knew what was going on in her mind?

Adrianne returned with a second muffin and sat next to her older sister. While Myron continued to squawk nonsense, Ellie watched the sisterly byplay, as well as the departing guests' reactions when they appeared to say their good-byes. Elsie and Connie, the older "aunts" from the Davenport, stopped with their dogs to give a tearful farewell, and Ellie promised to visit them and arrange a walking schedule as soon as she got back home.

Aunt Miriam, Uncle Scott, and Faith and Christian came by to pay their respects, as did the third group whose names all began with the letter R. And they promised to return if there was a memorial service for Dr. Kent.

The only people missing, that Ellie could remember, were "hunky guy," the man called Uncle Mickey, and Dr. B.

During the conversations, it was clear Vivian was the one with the level head, while the other three McCready women . . . Well, they were definitely in another world. After a few minutes of listening to them squabble, Ellie made a decision. "I think I'll go see how the dogs are doing."

"Oh, would you? And see if Maria's with them. I think they should all go for a walk on the beach." Arlene dabbed at her eyes with a napkin. "My babies are so upset over losing Martin."

The statement set up another round of suggestions, but they stopped talking when Detective Wheeling appeared in the kitchen doorway. Wearing a grim expression, he gazed at the assembled women and waited until Vanessa grabbed her oldest daughter's hand.

"I just got off the phone with the medical examiner, Ms. Millman, and I need to speak with you privately."

Arlene reached for Vivian with her free hand and entwined their fingers. "Anything you want to say can be said in front of my mother and sisters." She gave Ellie a hesitant smile. "And my guest."

Wheeling threw Vanessa a pointed look and cleared his throat. "There's no easy way to put this, Ms. Millman. Your fiancé was murdered."

Ellie and Vivian reclined in cushioned lounge chairs on the deck off their bedroom suite, resting in the late-afternoon shade with Rudy and Mr. T curled on the floor between them. Detective Wheeling's grave pronouncement had shocked everyone except Ellie, who'd been, bit by bit, putting the pieces of Dr. Kent's death together.

According to the detective, who was repeating the medical examiner, Martin Kent had died from blunt head trauma caused from cracking his skull on the walkway's brick border. Murder came into the equation because the ME had discovered a bruise on his chest that had come from a blow so powerful it had probably pushed the victim backward for the fall.

When Arlene heard the news she broke down and stumbled to her feet. Vanessa and Adrianne gathered her in their arms and rushed her to her suite, where the three women had remained. During that time, Viv had given Ellie her promised grand tour, taking her to every room in the huge house except the Suarezes' private quarters.

Rosa served lunch a few hours later, and Vanessa came downstairs, assembled a tray, and brought it up to Arlene. Viv and Ellie reclaimed Mr. T and Rudy and ate on the terrace, where they read the local rag, *Dan's Papers,* and discussed places they could visit that were nearby, so they could still be involved in helping Arlene.

Right now Viv lay with her eyes closed while Ellie thought about Detective Wheeling's news. Martin Kent was a sizable man, so she imagined that whoever had done the deed was strong, which meant the killer was most likely a man. Other than that, she had not a clue to the murderer's identity.

"What are you thinking about?" asked Viv a moment later.

Ellie raised an eyebrow. There was no point in trying to fool her best friend. "Dr. Kent."

Eyes still closed, Viv grinned. "I knew it. So you are working on the crime."

"I'm not 'working' on anything. I'm just thinking."

"Keep it up. You'll get to the bottom of the thing, like most good detectives do."

"I thought you said we were on vacation," Rudy muttered from below.

"Thinking doesn't mean I'm going to do anything about it," Ellie said to both conversations. "And I'm not detecting."

"But you are," Viv continued. "I just hope you figure it out fast. We were supposed to have some fun this week."

"What I'd like is a trip through Dr. Kent's office,"

Ellie admitted. "Just to see what he did in there, not to investigate. No one seems willing to tell me what type of medicine he practiced. We could probably figure it out by the type of magazines sitting on the waiting area tables."

"So, go inside. The only thing in your way is that yellow crime scene tape. Surely you know how to get through it without ringing any warning bells."

"The tape's no big deal, but Wheeling looked right at me when he said they'd arrest anyone who crossed the line for any reason. And your mom said he told her the cottage had to remain locked until the investigation was over. The last thing I want is to spend my first vacation in years in a prison cell."

"Did they set up a police guard?"

"Nope. We're on our honor. Your parents promised to keep it locked, and I believe them. No one is allowed in until the coast is clear."

"Like that's stopped you before."

"And that would stop you?" said Viv at the same time Rudy spoke. "I don't think so."

"Me, neither."

Ellie chewed her lower lip. There was no use arguing, especially when she was doing so with two unconnected minds. "There is one more thing bothering me."

"Oh?"

"Hunky Guy, our faux Agent Double O Seven."

"You know, I wanted to ask Arlene about him, but with all the activity I never got the chance. He told you he met Arlene shopping around town, and she invited him out of the blue. My guess is he finagled an invite on his own, and she was too flustered to do anything about it."

"My question is, why Wheeling didn't call him on it, and talk with Mr. Bond the same way he did the rest of us?"

"Maybe he did, but it was done at the police station."

"That's a possibility," Ellie said. "But why? If I could find a way to meet him again, I'd come right out and ask him, but it's not like I could walk next door and borrow a cup of sugar." Another guest came to mind, and she said, "And who, pray tell, is Uncle Mickey?"

"I have no idea, but Martin knew him, and I didn't see him anywhere around later, either."

"And that Dr. B woman?"

"She's someone he was in practice with a while back. Apparently they've stayed in touch and become best friends, though it doesn't sit well with Arlene. She told Martin he could invite Dr. B and Uncle Mickey because they were his only family."

"Okay, I'll forget about Uncle Mickey and Dr. B. I'd rather talk about Hunky Guy. Something's up with him. I just can't put my finger on it."

"Hmm. Maybe we could take an early-morning stroll along the beach tomorrow? We could lose track of time and just end up behind his house or something."

"That might work," Ellie agreed. "Finding out about him is my first priority after getting into the doc's office." It was then she decided to change the subject, just to get her thoughts off breaking into a crime scene. "I don't remember thanking you for the tour."

The place was huge, with three staircases leading to different second-floor sections of the house. The Suarezes lived in a four-room wing on the west side of the manor. The hall she'd walked through for last night's questioning led to Arlene's office and a library. The foyer, living room, sunporch, breakfast room, laundry, and kitchen made up the rest of the first floor, including a stairway that led to the upstairs and its five guest bedrooms and baths.

Though the Boston Terriers were allowed in every part of the house, they stayed close to Arlene, so Ellie hadn't been able to establish any type of personal communication with them. Their food bowls were in the breakfast area along with three dog beds, but there were three more identical beds in the living room, and another set on the back deck. It appeared that Myron, too, had the run of the place, though, according to Arlene, he enjoyed the foyer, kitchen, and rear terrace best.

His raucous squawks rang in her brain, and she echoed Viv's sentiments. Why would anyone want to live with a bird that repeated whatever it heard? It had to be like living in the midst of triplet three-year-olds. Even Rudy left the room when she and Sam got romantic. Weren't parrots supposed to be smart? Why would they want to watch humans interact, then scream out what they said in the throes of passion?

"You already thanked me a dozen times," said Viv, her eyes still closed. "And stop trying to change the subject."

"No, really, my thoughts were on this house. If it belongs to your sis, and Myron was so wealthy, why is she looking to marry for money again?"

"Ah, well, the way I understand it, Myron had kids from his first marriage and they got a lot of the cash and stocks. That's why Arlene got the houses, some of which were mortgaged, and sold them. She's set to live comfortably, but not as well as she wants."

"That sounds like Stanley's arrangement," said Ellie.

"He's left almost everything to his kids. Mother only gets a couple of mil. Not that she cares, of course, since she has enough money of her own. I guess that's one way to keep the children from starting a family feud after the last parent goes."

"Personally, I think Arlene's the type of woman who doesn't feel fulfilled unless there's a man in her life. I'd just like to see her happy with herself."

"What did she do when she lived here alone after Mr. Millman died?"

"I think she wrote astrology charts for friends and a few of the people she met in town. I know she chose the date for the wedding by reading the stars. Too bad she read her chart instead of Martin Kent's." Viv swung her legs around and sat up on the chaise. "I know she bought Myron right before the first Myron died. Then she met the doctor and he took her to a breeder to get her Bostons. And Rosa, Julio, and the girls have always been here, almost like Arlene's second family."

"Do the girls go to school?"

"Terry takes night courses at the local college, and works here in the house. Maria goes to high school, but she was having trouble over the last few months. I'm not sure what happened, but I gather she almost died from one of those street drugs popular with the younger crowd."

"That sweet little girl? On drugs?" Ellie found it hard to believe. "Wow, I guess you just never know."

"Funny, isn't it, how drugs seem to play a role in this debacle? I'm fairly certain Arlene is on them. I'm guessing Adrianne's taking them, and Maria had a problem, too. If this is what it's like to live with the rich and famous in the Hamptons, I'll pass, thank you."

"From the way Sam talks, the city has more drugs than what you'll find out here. I'm too busy to notice, but according to him and Rudy, druggies walk the streets of Manhattan right next to the normal folks and no one suspects a thing."

"All I know is I'd find it debilitating to juggle a drug habit. How can you make the money you need to buy the stuff if you're too hyped up or strung out to work? It would be a huge chore for me to hide it from my superiors, my coworkers, and my friends." She waved a hand in Ellie's direction. "And you'd know immediately."

"Probably, but maybe not. Remember, when we first arrived I thought Arlene was high from all the prewedding adrenaline pumping through her system. Could be she's hyped up now because she just learned someone murdered her fiancé." She shrugged. "I hate to admit it, but I'm a complete novice where drugs are concerned."

Viv took her turn at heaving a sigh, something she'd been doing often since they arrived. "Don't sweat it. Drugs are nasty business. You're lucky you never got involved with them or the people who take them."

"Can I ask you a question?"

Viv stretched, then stood and walked to the deck railing. "Of course you can."

"Even if it's about your sisters . . . and your parents?"

"The supercilious snob family? Sure, go ahead."

"Are you upset about that?"

Viv turned and rested her bottom on the railing. "What? That my father is an overbearing bore who thinks he's always right? Or that my mother thinks her two eldest daughters are paragons and can't see what they've become, even though it's staring her in the face?"

Mr. T stood on his hind legs and rested his forepaws on his mistress's knee. *"Tell her, Ellie. Make her see that those folks are the nut jobs and my girl's okay."*

Ellie rubbed her nose, attempting to come up with an answer that wouldn't hurt her best friend's feelings. "I do think your dad is a bit pompous, but considering his occupation, it sounds as if he had to be."

"And Mother? She's always treated me as if I was second best. The whole time we were growing up, Arlene and Adrianne were her perfect daughters, while I was her disappointment."

"Is that the reason you never tried to join Mensa? Afraid you'd fall short and prove her right?"

Viv bent and scratched T's ears. "Ha! I'd ace Mensa."

"Really? And you know this because . . ."

"Because when I was a freshman in high school, Mom had us tested by some specialist who did IQ studies. She wouldn't tell us our scores, but I sneaked into her office and found them. That's when I learned I'd outscored Arlene and Adrianne by twenty points." She crossed her arms. "It was one of the highlights of my life."

"Then why does your mother baby them and not you?"

"I've wondered the same thing, and I worked out a simple solution that I can accept. They did what Mom asked and I didn't. I never let her opinion influence me, and I think that made her angry, which put me on her shit list."

Rudy nudged Ellie's knee. *"Viv's story makes the ex-Terminator sound like a cupcake."*

"I'm sorry I brought up bad memories, Viv, but—"

"Hey, no worries. I've grown used to it. I have a great job, good friends, Dr. Dave and Twink . . ." She grinned. "And a fabulous best friend and her faithful companion.

What else does a girl need?" Viv walked over and sat next to Ellie on the chaise. "I'm good . . . really."

They remained side by side until Ellie checked her watch. "I'm starving. Think we can talk Rosa into letting go of some of that food no one got to eat last night?"

"I don't see why not. Besides, you're going to need your strength for later."

"Me? For what?"

"For breaking into Dr. Kent's office, of course."

Chapter 5

An ocean breeze blew in from the beach, filling the night air with a salty tang. Ellie, Viv, and the dogs were taking the long way around to the guest cottage so they wouldn't activate the security lights. They'd waited until all was quiet in the main house, Myron was under wraps in the foyer, and Arlene was in bed before they slipped down the back stairway. Lucky for them, the moon was bright, giving them enough light to find their way.

"I must be crazy, letting you talk me into this," Ellie whispered. "If we get caught—"

"Nothing will happen," Viv hissed. "Besides, you said you wanted in. What's the problem?"

"The 'problem' is Detective Wheeling. If he finds out I crossed the line, he'll throw me in the slammer so fast, I won't realize I'm there until Big Betty hits on me."

She couldn't believe Viv was the one who had encouraged her to break the law. But she knew her best friend was just trying to be supportive. She'd voiced her desire to see Dr. Kent's office, and Viv had come up with a way to make it happen. She'd even promised to take care of the fingerprints, so Ellie would be safe if the cops checked. But still . . .

"There's no way he'll find out," Viv said. "Stop whining and get down to business."

"You have the keys, right?" asked Ellie as they made a wide loop around the parking lot and headed for the far side of the building. According to Viv, that side of the house was protected by a stand of trees and, though it had no lights, was where they'd find the fuse box.

"You saw me take them off the board near the back door, remember?"

"Okay, okay. I just want to make sure we can get in."

"I know these keys work because I've used them before. Mom and Dad have a set, Adrianne has a set, I'm sure Dr. Kent had a set, Arlene keeps a set on her key ring, and this is the spare."

"Sounds to me like everybody in the Hamptons has access to the cottage."

Viv stopped walking. "Maybe you should take that as a clue. Anyone who was here could have gone into Dr. Kent's office."

The idea was so logical, Ellie decided to add it to her list. Wait, no! There was no list. She was on vacation. This little foray was just a bit of fun to stop the nagging questions knocking around in her brain. She tiptoed ahead while her best friend continued to whisper.

"If someone came up from the beach, no one would see them and they could have mugged the doc and escaped. And look at us. We're taking a route that's hard to see from the house. Anyone at the party might have done the same."

"We can talk about that later." Now in the shadows of the cottage, she inhaled deeply and took control of the situation. She spied the dim figure of a metal box mounted on the wall next to the air-conditioning unit. "Are you sure Adrianne and your parents are asleep?"

"They left the main house a couple of hours ago, and the second floor is dark. That's all I can say."

"And you're certain they're heavy sleepers."

"They were while I grew up. My guess is Adrianne took something from Arlene's pharmaceutical-grade medicine cabinet to help her get through the night. Maybe Mother did, too. Dad is the one we have to worry about."

"Great," Ellie muttered. The last person she wanted to be caught by while breaking and entering was Evan McCready.

"Come on, just do it. If he shows up downstairs, I'll take the blame." Viv flipped on her flashlight and zeroed in on their target. "Go ahead."

"Keep your fingers crossed that every fuse is labeled. We have to get those security lights turned off around the back entry or we'll never be able to get in without being noticed."

"I still think you should have worn gloves. What if I screw it up and forget to take care of a set of prints?"

Ellie rolled her eyes. "The only gloves in the house were those thick yellow ones Rosa uses for cleaning, and they wouldn't have worked. We made a deal, remember? I do the tricky business, while you wield the flashlight and wipe clean whatever I touch." She shrugged. "I have no idea if the cops would run another fingerprint scan, but I'd rather not chance it. Now hold that light steady. Here we go."

Viv did as ordered, and Ellie pulled the metal loop attached to the box. The door sprang open and they jumped. Then she peered at the breakers, relieved to find them marked.

"Hang on a second," she said, still examining the box. "It looks like they're already in the off position."

"Off? Are you sure?" Viv asked, her voice low.

"Fairly sure, but I'm not an electrician, so it's just a guess."

"The only people who've been out here are my family and the cops. I doubt they'd turn anything off."

"We should probably do something to check it out," said Ellie. "We need to know before we take the next step."

"So, which of us gets to run a test?"

"I don't—"

"No problemo. I'll do it," said Rudy.

"Me, too," added Mr. T.

The dogs had been so quiet, Ellie almost forgot they were there. After thinking a second, she came up with a plan. "How about using the dogs? If anyone sees them, then spots us, we can say we took them out for a last walk and they ran down here."

Viv gazed at the boys, sitting at attention between them. "I don't know about your little man, but T isn't trained or anything. How will they know what to do?"

"Trained? I'll show you trained, fool," mumbled Mr. T. Rearing up on his hind legs, he began to dance in a circle. Rudy immediately took to the idea and did the same.

Viv looked on in amazement while Ellie grinned. "See, T and Rudy already know what we want. This is their way of telling us they can help."

"I've never seen T do that before." Viv stared open-mouthed at her boy, then gaped at Ellie. "I don't know what to tell them or how. You're into canine-speak. You'll have to take the lead."

Ellie stooped and put a hand on each dog's head. "Just walk around the parking lot and circle the house. We'll watch from here."

"*Roger that,*" said Rudy.

He and Mr. T scampered to the lot while the girls squatted and peeked around the corner. When the lights remained off, they exhaled in tandem. Ellie gave a low whistle and the boys came running back.

"I don't believe it." Viv gave her Jack Russell a hug. "You are such a talented boy."

"Talented, nothin'. I'm a star," he reminded her.

Ellie hugged Rudy, then stood. "I say we go in around the back. That's the private entrance for both floors and it's where we found the body. It's also more secluded."

They crept along the dark side of the building while Viv trained the flashlight on the ground. The quartet slipped around the corner and Ellie raised her hand. The dogs immediately took a stand, one on each side of the door, their expressions as wary as if they were guarding a pharaoh's tomb.

"How do you do that?" asked Viv in a tone of frustration.

"It's a gift," mouthed Ellie. She nodded to the boys.

"We're on the lookout, Triple E," said Rudy, giving a doggie snort.

She waggled a finger at Viv, who passed her the keys. Ever so slowly, Ellie inserted the first key. When it turned, they opened the door and stepped into the dark foyer. She motioned for Viv to shine the flashlight on the office door, and Viv did as asked. Holding her breath, Ellie used the next key, and grinned. They were in.

They shuffled into the middle of the waiting room and surveyed the space, taking in the sofas, chairs, and tables that made up the area. Ready to find the doc's office, she stopped in her tracks. Laying a hand on Viv's arm, she shivered when the hairs on the back of her neck rose and her skin tingled.

Before she could speak something prodded her hard in the back. "Don't move," said a man in a dark and even tone.

Ellie swallowed, her mind a blur. "Who are you?" she whispered, attempting to look over her shoulder. Did the guy really have a gun? "What are you doing here?"

Viv tried to turn at the same time, and he pushed her forward. "Uh-uh-uh. Seems to me I should ask you two the same question. Now be quiet while I think."

"Think? What do you have to think about?" asked Viv, her voice wavering.

"Probably where he can shoot us," Ellie muttered.

He gave them each another jab. "I said be quiet."

It was then Ellie recognized the intruder's voice. "You know what? I don't think he has a gun," she said quietly in her best I-dare-you bravado. "I think he'll run if we turn around."

"You sure you want to do that?" asked the guy.

"Not me," squeaked Viv. "We should cooperate, Ellie. I don't want to die."

"There's not a chance of that happening." Spinning around, she faced their attacker. "Is there, Mr. Bond?"

"Mr. Bond?" Viv turned, too, and stared at their faux Agent 007. Her flashlight illuminated his chiseled face and the watch cap pulled low over his brow. "For Pete's sake. What are you doing here?"

"That's what I'd like to know," Ellie demanded. Her gaze raked his dark, long-sleeved polo shirt, then dropped to his hand and— Good Lord, he *was* holding a gun. "Is that thing the real deal?"

James Bond blew out a breath. "I should have known you'd be sticking your nose in here sooner or later." He pocketed the pistol and crossed his arms. "Didn't the police tell you to stay away from the crime scene?"

"They told me everyone had to stay away. I assumed that meant you, too."

"It did mean me, in a roundabout way. Now I suggest you leave and let me take care of business. Once I'm through, I won't bother—"

"What was that?" said Viv, her voice rising.

He laid a finger on his lips. Footsteps sounded from above, then stopped. A moment later the toilet flushed and footsteps again crossed overhead.

"That has to be Dad," whispered Viv. "He's getting up in years, so prostate problems abound."

"Really? I had no idea. It's not serious, is it?"

"Nah. Mom says he's on medication and doing—"

"Will you both please shut up," 007 ordered, his voice low and harsh. "And get the hell out of here."

Tired of Mr. Bond and his antics, Ellie grew bold. "Look, I don't know what you're doing here and I don't care. Just go away and leave us to do our thing."

He raised his hand and pushed aside their flashlight. "You're being ridiculous. I'm the one with the gun, and I just might decide to use it."

"Well, I don't think you will."

He focused on Viv. "Do me a favor and talk some sense into your friend. Tell her I mean business."

Vivian smiled. "You know what? I don't think you do. This is my sister's house, so I have a right to know why you're here." She made a move for the door. "Unless . . . maybe my dad should be the one to ask that question."

He again crossed his arms. "You two are certifiable. You know that?"

"I've been called crazy by better than you," said Ellie. "We want answers and we want them now."

Mr. Bond heaved a sigh, grabbed them each by an elbow, and steered them toward the door. On the way out, Viv stopped and wiped the doorknob. He pointed to the exit and the girls did as he indicated while he followed behind them.

"You actually expect us to believe you're just a nosy neighbor wanting to take a look at a crime scene? In the middle of the night? Because you have nothing better to do?" Ellie shook her head. "That's ridiculous."

"You forgot the nosy-neighbor-with-a-gun part," Viv chimed. "And you still haven't said that you have a permit to carry that thing."

They were gathered around the end of the dining table on the back terrace with Rudy and Mr. T at their feet. Between Viv's flashlight and the bright moon, Ellie could read every expression on James Bond's too-handsome face. Though he'd told several different-yet-connected stories to explain his presence in Dr. Kent's office, she hadn't believed any of them—a fact not lost on Viv.

"Maybe if you told the truth, we wouldn't be so

pushy," she offered. "It's not like we can do anything about it."

His smile was more like a sneer. "You two are a trip. I don't have to answer to you. And you're right, you can't do anything about it, because telling the cops will incriminate you as well."

"That's what I'm trying to say," said Ellie. "It's best we both keep quiet about tonight. Just clue us in on the real reason you were there."

Running a hand over his head, he swiped off his knit cap and folded it in front of him. Then he reached into his back pocket and pulled out a wallet.

"Please don't think about offering us a bribe," said Viv. "Because we can't be bought."

"I've got a feeling there isn't enough money in the world to shut the two of you up." He flipped open the wallet. "Here, this should do it."

Viv flicked on her flashlight and focused on the table.

Ellie stared at what appeared to be a badge tucked into one side of the wallet and an ID on the other. The circular badge had the letters DEA in the middle and a golden eagle with outstretched wings on top. On the other side was a card with a photo, but the print was too tiny to read.

"You work for the DEA?"

"I'm a special agent for the Drug Enforcement Agency. That's my identification."

She locked gazes with Vivian. "What do you think?"

"I haven't a clue. Does it look like Sam's badge?"

"Sam? Who's Sam?" he asked.

"Her boyfriend," said Viv.

"A detective I know," Ellie said at the same time.

"Great. You're a wannabe cop."

"I am no such thing," she huffed. "I'm just close to someone who's a homicide detective."

"She knows lots of someones," Viv added. "She has friends in high places. Very high places."

"Viv, please, give it a rest."

"Well, you do. Your current stepfather is a retired appellate court judge, you're dating Sam, you know Vince and that big-shot captain and—"

His gaze ping-ponged between the two of them. "What big-shot captain?"

"His name is Carmichael or something."

"Carmody?" He turned to Ellie. "You know Mitchell Carmody personally?"

"They're like this." Viv crossed her fingers. "She got him a dog."

"A dog?"

Ellie pulled Viv's fingers down. "Vivian, this is not the time to talk about Buddy."

"And why not? Getting him to adopt that Bichon was—"

"Not a part of this conversation." She again focused on the badge. The DEA was an arm of the Department of Justice, a federal agency that had its hand in everything the government watched over. If James Bond was truly one of their agents, Arlene could be in real trouble. "I've never seen a DEA badge before. How do we know this is real?"

"I guess you'll have to take my word for it until morning. Then you can call my superior."

Ellie frowned. The pieces were beginning to fit together. The way Arlene and Adrianne had easy access to drugs; the remoteness of Dr. Kent's practice; the cars coming and going in the parking lot. It all made sense now . . . sort of.

"Okay, let's say we buy your identification story. That still doesn't explain how you got inside the doc's office or what you were doing there."

He closed the wallet and tucked it away. "Dr. Kent's been under investigation for illegally prescribing and distributing Schedule Two drugs. According to a now-arrested pharmaceutical rep who incriminated a list of others, we have evidence he also kept a stash of drugs in his office where he was doling them out like candy." He gazed at Viv. "I had a warrant the night of the party, but I didn't want to make a big deal out of it. I was going to present it if I was caught, but then I found Kent and—"

"My sister would have been so embarrassed, especially having her fiancé arrested. She's been so depressed, I can't tell her about the doc's troubles."

"Have you taken a good look at your sisters? I doubt either one would be embarrassed. My guess is they're both regular users of Kent's contraband pharmacy."

Viv set the flashlight down and lowered her gaze. Then she looked up and brushed a tear from her cheek. "They're not—they won't be—"

"Arrested? That remains to be seen. I doubt they'll do any time, but they are involved in this case, and not just them. There are pharmacies in the Hamptons under investigation, and a couple more drug reps. The whole lot of them will be hauled in, once we get our ducks in a row."

"But the murder—"

"Screwed everything up. The first time I was in the doc's office, I hoped to grab his computer and take a look at his records. Then I was going to bring him in for questioning. Thanks to whoever killed him, I didn't get that far."

"You were there trying to scan his computer for prescription records?"

"That and anything else that would help me break the case. I figured he had the info on a spreadsheet, because the amount of crap he's suspected of doling out is mammoth. Trouble is, because of the murder the local cops have collected the goods. They told me they'd taken his computer and they were scanning it, but that doesn't mean he didn't have another one stashed away somewhere. They're out to find the killer, and they have jurisdiction, but we're playing tug-of-war with the evidence right now."

"Who do you think killed Dr. Kent?" asked Ellie.

He leaned forward and clasped his hands on the table. "Could be any number of people. A druggie hoping for a score, one of the pharmacists he was working with demanding a bigger cut, the disgruntled parent of a kid Kent's been supplying, even a hopped-up patient." He sat straighter in his chair. "I've been tracking Kent for a couple of months now, and when I heard they were hosting a party I finagled an invite from your sister. It was supposed to be my chance to see if he and one of the guests would have an incriminating conversation. I was hoping they'd talk business at the party, private business I could use for the arrest."

"And you don't have a clue who might have killed him?"

"I work alone, so it's impossible to be two places at once. When I heard your sister was expecting Kent on the terrace, I left the deck, went to the front of the house, and headed back around the grounds and the doc's parking lot. Then I waited at the side along the stand of trees—prepared to gather what I needed from his files—"

"Gather how?"

"Never mind how."

Ellie figured she'd worry about it later. "Get back to the murder. What happened next?"

He raised one dark eyebrow. "Quite a bit. I planned to go in through the front door as he went out the rear. Then I heard an argument, and it was a dilly. Lots of shouting and threats. Then a door slammed and it got quiet." Jim sat back in his chair. "I slipped through the front when I heard the rear door slam. Next thing I knew Kent was arguing again. I walked to the back door and tried to hear the voice, because I thought it might be the same man, but the tone was different."

Eyes shuttered, he placed his palms on the table. "I couldn't intervene without blowing my cover, so I waited them out. Then I heard another voice calling for *el doctor*, a string of Spanish, and footsteps moving away. It was then I figured I'd better at least sneak a peek, so I opened the back door. That's when I saw the body, bleeding out on the sidewalk. When I sidled over to take a look, and realized there was nothing I could do, I ducked into the bushes. Then you two showed up."

"You could have taken off before the police arrived," Ellie reminded him.

"And then what? All I wanted were the records—whatever he had on prescriptions and the purchases. I explained who I was when the cops got there, even told them about the arguments, and they said they'd cooperate, but they had to focus first and foremost on finding the killer." He cocked his head. "They confiscated Kent's phone records, calendar, and desktop computer, just about everything, but I was hoping to find something more so . . ."

"Are you willing to answer another question?" asked Ellie.

He blew out a breath. "Aw, hell, why not? You're in the middle of it now anyway."

"What kind of medicine did Dr. Kent practice?"

"Word on the street said he was a regular Dr. Feel-good, sort of like the physicians who took care of Anna Nicole Smith and Michael Jackson. He claimed to have the answer for a lot of troublesome conditions. Basically, he was in general practice, but advertised that he could help with depression and anxiety, work you through in-somnia, assist with anger management, even cure obe-sity. He had a pill for every problem, same as those physicians in Beverly Hills who treat the stars."

"And you're not concerned with who murdered him?"

"That's one too many questions." He stood. "I'm heading back to the cottage to lock up and reset the se-curity lights."

"What about taking a look around the office?"

"Who, me? Why, I'm shocked you think I'd go against Detective Wheeling's orders." He slipped the watch cap back over his head. "If anyone sees me, I'm just a friendly neighbor taking a midnight stroll along the beach." He headed for the stairs, then turned. "And by the way, finding the murderer is a job for the cops—not a cop wannabe."

"But my sister's the one who needs our help." Vivian had been so quiet, Ellie almost forgot she was there. "El-lie's solved cases harder than this one."

Shaking his head, he raised his eyes to the starlit sky. "You're not going to give it a rest, are you?"

"I—we—don't care about the drugs, but Viv is concerned about her sister. If the local police are on it, we'll be okay."

"Just remember to stay out of their way."

He charged down the stairs and Ellie blew out a breath. "Well, that was interesting."

Viv held her head in her hands. "Do you think we should believe him?"

"Believe what? That he's a special agent for the DEA?"

"Not the special agent part. That badge looked pretty official to me. I'm talking about Arlene and Adrianne, and the possibility of them being charged with drug abuse or whatever it's called."

Ellie knew nothing about the drug scene or the DEA's involvement in that kind of investigation. "I have no idea, but it did sound like he knew what he was talking about. Trouble is, someone needs to talk to Arlene, make her understand what her fiancé was doing."

"Wouldn't the police tell her?"

"I don't think they had a chance to. The second Wheeling said Dr. Kent had been murdered, she fell apart, ran to her room, and stayed there all night."

"Maybe he told Mother?"

"From the way I've seen the cops operate, they only give pertinent info to the people directly involved. Your mom and dad don't live here, and neither does Adrianne, so I doubt he'd tell them unless it was absolutely necessary."

"Oh, well . . . should we say something to her?"

"And if she asks how we know, how would you tell her we got the information?"

Viv rubbed her eyes with the tips of her fingers. "I

don't know. I just hate that I'm aware of something important and I can't share the information. Maybe, if she knew what Kent had been up to, she'd be able to shed some light on things."

"No one said we couldn't tell her about the investigation, but it would be awkward mentioning the DEA was involved if we had nothing to back it up. I'm not sure how to approach it exactly, except to wait for Detective Wheeling to show up again. If we were there, and we asked the right questions, that might give us a way to bring it all up."

"So I guess we should start by finding out when Wheeling is going to stop by, huh?"

"I guess." Ellie couldn't think. It was hours past her normal bedtime and she was exhausted from all the sneaking around. The fact that James Bond had scared the living daylights out of her didn't help. "Look, I know this is tough, but we'll handle it. Arlene isn't a bad person, she's just misguided. We'll work it out."

Viv sniffed back a tear and pushed from the table. "I know she's a pain; Adrianne, too. But after you, they're all I have. Just promise you'll help me sort this out. Please?"

Ellie walked to her side and gave her a hug. "Vivian, I'm on—"

"I know. You're on vacation."

"And so are you." Taking a step back, she gazed at her best friend and saw the exhaustion and desperation in her eyes. "I'll do what I can, okay? That's all I can say."

Chapter 6

Ellie stepped into her new one-piece chocolate brown Karla Colletto swimsuit. After taking a good look in the full-length mirror on the inside of the bathroom door, she smiled. She'd let Viv drag her up and down Fifth Avenue to stores that supposedly had designer togs for fifty percent off. After digging through the racks, she'd found a suit marked down because it was last year's model. The minute she saw it, she knew it was the right choice. Better still, it was under a hundred dollars, when it had originally listed for over two.

The gold piping accentuated her bust while shrinking her rounded tummy and flaring hips. The rich brown color also complemented her milky white skin and looked great with her coppery curls. She'd been worried about sunburn, but Viv had even found her an expensive sunscreen specially formulated for pale complexions.

All in all, she'd spent close to a thousand dollars on new clothes that day, but Viv had convinced her it was worth it. The Hamptons was one place you couldn't wear hiking boots or canvas casuals and still fit in with the trendy tourist crowd.

"Turn around again. I wanna see your bottom."

She gazed at Rudy, who was watching her from the fluffy turquoise throw rug on the sand-colored tiles. "And why, pray tell, is my bottom worth another look?"

"Because you'll be on the beach, and you might meet a man there. He'll want to inspect you from all angles."

She huffed out a breath. "I'm not interested in meeting a man, especially one who wants to inspect all my angles. I already have a great guy at home. I don't need to mess around with another."

"Sure you do. Who knows? He could be your Prince Charming—isn't that what the perfect man is called in the human world? And he's gonna want to check out your bottom."

"And why would I want to meet a Prince Charming whose barometer for finding his princess is her bottom?"

"'Cause he'd be a real man, not that wussy doofus dick you've fallen for. Now turn around."

Grinning, she did as ordered. As far as she knew, Sam loved her bottom, her middle, and her top, but she'd do anything to shut her boy up and get him off this crazy topic.

"You need more."

More bottom? "Okay, that's it. We're finished critiquing my figure. It's time to start our day." Determined to get moving, she charged into the bedroom. "We're supposed to meet Viv and T on the terrace for breakfast, then walk to the beach. We're on vacation, remember?"

"It didn't sound much like vacation last night. You were grillin' that DEA guy like a real cop."

"I was simply satisfying my curiosity about Arlene and Dr. Sleazeball. It didn't mean I had any intention of running my own investigation."

Sitting on the bed, Ellie grabbed her regular tote and the new straw bag she'd found when she bought the suit, and began transferring essentials: first, her cell phone, then her high-grade sunscreen that promised to bronze while it protected, a tube of lip gloss, a couple of dollars, tissues, two bottles of water, and a small folding dish. After adding her new peach-colored beach towel, she stuck her sunglasses on top of her head and stood.

"I don't get it. If we were home you'd be all over this case. What's wrong with you?"

"Nothing's wrong. It's just that I promised Sam I'd back off of sticking my nose where it doesn't belong, and Wheeling and Bond said the same thing. I thought about it and decided the cops could do their thing without me. Now give me a break and let me finish getting ready."

She slipped into her cover-up—a gauzy knee-length white shirt—slid her feet into sandals, hoisted the new bag over her shoulder, and headed for the door. "Let's get moving. We both need to eat, and we have to collect chairs and umbrellas before we hike to the beach."

"So, what are you gonna tell Viv?"

She knew what Rudy wanted, but decided to play dumb. "Tell Viv about what?"

"Stop actin' stupid. You just said you were thinkin' about last night. You should tell Viv how you feel and quit stringin' her along."

He was right. After their interaction with the shady 007, Viv had complained of "brain pain" and gone immediately to sleep. Ellie knew she should have confessed that she didn't think she should delve any further into this crime before her best friend closed her eyes.

"Viv's the one who's hot on this case. She went to find Arlene early this morning so she could talk to her about Dr. Kent in private." Taking the quickest way to the kitchen, they walked down the back staircase and into the rear foyer. "This is her ball game, not mine."

"Yeah, but she's askin' us for help. She doesn't have the nose for clues, like you and I do." He gave a doggie snort. *"Finding that doctor's killer is up to us pros."*

"Nu-uh. No way are you and I pros. Detective Wheeling is on it, and so is DEA Agent Bond. It would be foolish to step on their toes."

"But this killing seems more confusing than the others we've run across. Don't you want to know who did what?"

"V-A-C-A-T-I-O-N." She spelled the word carefully. "I can't be any more explicit than that. Now be quiet. We're almost in the kitchen." They went through the laundry room and into the eating area, where she again spied a lovely breakfast buffet. "Just give me a second to get your food out of the pantry."

"Are you talking to me, miss?"

She jumped when she heard the question. Then she saw Rosa sitting in a far corner of the breakfast area. Surprised to find her there, Ellie shuffled over. She hadn't seen the housekeeper since the night of the murder, but delicious food seemed to magically appear on the table for each meal, so she assumed Rosa's daughters had done the cooking while their mother dealt with Arlene.

"Um, no. I was talking to my dog." She smiled. "I do it all the time."

"Ah, *sí*. So does Miss Arlene." Sniffing, she dabbed her nose with a tissue. "She is *mucho* upset about losing *el doctor. Pobrecita.*"

The housekeeper appeared so forlorn, Ellie couldn't help offering comfort. Rosa had worked in this house a long time. The police must have questioned her, so there had to be something else on her mind.

"And what about you? Do you miss him, too?"

"El doctor?" Her cheeks turned dark red and her eyes narrowed. "No, never. He was not a nice man."

Shocked by Rosa's vehemence, she squatted to be on eye level with the woman. "You didn't like Dr. Kent?"

Rosa fisted the hand holding the tissue and set it over her mouth. "I'm sorry. I didn't mean what I just said."

"It's all right, really. I didn't know him at all, but I've heard things—things that make me want to agree with you." She crossed mental fingers and lowered her voice. "I heard Dr. Kent dealt in illegal drugs."

Eyes wide, Rosa sobbed into the tissue. "*Sí, sí.* He is the one who gave my Maria the pills that made her sick."

Ellie blinked. Maria was the teen who'd OD'd on drugs? And she'd gotten them from Martin Kent? No wonder Rosa disliked the doc. But could she have killed him?

"Oh, Rosa, are you sure about that?"

"I know because my daughter, she told me. She was cleaning the waiting room in his office and she heard some of his patients talking about how good they felt after taking his medicine. She sometimes gets—*como se dice—el dolor de cabeza*—what you call the migraine, so she asked him about the drugs, and he gave her something. For no money, he say. He just wanted her to—to—" She shook her head. "I cannot talk about it. Miss

Arlene, she might find out, and if she did she would be more sad than she is already."

If Martin Kent wanted what Ellie thought he wanted from the sixteen-year-old Maria, he was a creep, a pervert, and worse, a pedophile. Men like that deserved all the bad things that happened to them. "But the police don't know that Dr. Kent was the cause of her overdose?"

"No, no. She told them she bought the drugs from someone at her school, and made me promise to keep her secret. Miss Arlene, she has been so good to us since Mr. Myron died. Tomas left, and she let him return. He came back the night of the party, and now I am worried. Very worried."

"It's nice of you to protect Arlene, but don't you think it would have been better if she'd known the truth about her fiancé? From what you're saying, marrying him would have been a terrible mistake."

"At first, I tried to tell her, but every time I began, she changed the words to make it sound like Dr. Kent was a saint." Rosa shook her head. "I was going to tell the police, but Julio said no. He and Tomas would take care of it."

Take *care* of it? "What were they going to do?"

Eyes red, Rosa sobbed again, biting down on the tissue. *"Yo hablo demasiado.* I talk too much. I must go to work." She stood. *"Con permiso."*

Before Ellie could say a word, the housekeeper rushed off toward the back stairs.

"Now, there's a clue."

"Huh? What did you say?"

"I said 'clue.' Rosa just gave you a line on the killer."

"Tomas and Julio?"

"Duh, yeah. What else could 'take care of it' mean?"

Okay, so the phrase did have the sound of a clue, but what was it the men had planned to do? And had they already done it?

"I heard, but it could have meant anything. Tomas is Maria's older brother. He could have given her comfort, gotten her straight on the perils of drug abuse. Julio might have offered to send her to a family member to get her away from temptation." And out of Dr. Kent's clutches. "Stuff like that."

Trying to make sense of Rosa's words, she found Rudy's dry food in the pantry, removed his canned Grammy's Pot Pie from the fancy Sub-Zero refrigerator, and mixed his morning nibble. "Here you are. Finish up while I make myself a plate, and we'll go outside."

With the housekeeper's story still ringing in her brain, Ellie carried her coffee, scrambled eggs, croissant, and fruit to the back door, where Rudy was already waiting. "That was fast," she told him, shouldering her way onto the terrace.

"I was starvin'," he called as he raced ahead and touched noses with Mr. T.

"It's about time you showed up," said Viv, who was sitting at her usual place at the table. She pushed her empty plate aside. "I was afraid you'd gone back to sleep."

"Awwwk! Sleep take two. Awwwk! They'll help you sleep. Awwwk!"

Viv held her head in her hands. "That bird has chattered nonsense all morning. He's driving me crazy."

Ellie set down her breakfast and dug a knife, fork, and napkin from her tote. "Want me to take him inside?"

"I wish, but Arlene gave me strict instructions. Told me to bring him out here for some morning relaxation. Apparently, Myron needs a couple of hours in the fresh air every day in order to stay healthy."

Pulling her sunglasses from the top of her head, Ellie seated them on her nose and glanced over the dunes. "I can see why that would make him happy." She admired the sun sparkling on the ocean. "It's beautiful here, and the breeze is great. You won't have to force me to sit on the beach today."

"Awwwk! Force you! Awwwk! Don't force my hand, Marty. Awwwk!"

"Good Lord, did you hear that?" Viv's green eyes grew wide. "It sounded like someone threatening Dr. Kent."

Ellie blew out a breath. "Didn't you say he stayed in Kent's office while Arlene had the house painted for the wedding? Maybe he heard someone spit that out at the doc."

Viv turned toward the African gray. "Tell us more, Myron. Who threatened the doctor?"

The parrot moved his head from side to side and lifted his clawed feet as if dancing in place. *"Doctor, Doctor, give me the news. Awwwk! I've got a bad case of lo-oo-ving you. Awwwk!"*

"Good Lord, an ancient Robert Palmer tune. And Myron sang an oldie the other night, too. Could be that's all he's good for."

"That and eating M&Ms. He's one spoiled bird," Viv said, frowning. "Maybe he heard those words on a television show."

Silently agreeing, Ellie tried to turn the conversation back to their day. "I am so looking forward to this morning. A brilliant sun, warm white sand, and beautiful blue water—who could ask for more?"

Viv took a sip of coffee. "Me, for one. I spent some time with Arlene this morning. Alone time."

"I'm glad you did, especially without Adrianne and your parents. Were you able to make her feel less depressed?"

"I must have, because she didn't cry and she seemed more normal. When I got a look at her pupils, I noticed they weren't enlarged—" Viv put down her cup. "That's one of the signs of drug use, right? Enlarged pupils?"

"So I've heard, but maybe we could Google it to make sure. A person can find just about anything on that search engine." She'd used the site for a lot of her investigative work, especially when she'd checked out the poison used to kill Arnie Harris. "Does Arlene have a computer we can commandeer?"

"I saw one in the library when I was being questioned by Detective Levy, so that one might be good." Viv inched closer and lowered her voice. "I took a look in Arlene's medicine cabinet. Talk about an in-house pharmacy. It reminded me of a shelf behind a Duane Reade counter."

"Lots of little bottles?"

"Dozens. Some were marked with regular prescription labels, but many just had a white label with the type of drug written across it. I don't remember the names and I didn't have a pen and paper, so I couldn't copy anything down. I have no idea what any of them were for."

"Did you ask Arlene how she felt about the ME's ruling on Dr. Kent's cause of death?"

"Yes, and I was amazed by her reaction. She didn't

burst into tears or act upset, but she did say she couldn't imagine who would want to kill Martin. According to her, he was a man among men, someone who worked tirelessly to cure illnesses."

"And she didn't think it was odd that his patients came at all hours of the day and night?"

"According to her, that only proved how dedicated her fiancé was. Besides, she was usually busy in her study doing astrology stuff. I doubt she noticed the traffic."

Ellie thought about Sam and his job. He was gone all hours of the day and night, too, but she'd know if he was doing something out of character. Then again, maybe Martin Kent was acting *in* character, and Arlene simply didn't know him that well. Or she was lying to herself.

Viv peered out at the guest cottage, where her mother, father, and Adrianne were piling into their Cadillac. "I guess the family is going to Bridgehampton for the morning. Mom said something about it last night, but I never thought they'd be so thoughtless as to leave Arlene stranded."

"She's not stranded. You're here for her, aren't you?"

Viv rolled her eyes. "She and I aren't that close, at least not the way she is with Adrianne."

"That might change. You could try to forge a new beginning with your big sister while you're here."

"Do you think so?"

"I think you need to give it a try." Ellie watched the car back out of the lot and head up the curving drive. "Maybe they plan to pick up Arlene at the front of the house."

"I doubt it. Adrianne said she'd had all she could take of murder and mayhem, and intimated she was finished with Arlene for today."

"Awwwk! Murder! Don't make me kill you, Marty! Awwwk!"

Ellie and Viv turned and stared at the parrot. "Shut up, Myron," they said at the same time.

"Keep your mouth shut. Awwwk! Relax, relax, I tell ya. Awwwk!"

"Now what?" Viv said with a moan.

"Hello, baby. Awwwk! Baby love. Awwwk! My baby love. Awwwk!"

Ellie grinned. At this rate Myron was going to squawk through every oldie song ever recorded. Hearing a noise, she and Viv gazed at the door.

"Oh, good. You're both still here." Arlene, wearing a red string bikini and flip-flops, struggled through the entrance loaded down with beach paraphernalia. "If you're headed to the beach, I'm ready whenever you are."

Rudy, Mr. T, and the three Boston Terriers, Corey, Isabella, and Darby-Doll, had arrived at a truce and now lay curled on a large beach towel under one of the towering umbrellas. The canines had spent the past hour darting through the waves, chasing sandpipers and seagulls, and barking at anyone who walked past their section of shoreline. Even Rudy, who didn't usually take part in normal doggie games, had joined in and seemed to enjoy himself.

As for the girls, Ellie, Viv, and Arlene had situated the other two umbrellas so they combined the shade, which gave each of them a spot out of the sun. Viv was now walking the shore gathering sea glass, while Arlene lay next to Ellie.

The three women had talked nonsense while they slathered each other with sunscreen and bronzing gel, and Ellie finally got to see what she thought might be the real Arlene: an attractive mid- to late-thirties woman who'd buried two men she was fond of. Now, with this latest tragedy, she got the sense the deaths were beginning to sink in.

"Ellie, can I ask you something?"

"Sure."

"Do you think I'm a jinx to the men I care for?"

Oh, boy. "Um, well, I don't really believe in that bad luck, jinx theory like some people do. I'd rather believe in fate . . . or maybe destiny."

"Fate?"

"You know, what will be, will be. A plan of sorts that's already written for us. I believe in God, but it doesn't matter your religious faith. I think someone is in charge, directing our lives."

"Then you don't think Myron died because I cared for him, or that knowing me caused Martin to be killed?"

"Gosh, no. Love is a good thing." She repositioned herself to sit on her towel Indian-style. "I think you have to look at Dr. Kent's demise in a more realistic manner. He was dealing in drugs, or so say the cops, and that's the reason he died. You had nothing to do with it."

"I can't believe we're discussing this, but you seemed like family the moment you got here." Arlene heaved a sigh. "It's just so hard to see him in that light. I believe Detective Wheeling, of course, but poor Martin. To be so misguided that he'd pass out pills to anyone who asked."

"I doubt Dr. Kent was 'poor.' People today think having money is the only thing that will make them happy. The lack of it accounts for about ninety percent of the crime in this country."

"You seem so wise for your age." Arlene raised herself up on her elbows. "Do you mind if I ask you another question?"

Ellie grinned. "Oh, but I'm not wise. Just ask Viv, and she'll tell you about some of the 'unwise' things I've done lately."

"But you'll still answer another question?"

"Okay, but I can't guarantee I'll have a good answer."

Rolling over onto her back, Arlene said, "You and Viv are close, aren't you?"

"I hope so. I don't have any siblings, so I feel as though she's the sister of my heart."

"That's a very sweet thing to say. I'd like to think of her that way, too, but I'm afraid I've botched it."

"Botched it?"

"You know, waited too long to try and form a bond. It's my fault, really. I'm the eldest, so I should have taken it upon myself to be more interested in my baby sister's life, more caring, more thoughtful of her world."

Wow, that was quite a confession. But Vivian was the one who should be hearing this, not her. "I don't think it's ever too late to rework a relationship and form a bond. Viv's a wonderful woman. I'm sure she'd listen, if you wanted to talk about it."

"She was very kind this morning, trying to make me feel better about Martin." Arlene sat up and stared at the shore, where Viv was on her knees inspecting whatever had been washed up by the tide. Standing, she said, "Excuse me. I'll be back in a couple of minutes."

Ellie heaved a sigh. This was a good sign for Vivian. She wanted her best friend to be happy and content with her family, and growing closer to Arlene was a start. She leaned back and gazed at her legs, stretched out in front of her.

What the heck!

Slipping off her sunglasses, she gave her legs another once-over. Then she picked up the bronzing gel and compared the legs on the tube to the color of her own calves and thighs. Where had she gone wrong?

She tossed the tube on the towel and scrambled to her feet, ducking out from under the umbrella. She figured the blatant orange tone of her skin was probably a reflection from her peach-colored beach towel. When she stood in the sunlight, she'd get a better look.

She glanced at her arms, her hands, her fingers, and inhaled a second gasp. What in the world had gone wrong? A moan escaped her lips, and she bent to pick up the cause of her color catastrophe.

Hearing her mutter, the dogs woke from their naps and began to bark. *"Hey, Triple E, we got company,"* Rudy added to the chorus of barking canines.

She rose from her bottoms-up position. "Don't be silly. It's just me, not a stranger." The Bostons settled down, but Mr. T sniffed her legs, then dashed around her.

"The Rudster is right, fool," he chimed.

Ellie turned and practically bumped into Agent Bond's chest. Wearing mirrored sunglasses, a snug yellow T-shirt, and washed-out jeans that fit like a glove, he raised his lips in a smug smile.

"Forgive me for saying so, but you look a little strange. From the color of your skin, I'd say it was time you got out of the sun, Ms. Engleman."

She reached for her cover-up and pulled it on. "What are you doing here?"

"Enjoying the day, taking a walk—whatever you want to call it." He took her in from head to toe and back again. "Too much sun can be bad for you, or so I've heard."

"No kidding," snapped Ellie, again perusing the tube of gel. The list of ingredients, mostly chemical compounds, boggled her brain. With this much scientific jargon, it was impossible to tell if a person was allergic.

"Are you trying to find an antidote?" Jim asked, his tone teasing.

"What I need is a suggestion on how to get back to my normal skin tone. Maybe a bath in baking soda or some kind of cream or . . . something to get rid of this—this—"

"Orange skin?"

Slumping her shoulders, she nodded. "I look like a tangerine."

"Actually, that color would be good"—he snickered—"if you were a traffic cone."

Folding her arms, Ellie raised both eyebrows. "I'm happy to be so entertaining. Now go away." She dropped to the sand, still scanning the squeeze tub. There had to be something written on the back about what to do if one acquired an odd color.

When she looked up, faux Agent 007 was still checking her out . . . from all angles? Great. Rudy was right. This was just what she didn't need. "Don't you have something else to do? Like break into an apartment or arrest some drug dealers?"

"I was on my way to Ms. Millman's house when I saw you all out here. I got a call from Detective Wheeling."

That brought Ellie back to her feet. "Wheeling called you? If he arranged to meet you at Arlene's house, why didn't he call and tell her?"

"He said he tried, but no one answered."

"Not even Rosa or Julio?"

"According to Wheeling, no."

Telling herself that didn't sound promising, she gazed out across the sand and saw Viv and Arlene heading toward them. "I think it's time you told Ms. Millman who you really are."

He shrugged. "I guess there's no way to hide it."

The closer the women came, the wider Viv's eyes opened. "What the heck happened to you?" she asked, gazing at the parts of Ellie the cover-up wasn't covering.

"This is what happened to me." Ellie held up the sunscreen. "I can't believe I let you talk me into buying this overpriced tube of crap."

"That is not crap," said Viv, holding out a beautifully bronzed arm. "I used it, too, and look at me."

Ellie inspected Viv's arm, her long shapely legs, her creamy skin shaded a lovely tawny brown. Didn't it just figure?

"You do look great," Agent Bond said. "You, too, Ms. Millman," he added, taking in Arlene's string bikini.

Arlene smiled as she gazed up at the agent. "Why the formality, James? Don't you think neighbors should be on a first-name basis?"

When he stuffed his hands in his pockets, the bump in the back waistband of his jeans caught Ellie's eye. Good Lord! He was carrying a gun.

"We're neighbors for a reason, Ms. Millman. Let's collect this gear and return it to the house, where we can talk."

Chapter 7

Ellie, Viv, James Bond, and Detective Wheeling clustered around the terrace table, intent on Arlene, who was sitting calmly with her hands folded in front of her. One patrolman stood stoically at the entry to the kitchen, and another waited at the top of the stairs, each blocking an exit. Two more officers had already left to fetch Tomas Suarez.

"I can't believe Tomas would hurt Martin," said Arlene, her voice low, her lips thinned. "Are you sure about this?"

"Fedders and Alcott are bringing him in now," Wheeling said, his expression determined. "It would be nice if he told us what he knew."

Ellie was fairly certain of what would happen next, and decided now might be a good time to fill Vivian in on the proceedings. Focusing on the detective, she said, "If you don't mind, Viv and I will take the dogs down to the pen so they're not underfoot."

"Awwwk! Downtown! Things will be great when you're doooown-town. Awwwk!"

Petula Clark, thought Ellie. The woman would be less than thrilled to hear her greatest hit squawked by a parrot, even if it was a perfect voiceover. "Let's go, guys," she said, herding the canines like a Border Collie. "Everybody on the stairs."

"But I should stay here. Gotta sniff out those clues," yipped her boy.

"Me, too," groused Mr. T, staying at Rudy's side.

The Bostons simply obeyed without complaining, for which Ellie was grateful. Standing with her arms crossed, she gave the dogs an eye roll. "Come on, you two. Get moving."

Viv sneaked up behind them and stomped a foot. "You heard the lady. Down the steps and into the pen."

Myron screeched another round of Petula's song while the pups scampered ahead of Ellie. *"Hey, not so pushy, fool,"* T continued, trotting to the grass below.

"No way, Triple E. You need me up there," said Rudy. *"I'll be able to tell you what's really going on."*

She opened the gate and ushered the dogs inside, then squatted on the outside of the fence and laced her fingers through the mesh. "It's going to get crowded when the cops bring Tomas here," she said in a low tone. "And I can't treat you any differently than I do the Boston Terriers."

He propped his paws on the fence and licked her hand. *"Sure you can. I'm your boy."*

"I know, and you are, but not right now. Besides, I'm counting on you to stay alert and use your exceptional hearing to pick up on what's being said." She didn't really expect him to do that, but she did want to make him feel secure. Dropping her tone, she said, "You could talk to Corey or the female Bostons. Maybe they know something about Dr. Kent we should know." Hoping the comment would appease him, she stood. "I'll be back for you in a bit."

"Sounds to me like you've decided to take the case," Rudy called to her.

Ellie walked to Viv and laid a hand on her arm. "I have a feeling this is going to get ugly, so please don't say a word when we arrive up top. We might be able to get more info on the investigation by keeping our ears open and our mouths shut."

"Then you're officially on the case?" Viv asked, echoing Rudy's question.

With Rudy and Viv pushing her, Ellie felt she had no choice but to dive feetfirst into Dr. Kent's murder. She'd been thinking all day about her early-morning conversation with Rosa, and realized the housekeeper was a nice woman who'd gone through an ordeal with her daughter while trying to protect her employer. By refusing to incriminate Dr. Sleazeball, she was more than loyal, but there was no use covering for the doctor now that he was dead.

Unfortunately, Ellie had ignored much of what was probably important to the case because of the word "vacation." She had a lot of catching up to do if she was going to put all that had happened in order. "I'm seriously thinking about it," she answered Viv. "Now let's go up. And remember, no talking."

When they arrived on the terrace, the police escort and Tomas were already there. Sporting a day's growth of beard, the young man appeared sullen and withdrawn. Dressed in a formfitting white T-shirt and clean jeans, with his hands cuffed behind him, he was maybe five-foot-eight. His muscular build reminded Ellie of the middleweight boxers she'd met when she took the self-defense classes Sam had set up for her at a professional gymnasium last year.

But was he strong enough to have sent Martin Kent, a man who'd been at least six feet tall, sprawling backward so hard that he fell and cracked his head on the walkway?

Wheeling finished reading Tomas his rights, then said, "Okay, son, it's your turn. Is there anything you want to tell me about the night of Dr. Kent's death?"

Before he could answer, Rosa charged through the kitchen door and threw herself at her son. "*Mi hijo es inocente.* Tomas, he is a good boy. He did not do what you say."

When the arresting officers stepped near and pulled her away, she began to sob. "*No lo entiendo, te lo juro. Mi hijo es inocente. Le juró. Me prometió. Por favor,* please don't take my son."

"Awwwk! No lo entiendo. No lo entiendo," Myron squawked.

Shaking his head, Tomas said nothing.

Ellie threw the dopey bird a warning glance, but he continued screeching.

"Awwwk! Mi hijo es inocente. Le juró. Le juró. Awwwk!"

Rosa's sobs grew worse, her meaning clear. Her son was the light of her life. He never could have done what he was accused of doing. "Ms. Arlene, please tell them Tomas is innocent. He did not do what they say."

Arlene stood and squared her shoulders. "Really, Detective, Mrs. Suarez is correct. Tomas arrived home only a short while before the caterer found Martin. How could he have been the killer?"

"Arlene," Ellie began. "I think that's something for a lawyer to ask."

Arlene rounded the table and gathered the housekeeper in her arms. "Then I'll get him a lawyer, Rosa. The best money can buy. Where's Julio? He should be with you right now."

Where was Julio? It seemed strange that the man wasn't here with his only son, but Ellie kept the thought to herself. She raised a questioning eyebrow in Rosa's direction and the woman shook her head, as if to say "I will tell you later."

Wheeling gazed at the sky, then dropped his head and stared at the group. "Look, I understand you people don't want to believe the kid would do such a thing, but we have a motive and we have evidence. I suggest, Ms. Millman, that if you know a good attorney you have him meet us at the county lockup." The detective trained his eyes on Tomas. "Unless, Mr. Suarez, you want to say something?"

Ellie waited for Tomas to protest or make some sort of comment, but he stayed mum.

Wheeling nodded and the officers filed out with the young man between them; then the detective headed into the kitchen with James Bond on his heels.

Arlene helped the housekeeper into a chair and sat next to her while Ellie and Viv took seats on the opposite side of the table. When Viv tipped her head in Rosa's direction, Ellie got the message.

"It's not that bad, Rosa. Just a few months back, a friend of mine was found kneeling over a dead body with the weapon in his hand, and I helped him go free.

That's got to be more incriminating evidence than what they have on Tomas."

Arlene drummed her fingers on the table. "Viv told me you were an expert in unraveling murders, but were you actually able to find the killers and solve the cases yourself?"

Preparing to tell the truth, she swallowed hard. "That's not exactly how it always happens. On the last case, it was the dogs that recovered the evidence. I only—"

"Ellie's being too modest," Viv chimed. "She's helped solve several murders in the recent past, and she's on top of this one, too, aren't you?"

When Ellie didn't answer, Viv gave her an elbow jab. "Aren't you?"

"I guess I could be, if you really wanted my help."

"*Sí, sí*, Miss Ellie." The housekeeper wiped tears from her dark brown eyes, then pulled a fresh tissue from her apron pocket and held it to her face. "My son is innocent."

Ellie's heart clenched when Rosa's shoulders began to shake, signaling another round of sobs.

Arlene's eyes narrowed. "I can pay whatever fee you charge. Just name your price."

"I could never accept money for helping a friend in need," Ellie answered, slumping in her seat.

"What about if I promised to do what I can for your, um . . . skin condition?" Arlene offered, inspecting Ellie's face. "I know a secret or two you can try. I even have something in my beauty arsenal that might work."

"How can you resist an offer like that?" Viv prodded.

Recalling the way Agent Bond had laughed at the color of her skin, Ellie made a decision. She was enmeshed in this disaster whether she wanted to be or not. If hunting up a few more clues would get her complexion back to normal . . .

"Okay, I'll give it a shot, but please don't hate me if I'm not able to help. The doctor's office is probably the best place for me to start, but it's still a crime scene, and without access, all I can do is go over things with you and Rosa."

It was then Jim Bond returned to the terrace. His expression grim, he pulled out a chair and got comfortable.

"Let me get this straight," said Arlene thirty minutes later. "You're a DEA agent and you only made friends with me so you could get invited to our party, and gather evidence against Martin as a drug pusher." Frowning, she leaned back in her chair. "You know something, Mr. Bond? You really are a slug."

He shrugged. "I'm a man with a job to do, Ms. Millman. Dr. Kent was the slug. We have info from several reliable sources that say he sold to anyone who had the money, including minors." He glanced at Rosa, as if hoping she'd agree. When she didn't speak, he cleared his throat. "And don't take this the wrong way, but I believe you helped yourself to his medicine chest just as often as some of his so-called patients. If you fail to cooperate, you might be doing a little jail time yourself."

Arlene's eyes filled with tears. "You're bluffing."

" 'Fraid not. As of this morning, Detective Wheeling has agreed to cooperate fully with me on the investigation into your fiancé's business."

"What does that mean, exactly?"

"It means they won't make another move until I'm finished checking things out, which reminds me. The cops removed Kent's office computer and they're inspecting his records. I need to know if he had another computer—something small, like a PDA."

"He kept a data book, but I'm not sure where it is."

"Then I'd like to take a look inside your house."

Inhaling a breath, Arlene looked at Ellie. "Do I have to allow this man into my home?"

"Not if you don't want him there . . . but he could get a search warrant."

Arlene stared at the table, as if thinking; then she raised her head. "Get a search warrant, Mr. Bond. I'm tired of all your secrecy."

Agent Bond's expression hardened. "I have a question for you. Have you taken anything today? Say a muscle relaxant or a little Percocet? Maybe a pop of Oxy or Valium?"

Arlene brushed the tears from her flushed cheeks. "Unless you've checked my medicine cabinet, you have no idea what's in there."

"Oh, I have a very good idea," he continued. "You've had trouble losing weight, or you're anxious about a tennis tournament, or maybe a match at the polo field. How about the good doctor giving you something to help you sleep on the nights he worked late?"

Straightening her shoulders, Arlene said, "I think you'd better leave."

"I'm going. Just remember, Ms. Millman, that when the DEA is operating a case and we have probable cause, we can do what we want."

"Is that true?" she asked Ellie, her eyes wide.

Since this was the first time Ellie had been involved in a DEA investigation, she was clueless. "I'm sorry, but I have no idea what he can or can't do. This is why I told you I might not be of any help."

"Surely you have contacts," said Viv. "Maybe Sam could point you in the right direction or—"

Agent Bond stood, his chiseled mouth set in a grim line. "That's it. I refuse to sit here and listen to you women trying to come up with a plan that will allow a killer to beat a rap or find a way to get Dr. Kent off the hook. You're talking about the Drug Enforcement Agency, a division of the U.S. judicial system. Civilians have no right to poke their noses into our job, even if"—he stared at Ellie—"they're trying to solve a murder for a friend."

He moved to the stairs. "If you don't mind, I'll be on my way. If I continue to sit here, I'll have to arrest someone, and I have no intention of getting that involved with any of you."

"Jeesh, what a grouch," said Viv when the agent made it to the grass below. She gazed at Ellie. "I was serious when I mentioned Sam. Do you think he could at least give us some info on what the DEA can and can't do?"

Ellie knotted her fingers. If Sam thought she was messing in another murder, especially one involving the DEA, he'd probably drive to Montauk and drag her back home, then lock her in that padded cell he'd threatened her with a hundred times before.

"If I call him, I'd have to phrase every word carefully, more like I read something about the doc's arrest in a local paper, or heard about it through the grapevine, and I was curious. Otherwise, he'd never lend a hand."

"If you're dating a cop, you must have other connections in the police department. Think a minute." Arlene fanned herself with a tissue. "Damn, I'm hot. Is anyone else hot?"

Yes, the sun was shining, but it was close to one and

the terrace was shaded by the house. With the balmy breeze, it was quite comfortable on the deck. "Maybe you stayed too long in the sun," Ellie said, hoping that was Arlene's problem.

"I have to go to my suite." She stood. "The girls need lunch, Rosa, but after what's happened I don't expect you to do it. Where are Teresa and Maria? Maybe they can fix something for Viv and Ellie."

"Don't be silly," said Viv. "We're capable of feeding ourselves. Besides, I thought Rosa's daughters were cleaning the family apartment above the guest cottage."

Arlene used the tissue to blot invisible perspiration from her cheeks and neck. "Right. Okay, then. Rosa, go to your place and rest. Viv and Ellie can take care of things here."

The housekeeper trundled off through the kitchen. Arlene crossed her arms. "I guess I'd better call my attorney and have him recommend a good defense lawyer unless . . ." She glanced at Ellie. "Do you have any connections in that area?"

Ellie hunched forward. This was getting more involved by the minute. The only attorney she knew well enough to recommend was Joe Cantiglia's uncle Sal, and she doubted he had enough experience to assist with this disaster.

"Sorry, but no. The people I've helped all seemed to have their own legal advisers."

Arlene swiped the tissue across her cheeks again. "Fine. I'll call my man and see what he says. I'll probably take a nap after that, so don't go looking for me until dinner."

"But what about my—" Ellie began. "Skin?" she said to Arlene's disappearing backside.

"Don't worry. I'll tiptoe into her bedroom and take a look at her beauty supplies myself when we're finished eating," said Viv. "You're a saint for agreeing to do this. I'll help in any way I can."

"Just get my complexion back to normal, so people don't think I'm a tangerine." Ellie pulled an arm out from her cover-up and took a long look. "It's not getting any better."

"I don't understand why that happened. I used the same stuff and it worked fine on me."

"I'm a redhead. Maybe my skin is more sensitive than yours? Or maybe I used too much?"

"That won't fly. I'm the one who did your back and shoulders, and they're as orange as the rest of you." Viv peered at Ellie's face. "Take off your sunglasses."

When she did, Viv covered her grinning mouth.

"It's not funny." Ellie blew out a breath. Then she ran her hand through her curls. "Terrible, right?"

"Nah, but you do have those square white rings because of . . . well, you know."

"Oh, great. No wonder Mr. Bond refused to take me seriously. I look like an escapee from a freak show."

"It's really not that bad," said Viv, still smiling. "We'll find something, don't worry."

Ellie pulled her phone from the tote.

"Have you decided to call Sam?"

"I'm checking to see if he phoned me. That way, I can get back to him and he won't think I'm calling specifically for his advice on this murder." She thumbed through the numbers. "Nope. Just Mom, and she knows I'm here." Then a lightbulb clicked on in her brain and she hit speed dial. "Maybe I can get some info another way. Hang on a second."

"Awwwk! Hang on, Sloopy. Sloopy, hang on! Awwwk!"

Viv flapped her fingers at the chattering parrot. "Who are you contacting?"

"Give me a second and I'll— Hi, Dr. Bridges. It's Ellie Engleman. I need to get hold of Dr. Kingsgate," she said after hearing the medical examiner's phone message. "If it's not too much trouble, can you please pass this call along to her and ask her to phone me at . . ." She gave her number. "If I don't answer, tell Dr. Kingsgate to leave me a number where she can be reached."

"Dr. Bridges? How do I know that name? And who is Dr. Kingsgate?"

Ellie dropped the phone in her bag. "Dr. Kingsgate is the medical examiner Detective Wheeling said was handling this case. I met her when she was in training under Dr. Bridges when I bungled into Arnie Harris biting the dust."

"Stop putting yourself down. You haven't bungled into anything. You're exactly where you belong."

"Belong? You mean I'm supposed to be where the dead bodies are?" She gave Viv the evil eye. "Thanks a bunch."

"You know what I mean. They say the universe puts people in the right place at the right time, sort of like those characters in detective novels. Maybe that's what's been happening to you."

She thought about what she'd told Arlene: that she believed destiny was a huge part of everyone's life. But why in the world was it her destiny to be the real-life version of Nancy Drew or Miss Marple or whoever the heck else some dippy author dreamed up?

"Sorry, but I'm not buying it."

"Okay, then, what *do* you call it?" Viv leaned back in her chair. "And be honest."

What do I call it? Ellie continued to twist her fingers into a knot. "The opposite of what you think. I've been in the *wrong* place at the *wrong* time. Ask Sam. He has nothing good to say about my being involved in what he considers dirty business, and I'm not thrilled by it, either."

"Sam needs to give you more credit."

"Sam respects women who know what they're doing. The trouble is, most of the time I don't."

"But you do."

"How can you say that when I get things right maybe once in every thirty tries?" Ellie said. "Now let's have lunch, then go upstairs and try to bleach me back to a more human color."

Ellie raised a leg out of the bathwater and inspected her skin. Thanks to Viv and a ton of rubbing, her complexion had faded to a dull orange. Getting back to near normal had also taken a total body scrub with a loofah and something from Arlene's beauty arsenal that smelled like perfumed bleach, and two tub baths, each filled with three boxes of baking soda. She was still a little on the tangerine side, but the creepy color was barely there.

"That looks a lot better," said Viv from her seat on the commode lid. "How does your skin feel?"

"Like it's been rubbed raw, but I'll use that expensive Swiss body lotion of Arlene's to soothe the burn." She sighed. "I think we'd better drive to a drugstore and stock up on SPF sixty or I'm going to fry like an egg the next time I sit on the beach."

"Sure, why not? It'll be good to get out of the house for a while. Too many bad things happening here."

"Think we ought to ask Arlene to join us?"

Viv shrugged. "Probably not. She was sorting through pill bottles when I got to her room after lunch, and I know she took a couple of what she called relaxers. But I did see her empty bottles in the toilet and toss the containers in the trash."

"That's a good start. So you think she's asleep?"

"Yep." Viv stood and walked out the door. "You dry off and get dressed. I'll go start the BMW. I need to practice a little before we head into town."

"You sure you want Vivie to drive you again?" asked Rudy from his post on the turquoise throw rug.

Ellie opened the drain, stepped out of the tub, and wrapped herself in a fluffy towel. "I'm not about to get behind the wheel of that car, so yes. Besides, she's out there giving the shifting another run. How bad can it be?"

"Hey, that's for you to find out. I don't plan to get a second round of neck jerks until we go home."

She slathered her skin with Arlene's soothing body lotion, then walked into the bedroom and dressed in clean underwear. "What color do you think will play down the orange best?" She held up a creamy white short-sleeved T and a pair of red shorts she'd removed from a drawer. "How about these two?"

"Wear jeans and you won't have to worry about it."

"Hmm, maybe you're right." She pulled out a pair of color-washed denims and slid them on, then slipped the shirt over her head. "Makeup?"

"Not too much, in case it changes color when it hits that sandpaper-scrubbed skin."

Returning to the bathroom, she finger-curled her

hair, and grinned at him from the mirror. "You are too smart." After applying a bit of styling gel to her hair, she added a coat of mascara and a little peach lip gloss to their respective targets. "How do I look?" she asked, turning in place.

"Almost normal."

Relieved by his comment, she returned to the bedroom and put on her sandals. "You'll have to stay here. It's too hot to leave you in the car while we shop."

"Fine with me," said Mr. T from the pillow on Viv's bed. *"I'm taking a nap."*

"I want to go to the pen," said Rudy. *"See a little of the sun, smell that ocean breeze."*

"Fine. Come with me and we'll leave T here."

"I just hope those Bostons don't give me a hard time. That Darby-Doll keeps givin' me the fish-eye look."

"No fighting, please. Just ignore them all. They really are kind of cute, and Arlene has enough to worry about without you terrorizing her babies."

"Okay, fine, no arguing with the Bostons. Now let's get movin'. I could use a snack, too."

With Rudy following, she headed for the front stairs. Viv was right. They needed to get out of this house for a while. She'd get a bead on the town of Montauk, maybe do some shopping, and think of the clues. She might even buy a notebook so she could write down what she remembered of the investigation.

Too bad if Agent 007 didn't want her looking into the murder, because Rosa did, and so did Arlene. Surely, between her and Viv, she could come up with an overview of all that had happened since they'd arrived.

In the foyer, she peeked out the door and saw that the car was gone. With Viv practicing her driving technique, that gave her a chance to see if Rosa or her girls were around. She needed answers to a few questions before she took on the mystery of who murdered Dr. Kent.

"Maybe Maria will take you out back. You like her, right?"

"She's a cute kid. I can't believe that devious doctor was gonna do her wrong. Giving her those pills was bad enough."

After padding through the dining room and into the kitchen, they went out the rear door and onto the terrace, where Rosa was standing at the railing and staring at the beach.

After signaling Rudy with a finger to her lips, she cleared her throat to announce her presence and walked over to stand beside the housekeeper. "How are you doing, Rosa?"

Shrugging, Rosa heaved a sigh. "Not so good. I miss my son, and my Julio is not here. The girls, they are worried about their brother, and I am, too."

"Any idea where the girls are?"

"They finished the guest cottage and I sent them to the beach. They'll be here to help with dinner in a little while."

It was now or never, thought Ellie, taking a deep breath of the salty ocean air. "I know I asked you this earlier, but why is it you haven't told Arlene about what happened between Maria and Dr. Kent?"

Rosa clenched her fingers so tight her knuckles turned white. "Because Ms. Arlene doesn't need to worry about more bad things. With the doctor gone, my little girl is safe."

"I understand that, but don't you think it would be better if Arlene knew about some of the bad things her fiancé did? It might help her to come to grips with his death." She formed the next words carefully. "It could even get her to thinking about who might have wanted Dr. Kent dead, and that would help clear Tomas."

The housekeeper bit her lower lip. "You think that could be so? That it would help free my son?"

"I don't know, but I believe you should give it some thought. And remember, Arlene is your employer, but she's also your friend. I think she'll understand the reason why you didn't tell her about Dr. Kent and Maria when it happened, but I also think she'll be grateful to hear about it now."

"Since you are the one Ms. Arlene says will work to free my Tomas, I should probably do as you say. And I will, later today or this evening."

"One more question. I haven't seen your husband since this whole mess began. Where's Julio been?"

The housekeeper sniffed. "He is on a mission at our church, praying for our boy. A very special mission."

"Special? Can you tell me about it?"

"He is praying to *La Virgen.*"

"La veer-hen? I'm sorry but I don't understand."

"Not la veer-hen, you dip brain. The Virgin Mary," her boy corrected.

"He is promising a *manda* to *La Virgen Maria*, our Holy Mother," Rosa explained, as if echoing Rudy.

"Ahh." Ellie glanced down at her yorkiepoo and smiled. She knew about the Virgin Mary and respected her place in Christianity, but she had no idea about the other thing. "And what's a *manda*?"

"It's like a *juramento*, only different." The housekeeper sniffed. "He is willing to do anything to save our son."

"A *juramento*?"

She looked at Rudy and he gave a doggie shrug. *"That's a new one to me."*

A horn honked from the street, telling Ellie that Viv was ready to go. Relieved that Rosa knew where her husband was, and it didn't sound dangerous, she said, "I think we can discuss this later. Right now, Viv and I are going into town. Do you need anything?"

"Not for tonight, but maybe for tomorrow. I will let you know, yes?"

"Of course, yes." The horn tapped out a demanding string of bleats, as if Vivian would leave without her. "Viv can't wait, so I have to run. What time is dinner?"

"Unless Ms. Arlene changes the time, she usually eats at seven o'clock."

"Great, we'll be back. See you then."

Chapter 8

After checking out the *Yellow Book of Maps on the Hamptons*, Ellie decided to use a colorful and infinitely more interesting map she'd scrounged from a drawer in Arlene's kitchen. Reading it carefully, she chose to direct Viv to one of two stores in Montauk that appeared to sell what they were looking for.

"There's a White's Drug and Department Store on the map, but Montauk Drugs is closer," she told Viv as they passed Gurney's Inn, Resort and Spa on Old Montauk Highway and made a left onto Route 27.

"Fine by me. If we're lucky, they'll have what you need and we can be back home quickly. Maybe we can explore the other shops tomorrow or the next day," said Viv. "Just tell me when to turn."

Ellie checked the street names, which were easier to read on the more detailed map. "After we pass Emory, then Embassy, make the first right. That will put us on the circle. The drugstore should be on the right, too, somewhere near the Montauk Bake Shoppe."

"Very cute," said Viv as they turned into the center of town. "Looks as if we could spend an entire morning here checking things out."

"According to this business-sponsored map, there are way more summer shops in town than what you'd expect. There's even a Plaza Pet Supplies, and it looks adorable. Maybe we can stop there with the boys and see what's available when we make our next trip."

"Sounds fine to me." Viv steered the pricey car into a parking spot and they jerked to a stop. "Damn, and I was doing so much better," she ground out as the BMW shuddered and died. "This ride was an improvement over our trip out here from Manhattan, wasn't it?"

Ellie rubbed the back of her neck. "There was less spine snapping, so I say yes. You're getting the hang of it."

Viv removed the keys and opened her door. "Thanks, you're a pal." She waited for Ellie to step on the sidewalk and join her. "I know I've said this before, but I want you to know I'm serious. I can't thank you enough for agreeing to help my sister and Rosa. I'll never be able to repay you, but I've decided to cancel all the 'you owe me' pronouncements I've made in the past. After you solve this case, we're even."

Ellie laughed. "And if I don't solve it?"

"You're going to give it your best shot, right?"

"You bet, but I'll probably need help."

"Help? From someone besides me?"

They opened the drugstore door and stepped into cool air ripe with the scent of the ocean, probably from the display of burning scented candles set up to the left of the entryway. "I'll need another talk with Rosa and a first questioning with her girls. I even need to ask Adrianne a few details. I wasn't paying much attention, but I remember meeting people who seemed to disappear right before the body was found. To do this right, I'll have to get answers from everyone who was there, including your mom and dad, and maybe even the relatives who went home." Ellie took stock of the store while she thought. "Got any ideas on how I should approach your secondary family members?"

"You're talking about the people who were at the early party?"

"Yep. All of them," Ellie said, fingers crossed in hopes that Viv could offer a better idea.

"Hmm. Here's a thought. If you give me a list of questions, I can phone the R relatives and my aunt and uncle. I'll even try my non-aunts, Elsie and Connie, and take a shot at pinning down whatever they know."

"So that means Vanessa, Evan, and Adrianne are my job."

"That makes sense, don't you think?" said Viv. "They're the ones who are still here, and I'm too close to them to get a good read on their answers. Dad could be trouble, but Mom? Not so much. If you tell them it's for Rosa, they'll be more inclined to cooperate."

"Okay, you convinced me. I get the terrible threesome."

They scanned the aisles as they discussed the situation. "But I get the impression they refuse to believe their little girl was stupid enough to get hooked on uppers or downers, or fall in love with a pusher. That alone could shake up Mom and Dad—make them lend a hand."

"We'll see," said Ellie. She scoured the aisle directory.

The store was small and stuffed with merchandise, but they finally found a section selling flip-flops, towels, T-shirts, sand chairs, even boogie boards and plastic buckets holding shovels and sand molds for kids.

"Okay, there's the sunscreen," said Ellie, stopping at the end of the aisle.

While she inspected the offerings, Viv picked through a stand of sunglasses. "How do I look in these?"

Bent at the waist so she could check out the products, Ellie had to stand to do what Viv asked, and saw that she'd found a pair she liked, taken off her ultra-expensive glasses, and put the new ones on. "Too rectangular for your face," she said, giving her a once-over. "You need something round or oval." Ellie plucked a pair off the rack. "Here, these are twenty dollars and I bet they'll look great on you."

"Every pair on this rack is twenty dollars. I can't imagine wearing such cheap glasses." Viv slid them on and checked herself out in the mirror, scrutinizing her face from all sides. "You're right," she said, pouting. "These do look good."

"And they're as serviceable as those Jason Wus you paid two hundred and seventy-five for. Buy these for the beach and keep the designer brand for when you're out among the stars and celebrities of the Hamptons."

Returning to the shelves, she passed over all the expensive sunscreen products. She'd been that route and it had turned her into a human carrot. She needed plain old protection, something that had been around for years. Something people depended on.

Viv took the new glasses off and held them close. "Find what you're looking for yet?"

"Here's what I want," said Ellie, picking up a plastic bottle of Coppertone that promised complete SPF coverage. "Wasn't Brooke Shields the baby who first advertised this stuff when it came out years ago? How old is she, anyway?"

"I haven't a clue. Far as I'm concerned, as long as it keeps you from burning, it's a go. Is there a guarantee?"

"As good as any of the others. Now find me the school supply area, or the section that sells pens and notebooks."

They passed a mother leading two children, her arms full of kiddie Ts and underwear; a woman wearing a bathing suit and cover-up who carried a basket loaded with cleaning supplies; and a group of teenage boys balancing boxes of cookies and bottles of soda.

"I love places like this," she said to Viv. "It's one-stop shopping."

"Well, I'm not a fan."

"You're a snob," Ellie warned her. *And so much like your mother.* "One of these days you'll find out that some bargain brands are really as good as the designer stuff you pay quadruple for." She glanced down the next aisle and headed for the display of spiral notebooks. "Here's what I want. You check out. I'll be there in a minute."

Selecting two black palm-sized tablets that looked very much like the ones Sam, Vince, and every other Manhattan detective she'd met used, she held back a laugh. Rudy was going to get a charge out of it, but Sam would probably clap her in cuffs if he thought she was in true detective mode.

"What's so funny?" asked Viv when Ellie met her in the checkout line.

"Not a thing," she lied.

They stood behind the teenage boys at what looked to be the only open register. The older man ringing them up wore a white lab coat with a name badge, but Ellie couldn't read what it said. Blinking when she saw his face, she whispered to Viv, "How do I know this guy? He looks familiar."

Viv peered at the tall, jowled man handling the customers. "I think that's Dr. Kent's uncle Mickey, but I don't remember anyone saying he was a pharmacist. Do you?"

"Nope, but he may have a less important job, like a pharmacy technician or aide." Ellie and Viv moved up in line. "Do you think he'll remember us?"

"Beats me." Viv frowned. "You know, I think he was one of those people who disappeared a little while before the caterer found the doc's body. What do you think?"

"You're right and he's already on my mental list, though I thought I'd have to conduct a search to locate him," said Ellie, smiling. "This is why I need your help. If you're sure you didn't see him on the terrace before we went down the stairs, he'll stay a suspect."

"Unless he says he was in the bathroom," Viv added.

Oops, Ellie thought, that could be anyone's excuse, and how would she be able to prove them wrong? "Let's see what he says."

Now at the counter, Ellie got a better look at his name tag, which read MICHAEL FORREST, PHARMACIST, and under that what appeared to be an identification number. She set her spiral pads and sunscreen next to Viv's sunglasses. "Hi. Remember us?"

The man glanced up and focused on her face, then

spotted Vivian and gave a huge grin. "Why, yes, I do. You were at Arlene and Marty's prewedding celebration, which means you're from the McCready side of the family." He shook his head and his jowls wobbled. "Terrible thing, that. I gather you're still staying at the house? Have you heard any more about the killing?"

Ellie opened and closed her mouth. She'd been ignored for Vivie before, so she wasn't surprised. But how could she warn Viv that they should wait to question him until she'd had a chance to do a bit of sleuthing first?

"I remember someone saying that you really weren't Dr. Kent's uncle, even though that's what he called you. Do I have that right?" Viv continued.

"You have a good memory. I'm Uncle Mickey to most everybody around here. Been in business for a long time now. Between Fred Dwyer and me, we service just about everyone on this end of Long Island. Feel free to call me Mickey, too, if you like."

"Fred Dwyer?" asked Viv. "I don't remember him being at the party."

"He owns the other drugstore. Together, we take care of the locals and the summer crowd. I believe he was scheduled to come over with the second wave. I was Marty's best man, so I got invited with the first group. It was a real honor, I'll tell you. He was well liked by everybody. I can't imagine anyone wanting him dead."

When Viv asked, "How long had you known Martin?" Ellie tapped her toe with the tip of her sandal. It might not be smart to continue questioning him until they knew more about the pharmacist.

But it didn't matter, because Viv moved ahead. "I don't mean to be nosy, but Arlene is distraught. I was hoping to get a few old friends to stop by and offer comfort . . . that is, if you're an old friend."

Uncle Mickey accepted Ellie's credit card as he spoke. "Marty had been practicing around here for years. His original office was in Bridgehampton, but when he and Arlene got engaged, it was just natural that he moved to her place. Then again, I guess you already know all that."

He passed Ellie the receipt and she signed it while he spoke. "I thought maybe there'd be a memorial service. Didn't want to intrude on Arlene during her time of sorrow." He scanned Viv's sunglasses and accepted her card, too.

"I'm sure my sister will hold some kind of memorial, but she can't do anything until the ME releases the body."

Impressed at Viv's line of questioning, Ellie kept quiet. Why intrude when she was doing fine on her own?

"Right, right. I forgot about that." He handed Viv her card and a bag holding her glasses. "Guess I'll call first, feel Arlene out. If she sounds okay, I'll stop by. Nice talking to you." He nodded to the next customer in line, effectively telling them the conversation was over.

Ellie followed Viv out of the store and into the car before she said a word. "I thought I was on lead here?"

Viv started the BMW's engine. "I know, and I apologize. But when he looked at me and gave me that slimy smile, well . . . you know what I mean. I just figured he'd be more receptive to me." She checked over her shoulder, then looked in the rearview mirror and backed out onto the circle. "You're not upset, are you?"

Ellie snapped her seat belt in place. "Of course not. If we're going to work as a team, we'll take whatever assistance we can give each other. I'll question all the little old ladies. You can have the men."

"Oh, stop. You've been hit on by plenty of guys when I'm with you. It was clear he was more interested in me, just like I suspect our faux Agent Double O Seven is more interested in you."

Ellie choked out a laugh. "What?"

"You heard me," said Viv, a smile playing on her lips. "Mr. Bond would be asking you out if he didn't already think you were trying to ruin his investigation."

"He's working a case, so I doubt he'd want to hook up with anyone right now."

"Who knows? He might be in the market for a summer fling. He'd probably try to get into your pants if he hadn't heard about Sam."

"Vivian, that is so not funny."

"I'm being serious. You were too busy worrying about your tan cleanup to notice the way he looked at you on the beach. I've seen that twinkle in a man's eyes before. He definitely liked what he saw."

"There's no room in my life for another man."

"And he knows that, but it won't stop him from checking you out. Now, where's my next turn?"

"Take this left," Ellie said, still pondering Viv's words. "Then the first right. That's Old Montauk Highway. You know the way home from there." Sitting back, she crossed her arms and thought about Viv's outrageous assumption.

Her and James Bond?

It was too ridiculous to worry about.

"Good thing you got home when you did," said Rudy, gazing up at Ellie from the bathroom doorway. *"It was only a matter of seconds before I took out ol' Corey dog."*

"That adorable little Boston?" Ellie asked, swiping mascara over her lashes. "Why?"

"He was guarding all the water dishes. I'd walk to one, and Corey would rush over and stand in front of it, growling. He refused to back down when I called him on it."

"Well, that's not very nice." She added lip gloss, then walked past him and into the bedroom, where she checked out a drawer. "How about this?" she asked her boy, holding up a pair of white cropped pants and a navy-and-white-striped top. "Very beachy, don't you think?"

"Sure, fine. So, tell me, did you find out anything more about the night of the murder?"

She stepped into the pants and slid the shirt over her head before answering. "Not much. But we did end up in Uncle Mickey's drugstore."

"You mean that old guy with the bulldog face and droopy eyes?" He shook from head to tail. *"Didn't care much for him. He was one of the few people who never once gave us dogs a look-see."*

"Okay, so he's not animal-friendly. That doesn't mean he isn't a nice person. We should pity him, because he's missing out on one of the best things in life, just like Viv's dad is." Satisfied that she was decent, she slipped into her sandals. "You ready to go to dinner? I'll feed you. Then you can sit on the deck—where you will mind your own business, of course."

"Yeah, yeah, sure. Just watch Mr. T. He's been grumping about those Bostons again."

"I haven't asked yet, but I might as well. Did any of the Bostons talk about the night of the murder? Maybe see or hear a strange noise coming from the guest cottage?"

"Those three nut balls? All I know is they didn't like the doc. It was nothin' they could put their paws on, but Myron knew what he was really like, since he'd lived in the office for a couple of weeks before the party."

"You talked with Myron about Dr. Kent?"

"Not exactly. But he does a lot of squawking to himself, and I pay attention."

"And you'll tell me if he says anything interesting?"

"Trust me, if he's blabbing something important, you'll be the first to know."

They went down the hall and took the rear stairs into the kitchen, where voices from the terrace, along with squawks from Myron, filled the air. She pulled Rudy's dry food from the pantry and his can of wet from the fridge, took down a bowl and mixed his chow, then set it on a place mat in the eating area.

"Here you go. I'll check things out from the doorway. Come and get me when you're finished." With his nose already in the dish, Rudy didn't answer. She slipped out the door and stepped onto the deck to take stock of who was there.

Viv sat quietly, as if absorbing every word.

Arlene was so animated, she reminded Ellie of a set of chattering teeth. Talking to her mother and Adrianne at a nonstop pace, she was clearly on another prescription high.

Adrianne drummed the fingers of one hand on the table while she used the other to push the food on her plate in a circle with her fork, ignoring her older sister as if she couldn't wait to be excused.

Vanessa concentrated on her daughters as if she hadn't talked to them in years.

Evan manned the huge gas grill on the other side of

the terrace. Ellie wasn't sure what he was cooking, but it smelled delicious.

And Rosa, without her girls or Julio, stood in a far corner watching the proceedings through sad dark eyes.

Ellie closed the door when Rudy yipped. "You finished already?"

"Yep. Let's get movin'."

She chose a seat next to Viv. Rudy headed for Mr. T; they touched noses, then curled into balls and sat side by side.

"You seem quiet. Is anything wrong?" she asked Viv as she helped herself to a glass of icy lemonade from the huge pitcher on the table.

"I'm in detective mode and it's exhausting. How do you do it?" Viv muttered out of the corner of her mouth.

"Do what?"

"Keep track of everyone, pay attention to all the conversations, the sly looks and telling glances. Not only that, but thanks to Dr. Kent, my sisters are spending all their time living on illegal pills." She nodded to her left, where Arlene and Adrianne were arguing animatedly with their mother. "Which makes them impossible to figure out."

Ellie accepted the salad bowl Viv passed her and added a heaping portion of greens, tomatoes, feta cheese, and black olives to her plate. "I was afraid of that," she said in a subdued tone. "Maybe, after all this is over, your sisters can get some help at a—"

"Ms. Engleman," said Evan McCready, who had arrived at the table in silence. "I'm on grill duty tonight. We have rib eye steaks or fresh spiced shrimp skewers. What can I get for you?"

"I'm having a steak," said Viv, "but I'd be happy to share if you want both."

"That sounds like a great idea," said Ellie. "One shrimp skewer, please, and Viv and I will divide the food ourselves."

The senior McCready returned to his post without cracking a smile.

"What's up with him?"

Viv shrugged. "I think it's all the talk about Dr. Kent and the murder charge against Tomas. Dad's taking it all personally, as if he's the one to blame for not keeping an eye on things that night. Being ex-CIA, he feels he should have headed off a disaster. Thank God Rosa's holding up fine, but I hear her girls are a mess. And Julio's still MIA. No one's seen him since this morning."

"I'm sure Rosa knows, but she's keeping it to herself," said Ellie, not sure this was the time to tell Viv what she'd learned from the housekeeper.

Viv passed her a basket of rolls and she shook her head. "Dinner is my no-carb meal, remember? I have to do something if I want to look passable in my swimsuit."

"You look fabulous in that Karla Coletto. I'll be washing mine tonight—want to add it to my load?"

"Doing your own laundry?" said Ellie in a teasing tone. "Is the world ending?"

"Ha-ha. I'm just too lazy to take it to the town cleaner's when that big, swanky steam unit hanging out in Arlene's laundry will be free. It won't hurt me to do a load myself."

"I thought the washer and dryer was Rosa's territory."

"It is, but I don't want to add to her workload. She's got to be worried, even though she's putting on a good front, and the girls are frantic about their brother. It appears that Maria is taking it personally, says Tomas wouldn't have interfered if she hadn't taken the drugs to begin with. It's her fault if he did the deed."

"Are you saying the sisters believe their brother is a murderer?"

"I'm not sure. But Rosa finally told Arlene the real story behind Maria's overdose."

"Uh-oh. Now that Arlene knows the truth, do you think she can accept that her almost-husband was really a drug pusher?" *And a lecher?*

"I think so, but I'm not positive. As soon as I arrived on the terrace, the comments seemed to stop, but it looked as if they'd been talking for a while. Rosa's girls practically ran away when I showed up, and Mom dragged me into a description of what she, Dad, and Adrianne did on their afternoon out. It was all fairly odd, if you want my opinion."

"Of course I want your opinion," said Ellie. "You have to tell me everything you see or hear, no matter how insignificant you think it is."

"Right now my head hurts. Can we talk about it later?"

"Tonight, while we're doing the laundry?"

"Okay, fine. I've already made a list of the people I'm supposed to contact. I just need your questions."

Ellie took another sip of lemonade. "We can come up with a plan while the washer's running."

Evan carried a serving tray to the table and set it down in front of them. "Here you go, and make it quick. I have one more rib eye on the cooker and I don't want it to burn."

Viv slid the steak onto her plate and Ellie took the

skewer of shrimp. After dividing the food, they exchanged servings.

It was then Vanessa acknowledged Ellie's presence. "Ellie, hello. I don't mean to interrupt your discussion, but I didn't see you come out. Vivian tells me you had quite an exciting day." She squinted, as if appraising Ellie's skin. "You don't look all that bad to me."

"I'm better, thanks. Arlene had a few magic potions in her beauty arsenal, and the baking soda helped."

When Arlene stood and walked to the grill, Vanessa leaned forward as if sharing a secret. "This whole business about Martin being murdered because he's a drug dealer has everyone upset, but I did hear some interesting news. Arlene tells me you've agreed to help Rosa's son go free."

"Mother, I asked you not to bother Ellie just yet. She has to talk to some . . . people and get information first."

"I'm aware of that, Vivian, but I still wanted to thank her for offering assistance. Your father hasn't said a word, so I suggest you don't mention Ellie's involvement while he's around."

"But I do have to ask you both a few questions, Mrs. McCready," said Ellie, using her finger to follow a drop of condensation down the side of her glass. "It won't take long."

"As long as it isn't too intrusive."

"After we eat?"

"I'll ask him as soon as—"

Evan took that moment to sit next to his wife while Arlene returned to her chair. "What are you two yammering about?" he asked. "I believe I've already made my feelings known. I don't think anyone, especially a dog walker without one iota of police training, should butt into something that's the job of the local authorities."

"I realize that," said Ellie, cutting into her steak. "I'm only lending a hand because Rosa and your daughter made the request."

He raised an eyebrow and glared at Arlene, who was pushing her shrimp into a mound on her plate. "So I heard."

"Come on, Dad. Let it rest," said Viv. "Rosa and Arlene trust Ellie, and so do I."

Adrianne's fingers tapped out a disjointed rhythm on the tabletop. "I agree. The police should be in charge."

"I'm afraid it's not that simple," Ellie began. "The DEA is involved, and they mean business. The way I understand it, the good detective got orders to share with James Bond all that he knows, even though each of them is handling a different side of the investigation. And Wheeling isn't exactly happy about it."

"Ha! I'll just bet," said Evan, stuffing a slice of steak in his mouth. After chewing, he said, "Just make sure you don't step on the wrong toes or you could find yourself in jail for obstruction of an ongoing case."

"Wrong toes?" Ellie and Viv asked at the same time.

The senior McCready rolled his eyes and Ellie saw whom Viv got that trait from. "Don't you understand what people involved in a drug ring are like? They're dangerous, willing to do anything to make their sales quotas and keep their customers. If word slips out that you're on the lookout for Kent's killer, you could be next on the murderer's hit list."

Chapter 9

After dinner the group broke apart. Vanessa and Evan turned in early, while Arlene and Adrianne went to Bridgehampton to check out the little theater's summer schedule. With everyone accounted for, Ellie and Vivian decided it was time to compose the questions for Viv to ask the relatives who had left the morning after the murder. As soon as they finished, Viv disappeared to do her job and Ellie took Mr. T and Rudy on their after-dinner walk.

Now in the kitchen, she hunted the cupboards for a tea bag, found a box of Earl Grey, and brewed a cup with help from the automatic hot water tap on the island sink.

Inspecting the huge kitchen, she took note of the state-of-the-art appliances standing guard in the room. The kitchen had dark green marble floor tiles, matching granite counters, two sets of double stainless steel sinks, a stainless steel Sub-Zero refrigerator/freezer, a six-burner range with a separate grill area, and more cabinets than she could count. The space amazed her, but then so did everything about this house.

Cup of tea in hand, she walked through the eating area with its large bump-out enclosed by mullioned windows and stepped onto the deck. A breeze rustled the tall fronds of sea grass surrounding the yard, and she sighed, content with the smell of salt water wafting in from the east. She could live here happily, she decided, amid the sun, sand, and serenity. All she needed was Sam and Rudy by her side.

And the time to enjoy it.

This was her first real vacation in forever. Her ex-husband, the dickhead, had been too cheap to take any time off while they were married, and he couldn't understand why she needed a break. After all, he gave her everything he *thought* she needed, including membership to an upscale health club and money to buy designer clothes. All she had to do was walk the treadmill, follow her personal trainer's excruciating workouts, and keep herself runway-model thin, perfectly groomed, and politically correct.

Oh, and one more thing. He forbade her to own a dog.

She'd played by the dickhead's rules for ten long years, until she found him in bed with a client. Then all bets were off. She did a full-personality overhaul and rearranged her life so it was in line with what mattered most to her. Instead of saying yes, she said no. Instead of taking orders, she made demands. Instead of pleasing others, she worked to please herself.

She also ate real food, wore comfortable clothes, and interacted with people who cared about the same things she did. Her hellish workouts were replaced by enjoyable daily walks up and down Fifth Avenue accompanied by small, furry, four-legged creatures who needed her and, more important, loved her just for being her.

Besides forging a new and more balanced relationship with her mother, she now had a sister in Vivian, and a renewed friendship with Randall, a man who had watched over her for a short while after she'd lost her father. She'd found a career she loved and worked to make it a real business. Then she met Sam who, bit by bit, had inched his way into her heart and her life. They argued, they laughed, and they made love. She'd already decided she wouldn't trade him for a man like Brad Pitt, Ashton Kutcher, and Gerard Butler all rolled into one.

And, biggest blessing of all, she rescued a dog that turned into her best friend, her confidant, and her joy.

A moment later Viv opened the kitchen door, walked to her side, and leaned next to her on the railing. "Agent SS reporting for duty."

Ellie grinned. "I'm almost afraid to ask. What do the initials stand for?"

"Smart and Sexy, of course. I want to be a combination of Natasha from the *Bullwinkle* cartoons and Mata Hari." She held the extra notepad from Montauk Drugs. It was exactly like Ellie's, but it smelled of Obsession.

"And you're reporting on your latest assignment."

"Yes, but I'm afraid I didn't learn much," she answered, her voice heavy with annoyance.

"Did you reach everyone on the list?"

"Oh, yeah."

"And?"

"And nothing. I spoke to ten people and got just about the same story. The R people didn't remember anyone who was there, except for themselves and the

McCready family. No one recalled you, Rosa, her girls, James Bond, or Uncle Mickey and Dr. B. Some of them hadn't even met Dr. Kent. They knew he was dead, of course, but were shocked to hear he'd been murdered. Seems it takes a while for word from 'out east' to reach the big city."

"Really?"

She snorted. "Personally, I don't think they read. They just listen to the gossip shows on television."

"But they all seemed so friendly and talkative when they were at the party."

"Sure. Until they realized the people here couldn't do anything for them in a monetary or personal way. Then they wrote everyone off and went back to their self-centered, it's-all-about-me little lives."

"What about Elsie and Connie?"

"They were much sweeter. Asked if they should come out for whatever type of memorial service Arlene was planning. They even reminded me to remind you to make dog walking arrangements when you got back to town."

The info made Ellie dread her next task. "Guess that leaves me with your mom, dad, and Adrianne."

"Guess so." Viv turned and rested her backside on the railing again. "I brought the laundry down. You want to give it a shot, or do you trust me to take care of things?"

"I'll lend a hand. I've only heard about these expensive steam cleaners, never seen one in action." She followed Viv into the house and laundry room. "Wow," she said, eyeing the dials, knobs, and buttons on the front of the huge appliances. The washers and dryers in the basement of her building looked like kids' toys when compared to these professional machines.

Ellie sorted the laundry while Viv surveyed the directions posted on the washer door, then read a booklet tacked to the side wall of the room.

"Okay, it sounds easy enough. We'll do everything natural fiber first, like cotton and linen, then the lingerie and bathing suits. This guide says that things take half the time to come clean with less soap and zero trauma to the fabric."

"It sounds like a miracle invention." Ellie stepped back and let Viv measure the detergent. "Let's get something to eat while we wait."

Viv put her hands on her hips. "What about your no-carbs-after-dinner rule?"

"Certain fruits are okay. I saw a bowl on the island. Let's take a look."

Five minutes later, they were snacking on peaches. It was then Ellie said, "Okay, here's the plan. I'll corral Arlene after breakfast tomorrow morning and find out how much she knows about her fiancé and his business. I have no idea what she told Detective Wheeling, nor do I know if she plans a service now that she realizes her fiancé was a slimeball."

"She hasn't said anything about it to me, either, so I guess you'd better ask her." Viv cocked her head. "What do you want me to do while you're in 'questioning' mode?"

"Keep your mom and sister busy so Arlene and I can talk in private. After that, fix it so I can speak with Vanessa alone, then Adrianne. It doesn't have to be in that order, but I should use some logical sense of progression."

"What about Dad?"

Ellie shrugged. "I'll probably have to treat him as a hostile witness."

"That's a good description for him." The washer buzzed and Viv straightened. "Time to get that load in the dryer and the next one in the cooker."

They jockeyed positions and finished the chore. Then Ellie's phone rang and she pulled it from her pocket. When she didn't recognize the number on the display, she almost let the machine take a message, but she remembered her earlier call to Dr. Bridges.

"Paws in Motion," she said. "How can I help you?"

"Ms. Engleman? It's Dr. Kingsgate. Emily Bridges said you wanted to speak to me?"

Ellie covered the mouthpiece. "It's the ME. I'll take it on the deck."

Viv waved her approval and Ellie returned to the call, walking as she talked. "Thanks so much for getting back to me. I hope you don't mind the intrusion."

Dr. Kingsgate laughed. "You're not intruding. But Emily did tell me you were looking for answers, so I'm prepared. Fire away."

Groaning internally, Ellie frowned. Was she really that transparent? How nice that the local medical examiners considered her a pest. "I do have questions but—do you mind answering? I mean, is it against the rules for you to release info on a current case?"

"I assume you're talking about Dr. Kent?"

"Well, yeah. But how do you know that's the person I'm interested in?"

"You're in the Hamptons, correct?"

"Yes, Montauk."

"That's part of the territory I was assigned to after my training with Emily. And the only body I've worked on in the last two days is that of Martin Kent, a Montauk resident. I just put two and two together."

"You're finished with the autopsy?"

"I am."

"And you'd be willing to give me the cause of death?"

"Well, technically I shouldn't, but Emily swears you can be trusted. She also said that you had been involved in so many murder investigations over the past couple of months she thought the cops should hire you as a consultant. And since Detective Wheeling already got the report and made an arrest, well, it'll be public record soon enough."

"Great . . . I mean I appreciate it."

"So, what do you need?"

"I'd like an exact description of how the doctor died."

After a rustle of pages, Dr. Kingsgate said, "Okay, here goes. The cause of death was a subdural hematoma that resulted from blunt-force head trauma that, in turn, resulted from blunt-force chest trauma, causing the victim to fall backward against a hard surface."

"That blunt-force chest trauma thing?" Ellie asked, wanting to get it right. "It means he was either shoved or pushed in the chest, and that's what caused him to fall."

"You got it. There was a contusion on his chest, left side, middle, about four inches around. Whoever made that bruise did it with force; a punch with a closed fist, maybe one of those karate kicks with a heel."

"And that might have occurred in an argument, say a pushing and shoving match that got out of hand?"

"This was much more deliberate than pushing and shoving. Whoever did this knew that if they hit the doctor hard enough they might crack a rib and stop his heart."

Ellie thought a second. "Could you tell if the blow was done by a man or a woman?"

"My guess would be a man, because it was quite a bruise. If a hand was used, it had to be man-sized."

Ellie jotted the answer in her notebook. "One more question, Dr. Kingsgate, but you might not have the answer."

"I'll do my best. By the way, how about calling me Jordan?"

"Um, sure. And I'm Ellie."

"Glad that's settled. Now what's the question?"

"Detective Wheeling said they have evidence against Tomas Suarez. Do you happen to know what it is?"

"They don't tell us, you understand, so I've only heard through the grapevine, but I gather they found a knife with Mr. Suarez's fingerprints on it."

"A knife? But I thought you said the cause of death was blunt head trauma."

"It was. The knife was found on the floor behind the doctor's desk. They ran the prints and learned they belonged to the suspect. Knowing what they do about his younger sister, they figured he came home to avenge her. They fought when they reached the outdoors and Suarez punched his chest. When he realized the victim was dead, he took off without picking up the weapon."

"That sounds like conjecture."

"Yes, it does, but people have gone to jail for less. Right now they think they have a good case."

"You waiting for your pigeon to land, or what?" asked Rudy after climbing the stairs to the deck the next morning.

"Arlene is not a pigeon. She's a woman with a problem that I'm hoping to help solve. She's already told me she's grateful I'm going to work toward clearing

Rosa's son for the murder, and she's agreed to spend some time answering questions."

"Where is she?"

"Getting us both a cup of coffee from the kitchen. Very nice of her, if you ask me."

"She's the hostess. She's supposed to be nice."

Ellie narrowed her eyes. "She just lost her fiancé under trying circumstances, and she's been notified by the DEA that he was a drug pusher. That's enough to drive any woman to drink, if you ask me. Even I've been known to knock back a shot of something strong if I'm upset."

"Takin' a swig of something with a little kick to it every now and again is one thing. Popping pills to wake up, calm down, or fall asleep is different. She needs professional help."

"I agree, and Viv and I are going to make sure she gets it once this mess is over. Adrianne, too, if she'll accept it."

The back door opened and the three Boston Terriers trotted out, yipping and nipping each other in playful abandon.

"Oh, brother," Rudy muttered. *"Here we go again."*

"Be nice," said Ellie. She nodded to Arlene, who carried two steaming mugs of coffee to the table and set them down.

"Just let me get my gang settled and we can talk." After ordering her dogs to curl up on their beds, she pulled chew treats from the pocket of her gauzy white cover-up. "Can your boy have a rawhide?" she asked Ellie, passing one to each of her babies.

Rudy sat at attention and Ellie nodded. "Sure, and thanks for the coffee."

Arlene gave Rudy the chew and he hunkered down

to enjoy the treat. "Your dog is very sweet," she said. "But a little spooky. I know mine listen and obey, but your man? Sometimes I think he understands everything that's going on around him."

"Rudy is one of a kind," said Ellie. "I like to think he's special, in a very good way."

"My kids are special, too. I guess that's what every owner thinks about their dog."

"That's only natural if they love them."

After taking a deep breath, Arlene sat at the table. It appeared to Ellie as if she'd calmed down. She seemed less animated and more reserved, which meant, she supposed, that whatever drug she'd taken had worn off.

"Thanks for agreeing to talk with me," Ellie told her. "I know you're still grieving over losing Martin."

"Funny, but now that I know what he was doing, I don't really miss him. If my eyes had been open, I'd have seen that he was a sleaze. It makes me angry to think I was taken in by him," she said. "What he did to Maria was unconscionable. Adults are responsible for themselves, but an innocent teenager? He had no excuse for doing what he did to her."

"I'm sorry you had to find out about him that way, but better now than after you were married. Just think, it could have been your father's scenario. Whoever killed him could have come looking for him when the two of you were alone in the house, and killed you, too."

Arlene shuddered. "I've thought about that." She sipped her coffee, then set the cup down. "It's nice of you to want to help Rosa. She's been so good to me, especially since Myron passed away."

"Awwwk! Myron. That's my name. Awwwk! Don't wear it out!"

Ellie glanced at the bird dancing on his perch. "He's quite a character. Vivian told me he stayed in Dr. Kent's office while the house was being painted."

"I had to keep him safe from the paint odors, so Martin agreed to keep him." Arlene pulled an M&M from her pocket and walked to the African gray's perch. "Here, sweetie pie. Mommy's good boy."

The parrot picked the yellow candy from her fingers and brought it to his mouth. "*Mm-mmm good! Awwwk! Mm-mmm good! Awwwk!*"

"Martin said he didn't mind, but I'm almost positive he never got his favorite treat there." Arlene took her seat. "Now, where were we?"

Getting down to business, Ellie said, "Who do you think could have wanted Martin dead?"

Arlene's green eyes filled with tears. "I don't know. At first, when Detective Wheeling talked to me, he said it might be anyone he'd sold to or someone he worked with who wanted a bigger cut of his business. I still can't believe he prescribed pills like they were peanuts to anyone who asked or—or—" She shook her head. "I guess I've been fooling myself, knowing that he had so-called patients driving in at all hours and leaving just as quickly. I should have questioned his activities."

"And he never talked about his business associates?"

"Not a word about anyone. He liked his cars, of course, and he has a boat up in Sag Harbor. He gave me a five-carat emerald-cut diamond engagement ring. It was so huge, I was embarrassed to wear it. He had social connections here, but it was always his work that seemed to drive him." She gazed at her African gray. "There was a thirty-year age difference between myself and Myron. When I met Martin, I should have seen his flaws, but it was nice to be courted by a successful man more my own age."

"And you're positive Tomas arrived home only an hour before Martin's death?"

Arlene took another hit of coffee. "Rosa said so, and I believe her. I still can't understand why she wanted to save me pain by covering up what Martin tried to do to Maria. He was despicable."

"Despicable enough for someone in the Suarez family to want him dead?"

"They're good people," Arlene said, shaking her head. "I just can't see it."

Ellie had a final question, one she'd been thinking, but hadn't voiced out loud. "What about Julio?"

"What about him?"

"He's Maria's father. I imagine he was upset with Martin, too. Could he have gone to the doctor's office and gotten into a scuffle with Dr. Kent and killed him?"

"I know he's strong, but Julio is also gentle and soft-spoken. I don't believe there's a mean bone in the man's body. Rosa said he was with Tomas in the house, and I believe her."

"Maria was his baby. What if he called Tomas home and talked him into helping him avenge the wrong Martin had done?"

"I wouldn't know anything about that."

"I haven't seen Julio for almost twenty-four hours now," said Ellie, carefully broaching her next question. "Rosa told me he'd been at church making something called a *manda.* Do you know what that is?"

When Arlene raised her head, her eyes were filled with tears. "I have no idea." The hand holding her coffee cup began to shake. "All this questioning has worn me out. I can't talk any longer. I need to go upstairs and lie down." She stood before Ellie could say another word. "Come on, babies. It's time to go up with Mommy." She pushed through the kitchen door, held it open for the Bostons, and disappeared.

"I haven't seen Adrianne since we finished breakfast," said Viv as she and Ellie shared space under a beach umbrella on the shore. "Mother said she was around somewhere, but she hasn't answered the cottage phone or her cell, and when I asked Dad he said she wasn't up there."

Ellie had spoken with Vanessa McCready immediately after lunch, but had no luck garnering any more information than she did from Arlene. According to Vanessa, she'd been on the porch entertaining the McCready relatives, not paying attention to where any one person was. She figured Arlene had everything under control. It was her daughter's night, after all. What else was a mother supposed to do?

Viv had kept Adrianne busy during the time Ellie spoke to Vanessa, but the middle sister had somehow still managed to escape just as Ellie was about to sit her down for a talk. They'd searched high and low and eventually given up, deciding instead to spend time in the late-afternoon sun.

Now that they'd been on the beach for about an hour, Ellie decided to make a careful inspection of her legs. After doing so, she breathed a sigh of relief. Her traffic cone orange extremities were almost back to normal and had, in fact, turned a decent shade of brown. Maybe tomorrow, she could again sit in the sun and leave the Hamptons looking as if she'd actually enjoyed a week at the shore.

Glancing to her left, she noted that Viv was still using the same expensive bronzing gel, and turning a beautiful shade of gold in the process. *Stop fussing about your skin and Viv's and get back to business*, she told herself.

"Strange how Adrianne never seems to be around when she's needed, isn't it?"

"I know," said Viv. "Then again, she always was a bit of a Harry Houdini. Whenever the three of us got into trouble, Adrianne always took off right before we were caught, and in the end only Arlene and I would get punished. She'd turned her disappearing act into an art form by the time she was eight."

"I imagine she'll show up for dinner, don't you?"

"Of course. And if she doesn't I'll make Mom confess to what's going on with her. They were all willing to be questioned this morning, so what's changed since then?"

"She's your sister," said Ellie. This vacation had opened her eyes to Viv's smart-ass comments about her family. While Vivie was agreeable, witty, and real, the rest of her family was dour and sarcastic in the way they treated others. "Though it's hard to believe you were swimming in the same gene pool."

"I'll take that as a compliment," said Viv. She stood and stretched, then slipped her cover-up over her bikini-clad body. "How about we make a quick stop before we go to the house?"

Ellie gathered her towel, shook out the sand, and stuffed it into her bag. Then she commandeered Viv's tote bag while Viv took charge of the umbrella. "I can only hope you want to go where I want to go."

Viv plodded through the sand in the direction of the guesthouse with Ellie beside her. "Am I getting warm?"

"You're on fire. I've wanted to see the inside of his

office all day, and not to belittle your father, but I'd like to see for myself if Adrianne is there."

They reached the rear of the cottage, and propped the umbrella at the back door. "Your mother said the cops have given permission to leave the place unlocked, correct?"

"Yep, and guess what."

Ellie opened the entrance door. "What?"

Viv reached into her bag, and pulled out a key.

"That will get us into Dr. Kent's office?" Ellie asked.

"I've been carrying it around, hoping you'd want to stop in, but I figured that would be useless now that the cops and Mr. Bond have tramped around inside." She stepped to the door that led to the second-floor apartment. "And just to show how much I love you, I'm willing to check the guest quarters while you inspect the doc's office. What do you think of that?"

"You're a pal," said Ellie.

She held out her hand and Viv dropped the key in her palm. "I'll be back in a couple of minutes to join you."

She unlocked the office door, then peered into Dr. Kent's waiting room. The decor, a mixture of beach casual and antique oak, was comfortable yet had an air of money about it. Glass-topped tables held groupings of magazines and clusters of seashells, while wicker baskets and framed seascapes blended perfectly with the cream-colored walls and ocean blue drapes.

She started in the kitchen, happy to see that the usual grit left behind when a crime scene was dusted for fingerprints was gone. No wonder Maria and Terry had been missing for the entire afternoon yesterday. It must have taken hours just to clean the place after the cops had made a thorough search.

She first opened the cupboards and moved glassware and dishes, then checked the fridge, which was empty, and peeked inside an equally empty dishwasher. She gave a final inspection of the pantry and headed for the bathroom, where she found things to be in order, as well.

Back in the living room, she looked under the sofa, took stock of a bookcase, and shoved a few chairs around. Then she sighed. She was terrible at running a search. All she knew was what she'd seen on cop shows, and she hardly ever watched those. Why in the heck did she think she'd find anything after professionals had done their job?

Opening another door, she found herself in an examining room, complete with a raised table topped with a roll of white paper and a pillow. Looking into an empty glass-fronted cabinet, she guessed it had contained the drugs that the police confiscated; then she checked the drawers and a smaller cupboard, but all she saw were cotton swabs, tongue depressors, and other bits she expected belonged in a doctor's office.

Growing frustrated, she opened the next door, pleased to find Dr. Kent's actual private space. A massive mahogany desk sat against one wall, complete with a beautiful leather chair. Hanging on the wall behind the desk were the usual diplomas giving his credentials: Princeton University, a medical degree from Johns Hopkins, and an internship at Beth Israel, plus a few more framed documents from a variety of hospitals around the country.

A credenza sat below the wall of diplomas, and she opened it. One side had the innards for hanging file folders, but there were none. The other side was a shelved cabinet, which was also empty, and she decided it was probably another storage area for his giveaway drugs.

Steps on the stairs told her Viv was on her way down, so she continued her perusal. Rounding the desk, she scanned the room, but stopped short when she saw what was on the wall opposite the desk.

From where Dr. Kent sat during his working hours, he would see this picture every time he raised his eyes.

"Find anything?" asked Viv, entering the office.

Ellie swallowed. "How about you tell me?" She jutted her chin toward the wall holding a painting of a woman in profile.

Viv glanced in the direction of Ellie's gaze and gasped. "Holy hell. How did that get there?"

"Looks like the painting was hung with a particular purpose," said Ellie.

"Ya think?" Viv's tone dripped sarcasm.

"Is that who I think it is?" Ellie continued, still in shock.

"See that tattoo, the butterfly on her lower back?"

"It's pretty hard to miss, and it appears to be more on her upper right buttocks, if you ask me."

"Whatever. All I know is she got that the summer she left for college. Dad never saw it, but Mom had a fit. There's no doubt in my mind. That's Adrianne."

Chapter 10

"She's completely naked," said Ellie, still surprised by the painting.

"No kidding."

"Why do you think it's here?"

Viv *tsk*ed. "Check out the view in this room."

Ellie turned and again zeroed in on Dr. Kent's desk. "Maybe she did it for practice? Like she was supposed to submit a self-portrait to a contest and she had to do a mock-up, and she wanted the doctor to be the judge."

Viv looked at her as if she had three heads. "You're joking, right?"

"Well, what other reason would she have for putting a naked self-portrait on her future brother-in-law's wall?" The question made perfect sense to Ellie.

Viv put her hands on her hips. "I never thought I'd say this, but I think Sam is right. You truly are a Little Mary Sunshine." She looked around the room and focused on the barge-sized leather sofa. "Want to hear my theory?"

"Ah . . . sure." Ellie continued to stare at the painting. Adrianne's long dark hair swung down her back, her profile perfect, her figure lithe. She was beautiful in a look-at-me sort of way, though Ellie felt it was all superficial. To her, the truly attractive women were the ones who had no idea of their striking appearance or, if they did, wouldn't let it get in the way of their being a nice person. It was one of the reasons she liked Vivie so much.

"I think she did it to get back at Arlene," Viv pronounced.

"To get back at Arlene? What did her older sister ever do to her?"

Viv turned, grabbed one of the chairs in front of the doctor's desk, jerked it around to face the painting, and plopped herself down. "Jealousy, for one thing."

Ellie pulled the other chair in place and copied her friend's actions. "She's jealous of Arlene? But why?"

Shaking her head, Viv rolled her eyes. "Because Arlene has money and Adrianne doesn't. Plus, she's had a husband and was on her way to number two."

"Adrianne's never been married?"

"Nope, and I doubt it will ever happen. And before you ask why I think that—" Viv crossed her arms. "It's because she's a bitch, plain and simple."

"That's not a very nice thing to say about your sister, Vivian."

"That kind of truth rarely is. Adrianne's always been jealous of Arlene, and me, if you want to know."

"Do you really think so?"

"Don't make a decision until you hear my reasoning.

Before each of my divorces, I called Mother to let her know what was happening in my life. I'd hear from Adrianne a week later, and she'd ask me how things were going. I'd fill her in and she'd sound so sympathetic I'd break down. Once I even cried. I found out later from Mom that Adrianne knew all about the divorces before she phoned me." Viv blew out a breath. "She called me because she wanted to bask in my misery and feed off my lousy luck. It made her happier with herself."

Ellie couldn't understand why any sister would be glad to hear that another sister's marriage had failed. She'd been through each of her mother's divorces and knew it was a terrible time for a woman. And even when she'd known that divorcing her dickhead ex had to be done to save her mental well-being, it had been a trying and miserable experience. "Have you discussed it with Arlene?"

"I told her, and she started out talking just like you, but when it happened after my second divorce, and I clued her in, she had to agree."

"I still don't get the reason for this portrait."

"Think, Ellie. It'll hit you in a minute."

It only took her about thirty more seconds to see the light. "Oh."

The corners of Viv's mouth turned up, but the smile didn't reach her eyes. "Oh is right. How else could you hurt a sister you're jealous of without doing her physical harm? Even if Arlene never came to the doc's office, and it's obvious she hasn't, Adrianne would know that she'd had an affair with her sister's husband, and he would be reminded of her every day. The ultimate slap in the face, if you ask me."

"So you think they slept together?"

"Oh, Lord, of course they did. Probably right there on that huge couch. I'd expect nothing less from a man who tried to screw a sixteen-year-old child."

Ellie stared at the picture while Viv's words sank in. The likeness, painted from Adrianne's butt to the top of her head, had her body turned just enough to showcase one curvy breast with a fully erect, pink-tipped nipple. Now that she understood what Viv meant, she realized the provocative expression on Adrianne's face was more of a see-what-I-can-do challenge to her older sister than a teasing expression for Dr. Kent.

"How long do you think the affair went on?"

"Best guess, almost from the day she arrived to paint the artwork in Arlene's house."

"Three weeks, and Arlene never caught on?"

"Guess not. She was probably so hopped up on drugs and wedding plans she had no idea. And the sleazy doctor, well, he might have figured it was one last fling before he tied the knot . . . or until the next opportunity presented itself."

Ellie rolled her neck to work out a kink. "I never thought I'd say this, but I'm relieved the man is no longer with us."

"I imagine a lot of those women looking for happy pills said yes to his advances just so they could get their drugs."

"That's no excuse for a woman having sex with a married man," Ellie said. "Believe me, I went through it, and I don't think I can ever forgive Cherry for sleeping with my ex."

"It takes two to tango, kiddo."

"I'm well aware of that, but I can't imagine any woman sleeping with Larry Lipschitz, CPA extraordinaire, because they needed to have their taxes done or their checkbook balanced. At least he and Cherry got married."

"Lucky her. Now she's the one who has to work her ass off with a personal trainer and keep her hair highlighted and her makeup perfect twenty-four/seven."

"And live without a dog."

"Cherry Abrams wanted a dog?"

"I don't know," said Ellie, shrugging. "But I think about it sometimes, and figure it's exactly what she deserves for doing what she did."

"Wow. I'm impressed. I think that's the first totally mean thing I've ever heard you say about anyone."

"And I already feel guilty for it. I can't imagine anyone who loves dogs having to live without one." Ellie sniffed back a tear. "I'd have no life if I didn't have Rudy."

"You'd have Sam."

"I doubt it. I only met Sam because I was walking dogs, and I never would have done that if I didn't have my boy."

"Hmm. Maybe you owe Cherry a huge thank-you. If she hadn't slept with the D, you wouldn't have found them in bed together, and you might still be dogless and married to a dickhead."

Ellie grinned, though she knew she shouldn't. "When you put it that way . . ." She turned her head and again faced Adrianne's backside. "What are we supposed to do about this?"

"Do?"

Ellie raised an eyebrow. "Yes, do. Should we call Adrianne on it or tell Arlene? I can't believe she's never been in here to see it."

"Like I said, Adrianne probably only did it over the last three weeks, and big sis was too busy planning the wedding to pay attention." Viv stood and put the chair back where she found it. "Guess we should go to the house and get ready for dinner. I don't want anyone to come here looking for us until we decide how to handle this."

Ellie righted her chair and followed Viv to the foyer. Once there, she locked the office door. They walked to the exit, picked up their tote bags and the umbrella, and headed back to the house.

She had a lot to think about. Worse, knowing what she did, she had to quiz Adrianne about the night of Dr. Kent's murder.

Vanessa, Evan, Vivian, and Arlene drove into Bridgehampton after dinner looking for a shop that sold ice cream. Adrianne cried off, saying she had a headache, and Ellie saw her chance for some time alone with the middle McCready sister.

"Adrianne, can you give me a couple of minutes before you go to the cottage?"

Stopping in her march to the stairs, Adrianne tugged on her formfitting, off-the-shoulder top. The night was cool, Rosa and her daughters had cleared the terrace table, and there was no one else around. "I guess." She planted her shapely butt, clad in tight black capris, in a chair. "What do you want to talk about?"

Ellie tried for a smile. "The night of Dr. Kent's murder."

"I figured you'd get around to me eventually, but I really have nothing to say."

"You were upstairs in the cottage when he was killed, correct?"

"Yes, but I'd been asleep. The party gave me a headache, and I took a muscle relaxant to get rid of the tension. Detective Wheeling knows all this, by the way, and he's satisfied that I can't be of any help in the case."

This headache thing was getting old. Ellie couldn't believe a woman like Adrianne wouldn't be more creative when she lied. "Dr. K gave you the drug?"

Adrianne smiled, but it was forced. "Of course."

"Do you think you were the last person to see him alive?"

"I doubt it. There were a couple of patients in the waiting room when I left to go upstairs."

"And you never heard an argument?" Ellie asked, thinking of what James Bond had told her.

"The music coming down from the house sort of muffled things and the pill knocked me out. Sorry, but that's about all I can say." She stood and walked to the stairs. "I think we're done here."

"Viv and I were in Dr. Kent's office today," Ellie said, hoping to see some reaction from the woman.

Adrianne slowly turned around. "Really? Did you find anything interesting?"

"I had hoped to find a clue to his killer. Instead we saw some very engrossing artwork."

"I imagine you did." Her smile reminded Ellie of a snake. "Marty loved that self-portrait. He said he'd never take it down. He told me it held the secret to his success. Marty—"

"Awwwk! Marty! Awwwk! Do it again, baby. Yes, just like that! Awwwk! Just like that!"

Myron's chatter echoed that of a woman in the throes of passion, and now that Ellie had been around her for a while, the voice reminded her of Adrianne's.

Nostrils flaring, Adrianne shot the African gray a dirty look and huffed out a breath.

"So you and Dr. Kent had sex in his office." Ellie made the question a statement of fact. "When Myron was in the room."

"The little pecker watched everything. According to Marty, he was very entertaining. Some of his patients liked to try to make him talk, especially when the stupid bird would repeat things in their exact voice."

"But you didn't enjoy it?"

"It wasn't on my how-to-get-a-laugh list, but who cares? That bit of passion could be any woman's voice." She turned back to the stairs. "And if Arlene figures it out, what can she say?" Stomping down the steps, Adrianne disappeared.

"What a piece of work." Rudy crawled out from beneath the table, where he'd been sitting at Ellie's feet.

"I know. Poor Arlene, trusting her sister without knowing she'd been sleeping with her fiancé."

"Makes Vivie look like a champ, doesn't it?" Rudy spouted with a yip.

"Makes my girl rise ten levels above the rest of her dip-wad family," T said with a growl. *"Vivie is tops in my book."*

"You know I agree with you. I just wish there was some way to make sense of this mess." She dug a pen and her spiral pad out from her bag. She'd never asked Sam exactly what it was he wrote in his many tablets, but now she wished she had.

"Guess I have to look at my notes and see if anything else makes sense."

She'd written the name of every person who'd been at the party, starting with the immediate family, then given each of them a page for notes. The four R guests had been Viv's job, as well as an aunt and uncle, their children, and Elsie and Connie. She'd received Viv's report on each of them and scribbled a "no comment" on every page.

Flipping to her suspects, she checked all she'd written after her talk with family members Arlene, Vanessa, Evan, and now Adrianne. She copied what she remembered of Adrianne's explanation of the painting, ending with "Marty said it was the secret to his success." Odd that he said the painting was the key and not Adrianne herself, but did it really make a difference?

She still had to corner Julio, Tomas, Maria, Teresa, and, just to be thorough, Uncle Mickey and Dr. B. Tomas was already in jail and his knife was found at the scene. It was easy to imagine the hot-tempered young man having an argument with Dr. Kent over his younger sister and threatening him with a knife.

Could he have dropped the weapon in a scuffle, followed the doc out, and found his father waiting? Would Julio have been angry enough to shove Kent so hard he went flying backward and smacked his head?

Both men knew the area. Tomas had lived there off and on for years, and Julio maintained the property. Surely he'd taken the route on the far side of the cottage, where it was hidden from view, a hundred times before. They could have run around the parking lot and steered wide, then entered the main house through the front and acted as if they'd been inside all along. With so much activity going on outside, who would see them?

"I can tell you're thinkin'." Rudy sniggered. *"There's smoke comin' outta your ears."*

"Very funny." Ellie gazed at him. "You're not keeping

anything from me, are you? Did you notice anybody heading down the walk to Dr. Sleazeball's office during the party?"

"Those pains in the butt, Greta and Coco, were yapping. Kept trying to get Mr. T and me to play, but we ignored them." He put his paws on her thigh. *"I saw a coupl'a men walkin' down the path as the night wore on, but I'd never recognize them by their backsides."*

"How about a scent? Or their hair?"

"Too far away when we saw 'em," said T.

"Maybe if you took me to the dog psychic, Madame Orzo, she'd help me remember," Rudy whined.

"There's no time for me to get you back to the Village for a session with the woman. Just use your own brain and think, but not too hard. Something might come back to you."

Ellie wrote what little she could on the pages. She had to speak to Julio, and there had to be some way she could question Uncle Mickey and Dr. B without arousing their suspicion. Adrianne had been no help, but—

What was it Adrianne had said? She'd gotten a sedative from Dr. Kent, and when she left his office two or three patients were still in the waiting room. Who were they, and how could she get their names?

Glancing up, she noticed that the outdoor lights had automatically brightened, which meant darkness was almost upon her. She stood, prepared to go into the house and turn on the lights for the terrace; then she heard footsteps. Rudy and Mr. T growled at the same moment and stalked slowly to the stairs.

Ellie flipped on the rear lights and James Bond blinked in the surprising glow. Wearing a more formal but still resort-casual dark green T-shirt and khaki pants, he looked as handsome and cocky as ever. He straightened at the bright flash, his dark eyes focusing on the back door.

"How did you get here?" she demanded.

"I walked down the beach, of course, and followed the path up. You have a problem with that?"

She stepped onto the terrace. "No one's home, so you might as well leave."

His full lips curved in a grin. "You're here, aren't you?"

She propped her back against the doorframe. "Yes, but I'm not in charge of the house. I can't let you in and I've already answered all your questions, so—"

He pulled a folded piece of paper from his back pocket and snapped it open. "Oh, but you can let me in. I have that search warrant Ms. Millman challenged me to get."

Growling, Rudy and T scuttled in front of him. *"We got him, Triple E. Say the word and he's toast."*

When the dogs threatened, Agent Bond took a step in reverse and slapped his hand over his lower back. "Hey, call off the mutts!"

Ellie stifled a smile and tried for serious. "There's no need to reach for your gun, Mr. Bond. They're just protecting me."

"He's sweatin'. I can smell it," Rudy snarled.

He stared at the dogs for ten seconds, then slowly moved his right hand back to his side. "How about calling me Jim? This whole Agent Double O Seven thing is getting old." Before she answered, he waved the warrant, his voice all business again. "And I can assure you this is on the level."

"You want to use it now? Tonight?" Detective Wheeling had already searched the house. What was

Agent 007—Jim—looking for? "A little late, don't you think?"

Keeping an eye on Rudy and T, he took a step closer. "The local cops gave me the findings on their search, and they collected only one computer, which Kent kept in his office. I'm hoping to find something smaller, maybe a PDA, whatever he used to store his records in. The desktop had none of that, but I need the personal one. I'm hoping to find it in Kent's home office." His lips thinned. "I also want to check out Ms. Millman's medicine chest for myself."

"And I'm supposed to let you in?"

"You could, but it's not necessary. The door isn't locked and you and the dogs won't block my way—" He stopped when Rudy and T began a second round of growls. "Come on, call off the mutts and cooperate."

She had no right to refuse him. He was an agent for the DEA and the doctor was dead. Jim had already told her he wasn't interested in finding the murderer. All he wanted was a look at Kent's personal records so he could capture the rest of the slime in the doc's drug ring. But she did feel protective of Arlene, who, aside from that one negative comment about weight, had only been polite and kind to her, and she was trying to repair the relationship she had with Viv.

Ellie gazed at the guesthouse and saw the lights on the second floor. "Adrianne is in the cottage. Why don't you talk to her? She's a family member, and she could let you in."

He set his hands on his hips. "The woman is useless. She told me she had a prescription for every Schedule Two drug she was taking, and it checked out. Interestingly enough, they were all filled in the Montauk pharmacy in the past three weeks. I really don't want to ask her permission to do what I already have the authority to do."

Ellie remembered Viv saying that Arlene had cleaned her medicine cabinet and tossed out a couple of dozen bottles of pills. Though her older sister might not have any smarts in choosing the right man, she was a member of Mensa. Surely she had gotten rid of anything incriminating.

"Are you going to arrest Ms. Millman?"

He crossed his arms and his biceps flexed, filling out his shirt and shaping each muscle. "I don't plan on it, but she could be in trouble. Her sister, too. It depends on what I find inside."

"And this has nothing to do with the murder?"

"Awwwk! Murder! Awwwk! Don't make me do something you'll regret, Marty. Awwwk!"

Ellie spun around to face Myron. She knew the voice he was imitating. She'd heard it somewhere before, but where? Just then her phone rang. Surprised by the tone, she automatically reached into her tote and pulled out the cell. When she checked the caller ID, she gave a mental eye roll. Leave it to Sam to pick tonight for a chat. Dropping it in the bag, she let the call go to voice mail.

"You could have taken it out here," Jim said, cocky as ever. "Then again, I guess you already know that."

She took a step forward to show him she wasn't intimidated. "How would you know what I know?"

"Awwwk! I know, I know, I know! Awwwk! I know! I know! Awwwk! Ain't no sunshine when she's gone. Awwwk!"

He grinned. "Ol' Myron does a good job with Bill

Withers, doesn't he? 'Ain't No Sunshine' is a golden oldie."

No one had told Ellie what to do with the dopey bird, but someone always brought him in when it got dark. Since she was the last one on the terrace, she felt it was her turn to take care of the African gray. And the boys, before they did something they'd be sorry for.

Shrugging, she decided to ease up on faux Agent 007. He was correct. She couldn't stop him from entering the premises. "Back off, you two. We have to let Mr. Bond in."

She picked up Myron's pedestal and her verbal sparring partner shot past the guard dogs. "Here. I'll take that." His fingers wrapped around hers, and just as quickly, he let go and backed away. "Sorry. Put it down, and I'll do the job."

Heat flamed up Ellie's neck and crept over her cheeks. Good thing the terrace lights cast shadows or he'd see her blush, which would only make her turn a darker red. If she was still the color of a traffic cone, he might not notice, but she was almost back to normal. . . .

She took a step of retreat and held open the door. "We can bring him in the kitchen. He has a cleared spot there."

The dogs marched in first. Then Jim carried in the perch and stepped aside to let Ellie lead the way. She flipped on the kitchen light and aimed for Myron's special area while the bird squawked another round of phrases.

"Awwwk! Don't make me hurt you, Marty. Awwwk!

"Ahh! Ahh! Ahh! Awwwk! That's it. Do it to me. Awwwk!"

She was fairly certain the female voice belonged to

Adrianne, but where had she heard that male voice? Arriving at Myron's post, she pointed a finger. "Just set him down and give me a minute. He gets a slice of apple as a nightly snack."

Jim edged past the dogs and headed into the dining room. "You do what you have to. I'll get started."

"We can still take him down, Triple E."

"The fool has no idea who he's dealin' with."

Ellie pulled an apple from the fruit bowl, rinsed it, and cut off a slice. Dropping to one knee, she gave each boy a chunk while whispering, "The man had a gun. He might have shot you both. Now be good."

Standing, she chopped off another slice and brought it to Myron, who took the apple with his beak. "Tell me, Mr. Smarty-pants. Whose voice was that you mimicked a minute ago?"

Myron took a bit of the apple, then passed it to his clawed foot, chewing as he stared at her.

She returned to the counter, cut two more slices, and tossed them to the boys. "You're an animal. Can't you talk to that crabby-assed bird?" she asked Rudy. "That might solve some of the mystery."

The dogs chomped the apple down and sat at attention. "Really, think about talking to him for me, please?"

"Sorry. No can do," said Rudy, licking his muzzle. *"That parrot reminds me of a lawyer; all talk and no common sense. They both talk bird-speak and I don't."*

"Well, I don't 'speak bird,' either, and you're a lot closer to him on the evolutionary chain than I am." She wiped the countertop with a sponge and rinsed it out, then washed her hands. "Guess I'd better go find Agent Double O Seven before he gets into something he shouldn't." She walked to the rear staircase. "You two, go up this way and head straight to bed. No snooping or annoying Jim."

The dogs grumbled, but did as told. Ellie wanted to see what Jim was doing, so she followed his tracks. If he found something in the doctor's office, she wanted to know about it. When she arrived in the foyer, she caught a glimmer of light from the hall that led to the library and Arlene's office and figured he'd gone there first. Then she took a better look and realized the area was still fairly dark. She stepped toward a side table holding a lamp. She'd need more wattage to find her way into the hall.

"Hey, Jim, have any luck?" she called out. When he didn't answer, she opened her mouth to give another shout. The hall turned dark as a tomb, and before she could speak, a large figure came rushing toward her.

Plowing into her like a pro linebacker, the man shoved her out of the way and knocked her into the table, where she fell flat on her ass. Glass crashed as she hit the floor and she banged her head on the way down.

She saw stars. Footsteps pounded down the stairs and the dogs barked. A moment later everything went black.

Chapter 11

Muscled arms held Ellie tight, but in a good way. When something cool pressed against her left temple, a flash of pain shot into her brain. She struggled to get away, but those same arms tensed around her, keeping her in place.

"Sit still and let me clean you up a little."

Another familiar voice . . . it was . . . it was . . .

She opened her eyes and slammed them shut. Damn, the light was bright. Moving, she felt another pain hit her and slumped into those warm, hard arms.

"Do you think anything's broken? Can you talk?"

"Head hurts. Don't wanna," she said with a moan.

His chest shook and she knew he was laughing.

"I can't believe a big tough girl like you would let a little pain shut you up."

Big girl? Was that another crack about her weight? "It's my head, not yours, bozo."

"Ah, there's the woman I'm used to dealing with."

She sat up and this time the arms let her go. Wincing, she cracked open her eyes, hoping to fend off that darned bright light. Through a haze, she saw khaki-colored pants crouched beside her outstretched legs. She blinked, her eyes opening wider, and let her gaze wander up a flat stomach and chest to well-formed shoulders, a corded neck, strong jaw, and . . .

What was she doing in the arms of James Bond, with his *GQ* face just inches from her nose?

Pushing him away, she groaned. "What the heck did you do to me?"

He chuckled. "Me? Not a darn thing. I heard a crash and came down the stairs as fast as I could. Stupid dogs almost tripped me when they raced from behind me to the bottom of the steps. They took off out the door and I haven't seen them since."

"What!" She groped against him. "I've got to get Rudy. And T. It's dark. They don't know this area." Rising to her knees, she put her hands on the floor to push herself up. Pain sliced her left palm and she hissed.

"Slow down and take it easy. There are shards of glass all over the place." He grabbed her upper arm. "Here, lean on me and I'll help you to stand."

Ellie found her footing and swayed right into those rock-hard arms again.

"Hey, you're not going to pass out on me, are you?"

She shook her head and a jackhammer started pounding double time in her brain. "No, I'm okay," she lied. "I have to find my dogs."

"Screw the dogs. You've got a knot on your temple the size of an egg, and now you've cut your palm. Sit here and hold this towel on your head while I take a look outside."

He moved a rattan side chair out of place and tucked her into it. She blinked in the light as he walked through the foyer and disappeared. It gave her time to survey her surroundings. The glass-topped table next to the chair was overturned, the crystal vase that had sat upon it shattered on the hardwood floor, while seashells lay scattered alongside the glass.

Checking the towel he'd handed her, she saw traces of blood. Her blood. What the heck had happened?

She reached back in her memory, hoping to recall something of the night. Jim Bond arrived while she was on the terrace and waved a search warrant. Myron sang and squawked, so she brought him inside and gave him and the dogs a piece of apple. Jim left to do whatever, and she sent Rudy and T up the rear stairs, and followed Agent 007 to the front of the house.

She saw light filtering from the hallway and figured he'd gone to the doc's office first. When she called, he didn't answer, so she opened her mouth . . .

And a human steam engine ran her down.

"Well, crap," she muttered, dabbing at the lump. Wincing, she laid her head on the back of the chair. If the door had slammed, and she thought it had, how did the dogs get out? And what did Rudy think he was doing? Despite his bravado, he was as inept at catching a burglar as she was.

She pictured the dark hulking shape that had run at her as if she were invisible.

Heaving a breath, she held the cool towel to her temple. Jim was right. The lump was big and it hurt.

Forget the jackhammer. If she didn't know better, she'd swear the entire cast of *Riverdance* was giving a run-through performance inside her skull.

She closed her eyes and tried to relax. Moments later something furry landed in her lap.

A slurp of wet stroked her cheek, and she smiled.

"Hey, you okay?"

"I'm fine. Just got run down by some idiot and hit my head. Where were you?"

Rudy nuzzled against her chest. *"T and I were checkin' out Agent Ass-wipe and we heard a scuffle. When we headed down the stairs, we saw a guy run out the door, so we took off after him."*

"I thought I told you to go straight to bed."

He gave her cheek another lick. *"Yeah, well, lucky for you that didn't happen."*

She ran her free hand down his head and back, then wrapped him in her arm. "Don't ever scare me like that again, you big knucklehead."

"Scare you? How do you think T and I felt when we heard the racket and saw you crumpled on the floor? No guy is gonna do that to my girl and get away with it."

"Is Twink here?"

"Mr. T is ready and waitin'." The Jack Russell set his paws on her knee. *"We would'a caught that fool if he hadn't taken off in a car."*

Footsteps sounded in the foyer and she whispered, "We'll talk later. Hush for now."

"Who are you talking to?" asked Jim.

"Myself. I've been trying to piece things together and I think I have a handle on what happened." She forced a weak smile when he stood in front of her. "Thanks for finding the boys."

"They found me."

She arched an eyebrow at Rudy and moaned at the pain. "What they're good at finding is trouble."

"My guess is whoever slammed into you left a car running out front. The dogs just missed him, but they chased the car."

Jim squatted beside the chair and Mr. T showed his teeth.

"Keep your distance, fool."

She patted his head. "*Shh*, no talking."

Jim pulled back out of striking range. "He's not talking. He's growling." He took her hand and removed the towel from her head. "You're going to have a mother of a bruise come morning. Give me that and I'll get more ice. We can go over things when I get back."

He left and she patted her thigh, signaling Mr. T. He jumped up next to Rudy and she held both dogs tight. "You two are the best." She squeezed until they wriggled. "Tell me what you remember, but make it fast."

"He was a big guy. When he slammed the door, it bounced back and smacked the wall," muttered T, his muzzle against her chest.

"He got to his car before we did, so we just missed jumpin' up the side and getting a look at his face. He took off like he was drivin' at NASCAR." Rudy gave her chin a lick, then pushed his nose into her neck. *"We tried, Triple E, but he got away."*

"It's okay." She rubbed their heads. "You boys did good. Could you recognize him by his scent if you met him again?"

"He smelled like medicine," said Rudy.

"Medicine?" Dr. B immediately came to mind, but why would she be here robbing the house? Was she big enough to slam her down like a linebacker? "A doctor smell?"

"I guess. It was like chemicals."

Great. Ellie heaved a sigh. "How about the car? Did you notice anything about it?"

"It was big and black," T said. *"And it had one of them emblems on the trunk. Like an upside-down Y."*

A Mercedes, thought Ellie. There were probably five thousand in Montauk alone. "That's good."

"Talking to yourself again?" Jim asked, walking to face her. "Here, tip your head a little and set this on the bump."

"It feels better." She placed the towel on her head and winced when the weight of the ice settled. "Don't they have a bag of peas in the freezer?"

"Peas?" He frowned as if he thought her crazy. Then the light dawned. "Oh, yeah. I didn't check, but I will."

The sound of footsteps came from the foyer. Then Rosa peeked into the room. *"Dios mio! Señorita Ellie. Qué pasó, pobrecita? Estás bien?"*

"Sorry for the mess, Rosa," Ellie began. "I think I interrupted a burglary."

"*Es* okay. I get the broom—"

"Forget about the broom, and find me a box of Band-Aids or something I can use to make a butterfly wrap." Jim stood. "And don't touch a thing until I give the okay. This is a crime scene. I'm calling Wheeling."

Ellie lay in bed, a bag of frozen peas balanced on her left temple. T was under the covers on his mistress's bed and Rudy was next to her, licking her cheek. Viv was finishing up in the bathroom.

Between what she recalled and what Bond remembered, Detective Wheeling had pieced together his version of the incident.

The family had left, but she'd stayed on the terrace at the rear of the house. When it grew dark, no one was inside to turn on the lights, so the house looked empty. Someone, probably one of the doc's "patients," needed a hit and decided to check his office for prescription pads, spare drugs, whatever he could find. He broke in and went to Kent's home office.

Then he heard Jim going up the stairs, and made to leave. That's when she called out and he realized he was trapped. Head down, he raced down the hall and smashed into her, dropping her like a rock. On her way down, she knocked her head against the table, which broke the vase and sent things flying. When the dogs heard the commotion, they took off after the intruder, but had no luck catching him.

Ellie thought it a plausible explanation, though her own theory was better. What if the burglar was the murderer, and he was looking for evidence that might incriminate him? Since Tomas was already locked up, that would prove the kid was innocent, and the real killer was running free.

But Wheeling didn't buy it and reminded her they had enough evidence to bring Tomas to trial. They were more inclined to believe it was a patient looking for a stash of drugs.

Viv took that moment to arrive in the bedroom wearing a soft cotton nightshirt that fell to her knees. Walking to Ellie, she peeked under the bag of peas and *tsk*ed. "It looks like someone took a battering ram to your face. I just hope the cut doesn't leave a scar."

Ellie fingered the lump and felt the butterfly bandage holding her skin together. "Jim said it wouldn't if I left it alone for a while."

Viv smiled. "Agent Bond to the rescue? I told you he has the hots for you."

"Don't be silly. He was here and he knows first aid. What else would he do?" She grimaced. "I don't want to know how bad the rest of it looks, but tell me anyway."

Viv narrowed her eyes and peeked again. "The egg is huge, sort of like the jumbo size you can buy at Gristedes. The purple color goes over most of your forehead and it's starting to cover your eye." She raised an eyebrow. "Do you need help with the pain?"

Ellie shrugged, which caused another *Riverdance* rehearsal. The egg was throbbing like a son of a gun. "Gee, I don't know. Do you think Arlene has something that'll make me comfortable?"

"Don't be sarcastic. You need it, so you're not abusing drugs. Give me a minute."

She disappeared out the door and Ellie sighed. "Yippee. I'm about to hop on the druggie train right alongside just about everyone else in this house. I might as well tell Jim to arrest me now."

"That's not true," said Rudy, curling next to her hip. *"It's only for one night, so you can sleep."*

"Yeah, I know. But I don't want to fall into the trap most people do when they start taking the prescription-only stuff Jim keeps blabbing about."

"You got me, and I'll make sure that won't happen."

Viv reappeared with her hand cupped. "I got you a Valium and a Percocet. One to help you relax and one for the pain. Hang on while I get a glass of water."

Ellie groaned. She did not want to start using drugs,

but the Riverdancers that had taken residence in her brain had another idea. The more she worried about the drugs, the faster they clogged.

The side of the bed dipped and the dancers moved in double time. "Here, sit up and take these."

She opened her eyes and saw Vivie, her face screwed with worry, sitting on the edge of the bed, a glass in one hand and two pills cupped in the other.

Struggling to sit upright, Ellie let the peas slide to the bed. Then she took hold of the cup, reached for the pills, and swallowed them down.

Viv gave a tentative smile. "You should feel better in about twenty minutes. I want you to sleep until noon. Don't worry. I'll keep tabs on you, make sure there's ice on that lovely purple mask, and keep track of your breathing. That sort of thing."

"Thanks," Ellie mumbled. "You're a pal."

"That's what I'm here for." Viv stood and the mattress evened out. Then she collected the bag of soggy peas. "Give me a few minutes to get rid of these and find more. If you lie on your right side, I can set the next bag on the bruise without disturbing you. Just relax and let the medicine take you away."

Ellie did as she suggested, turning to her right, and Rudy got comfortable behind her thighs. *"How you feelin'?"*

"Unless somebody gives me a shot of morphine or Demerol, I doubt anything will work to make the ache go away. What I really want is Sam."

"The Defective Detective? What am I? Chopped liver?"

Reaching back, she scratched his head. "Not for comfort, silly. Because I need to talk to someone about tonight."

"You do have that dick of a DEA agent. He seemed pretty chummy when you were comin' out of it."

"He was being conscientious, that's all." She closed her eyes and envisioned him holding her gently, his chiseled mouth just an inch from her lips. "He's turning into a nice guy."

"Be careful with 'nice.' It might be a trap."

"Stop talking crazy and go to sleep."

"I'll do that after Viv gets here, freezes your brain, and douses the lights. Until then, I'm on watch duty."

Ellie smiled and closed her eyes. The Riverdancers' clogging had slowed. She was safe as long as Rudy was here to protect her. And Viv. And Jim Bond, too.

Rosa was nice, caring for her after the fall. Arlene had been nice, and Vanessa and Evan McCready, too. Adrianne hadn't showed her face, even after two cop cars arrived with their lights flashing, but Adrianne might be nice, too.

She heaved a contented sigh.

Viv walked in and Ellie grinned. "Hi. You're the best friend. How can I ever thank you for being so nice?"

"Looks like the pills are working, huh, Rudy?"

"Don't talk to Rudy." Ellie yawned. "Only I can do that."

Viv placed a bag of frozen vegetables on her temple. "You used up all the peas. We're down to sweet corn."

"Sweet corn is nice." She snuggled into the pillow, relieved to find the Riverdancers were taking a break. "Did I ever tell you my secret?"

After flicking off the lamp on each nightstand, Viv sat on her bed and gazed at Ellie through the moonlight floating in from the French doors. "You have a secret? I find that hard to believe. You tell me everything."

"I do, I do. And it's . . . nice." She giggled. "Nobody knows, but I can talk to Rudy and T, all the dogs I walk, really, and they talk back to me."

"Uh-huh. And I talk to my plants. It helps them grow."

"You don't believe me," said Ellie, wounded that Viv would laugh at her deepest and most unusual secret. "But you're still nice."

"Okay, I'm nice, the dogs are nice, the sea grass is nice. Even the sand fleas have something to be thankful for. Now go to sleep."

Ellie's eyelids drooped. She felt light, as if she were filled with helium and floating above the room. She'd told Viv her secret, and Viv hadn't said she was crazy. Vivie was nice. Detective Wheeling was nice. James Bond was nice, too. Right now the whole world was . . . nice.

But Sam was the nicest, and she missed him. Maybe she'd call him tomorrow and tell him about tonight.

Ellie turned over and stretched. Moving a hand, she found Rudy and gave him a good morning scratch. Then she stretched again and her head started to hammer. Worse, she had to pee.

That made her groan. There were peas. Then there were pees. Only this kind of pee was different from the peas she'd had last night. Really different.

Sitting up, she swung her legs over the side of the mattress and sucked down a gasp. What had happened to her head? It felt as if the entire tympani section of the New York Philharmonic were performing in her skull.

Her feet were on the floor, but she wasn't sure if she could or should stand. She opened one eye and spotted a bag of what was once frozen corn plopped on the cotton rug under the nightstand. Had she sleepwalked and robbed the freezer?

Robbed? The word set off an alarm bell, adding to the racket in her brain. She raised her hand to her head and cried out. *Darn but that hurt.* The word "robbed" snaked into her brain again and another warning bell rang, loud and clear.

She'd been involved in a robbery? Wait—no—not that. A burglary.

She gave herself a mental pat on the back for knowing the difference, then frowned. Who the heck did she burgle?

The balcony door opened and Viv stepped into the room. "I thought I heard you moving around. How do you feel?" She didn't wait for an answer, but walked closer and put her hand on Ellie's head.

"Ow! Hey! No touching!"

"I just want to see how things are this morning, or should I say this afternoon? Now hold still."

This afternoon? Ellie's gaze shot to the clock on her nightstand. No, that couldn't be right. "It says one thirty."

"Good for you. You can tell time. At least your brain is still functioning."

Wrinkling her nose, she glanced up. "Very funny. What the heck's wrong with me?"

"You mean you don't remember? Well, that's a bummer."

"Tell me, please. For some reason I'm a little mixed up."

"If that's all, you're lucky," said Viv, sitting on her bed. "You crossed swords with a burglar here in the house last night." She recounted the incident. "Your new best friend, Jim Bond, called Detective Wheeling and took care of you until we got home."

"Are you telling the truth?" asked Ellie. "Or are you just trying to confuse me?"

Viv used a finger to cross her heart. "Truth, honest. And if you want a real treat, go look in the mirror."

Remembering she had to use the toilet anyway, Ellie stood and swayed on shaky legs.

"If you need help, just say the word." Viv stood and took a step toward her. "I'm here for you."

"No, no. I'll be fine." She shuffled forward, fighting to keep her legs in working order. Then she raised a hand to brush the hair out of her eyes and flinched. Touching her left temple, she cursed. It felt as if someone had glued half a lemon to her head. A very painful lemon.

Hobbling into the bathroom, she aimed for the commode and plopped down, grateful that her plumbing was working full tilt. Right now she'd bet money that every part of her body had been run over by a semi going seventy on FDR Drive.

Finished with business, she stood and used the bathroom counter to help keep her steady while she walked to the sink. She needed to brush her teeth, rinse her mouth, take a couple of aspirins, maybe douse her head under cold running water.

Raising her gaze, she came face-to-face with the woman in the mirror. Her fingers moved of their own accord, gently probing the huge bump on her purple forehead, the dark circle under her left eye, the flush of color on her cheek.

She closed her eyes and counted to ten, positive her swollen face was a trick of the mind. Viv had said she was in for a treat, and her brain had played along.

When she took another look, she groaned.

"What! What's wrong?" asked Viv, running to the

bathroom door. Watching Ellie inspect her face, she grinned. "I told you you were in for a treat."

"This isn't a treat, it's a disaster." She braced her hands on the sink and hung her head. Bit by bit, the events of the night before washed over her. She remembered everything, including getting whacked by a human speeding semi.

"Oh, God," she said, moaning. "It's all coming back to me."

She looked in the mirror and saw Viv standing by her side. "You sound like Myron imitating Celine Dion. But it's good that you remember." Viv stuck a hand in the pocket of her shorts and pulled out two tablets. "You want the quicker fixer-upper again?"

"What? No!" Ellie shook her head and the cast of *Riverdance* started up again. "Give me a couple of ibuprofen and I'll be fine."

"Okay," said Viv, opening a drawer. She smacked a bottle on the counter. "Here you go. I'd take three, just in case."

Ellie did as she suggested, brushed her teeth, and hobbled into the bedroom. "I'm going to take a shower. Come in and get me if I'm not out in ten minutes." She dug underwear from a drawer. Rudy jumped off the bed and followed her into the bathroom. Setting the bra and panties down, she turned on the shower and waited for the jets to steam the stall.

"You gonna be okay in there?"

"I think so. But if I'm not, go get Vivie, would you?"

He dropped onto his favorite rug and stood guard. *"Sure thing. But take it easy. You got all day to line up what happened last night to the murder."*

She stepped into the shower and let the warm water

wash over her, melting her misery under the stinging spray. Scrubbing with a loofa, she rubbed away all the aches and pains and pretended they'd never been there. Then she carefully washed her hair, keeping her hands off the lump.

Outside the stall, she dried off and slipped on her panties and bra. Then she used a blow dryer and finger-combed her curls until they were springy. Heaving a huge sigh, she stood tall and went into the bedroom.

Chapter 12

Stretching out on the chaise, Ellie reached for her drink, a glass of plain iced tea with a sprig of mint and a slice of lemon. After taking a sip, she basked in the salty breeze and scanned the shaded terrace. Rosa had gently attached another butterfly splint to the small gash on her forehead, and given her a second dose of ibuprofen. She was comfortable and pain free.

She'd tried to get Rosa to talk further about *el doctor* and the night of the murder, but the housekeeper had pleaded busy the first several times Ellie had broached the subject, which made her realize there was no use making Rosa, who was stressed, discuss something so painful. Maria, Teresa, and Julio became her next targets, though she hadn't seen any one of them since she'd settled on the deck.

At the sound of footsteps, she focused on the stairs. Viv's head appeared, then the rest of her, dressed in a tiny yellow bikini. When she hit the terrace floor, she dropped her tote bag on the table and pulled on her cover-up, a one-piece long-sleeved T-shirt that fell to midthigh.

"You're awake," said Viv. "That's a good sign."

Ellie envied her best friend's golden bronze skin. She'd acquired a bit of color after the tanning debacle, too. The pale brown of her skin was better than traffic cone orange, but the iris purple of her face sort of put a damper on the tan. "I see you got a little more sun," she said to Viv, trying to keep the envy from her voice. "You look great. Just like you're supposed to after a summer vacation in the Hamptons . . . unlike me."

Viv eyed her and shrugged. "Don't be so down on yourself. The purple will fade in a couple of weeks, and the lump's already smaller. We'll sit on the beach again tomorrow, and you'll get a bit more of a 'back from vacation' glow, too."

"I'm not worried about the lack of a tan, but Sam's going to go bananas when he sees my face. I've been trying to come up with a story, but I'm a terrible liar. So far I haven't thought of anything I can say that he'll believe." She sat up and swung her legs over the side of the lounge chair. "What time is it?"

"Hang on a second. I'll check." Viv went through the kitchen door and returned a few minutes later with her own glass of iced tea. "It's five thirty, and Rosa's cooking. She said it's something soothing to help energize your system—Arlene's, too."

Rosa had clucked over her from the moment Ellie had taken position on the lounger. Like a perfect mother hen, the housekeeper had delivered iced tea, a midafternoon snack, and a pillow for her head. She'd even brought Myron inside so his squawking wouldn't disturb Ellie while she slept.

"Rosa's been a doll through all of this. What's up with Tomas? I tried to ask her about the bail hearing, but she clammed up whenever I opened the topic today."

"Terry and Maria took over her chores while you were asleep this morning so Rosa, Julio, and Arlene's attorney could meet at the courthouse. The boy is home, thanks to Arlene, who put up a bond. It was half a million. Can you believe that?"

"Wow. Did they give a reason for the huge amount?"

Viv carried a chair to the chaise and took a seat. "Rosa finally told Arlene that her son had a record, which is why they got his prints off the knife so fast. It was penny-ante stuff, but he's been hanging with a gang. The DA argued that he was a flight risk, thus the outrageous amount."

"And Arlene didn't care?"

"Far as I know, she told the attorney to do whatever was necessary to free the kid. He's home right now, helping his father with the landscaping work around the guest cottage."

"Then Julio's back. You've seen him?"

"Yep. I guess he's the next person you want to talk to about the night of the murder, huh?"

Ellie reached into her tote, pulled out her spiral notepad, and flipped the pages until she arrived at the blank sheet with Julio's name at the top. "I know it's not going to be easy, but I have to question him. Did he mention where he's been for the past twenty-four hours?"

"Sort of." Viv took a long swallow of tea. "Arlene said Rosa told her he'd been in church, praying for his son, but that really wouldn't account for the entire time."

"I doubt it. Has Wheeling been around?"

"He was over this morning. Told Arlene they were

releasing the doc's body to her because Kent's brother called and told them he was in the process of sending a letter of release giving Arlene full control. Needless to say, she's in a tizzy. Says she and Martin discussed a will, but never got one on paper. It's not only his body. He owns two cars, a huge boat, and office furniture and equipment. She tried the brother herself, with no luck, so she's having the doc cremated as soon as the letter arrives."

Fingers crossed, Ellie asked, "Is she planning a memorial?"

"I guess so. Why?"

"Because—well—I think his killer was someone here at the party that night. And everybody who was here said they'd come to a memorial, if one was held."

"It's possible. Wheeling says they've done a thorough check of the patients listed in the doc's appointment book, and they all had a decent alibi for the night of the party. And here's a bit of news." Viv lowered her voice. "Mr. Bond finally told the detective that he'd broken into the crime scene the night of the murder and heard Kent arguing with someone."

"Really?" Ellie bit her lower lip. "Did he say anything about you and me doing the same thing while the crime scene tape was up? And when did he say it?"

"After the burglary, when they went over who might have sneaked inside and why."

Ellie cocked her head. "You still haven't said. Did Jim cover for us, or did he squeal?"

Viv *tsk*ed. "You're starting to sound like a character in one of those ancient Humphrey Bogart movies. No, he didn't 'squeal.' He kept us out of it." She smirked. "He likes you."

"Now you're starting to sound like a fifth grader." She sighed. "I only hope Wheeling never hears that we broke into the doc's office the same night Jim did."

"As long as Agent Bond keeps quiet, I don't see how he'll find out."

"Too bad we ran into him there. I really would have liked to check out Kent's office early on after the murder, instead of two days later. And I still wish Rosa would give me a better explanation of where Julio's been and what he's been doing. Maybe she doesn't know her son or her husband as well as she thinks she does."

"I still buy your explanation. Tomas was the first person to argue with the doc, but he ran, and the real killer was lying in wait. And don't worry. I didn't say anything to Arlene about us crossing the tape, either. I figured it would just open up a whole new can of worms." She straightened in her chair. "See, I'm getting the hang of things. Following in your footsteps as a private investigator."

Ellie's shoulders slumped. "Maybe we should both go back to being ordinary citizens. I'm worried that things could get more violent than they did last night."

"I don't give a fig about the violence. Rosa is distraught over her son's arrest, and Arlene is still coming to grips with Dr. Kent's illegal practices. Which means they need our help."

"When do you think we should clue her in about the painting?"

Viv ran a hand through her long dark hair, then pushed her pair of twenty-dollar sunglasses to the top of her head. "I've run it through my brain, and I don't know what to do. If Arlene blows her cork and confronts Adrianne, it might start 'the great catfight of 2012.' And Mother is going to flip, too."

"I asked Adrianne about it last night when I had her in my clutches," Ellie confessed. "It didn't seem to bother her a bit that we knew about the portrait."

"Sounds like Adrianne. Did you press her about seeing or hearing anything while she was resting during the party?"

"Sure did. She claims she didn't hear a thing."

"Do you believe her?"

"Now that I've gotten a better read on her? No."

Viv's green eyes grew wide. "Oh, my God. Do you think she killed Dr. Kent?"

Ellie blew out a breath. "I don't want to think it." Viv and her family would be gossip fodder for the scandal sheets for sure if word got out that the middle sister of a local resident killed her older sister's fiancé. It was bad enough drugs were involved. With the sleaze element, every newspaper in town and every TV tell-all program would jump on the story, and the entire McCready family would be dragged into the middle of the mess. "I just can't imagine her being strong enough to knock a well-built, six-foot-tall man backward like the killer did."

"I agree. Adrianne is a brat, but she doesn't have the strength to push that hard. But she did take a martial arts course to 'strengthen her inner core,' as she puts it." Viv shook her head. "And what about a motive?"

"They could always say that when the doc told her their affair was over, she wanted to get back at him."

"It's possible, but that's not Adrianne's MO. She would have slashed Kent's tires or keyed his Mercedes, maybe even trashed his office before she'd get that physical."

Ellie set her iced tea on the side table. "I don't think we need to spell anything out to Arlene. Once she sees the painting, she'll figure out the affair for herself."

"You're probably right. She needs to know everything."

"Then we'll tell her tonight?"

"Uh, okay."

"Without your mother, father, or Adrianne present."

"That might be difficult."

"We can wait until they go to the cottage."

Viv leaned forward in the chair. "But you'll be with me when I do it, right?"

Ellie put herself in Viv's shoes before she answered. If she was attempting to rebond with her big sister, this could be an important step. "Not a problem. I'll give moral support and sensible reasoning if you need it."

Dinner that night was a choice of warm crab chowder or chilled gazpacho, a wonderful tossed salad, and crusty, fresh-from-the-oven bread. Ellie ate her fill, then sat back and watched the McCready family dynamics at work. To her mind, except for Adrianne, they were getting along more like a caring unit than an angry group of folks who just happened to be related.

"How are you feeling, Ellie?" Viv's mother asked for the fifth time that night.

"Awwwk! Feelings. Oh-oh-oh, feelings!" squawked Myron. *"I feel a headache coming on. Awwwk!"*

"I'm fine," said Ellie, ignoring the idiotic bird Arlene had returned to the terrace. "I just have to be careful about touching my temple. It's no big deal."

"Awwwk! Deal me in, baby. I'm game for anything. Awwwk!"

Arlene stood and pulled an M&M from her pocket. "Give me a minute. This should calm him down."

Myron grabbed the candy in his claw, brought it to his beak, and began to eat.

"He's so much more agreeable once he has his favorite snack." Arlene returned to the table. "Now, where were we?"

Evan McCready had kept his gaze trained on Ellie almost the entire evening, and she imagined it was because of her charming purple face. Now he said, "I may have been a bit gruff with you when this whole mess started, my girl, but you've won me over. I should have said this earlier. You were very brave last night, confronting that burglar."

Wow, thought Ellie. High praise coming from a man who had sneered and growled at everything and everyone just a few days ago. "Thanks for saying so, Mr. McCready, but I really haven't done much yet."

"Nonsense," said Vanessa. "You stopped that man in the midst of a robbery. If you'd hit that table any harder, you might have more to worry about than a cut and a bruise. You could have been killed."

"Killed! Awwwk! I'm gonna kill you, Marty! Awwwk!"

"Oh, dear." Arlene stood and delivered the African gray another M&M while Ellie thought. She needed time to figure out whom that voice belonged to. "Mr. Bond was there to take care of things, and the dogs helped, too. They're the real heroes of the incident."

Mr. T hopped onto Viv's lap and she cuddled him close. "Dad knows what the boys did. He might even be coming around to making friends with Twink." She kissed his pointy muzzle and he licked her lips. "Isn't that right, sweetie?"

T pulled back a bit. *"It's Mr. T to your old man, Vivie, and don't you forget it."*

"Awwwk! Woof! Woof! Woof!" Myron barked, sounding exactly like a Boston Terrier. *"Awwwk! Awwwk!"*

Evan McCready stood, grabbed the African gray's perch, and marched into the kitchen while the women laughed. He returned a minute later and took his seat. "I wouldn't go that far, Vivian, but I do see the advantage in having a dog for protection," he continued as if he hadn't left the terrace. "Even a small one."

"And Twink is the best." Viv scratched his ears. "Aren't you, baby doll?"

Mr. T wriggled from her arms and jumped to the deck. *"Hey. No more with the mushy stuff in front of the family."*

"And what about me?" grumped Rudy from below the table. *"I deserve a pat on the head, too."*

Ellie tamed her smile into a modest grin. "Both the dogs were brave. Has Vivian told you about the time Rudy dived onto a woman while she held a gun on me?"

Evan nodded. "She mentioned it, but at the time I thought she was just selling me a tall tale. I can see now that your dog would be game enough to protect you from any bad situation."

"Ahh, that's more like it."

"And on that happy note, I think it's time we retired, don't you, dear?" Vanessa asked her husband. "Ellie needs her rest, and so does Arlene."

Adrianne tossed her napkin onto the table, stuck out her lower lip, and stood. Walking to the stairs, she stomped down the steps without saying good-bye.

Vanessa heaved a sigh. "I'm afraid this has hit Adrianne hard, though I'm not sure why. She's been acting unusually quiet since Dr. Kent's death."

"If you ask me, she's been sulking like a twelve-year-old," said Viv. "I bet she wants to party at one of the clubs in Bridgehampton, but she doesn't want to go alone, and she knows none of us will go with her. It's typical Adrianne bullshit."

"Now, Viv, leave your sister alone. She's trying."

"She's *trying*, all right," Viv muttered. Then she smiled at her parents. "I have an idea. How about if we all go into town and have lunch at the American Hotel one day this week? I hear it's a Billy Joel hangout. Maybe we'll see him there."

"That's an excellent idea, dear. Evan, what do you think?"

The senior McCready swallowed what Ellie thought was a laugh. "Fine, if that's what you ladies want." He gazed at his oldest daughter, who had been quiet through the past exchange. "Think you can handle a public outing, Arlene?"

"If I'm with you all, then yes, but I need to ask a question and I'd appreciate your honesty."

Viv locked gazes with Ellie, then said, "Shoot, sis, and we'll do our best to help."

Arlene took a deep breath. "It's about a memorial for Martin. I've been told word has already gotten out that he's under investigation by the DEA, and the whole of the Hamptons knows he was murdered because of it." She sniffed back a tear. "I hate the thought that I came this close"—she held two fingers an inch apart—"to marrying a drug dealer, but I feel I have to show some kind of farewell to my fiancé. Now that his body's been released, do you think I should actually offer a memorial service?"

Good question, thought Ellie, and one she and Viv had discussed at length. No one spoke, so she took control. "I know I'm not family—"

"Oh, but you are," said Vanessa.

Arlene dabbed at her eyes. "Mother's right, Ellie. You've been a trouper through this entire episode, especially in agreeing to help free Tomas. Please, speak your mind."

"Okay, but listen to everything before you comment." She steeled herself for their opinion. "I promised to assist in finding the real killer, and I've come up with a theory. I think there's a good chance the killer will be here if there's a memorial."

"What are you saying?" asked Vanessa.

Evan laid a hand on his wife's shoulder. "The girl's right. Haven't you ever heard the old saw—'the killer always returns to the scene of the crime'?"

"That's what I'm hoping for," Ellie answered, relieved that she had someone in her corner besides Vivian. "I've done a bit of investigating and tried to put the pieces together. I think Arlene needs to call everyone who was at the dinner that night and ask them to attend as a personal favor. I'm hoping that might stir the pot a little, and the killer will show. If we ask the right questions, he may incriminate himself."

"I've been in on everything Ellie's done, and I agree," added Viv. "She knows what she's talking about."

"So you'd be willing to help, Mr. McCready?"

The man gave his first full-blown smile of the weekend. "What I think is it's about time you called me Evan, young lady. And I do agree. With Agent Bond and

Detective Wheeling here, plus me, of course, I'm sure we'll be able to handle anything that comes up, including a visit from the killer."

"I'm not sure Mr. Bond or the good detective will want our interference," said Ellie. "My guess is whatever we decide to do will have to be done on the QT."

Vanessa's smile told Ellie exactly what she was thinking. "Then we'll all be undercover?" She clapped her hands. "Oh, I can't wait. It sounds like fun."

Vivian, Arlene, and Ellie sat around the terrace table, each woman digging into her own personal-sized container of Caramel Cone. Viv had made a run to the local grocery store when Ellie said she needed something cold for her head, which wasn't exactly what she meant, but the frigid ice cream was working like a charm at the moment.

"This is fabulous," said Arlene, licking her spoon with gusto. "I had no idea anyone made ice cream that tasted this good." She dived in for another helping and swallowed it down. "And my babies think so, too."

She dug into the container, careful to avoid the bits of chocolate, and passed a waiting Boston Terrier a spoonful. Then she giggled. "Thank God Father's not here. He'd have a cow if he saw me feeding the gang from my own spoon."

"Oh, pooh," Viv said. "Daddy would have a cow over anything you did with your dogs. I think tonight's the first time I've ever heard him say a kind word about any canine." She raised her carton in Ellie's direction, giving her a toast. "And we owe his change of heart to you, my friend. And Twink and Rudy, of course."

"Why, thank you," said Ellie. "It was great to see him

act like a real dad tonight. Not to be insulting, but has he always been cranky?"

"I think he's felt sort of useless since he retired. Playing golf can get boring after a while, and the projects Mother comes up with? Well, they're not exactly the type to keep an ex-spy busy."

"I bet he'd even adopt you as a fourth daughter, if we asked him," said Arlene. "Because I've never heard him sing anyone's praises until he warbled yours. That is, if you wanted him to."

"Ah, no, thanks," said Ellie. She had Randall and Judge Frye, who treated her like their own daughter, and that was all the fathering she could manage in her life at the moment. "But I am happy your dad's taken a liking to me. More important, he thinks I'm doing a good job with this case. Too bad I have yet to find anything useful."

"Knowing Dad, he wouldn't say so unless he meant it." Arlene downed another scoop of Caramel Cone. Then she carefully picked around the chocolate bits and fed a scoop of ice cream to Isabella and one to Darby-Doll, her female Boston Terriers. "I'm going to have to buy this stuff by the case. Right, Corey?" she asked her male dog. After giving him a final spoonful, she capped her tub and stood. "It's getting late. I should probably get to bed. I have to plan a memorial service for a criminal tomorrow."

Viv glanced at Ellie, as if to say "now's the time," and walked to stand at her sister's side. "Arlene, Ellie and I have something personal we need to discuss."

Arlene shrugged. "Sure, why not? Especially since it seems like I no longer have a personal life. Do you know that I haven't received a single phone call or card from the women I thought were my friends?"

"But I'm sure you will—"

Raising a hand, Arlene said, "No, I won't, and I've already figured out why. Those women were only pretending to like me because of Martin. They got their drugs from him, and they used me to stay in touch."

"I don't mean to pry, but what about the drugs? I know you used them to get you through the last few weeks, and that's your business, but—are you still taking them?" asked Ellie.

"You're not prying. You're asking because you care, and I appreciate that." She heaved a sigh. "I've been trying to slowly wean myself off. I plan to take half of my usual dose to get to sleep tonight, and that might go on for a while, but I'm determined to get through the day without any of the 'happy pills' "—she used air quotes around the last words—"if it's the last thing I do. I want my life back."

Viv squeezed her sister's shoulder. "I'm so proud of you."

Arlene's cheeks colored. "Thanks. I'm proud of me, too. And guess what I've decided to do."

When Ellie and Viv didn't answer, she smiled. "I'm going back to my first love . . . astrology. I'm set financially, and I've decided I don't need another man in my world, at least for a while. I'm going to advertise in *Dan's Papers* that I'm available for charting horoscopes and let the ad run year-round. I'll meet new people—people who are interested in the things I'm into, not people who want me because my lover is a pill pusher."

"Wow," said Ellie. "That's a real life-changing decision."

"And it sounds wonderful," added Viv. "You haven't read my chart since I was in high school. I want to be your first client."

"Nope. I already have a first client . . . if she wants to be." She focused on Ellie. "What do you say? Want to be my first new customer—for free?"

Ellie blinked in surprise. "Sure. I guess so." She'd never had her horoscope read, but it sounded like fun. "Uh, when this is over?"

"Great. I just need your date, time, and place of birth. I'll do the rest."

Viv raised her chin, and Ellie nodded. "Ah, sis, we're not exactly finished with the personal stuff. There's something else you need to know."

Arlene cocked her head. "Oh, Lord, now what? Please don't give me any more bad news. I don't think I could take it."

"We're not sure it belongs in the 'bad' category, but Ellie and I think it's important. And you shouldn't see it alone."

"You can't just tell me? I have to go somewhere to see it?"

Ellie capped her Caramel Cone, gathered the other two cartons, and headed for the kitchen. "Don't worry. We're only going to the guest cottage. I'll just put these in the freezer and walk down with you and Viv."

"Then it does have to do with Martin." Arlene frowned. "What the hell else did the bum do?"

Ellie left Viv with the task of preparing her sister for a sight she had to see. Standing in front of the freezer, she stored the Caramel Cone and shut the door.

"You think she's ready for this?" asked Rudy, who had followed her inside.

Ellie scratched her boy's ears. "One can only hope. She sounds fairly pulled together. If she falls apart, Viv will be there for her."

"Poor Vivie. She's takin' a big chance, showing her sis something so freakin' rude."

"I agree, but it serves Adrianne right. How dare she pretend to care for her sister, then deceive her in such a rotten way? Imagine, sleeping with your sister's fiancé and acting like it's perfectly okay."

"I hear you."

They arrived at the kitchen door and Ellie saw Viv and Arlene standing close and talking quietly. "Are you sure you want to come with? You could go up to bed and I'll let you know what happened tomorrow."

Rudy snorted. *"Are you kidding? I wouldn't miss this for all the Milk-Bones in the world."*

Chapter 13

The outdoor lights marking the brick walkway glowed steadily, guiding the girls and the five dogs to the guest cottage. Arlene had taken the keys off the board at the terrace door because the bag holding her regular key ring was in her bedroom. Viv told her they'd already used these same keys twice. Once when they crossed the crime scene tape, and again when they found what they thought she should see.

As they walked, the dogs bounded off the path, sniffing tufts of sea grass, lifting their leg or squatting, then racing in whatever direction their senses took them. Even Rudy, who rarely participated in canine antics, wandered with abandon. It appeared they were all happily up for following their mistress to wherever she was going.

Now at the cottage's rear entrance, Arlene stopped and gazed at the path that circled the back of the building. "Is this where they found Martin's body?" she asked, gazing at the broader area of bricks holding a dark-colored stain just outside the door.

"That's where Dr. Kent was when Viv and I got here, yes."

Arlene nodded toward the hidden corner. "And Agent Bond was there, behind those pine trees?" She bit her lower lip. "Lying in wait."

"It did seem that way," said Ellie, "though he explains it differently. He says he was preparing to come in through the front door when he heard the argument, so he waited until a door slammed. He entered the building, but before he could search, the doc started arguing with a second person outside. Next thing he knew, the caterer was crying for help. By the time he got back here, Dr. Kent was dead. There was nothing he could do, so he ducked behind the pines until we arrived."

"Or so he said," Viv added.

"Do you believe him?" Arlene asked, her voice trembling.

"We don't have any reason not to," said Ellie. "He's a law enforcement officer. Why would he kill Dr. Kent, when he needed the doc to get the details of his drug ring?"

Wrapping her arms around her shoulders, Arlene shuddered. "And to think, I almost married that monster."

Viv hugged her close. "But you didn't. In a way, the murderer saved you."

"Now, there's a gruesome thought," said Ellie. She gazed at the darkening sky. "It's getting late. We should go in."

When Arlene raised the keys, her hand shook. "Can you do it, Vivie? I'm too nervous."

"I can't believe you've never been in here," said Viv, accepting the keys.

Arlene blew out a breath. "After the remodeling, I dropped by to make sure the guest suite upstairs was in order, and Martin gave me a quick tour of the downstairs, but that was it. He never invited me back, and once Maria and Terry took over the cleaning responsibilities I didn't have a reason to return."

Ellie gazed at Viv, who nodded. "I know you don't want to be here, but you really should see what's inside."

"I just want you to think before you react," said Viv. "Because it'll probably impact you in a negative way." She gave Arlene another hug. "But don't worry. Ellie and I are confident you'll handle it."

After opening the door, Viv stood aside to let the entire group enter the foyer. They headed straight for the office and unlocked that door. Then Viv took her sister's hand and led her into the waiting area while the dogs scampered beside them.

Ellie turned on the light. "How are you doing, Arlene?"

"So far, so good. It's just that . . ."

"Hang in there, big sister. Ellie and I discussed it and we think it's best you do this now when you have company, instead of later when you'll be alone."

After scanning the room, Arlene sighed. "So, this is where he did his dirty business." She sat on the couch and riffled through the magazines centered on the coffee table, picking up a copy of last week's *Dan's Papers*, then a *Town and Country*, then a *Vanity Fair.* "He certainly gave his patients the newest and best reading material, didn't he?" she asked of no one in particular.

She eyed a large empty jug sitting on a credenza.

"Rosa told me he insisted the girls kept that filled with iced lemon water. What an idiot, giving his customers amenities while he fed them poison."

Viv sat next to her on the sofa. "This isn't all. You need to see his office."

Arlene gazed at the open door across the room. "You expect me to go inside?"

"You should be aware of everything he was into," said Viv. Standing, the sisters held hands and went into the doc's private office with Ellie and the dogs following. Once inside, she again took care of the lights while Arlene scanned the room.

A moment later, Arlene stiffened and headed toward the far wall. Ellie held her breath. Viv turned and gave her an eye roll, then walked next to her sister.

"I don't—I can't—" Arlene whispered, staring at Adrianne's self-portrait. Then she straightened her spine like a general preparing to declare war. "I'm going to beat her to a bloody pulp."

Viv placed her hand on Arlene's shoulder. "No, you're not."

As if deflating, Arlene slumped against her, and Viv led her to the oversized leather sofa, where she stopped and stared.

"Put the pieces together, sis. Don't make us tell you what we believe happened here," Viv said in a quiet tone.

Arlene sneered at the sofa as if it were riddled with vermin, then sidled to one of the two chairs in front of Dr. Kent's desk and turned it to face the portrait, much as Viv and Ellie had done the evening before. Solemn-eyed, Viv followed suit while Ellie shuffled around the desk and dropped into Dr. Kent's plush leather chair.

When Arlene propped her head in her hands and

began to cry, Ellie opened a drawer, found a box of tissues, and passed the box across the desktop to Vivian.

"I'm so sorry, Arlene." Viv handed her a tissue.

Time passed while Arlene cried and Viv offered comfort, holding her close while the tears flowed. Even the dogs acted as if they knew this moment was important. Toning down their antics, they padded near their owners and sat at their feet.

Rudy found his way around the desk and rose on his hind legs, resting his paws on Ellie's thigh. She smiled at him and he jumped into her lap.

"This is serious stuff, huh?"

She caressed his head. "Very," she said in a hush. "So no talking."

Minutes passed, while Viv and her sister spoke in whispers. Then they turned their chairs around and faced Ellie. She put Rudy on the floor and gave a half-hearted grin. "Are you okay?"

"I'm getting there," said Arlene. She rubbed her red nose. "Who else do you think saw the painting?" Her voice sounded strong but soft.

"Detective Wheeling, the EMTs, and the forensics crew. Agent Bond, Maria, Teresa, Rosa, and Viv and I, for certain," offered Ellie. "We have no idea if your mother and father dropped in after the crime scene tape was removed."

Arlene raised her gaze to the ceiling. Then she grabbed another tissue and blew her nose. "Well, now, that's abso-fucking-lutely great, isn't it? Though I can't believe Mother would have seen this and not commented." She heaved another sigh. "There's no way I can shut them all up, especially the police team. What will I do if word gets out?"

"I don't think you need to worry about that," said Ellie. "The investigative crew is ordered to secrecy when they work a crime scene. They're not supposed to give details to reporters or gab about what they found to friends or family. Every once in a while someone slips up, and you can't control that, but—"

"A story or photo might still leak out." Arlene dabbed at a tear that escaped her tissue. "Great."

"If you ask me, that thoughtless painting is nothing when compared to what Dr. Sleazeball did to Maria and some of the women who wanted what he had to offer. And I'm betting gossip about those exploits will get out before anyone mentions Adrianne's tacky self-portrait. Let's see if anything's written in the next issue of *Dan's Papers* and worry about it then," said Viv. She gazed at Ellie. "I think we ought to leave before someone from upstairs hears us and decides to come down."

Ellie agreed and stood. Arlene grabbed another fistful of tissues and did the same. "With so much to think about, I'll never get to sleep tonight. Which means I'll be back to taking more drugs." She inhaled and her entire body shuddered. "I hate the thought that even after his death, Martin is able to manipulate me. I'm afraid—"

"There's nothing to be afraid of. We're here and we'll take care of things," said Viv as they closed the rear door.

"I'm not afraid of the killer. I'm afraid of this damned addiction. I have to find a way to toss those pills in the trash and still hang on to my sanity."

"There are places you can go to for help," said Viv, locking the outer door. "We'll find a good doctor and get you a professional recommendation."

Arlene walked between Ellie and Viv as they followed the brick path home. "I don't know why I'm asking this, but what about Adrianne?"

"You don't have to go to the same center. There are plenty of places that give exceptional care," said Ellie.

"I don't know how I'm going to face her in the morning."

"Just try to get a good night's rest. Adrianne might not even show until dinner. We'll tackle it then." The dogs raced up the stairs to the deck with the three women at their heels. "Think about it carefully and do what you feel is right."

The next morning, Ellie and Viv awakened with a new idea in mind. They'd talked for an hour before drifting to sleep last night and come up with a plan. Because of the activity surrounding Dr. Kent's death, they hadn't been able to visit any part of the Hamptons except the Montauk drugstore. It was time they canvassed a few of the area's hot spots, found a way to catch a bit of gossip, maybe stop in some local stores and hear what was being said on the streets.

"How do I look?" asked Viv, pirouetting on her bronze-colored Mephisto sandals. She wore a pair of tan, ankle-length linen slacks, a silk, off-the-shoulder white T, and a bronzed leather belt to pull her outfit together.

"Very in-style," said Ellie, though she hadn't a clue if Viv's clothes were "in" or "out." All she knew was they were mostly Ralph Lauren, they were expensive, and Viv looked great in them.

"I'm wearing the opposite. White cigarette pants with a brown, long-sleeved, scoop-necked T. But my sandals are Dansko Sigrid ankle straps. Think anyone will care?"

"The only thing they'll notice about you is that purple face and swollen eye." Viv checked her out. "Wow, it's gotten worse, not better."

Ellie's shoulders slumped and she dropped to her bottom on the bed. "You really know how to make me feel special."

"Oh, stop." Viv whipped the twenty-dollar sunglasses from her bag and passed them over. "Here. Fix those curly locks to cover your forehead and wear these. And don't take them off, even if we're inside. If we're lucky, you'll look more like a girl with a hangover than a battered woman."

Ellie stepped into the bathroom and stared in the mirror. She'd tried not to look at her face this morning because it was so ghastly. She never gave a thought to what any strangers would see if they gazed at her straight on. Frowning, she added tinted sunscreen to her face, careful not to press on her bruises, then added mascara and gloss.

After dabbing a bit of gel on her fingers, she pulled a couple of curls down to cover her left eyebrow. Then she fluffed her hair, slipped on the sunglasses, and took another look. *Oh, Lord, nothing is going to make it better.*

Standing tall, she returned to the bedroom. "I'm afraid this is the best I can do."

Viv covered her lips with a hand, but her grin sneaked out from behind her fingers. "Sorry. I guess we'll just have to live with it. But remember—keep those sunglasses on and try not to make a spectacle of yourself. We're not clubbing. What can people expect for a simple breakfast and a day of shopping?

"I just need to make a potty stop. Think you can bring the dogs down to the pen? I'll meet you there in a couple of minute, and we can get going," said Viv, stepping into the bathroom.

"I don't suppose we can come," said Rudy as he and Mr. T followed Ellie down the rear stairs.

"Sorry, but no. It's going to get too warm to leave you in the car."

"We're tough. We can take a little heat," said T, his tone full of bravado.

"You two are about as tough as day-old marshmallows where the weather is concerned. I'll fix you both a morning nibble while I wait for Viv."

When they entered the kitchen, Terry and Maria were setting up the buffet and Rosa was at the stove. "Good morning," she said to the trio. This might be a good chance to begin her questioning of the Suarez family. "I'm glad you're all here. Can you spare a few minutes?"

Rosa made eye contact with her daughters, and they sat at one end of the large breakfast table. "Give me a second," said Ellie. She took the boys' food and bowls from the pantry and poured them each a bit of kibble, then carried it to a floor place mat. Joining the Suarez women, she asked, "How are you all doing?"

"A lot better than you, is my guess. Do you still hurt?" asked Terry, the older sister, scanning Ellie's bruises.

"Ibuprofen does wonders," she answered. "And it helps if I keep my hands off, but that's hard to do because it's starting to itch. Now, what's up with you three?"

Terry stiffened her shoulders. "I'm fine, but Maria's a mess. And Mama and Papa aren't so great, either."

Maria sniffed away a tear. "Sorry, but I still feel responsible for this whole mess. If it weren't for me—"

Terry grabbed her hand. "Stop talking like that. Ellie is going to make sure Tomas goes free. Dr. Kent was a monster. Whoever killed him did the world good."

"Viv and I will do our best to figure it out. Now, what about Tomas?"

"He is *mucho* upset," said Rosa, pulling the ever-present tissue from her apron. "He doesn't understand why that detective isn't listening to his story." She blew her nose. "Miss Vivian, she says you are an expert with things like this. Why won't the *policía* listen?"

"Over the past year, I've learned that's the way they do things," Ellie answered, sorry she had to give them this bit of news. "The police look for the obvious answer, and when they find it they're finished. Unless the lead detective has a reason to be suspicious, they usually let the arrest and the evidence stand and go to trial."

Rosa gave a halfhearted smile. "And that is the reason you are trying to help my son? Because you are suspicious?"

"More than not trusting Detective Wheeling's decision, I believe in you, and Julio and the girls." She made eye contact with Maria and Terry. "You're decent people and you believe Tomas is innocent, which means I do, too. That's why Viv and I won't be eating breakfast here, maybe not even lunch. We're going to look for clues."

"Clues, but not here?" asked Maria.

"Yep, so I need to talk to you both, all right?"

When the girls nodded, Rosa said, "I must still prepare food for *la familia*. I will only be a short distance away."

Ellie pulled a pen and the black spiral notepad from

her tote. "The way I understand it, the two of you were the main caretakers of Dr. Kent's office. That means you saw who came and went to him on a regular basis, correct?"

"Maria and I split the duties," Terry told her. "I'd take the afternoon shift, which was mostly cleanup. Maria did the morning, made sure the waiting room and public offices were presentable, refilled the lemon water, that kind of thing."

"I'd like you both to think hard. Best guess: Which of the doc's clients did you see in his office the most? Better still, did you ever hear him arguing with anyone? Or maybe complaining to himself after a patient left?"

"He always treated his patients, who were mostly women, I might add, with charm. You know, holding the door open when they left his office, complimenting them on their hair or clothes, that sort of thing," said Terry, a smile lurking on her lips. "They all seemed to love him, but I'm pretty sure I know which ones he screwed."

Rosa *tsk*ed from across the room. "Teresa, be careful what you say!"

"Really?" Ellie said at the same time.

"It's true, Mama. Many of those wealthy women used sex as a way to secure their pills. And their names could help our brother." Terry gave a full-blown grin. "Right, Ellie?"

"Uh, possibly." And maybe, if she got the sisters talking, something inconsequential might slip that would lead her to the killer. "I'm ready for the names when you want to give them."

Terry rested her chin in her palm, thinking. Then she began a slow recitation. Several of the names were vaguely familiar, but she'd have to ask Arlene who the women were. In all, she was given eight names. "And you're sure he was sleeping with them?"

"Almost positive. They were always the last patients of the afternoon, and most of the time I'd be here when they left. The doc would walk them out of the office while they straightened their clothes and giggled. Sometimes, they even shared a kiss before he opened the front door."

"And you're certain this is all of them?"

Terry swallowed. "Yes, except for—"

"Enough!" called Rosa, staring daggers at her eldest daughter from over the island sink.

"It's all right, Rosa," Ellie offered. "We know about Adrianne. We saw the painting on the office wall."

Terry and her sister heaved a breath. "I'm glad that's out. I hated keeping the information from Arlene, but I thought it would hurt her more to know—"

"That her sister was sleeping with her fiancé. You bet it would," added Maria.

"Okay," said Ellie. "Anyone else?"

Maria crossed her arms. "Uncle Mickey usually stopped in first thing most mornings. He and Dr. Kent talked loud enough for me to hear, but I never really paid much attention, so I don't know what they said. Uncle Mickey always seemed jolly when he left, so I'm not sure they were arguing. And Dr. B came with him once in a while," she said. "Did you talk to her?"

"Uncle Mickey and Dr. B are already on the list." Footsteps and voices rattled on the terrace. "It sounds as if the family has arrived for breakfast, so I have to run." She gazed at both girls. "If you think of anyone else, let me know."

Viv walked into the kitchen. "Hi, girls. Ellie, you ready?"

Ellie tossed her notepad into her bag. "Looks like Viv and I are off." She grinned at Rudy and Mr. T, sitting in a corner of the eating area. "Maria, would you mind putting the boys in the back pen?"

"Those cuties? No problem."

"Oh, and one more question," said Ellie. "How about giving us the skinny on where all the society people hang out? What are the most popular places for breakfast and lunch?"

Ellie sat with Viv at a waterside table at the Oasis Bar and Restaurant in Sag Harbor, drinking what she hoped was their last glass of wine for the day. They'd arrived after the lunch crowd cleared out, so most of the prime tables were free, which gave them a great view of the harbor and its resident boats, including the one that belonged to Billy Joel.

And giving the fleet such a simple description made Ellie grin, because most of the "boats" were yacht-sized with enough space to sleep ten or twelve belowdecks and more topside. She'd even heard people talking about a party they'd attended with forty or so guests on deck, and an on-site crew that consisted of a captain, a personal chef, and a brigade of crewmen.

Viv nursed a merlot recommended by the waitress, while Ellie held tight to a glass of sauvignon blanc, refusing all offers of a refill. This was their fifth restaurant of the day. They'd stopped at the Golden Pear Café, a delightful cafeteria-style spot in Bridgehampton, for breakfast, and another place called the Bagel Bin after that. They also had lunch at the American Hotel here in

Sag Harbor, stopped at another place for dessert, and arrived at the Oasis for drinks.

Oddly enough, not a single person had given her swollen face a glance. Instead of wondering about a stranger, these women seemed more interested in what was going on in their own lives. They clustered at tables talking while they ate, but each group seemed to clam up whenever Ellie and Viv took a seat nearby. One group even left and huddled around a table outside to finish their conversation, which was, to Ellie's mind, a direct insult.

But she refused to obsess, racking her brain for some way to begin a casual conversation with anyone to see if they knew Martin Kent.

In between restaurant-hopping, they'd wandered the downtown areas of several small villages, where Ellie tried her best to listen to the women chatting in the clothing stores while Viv shopped. Stories about Prince William and Prince Harry attending a polo match on Governor's Island in support of a charity that aided the children of an impoverished African nation abounded, but there were also a few references regarding Dr. Kent accompanied by knowing looks whenever someone mentioned his death. And there was no talk of who might have killed him or who the replacement for their drug needs would be.

She was about to confess to Viv that she was out of ideas when their waitress approached with the tab. She reached for her wallet, but Viv intercepted the folder, pulled out her debit card, and tucked it in the slot, then added a hundred-dollar bill to the inside pocket.

Ellie realized anything she said at this point would be considered rude, so she shut up and let Viv do her thing.

"This is all yours, Kileyanne." Viv handed the folder to their server, a young woman of about twenty wearing the usual waitress garb and a ton of eye makeup. "I was wondering if you could do us a favor."

Kileyanne checked the folder and grinned. "Sure, just let me take care of this first."

"I know you have money to spend," Ellie whispered when the waitress sauntered away. "But that tip was four times the amount of our bill. What's up?"

Viv shook her head, sending her straight dark brown hair rippling in the light bouncing off the peaceful water of Sag Harbor. "We tried it your way all day, and nothing worked, so I thought it was about time we used my method."

"And your method is . . ."

"Couldn't you tell from all the blather we've listened to today? Money talks and bullshit—well—you know what it does. Now hang tight and watch a master at work."

Sitting back in her chair, Ellie prepared for the show. Viv could be quite the actress when she put her mind to it, which meant the next ten minutes might be fun.

Kileyanne returned with the receipt and handed it to Viv. Then she pulled out a chair, sat down, and raised her chin toward the bartender. "Chuck says I have a couple of free minutes. So, what's on your mind?"

"My friend and I"—Viv tipped her glass to Ellie—"had an appointment with a doctor over in Montauk this morning, and when we got there the office was shut up tight with a sign on the door that said he was closed. We were wondering if maybe you knew what happened to him."

"You must mean Dr. Kent," Kileyanne said, her voice low.

"He's the one. Did you hear why he closed up shop?"

She glanced around the room. All the tables were empty, except for one near the door, where a man sat with his back to them. "He was murdered."

"Murdered?" said Ellie, playing dumb. "How? Do they know who did it?"

Kileyanne pulled a blue packet of sweetener from a holder on the table. "Word is, the cops arrested a kid who lived on the property, but the 'in' people have a different idea. Some of them think he was killed by a disgruntled patient."

"A patient?" Ellie blinked her surprise. "Then it could be someone people around here know?"

The girl shook her head. "I'm on the other side. I think it was a business partner. You know—like a supplier."

"Any idea who that might be?" asked Viv.

She twisted the packet in her fingers. "Not me, but I do know who's making money now that he's gone."

"Really?" said Viv. "And is it someone who's in his same line of work?"

"Line of work?"

Viv lowered her voice. "You know, they're willing to help women with . . . problems. Anxiety, depression, weight loss. All the things that bring a girl down."

"Oh, that." Kileyanne again glanced over her shoulder, as if making sure no one was listening. "Try Dr. Bordowski. But she goes by Dr. B," she said, her voice dropping a tone." I've only heard about her, and I've never visited her for a—er—a problem."

"Of course not," said Ellie, hoping to win the girl over. "Do you happen to know where this Dr. B's office is located?"

Kileyanne tapped the packet on the table, then set it back in the metal holder and straightened the group of condiments. "She's on some side street in Bridgehampton, but I don't know the exact address." She checked out the room again before speaking. "My girlfriend Amy, we're roomies at the same college, she goes to Dr. B for help losing weight. Nothing seemed to work, so she asked around and a lot of the girls said to go to her or Dr. Kent. She told me yesterday she's lucky she started with Dr. B, so she didn't have to go through the mechanics of getting a new prescription."

"What's your friend—Amy, is it?—what's she been taking?" asked Viv.

"It's two things, really. One to stop her from feeling hungry and another drug to help her fall asleep. That one really zonks her out." The bartender rattled a glass, then cleared his throat, and Kileyanne jumped to her feet. "Sorry. I have to go. Good luck, and thanks for the tip."

The girl walk into the kitchen and Ellie took a survey of the room, noting they were now the only customers. The man sitting at a table near the door had left. "Maybe we should go. We found out what we needed."

"Aren't you forgetting something?" Viv picked her bag off the table and headed toward the exit. "A very big something?"

Ellie held back a laugh. "Will a 'thank you so much, Vivian, for the brilliant idea of talking to our waitress' do? Because without your genius idea, we'd still be strolling around stores that charge exorbitant prices for clothes while listening to semisocialite bitches crab about their inadequate allowances." She raised her nose in the air. "I can't believe Daddy is insisting I get along on just four thousand a week," she said in a thick Long Island accent.

Viv giggled as they left the Oasis and headed for their car. "That's close enough." She unlocked the door and they slid inside, where Viv started the engine and cranked the air up to high. "So, thanks to me we know that good ol' Dr. B, or Sabrina Bordowski, had a hand in whatever it was Kent was running, and probably Uncle Mickey, too. I swear, people should pay less attention to complaining and more to being kind to their servers. Those people hear everything, yet no one gives them a second look. I bet they know enough secrets to extort millions."

"You're probably right. Just imagine the flap there'd be if one of them decided to write a book." Ellie checked her watch. "I guess we'd better get back to the house for dinner, though I doubt I can eat a thing." She snapped her seat belt in place. "I haven't had this much food in ages."

"I know, but it was worth it," said Viv, pulling out of their parking spot. "Besides, one smell of Rosa's delicious cooking and your appetite will be back in no time."

"You're probably right," Ellie agreed. "What do you think is happening at home?"

"Any one of a million things. But my guess is Arlene's waiting for us to return before she confronts Adrianne."

Chapter 14

Ellie took a quick shower, tamed her curls, and got dressed for dinner. After pulling on black linen shorts, a silk lime green T, and a matching sweater, she checked herself in the mirror, happy to see that her wardrobe didn't look too shabby. Of course, it couldn't hold a candle to Viv and the Ralph Lauren pieces she had packed in her five Louis Vuitton suitcases, but what she owned did appear colorful, clean, and up-to-date.

And it was important she look her best tonight, because she was preparing to referee a knock-down, drag-out fight during what would be a very important evening in the McCready family's life.

"*Stop fussin',*" said Rudy, who was perched on the foot of their bed. "*You look fine to me.*"

"Thanks, big guy, but this bruise is a bummer. I can wear sunglasses when I'm out in public, but it's a different story when I'm on a shaded deck with friends."

She checked her cell phone, saw that there were three

messages from Sam, and set the phone on vibrate. Then she dropped it in her pocket. "I have to make a point of calling Sam before bed tonight."

"Detective Doofus is checkin' up on you, I bet."

"Sam is not 'checking up on me.' We haven't talked in a couple of days. I miss him, and I'm sure he misses me." She gave him the evil eye. "And stop calling him a doofus."

"Okay, okay. No doofus, but I'm still gonna use demento. That's one of my favorites," he told her, adding a sneeze to finish the pronouncement.

Ellie sat next to him and gave his ears a rub. "We'll see. Now tell me about your afternoon. Did you learn anything that might help with the case?"

He lay down and put his head on her thigh. *"A couple of things went on. First, there was still a lot of traffic parading in and out of the dead doc's parking lot. Most folks read the notice and drove away, but a few walked up here and bothered Rosa."* He snorted. *"She was cool with it. Told 'em* el doctor *had died and she had no idea who they should see for their problems."*

"Smart woman, and nice to hear that she kept them from bothering her boss. Arlene's going to have enough on her plate when she confronts Adrianne tonight." She ran her hands down his back and he rolled over for a belly rub. "Anything else?"

Rudy wriggled under her scratching fingers. *"Oh, ooh, yeah, right there—riiiight there."* He stretched out his back legs and she ran her hand up and down his tummy, hitting all the good spots. When she finished, he stood and gave another sneeze. *"I'll take a second round of that before bed, if you don't mind."*

"Of course I don't mind. Now, what else did you learn?"

After giving a full body shake, he plopped his bottom on the mattress. *"Julio and Rosa talked. I found out what that* manda *thing really is."* He raised his muzzle. *"And it's darned special, if you ask me."*

"Since when did you learn to speak Spanish?"

"I thought you knew. I'm bilateral."

Ellie smothered a smile. "I think you mean bilingual."

"Whatever. And I learned more when Tomas joined them. He went over exactly what he did that night in the doc's office and swore to 'em it was true."

"Really? And did it happen the way we thought? He threatened the doc with the knife, they argued and he dropped it, and then he ran and the doc followed him out? But he escaped, leaving Kent to contend with the real killer?"

"You got it. Tomas didn't see anyone lying in wait, but there must'a been, just like you thought."

"And the *manda* explanation? Did it make any sense to you?"

He gave a doggie shrug. *"I have a handle on it, but it's hard to explain. It's got something to do with that* juramento *thing. It's a special promise of some kind made to the Virgin Mother. Ask Rosa. She knows."*

"I can only hope she does. Maybe I should ask Julio? Or Tomas?"

"I wouldn't waste my time on that kid. He's got a chip on his shoulder the size of an overstuffed burrito. He needs to make that trek to Mexico City on his hands and knees when this mess is over."

"He'll have to do what!" asked Ellie, standing.

"Never mind. Rosa will tell you." He jumped off the bed. *"Let's get movin'. I'm starved and I can't wait for the show to begin."*

Ellie bit her lower lip. Tomas had to crawl to some place in Mexico City? She needed Rosa to explain that one to her, but it would have to wait until later. All she could focus on now were the McCready sisters.

She and Rudy left the bedroom and took the back stairs down to the laundry room. "I just hope Viv has the good sense not to provoke anyone, or we'll have World War Three on our hands."

"You know Vivie. She does what she wants. But I heard you tell her to hang loose until we showed up."

"Some witness you are, when nobody but me can hear you." They landed at the bottom of the stairs. "That's no help for my case at all."

"Then I guess you don't remember the stuff you said when you took those drugs after you were attacked."

"I don't want to talk about those drugs. All they are is trouble—trouble I don't need. And what about the 'stuff' I said?"

Rudy gazed up at her, a smile creasing his doggie lips. *"You told Viv you talked to us canines."*

Ellie's mouth dropped open. "I did what?"

"Aw, it was nothin'. Vivie didn't believe a word of it. She was so worried about your condition, all she did was make some dopey comment about sand fleas."

"Are you sure?"

"Duh, yeah. She blamed your crazy talk on the drugs and laughed it off." He gave another head-to-tail shake. *"What human in their right mind would believe such a lame story?"*

"Okay, great. If she says anything, I can act like I don't remember, which I don't, and play dumb."

"You're pretty good at that, too," he answered with a yip. *"Now hurry up with my dinner."*

Ellie rushed through the mechanics of preparing his food. There wasn't a soul in the kitchen, which meant everyone was on the terrace, and that was strange, because from what she could overhear, there was very little conversation taking place outside.

After setting Rudy's dinner on a place mat, she tiptoed to the back door and peeked out the window.

Viv and Arlene sat on the far side of the table with an empty chair between them that Ellie assumed was for her.

Vanessa's and Adrianne's backs were to the door, so it was difficult to gauge their thoughts.

Evan McCready, at the head of the table, seemed to be the only person enjoying his meal, a shrimp, avocado, spring greens, and vegetable salad.

And Rosa circled the group with a basket of rolls, going from person to person with her offering.

"What's goin' on out there?" whispered Rudy.

She jumped at the sound of his voice and put a finger to her lips. "*Shh.* Are you finished already?"

"Yep, and prepared for the opening act. You bringin' the popcorn?"

"That isn't funny." She ignored her phone, which had started vibrating in her pocket. This was not a good time to talk with Sam. Squaring her shoulders, she pushed open the door and walked around the table.

Vanessa's eyes grew wide when Ellie took the seat between Viv and Arlene. "Oh, you poor thing! The bruise has gotten darker. How are you feeling?"

"About as good as I can for looking so battered. My face doesn't hurt, but my temple does, especially if I touch it." *Or sneeze or move my head.* When she smiled a hello to Adrianne, the woman ignored her. Too bad someone hadn't given the middle sister what she needed while growing up—a smack upside her head. "Did Viv tell you what we did today?"

"She's been talking about it," said Vanessa.

"I've only met Sabrina Bordowski a few times," Arlene began. "Now that I think back on it, she and Martin did seem a bit . . . close. I will admit, I often wondered if they were . . ." Letting the statement hang, she gazed at Adrianne and stiffened. Then she put a hand on Ellie's thigh, as if preparing her for the next sentence. "Maybe you know who else Martin was sleeping with, sister dear, seeing as you were number one on his list."

Vanessa inhaled a gasp. "Arlene! What are you saying?"

"Awwwk! Arlene! Do what I say! Awwwk!"

Ignoring Myron's inane squawking, Viv leaned back in her chair. "Come on, Mom, get real. Haven't you figured it out yet?"

Adrianne sneered, her expression turning downright ugly. "Don't 'sister dear' me, Arlene. You were the one he planned to marry."

"Awwwk! Goin' to the chapel and we're gonna get ma-a-a-ried! Awwwk! Goin' to the chapel. Awwwk!"

"One of you had better tell me what you're talking about, or I'll—I'll—"

"You'll do what? Send us to our room? Take away our allowance? Really, Mother, get a life," said Adrianne.

"Maybe I should say the same to you," snapped Arlene. "But get one of your own, instead of stealing mine."

Vanessa pushed away from the table, stood, and placed a hand on her husband's shoulder. "Evan, what are they talking about?"

"Awwwk! Everybody's talking at me. I don't hear a word they're sayin'. Awwwk!"

"Will someone please shut that bird up!" cried Vanessa.

Rosa rushed to the parrot and carried him inside.

The senior McCready glared at his daughters. "I have an idea, and it infuriates me." He focused on Adrianne. "I believe you owe your older sister an apology."

Adrianne crossed her arms over her bright yellow tank top. "I don't owe her anything. She has everything she wants already. I wasn't the only woman Marty slept with, but I was the best. He told me my portrait held the secret to his success, and she should know it."

Vanessa dropped into her chair. "Portrait? What portrait?"

Rosa returned to the terrace and set a plate of the shrimp and avocado salad in front of Ellie.

Viv sat up straight, as if preparing to march into battle. "We saw the painting, Adrianne. It was a cruel and tacky thing to do. So low-class."

"What is this painting you're talking about?" asked Vanessa.

Arlene seemed to deflate like a balloon with a slow leak. "Adrianne painted a nude self-portrait and hung it on the wall in Martin's office—and it's a direct slap in my face."

"It's always about you, isn't it?" Adrianne thumped the table with a fist. "You're nothing but a self-righteous prig."

"Hey, stop right there," said Viv.

Ellie opened her mouth to speak, but Arlene shook her head. "I can handle it." She stared at her sister with her green eyes blazing. "I want you out of the guesthouse tonight. You are no longer welcome in my home or my life."

"Do somethin', Triple E. Adrianne can't leave until after the memorial," Rudy reminded her from under the table.

Her boy was correct. Adrianne was still on her suspect list. Though it was difficult imagining her as the killer, she was tall with ripped arms and a toned figure. With the right amount of anger and leverage, she could have pushed the doctor hard enough to make him fall.

"Arlene, just a minute," Ellie began. Then she realized she couldn't say what she wanted.

"Yes, think a minute, Arlene. We drove your sister, so she has no way home. I want the two of you to talk this through here and now," ordered Vanessa.

Viv hissed out a sigh. "This is between Adrianne and Arlene, Mother. You need to stay out of it."

"What I need is for my girls to get along like sisters should," Vanessa said. A tear slid down her cheek and she dabbed it with her napkin. "After Evan, you three are all I have in the world. I want you to be happy and—"

"Sorry, Mom, but that's only going to happen when you start treating Adrianne like a grown woman and accept what she's become," Vivian interrupted.

"What I've become?" Adrianne stood. "You should talk, little sister-with-the-big-job-and-salary. Too bad you can't hold on to a man, either."

"Hey, wait one second—" Ellie said, protesting for Viv.

Adrianne focused on Ellie as if she were fresh prey. "You have nothing to say in this, Ms. Big Ass. Who do you think you are, barging into our family business, then bragging about how you could find Marty's killer? You're nothing but a dog walker masquerading as something special."

"Did she just call you Ms. Big Ass?" Rudy yipped, snaking between her feet to stand clear of the chair.

Unable to speak, Ellie blinked her shock.

Evan McCready grabbed his daughter's forearm. "That's enough, Adrianne. It's cruel and it isn't true. Now you have three people to whom you owe an apology."

Ignoring her father, Adrianne scanned the table. "I'm not leaving until after the memorial. I hear our intrusive guest is planning to pull a rabbit out of her butt and reveal Marty's murderer. I wouldn't want to miss that show for all the money in the world." Rounding her father, she stumbled into Rudy, who was blocking her way, and shoved him aside with a jab from her foot. Then she marched down the stairs with her Louboutins thundering.

Panting, Rudy jumped into Ellie's lap. *"Did you see? Did you see! She kicked me. Me! An innocent pooch. The nerve!"*

Ellie hugged her boy close, then pushed her dinner plate to the middle of the table. This battle was pretty much what she had expected, but when her dog was threatened, well, that was it.

"I'm okay, Triple E. But we gotta show her we're right. We'll do it on the night of the memorial, when we announce the doc's killer."

Raising her gaze, she found that all eyes were on her.

"Oh, Ellie, I'm so sorry you had to hear that," said Vanessa.

"I apologize for my rude and crude sister, too. You were here in support of me. There was no need for her to verbally abuse you the way she did," said Arlene.

Viv smiled and threw an arm around her shoulder. "The girl is tough. She can take it."

"Still," muttered Evan. He fisted his hands. "I'm going to the guesthouse to speak to my spoiled brat of a daughter. Vanessa? Are you coming?"

After the McCready parents left the table, Viv blew out a breath. "If you ask me, once she did that to Rudy, she was toast. You should have used those lessons in self-defense to flatten Adrianne and show her who's boss."

Arlene shook her head. "That might have been interesting, seeing as Adrianne's been into kickboxing for the past year."

"Did ya hear? Did ya hear?" Rudy snapped out. *"She could'a learned one of them fancy kicks and slammed Kent in the chest."*

Ellie again cupped Rudy's muzzle. He was right, but she couldn't think about it now. "I'm more angry about my dog than I am about the Ms. Big Ass comment," she admitted. So what if she wasn't a size 6 anymore? She'd checked her bottom before buying her new swimsuit and there were no ripples or orange peel skin that came with the cellulite so many women complained about. "But she was definitely rude."

"That's Adrianne for you. She's always thought the world revolved around her and everyone else was second best." Viv grinned. "And stop internalizing. Your ass is fabulous. Just ask Sam." She smirked. "Or Agent Double O Seven."

Arlene's expression slipped into solemn mode. "Ignore Adrianne. That's what I plan to do. Everything she says is mean-spirited. Viv's right, by the way. You do have a great ass."

Before Ellie could speak, Rosa began clearing the table. Arlene stood and so did Viv. "Come on, let's go inside and have a glass of wine. Arlene will break out the good stuff. We can get mellow and figure out how to get back at Adrianne."

Ellie's phone began to vibrate, so she shook her head. "I'll catch up with you later. I think Sam is looking for me, and it's time we talked." She pulled her phone from her pocket and saw the signal for another voice mail message. "He's left a bunch of messages, so I guess I'd better respond."

Before phoning Sam, Ellie ran her hands over her boy. She'd checked Rudy for bruises or sprains, and he was fine, but he was also rabid mad. Adrianne had taken him by surprise, and he wanted revenge. Ellie had calmed him down, but he was still pacing the terrace and complaining in short woofs and gruffs.

Sam had to have free time to be so insistent about calling her, and that wasn't the norm in his line of work. He was usually at a crime scene, in the station questioning a suspect, on surveillance duty, or filling out the reams of paperwork needed to close a case. Anything was possible, and she found that way of working challenging, tiring, and defeating.

The few times she'd been on the hunt for a killer, it was only because she was helping a friend. She was not on the NYPD payroll, nor did she ever plan to be. She valued her friends and felt she could never have enough, which was all the reason she needed to lend a hand when they were in trouble.

The thought of being a New York City detective made her skin crawl. She'd heard about some of the crime scenes Sam had worked, and his description was enough to make her stomach turn. She never wanted to walk through pools of blood, see shattered bodies, or try to figure out why some maniac had butchered a wife, child, or friend.

And she could never carry a gun or harm anyone in the course of seeking a killer.

"You about ready to go in?" asked Rudy from underneath the table. *"I smell a storm comin' on."*

"You're just tired because you've spent a lot of energy nursing a grudge. I plan to stay out here and give Sam another try, but I can open the door and you can go up."

She inhaled deeply and caught the scent of ozone, a sure sign of dangerous weather. Staring into the sky, she saw a mass of churning clouds obscuring the moon. It seemed as if Rudy was on a roll, his instincts about the storm, about Adrianne, about the whole murder business.

"You know, I think you're right about that storm, but I bet we have another hour or so before we need to worry. You can still go up and find Viv and Mr. T, if you want. They'll give you a cuddle while you wait for me."

"I wouldn't leave you here alone for all the Dingo bones in the world," he said, putting his nose on the edge of her sandal. *"We're a matched pair, remember?"*

"Okay, just give me a minute to try Sam one more time. He might be—"

"Who are you talking to, Miss Ellie?" asked Rosa, slipping through the kitchen door. "Is getting dark and the weather people say we will get a big storm. You should be inside."

"I'm just trying to make sense of Adrianne and what she did to her sister, for one thing. Then there's finding Dr. Kent's killer to save your son. I'm afraid I haven't gotten very far with that problem."

The housekeeper took a seat at the table. "Ah, *sí*, I was afraid of that. The *policía*, they have evidence and motive, correct? And that is all they need to bring my Tomas to trial."

"Unfortunately, yes." Ellie forced herself to chat, even though she was exhausted. "I wanted to ask you about something you said earlier, when you talked about a *manda.*"

"Ah, *sí*, the *manda.*" Rosa nodded. "It is special, something we do to ensure what you call a happy ending to a challenge or a battle."

"And you said it was like a *juri*—"

"Jur-a-men-to," Rudy muttered.

"Juramento." Ellie corrected herself. "Sorry, but my Spanish is almost nonexistent."

"I understand, so I will explain, yes?"

"Please do. I need all the assistance I can get if I'm going to free your son."

"Ah, but my Julio, he has already gone to the highest giver of help. The one who can do the impossible for her believers. The *Virgen.*"

Though she pronounced the word as "veer-hen," Ellie knew whom she meant. "The Blessed Mother?"

"*Sí, sí.* A *juramento* is a promise to a saint when one of my people wants to stop drinking. A *manda* is like that, but it can be for anything."

"So Julio made a *manda* to the Holy Virgin."

"*Sí.* When our boy is freed, he and Tomas promise to go home to Mexico City, where they will crawl on their knees to the Altar del Perdón in the Catedral Metropolitana in gratitude."

"Wow, that's some promise," said Ellie, clasping her hands together on the table.

"Told ya so," Rudy gruffed.

"But it will be well worth the trip, if our Tomas is proven innocent. And we will owe you a year's worth of prayers in thanks, as well."

"That's fine with me. I don't think you can ever have too many prayers," Ellie said, trying to hide the emotion welling in her throat. "I'd appreciate that."

"It will be the least we can do for someone who is so willing to save our boy." Rosa stood. "Can I get you anything before I retire? Hot tea or some lemonade?"

"A cup of Earl Grey would be nice. Thank you."

"Sí, un momento."

Rosa left, and Ellie used the time to dial Sam, who answered on the first ring.

"Hey, babe. How are things?"

She leaned back in her chair. She hated lying to anyone, especially Sam. "Fine . . . just great. . . . How about you?"

"What's wrong?" he asked after a full five seconds.

"Wrong? What makes you think something's wrong?" Ellie swallowed. "Everything is wonderful."

"Aha. So why do I think you're lying?"

"I'm not. Though I did have some problems with that pricey sunscreen Viv talked me into buying. My tan isn't exactly what I was hoping for."

"Sorry to hear it. But you knew it would be tough to tan with your fair skin and red hair. Maybe next time you want some color I'll be there to put on the sunscreen. Besides, having a suntan is no big deal."

"I was just hoping. How are you?"

"I grabbed a crappy case the other day, so I've been busy, but Vince is on call so I have a break. Since we're in a storm situation, I thought maybe I'd drive to Montauk early tomorrow morning and spend a day with you, seeing as you'd probably be housebound."

Eeek! "What? No!" She sucked air into her lungs. "I mean, this isn't a good time. There's been a death, so we're holding a memorial service and—"

"A death? Who died?"

Ellie slumped in her seat. Sam sounded suspicious. Too suspicious. "A—a—friend—of the family. No one important."

"You're going to a memorial service for no one important?"

"Well, they weren't important to me, but they were to the McCreadys so I'm tagging along," she said, proud of the half-truth. "In support of Viv, of course."

"Too bad, because I only have tomorrow. After that, Vince is taking a day off. It's raining buckets here right now, but word is the storm is moving your way. Damn near a hurricane when it started out, but it's quieted down some. You be careful tomorrow, you hear?"

"I hear." She heaved a sigh of relief. "I miss you, Sam."

"I miss you, too. Just take it easy. You deserve a break. Maybe next year, we can go somewhere together. Then I'd be the one to help you into and out of that new swimsuit."

Her insides warmed. Sam had already given her a hand getting out of her Karla Colletto after she'd modeled it for him at home. They had their issues, like all couples, but intimacy had never been one of them. "We could rent a house for a month, if I found a walker friend to take all the dogs." *Or a decent assistant.* "I'll work on it."

"Just make sure it's a place I can afford on my own. I

could get a week, but if you wanted to stay longer I'd commute the rest of the time."

Since they'd started living together, Sam had insisted they do the extra stuff on his NYPD salary, and not what she earned as a dog walker, and she tried to accommodate him. They didn't talk money often, but the fact that her mother was well off and she was mentioned in the judge's will was a sore spot. He wasn't happy that she made more walking dogs than he did as a cop, and though he never complained out loud, she knew it bothered him.

But there was no way he could afford a month's rental "out east." "I'll look around and see what I can find."

"You do that, and give me a call when this memorial thing is over. I miss you."

"I miss you, too. See you soon."

Rudy growled as she snapped the phone closed; he raced to the top of the stairs. *"Heads up, Triple E. I smell trouble."*

"Storm trouble or people trouble?" she asked, turning around in her chair.

Instead of answering, he growled a louder warning.

Chapter 15

The wind picked up just then and a tingle rippled down Ellie's spine. Jim Bond's head appeared, followed by his tall, muscular body. Tonight's attire, a pale blue golf shirt and black slacks, was trim and dress casual, as usual. He stopped on the top step and glared at Rudy, but he showed progress by not reaching for his weapon.

"If you want Arlene, I'm afraid you're too late. She's already gone to bed," she said, glad to see that Rudy was holding his temper.

Jim's lips drew into a line. "Is there a secret code or some special word I need to know so your dog will let me pass?"

"Yeah. It's 'I surrender.' Then you toss your bazooka over the terrace." Rudy gave another growl, this one more menacing. *"Got it, dickhead?"*

Ellie smothered a smile. "Enough, Rudy. Let the man walk by."

Rosa came out, took one look at the DEA agent, set

down Ellie's tea, spoon, and napkin, and raised a finger. "I be back."

Jim sauntered to the table and commandeered a chair. "You keep telling me your dog is friendly, but I've yet to see it."

"He is nice, but he's also protective. If he thinks someone is going to hurt me, he's on top of it."

"Just what you need, living in the big city like you do."

She inhaled another draft of ozone-filled air, dunked her tea bag a few times, and wrapped it around the spoon. "Like I said, Arlene's already gone. You really should make an appointment instead of showing up unannounced this late in the evening. Especially with bad weather on the way."

Rosa brought the agent the same drink setup she'd given Ellie, waved a good-bye, and shuffled into the house. Ellie sipped her drink while Jim fiddled with his tea. She wasn't about to speak. He'd come here without an invitation. She could wait him out all night if she had to.

"Glad to know you're aware of the storm. This end of Long Island is supposed to get hit with the remnants of the latest hurricane," he told her. "It won't be crippling, but they are expecting a lot of wind and rain."

"Sam already called to warn me, but I could tell by the eerie atmosphere something big is brewing out there. With all that's been going on, weather is the last thing I've been worried about."

"Your face looks better," he said, raising a hand toward her forehead. "The swelling is down and the bruise is clearing up. Does it still hurt?"

"Only when I laugh," she answered with a frown. "Now tell me what you want and make it quick. I'm finishing this tea and calling it a night."

"So you heard from your boyfriend the cop," he said, smiling.

"We hung up a couple of minutes ago." She took a long swallow of her tea. "Now tell me, Special Agent Bond, why are you here?"

He downed a bit of tea, too, then set the cup down. "Okay, I'll get right to it. I talked about you with one of my law enforcement friends today. A guy named Mitchell Carmody."

Ellie inhaled a gasp. "You and Captain Carmody talked—about me?"

"Look at it from my point of view." He leaned back and crossed his arms. "You forced my hand. You've been getting in the way of this investigation, and I had to speak to someone who might know where I could find your 'off' button, before I arrested you for obstruction. Sad thing is, it didn't work."

Since Sam hadn't mentioned a meeting, he had yet to hear from the captain. But there was still a chance Carmody would read him the riot act and order him to do something about his over-the-top girlfriend or—or—

"What do you mean—it didn't work?"

"Well, it seems the captain can do nothing but sing your praises. He says every once in a while you get a wild hare, his words, not mine, and go off on your own, but basically you have a good nose for sorting things out."

"He told you that?"

"I knew Carmody was an upstanding guy the minute he agreed to take Buddy," muttered Rudy.

She tapped him with the toe of her sandal. "I had no idea he felt that way about me."

"Trust me, he does." Jim shrugged and his biceps flexed. "But there is one thing you're not good at."

"And that is . . ."

"Picking up a trace. I followed you and your pal Vivian to all five restaurants and bars today. I didn't mind it, of course. Got a chance to eat some good food, have a drink or two, even get a look at how some of the super wealthy occupy themselves while they're on holiday." His lips turned up at the corners. "It was the shopping that drove me nuts."

"If you'd taken me with, like I asked, I would'a smelled him out," Rudy said, jumping into her lap.

She cupped her hand around his muzzle. "You're telling me you went to the Golden Pear Café, the Bagel Bin, the American Hotel, the Corner Bar . . . and the Oasis?"

"And all your stops in between, so there's a few things I need to know, starting with where in the hell did your friend Vivian learn to drive?"

She drummed her fingers on the table. "That's none of your business. What else?"

"Hey, don't get angry. I already told you I'm not going to arrest you . . . yet."

"You have no reason to arrest me, and we both know it." She pushed from the table, and Rudy leapt to the floor. Then she gathered the teacups, spoons, and napkins. "I've had a rough day. I really need to go in and get to sleep."

"Then you're not going to tell me what you found out when you got that waitress—Kileyanne, was it?—to talk to you?"

Ellie opened and closed her mouth. Another gust of wind blew curls into her eyes and she shook her head. Stacking the dishes and napkins in her hand, she marched to the door with Rudy following behind.

"Hey, wait. I need help with something, and if Carmody trusts you, well, that's good enough for me."

She turned on her heel. "You're asking me for help?"

He stood and took a step toward her. "Don't get excited. It's just a small favor. I'm trying to find a PDA or maybe a notebook, anything Kent could have used to record his illegal transactions. I've looked in all the right places with no luck. I even talked to Ms. McCready, and so has Wheeling, but since he has a case for the killer, he doesn't need more. I thought maybe, with you in the house, you might have seen something I missed."

"In the library? Or his office?"

"Anywhere. Kent was a slick operator, but even he had to keep records. Nothing showed up on his personal computer, so it has to be somewhere around here."

Ellie thought a second before answering. She could talk to Rosa, who knew the house as well as anyone, take the time to search, maybe let Rudy sniff out a clue. "I'll see what I can do, but I'm not promising anything."

"Fine. That's all I ask." He moved closer and she opened the kitchen door. "So it's good night, then?"

"You bet it is, bozo-brain."

"Ah, yeah." She ducked around the door and slipped inside. Jim was giving off a vibe she planned to ignore. She had Sam, and he was the only man for her. "I'll get back to you if I find anything."

The next morning, Ellie stood near the six-burner range, gazing out the breakfast area's bay windows. The hurricane that had developed somewhere in the mid-Atlantic over the past week had worn itself down to summer storm level overnight. Its route had bounced it off the

Outer Banks, where it skirted around Virginia Beach and the eastern shore, and had made its way up the coast, hitting New Jersey, New York, and Long Island.

"I guess with all that was going on around here, we forgot to pay attention to the weather forecast," said Viv, rearing back from her scan of the yard. "It's a good thing this storm lost some of its punch, or we'd be getting walloped."

"If I was home, I would have been on top of things. I usually check weather info every night before bed to make sure I'm prepared for walking the dogs the next morning." Ellie accepted the omelet Rosa made for her and inhaled the yummy aroma of onions, tomatoes, Swiss cheese, and sausage wrapped inside fluffy eggs. "Waking up to whatever the weather brings must mean I'm really on vacation."

She sat next to Viv and took another look out the window. Water cascaded down the panes while, farther out, the prevailing wind bent the sea grass almost to the sand. That cleared their view of the dunes and allowed a peek at the waves crashing against the shore.

On the right side of the yard, the guest cottage stood alone. If not for the three cars in the parking lot, one would think the house had been abandoned by its residents and left to the pounding of the storm. Ellie wondered how the family members inside were getting along after the past evening's tumultuous discussion.

"What happens in the guest cottage on days like this, when they can't make it to the house for meals?" she asked no one in particular.

"They can come up if they want. There are umbrellas, raincoats, and other foul-weather gear in the closet under the stairs," said Viv. "But after last night, I'm sure they'll just hunker down and stay inside until the storm passes."

"The refrigerator is fully stocked," said Rosa. "Ms. Vanessa has all she needs to make a good breakfast, and the freezer is filled with meals that can be thawed and heated."

"Do you see to that as part of your housekeeping duties?" Ellie asked her. "Or does the job fall to the girls?"

"*Sí*, is my job to make sure everything is prepared, but my girls, they carry it there and put the groceries away. It is one of their chores to make sure the cottage is ready for guests."

Ellie moved closer. "Does this house have a safe, or maybe a secret drawer in one of the desks?"

Rosa cocked her head, thinking. "No safes, but I could check the desks for you. Maybe you should ask Arlene?"

"I hate to bother her. It's just that I feel as if we've missed something that might help with Tomas's case."

"And you think this secret drawer could hold a clue?"

"I do, but I have to go out this morning to see—"

Thunder rolled, sounding too close for comfort, and Ellie jumped. When it ended with a loud *"Awwwk! It's raining men! Awwwk!"* she knew she'd been fooled.

"Darn that bird," muttered Vivian. "I would have sworn that noise came from Mother Nature, not a parrot."

"He is amazing," said Ellie, walking to the table. "Too bad he wasn't a witness to Dr. Kent's murder. He'd probably identify the killer with a single squawk."

"Better still, he could be questioned. In the three weeks before the wedding, he must have heard all manner of shady stuff: arguments, love talk, drug deals—anything the doc discussed with his patients and pals." Viv sighed. "Instead, he's just a nutty bird."

"Awwwk! Sometimes I feel like a nut! Awwwk! Sometimes I don't. Awwwk!"

"Nutty is right," Ellie agreed when Myron spouted the last comment. "I'm betting most of those passionate moans he likes to repeat were made by Adrianne and the doc's patients, and not Arlene. Can you imagine how she must feel hearing her fiancé making love with another woman?"

"Awwwk! All you need is love! Awwwk! Love, love, just a little love. Awwwk!"

The patter of paws echoed from the dining room, announcing the Boston Terriers. A few seconds later the canine trio and Arlene sauntered in, the dogs and their owner dressed in bright yellow hooded slickers and boots.

"The babies and I are taking a walk and I have extra raincoats. Do either of your guys want to go with us?"

A wave of guilt washed over Ellie. She hadn't done much in the way of walking any dog, including her own and Mr. T, since she arrived. Maybe this was the time to show her thanks to Arlene by offering to do the job for her.

"Why don't you let me take them? I owe you so much for allowing me to stay here with Viv." She stood. "Really, I don't mind."

"But I do," Rudy gruffed from under the table. *"I already did my business and got soakin' wet for it. I won't need another out for a while."*

"You wouldn't catch me dead dressed like those three buggy-eyed nitwits," said Mr. T. *"They look like four-legged bananas."*

"Don't be silly," Arlene continued, oblivious of the canine commentary. "I need the exercise. All I've been doing is sitting around feeling sorry for myself. My hope is to walk off some excess energy, which might help me concentrate on the details of Martin's memorial." She locked gazes with her sister. "I don't think I can put it off any longer."

"I hate to ask, but has he been cremated?"

"I talked to the funeral home today, and they're taking care of it. They said the remains will be ready by tomorrow."

"And you'll be able to handle it?" asked Viv.

Arlene shrugged. "Ellie said holding it might be what we need to flush out the murderer, so I'll have to. Trouble is, I'll own his ashes when it's over. What am I supposed to do with that kind of reminder?" She shrugged again. "Are you sure your boy doesn't want to go out?"

Viv peeked under the table, saw T licking his privates, and *tsk*ed. "Twink is busy doing what male dogs do best. He'd hate me if I moved him now, but thanks."

"Okay." Arlene headed for the front of the house. "I'll eat when I come back, Rosa. How about an egg white omelet with some veggies and a cup of fruit? Diced watermelon, peaches, bananas—anything will do."

Rosa began the breakfast while Viv grabbed her and Ellie's coffee cups. "I'm getting us a refill. You need anything else?"

"How about a new clue to the killer's identity?" said Ellie, thinking ahead to the planned memorial. The McCready family expected a miracle, and she was far from living up to her promise of unveiling the killer. Why had she allowed Viv to talk her into investigating this crime?

"Hey, I just thought of somethin'," said a voice from below.

Ellie ducked down to face her yorkiepoo. "Yes?"

"Did you ever notice the difference in the way people talk about Dr. Kent?"

"A difference in the way people talk about him? Sorry, but I'm not following you," she whispered.

"For instance, whenever that dopey bird does the humpin' hamster talk or squawks out the threats, he says 'Marty.'" Rudy put a paw on her knee. *"But when Arlene talks about him, she calls him Martin. Don't you think that's odd?"*

She reached down and scratched his ears. "Now that you mention it . . ." Pulling her spiral pad from her tote, she flipped pages. "Give me another example and I'll see where it fits."

"That mean sister, the one who kicked me, she said Marty plenty of times."

Ellie searched her brain for Adrianne's snotty remarks and came up with "Marty loved that self-portrait. He said it held the secret to his success."

"People were knocking on Marty's office door at six a.m."

"You've been bragging about how you'll find Marty's killer."

"Okay, so Adrianne called him Marty. I still think the chance she murdered him is slim to none."

"Then what about those threats Myron squawks? That's a man's voice."

"Or maybe a woman's. I don't remember." She flipped pages and went to all of her suspects, trying to recall how they'd referred to Dr. Kent. Rudy was right, but she'd never connected it. She'd talked to a lot of people, so who besides Adrianne had called him Marty?

Viv returned with their brimming coffee mugs and took her seat. "I know I've said this before, but I can't thank you enough for helping us out, especially after you were assaulted. And then insulted by my sister. Just let me know if there's anything you want me to do and I'll take care of it."

Ellie heaved a sigh. Viv acted as if finding a killer was nothing more than putting a puzzle together, which it was, only this particular box contained lots of missing pieces. She was in this difficult position because "friends helped friends" and "a promise is a promise" were codes she tried to live by.

"The best thing you can do is lend Arlene a hand in planning the memorial."

"I can definitely do that," said Viv, taking a sip of coffee. Then she scanned Ellie's face. "The bruise is turning yellow around the edges. I'm no expert, but I think that means it's healing."

"Probably," Ellie answered. Still flipping through her notebook, she realized there was one person she hadn't questioned. "You know, maybe I should visit a doctor and get the diagnosis from a pro. Who knows? I may be offered a prescription for happy pills to help with the pain."

Ellie searched the Hamptons' phone directory, took down Dr. Bordowski's address, and called the office number. A recorded voice told her that despite the storm, Dr. B was holding office hours and no appointment was necessary. After taking a shower and donning decent clothes, she borrowed a slicker from Arlene and took the BMW keys from Viv.

It was about time she did some detecting on her own. She needed to earn the trust Arlene, Viv, Rosa, and the girls had given her. Thanks to the bad weather, she figured the roads would be fairly clear of cars, so she could drive without scaring the bejesus out of herself or any of the "out east" residents. She was a big girl, she had a license, and if Viv could do it, so could she.

Now out in the driveway, Viv leaned into the driver-side window. "Are you sure you want to do this alone? I don't mind coming along."

"You already have a job helping Arlene arrange Dr. Kent's memorial. And remember to invite Jim Bond and Detective Wheeling, too. If anything exciting happens, we'll need police backup and they're the primaries on this case."

"Got it," Viv said in a cheery voice. She kept her head inside the window, though her rear end was getting soaked by the falling rain. "Go on, start the engine. I need to know you can at least do that before I let you leave the driveway."

Ellie puffed out a breath and fastened her seat belt. "All right already." Keeping everything in neutral, she stepped on the clutch and turned the key while the engine hummed to life. "Satisfied?"

"So far," said Viv. "Do you remember what I told you?"

"Yes, I remember. I can do this on my own. If I need you, I'll hit the horn."

"Ooo-kay." Viv stepped back and raced up the front steps. "Be careful," she yelled before she ducked inside and slammed the door.

First things first, thought Ellie: *Get familiar with the car, find all the knobs and switches, and make sure I know how to use them.* She stared at the cluttered dash and steering wheel column, found the windshield wipers, and turned them on. Playing with their speed, she smiled when she got the blades moving at a nice even pace.

Then she spotted the headlights and flicked them on. After that, she rolled the windows up and down a couple of times. The rain had lessened. If it stopped, it might be nice driving with fresh air tousling her curls and cooling her overworked brain. And speaking of cool . . . The interior of the beastly BMW was warm, the front and side windows steamed. After locating the defroster, she turned it on.

Already exhausted from fussing with the dashboard buttons, she heaved another sigh. Manhattanites had it right. Sit back and let the buses, subways, and cabs get you where you needed to go. There was no messing with engines, stick shifts, or foggy windows. You could sit back and read a newspaper or talk to a friend without a care, and still reach your destination in one piece.

Easy-peasy and less nerve-racking than having to actually drive.

Last step, she told herself, and it was the "big one." Time to use the clutch and move the gearshift into place. After sliding through each gear a half dozen times, she checked the windows. The heat vents had done their job and cleared the fog, so it was time to take off.

What was it Viv had said? Driving a car was like riding a bicycle? Once you learned how, you never forgot?

Repeating *nice and easy* in her brain, she needed only three tries to back out of the parking spot and execute a K-turn so she was facing the street. *Not that difficult,* she thought, moving the car into first gear. *Just ease up on the clutch and give it a little gas.*

The engine died and her neck snapped in place, making the bump on her temple throb and her teeth clatter.

Try it again, only this time move slower. You can do it.

Inching out of the drive, she turned onto the road and exhaled. *Now for second gear. Clutch, shift, ease up, give the engine gas, and go.*

She repeated the effort and slid into third. When that worked, she eased into fourth. If she was careful, she could stay in this gear for the entire drive. So what if the posted speed limit was fifty? There were no cars on the road. If someone came up behind her, they could just go around.

She passed through the nearly deserted Amagansett, gliding along in fourth gear and damn proud of herself. So far, she'd hit every green light and no one had crept up behind her to hurry her along. The hard part was next. East Hampton was a larger village with more lights and a tricky intersection she'd have to traverse to stay on Route 27.

Up ahead, the light flashed from yellow to red and her heart rate accelerated. She hit the clutch, moved into neutral, and stepped on the brake, then coasted to the light. When it turned green, she stepped on the gas, which was definitely *not* the right thing to do. She wasn't in gear. All the BMW's roaring engine did was catch the attention of a few folks wearing rain gear and waiting to cross at the light.

She jiggled the stick shift into first and eased up on the clutch again, causing the car to jerk and die in the middle of the intersection. Someone behind her honked and she rolled down the window, waving a hand, encouraging them to pass.

The next thing she knew, a blue light was flashing behind her. She checked the rearview mirror and the cop car shot out its *Whoop! Whoop! Whoop!*

Filled with trepidation, Ellie searched her tote bag

for her wallet, which held her license. When she glanced in the mirror, the officer was talking on a radio and she imagined he was calling in the car's plate.

She reached into the glove box and pulled out the rental agreement. Taking deep breaths, she willed her stomach to be calm. Then she flipped down the visor mirror and took a look at herself. *Yeech!* Her face was a mass of color, mostly blue and purple, but there was a bit of that ghastly yellow-green Viv had mentioned earlier.

Even though rain and clouds filled the sky, she slipped on her sunglasses, hoping he wouldn't notice the shocking condition of her face.

"License and registration, please," said the officer when he got to her door.

Ellie had the paperwork waiting.

He scanned her license and rental agreement. Then he inched down and gazed at her through the window. "Are you having trouble with your vehicle, miss?"

Ignoring her twitchy stomach, Ellie smiled. "Just a little. It's a rental, and I'm not used to a stick shift."

He raised his eyebrows and gazed at her. "Would you mind removing those sunglasses? I like to look a person in the eye when I talk to her."

She did what he asked, but her feeble confidence took a nosedive when he got sight of her face. No doubt about it, this was going to take a while.

Chapter 16

Ellie found Dr. Sabrina Bordowski's office on Newtown Lane, just off Route 27 in East Hampton. After parking head-on in the spacious lot next door to the office, she took a couple of deep breaths. She'd finished her session with Officer Pat O'Brien—no kidding, that was his name—just minutes ago, and was still a bit shaken. Though he'd given her a short lesson on shifting the BMW in a more efficient manner, he'd also given her a warning for careless driving.

His instructions had been insightful, and Officer Pat was sweet yet firm, sort of like a fresh summer peach. Too bad Viv hadn't been in the car. She'd have eaten him up for sure.

The sign identifying Dr. Bordowski's place of business was small and unassuming, its information clear: DR. SABRINA BORDOWSKI, M.D., ADULT GENERAL PRACTICE. If she was into supplying drugs the same way Dr.

Kent had been, this sign had to be one way she protected herself from selling to minors.

She checked the parking lot, taking note of the Mercedeses, Jags, and Audis surrounding her. A few spaces down, a petite, dark-haired woman quickly exited a bottle green Rolls-Royce. Slamming the door with a thrust of her size-2 hips, she brushed off her white designer jeans while she raced to the building in the light rain.

Ellie slipped from her BMW and followed Ms. Dolce & Gabbana. She'd seen the complete outfit, including the woman's sleeveless D&G floral-print top, while gawking at an online Web site with Viv. Even on sale, the two pieces cost over a thousand dollars. No doubt about it, Dr. Bordowski's clientele was pretty much the same as Dr. Kent's had been. In fact, she'd bet money Dr. Bordowski had picked up a few of the deceased doctor's patients already.

Walking a short distance behind Ms. D&G, Ellie entered the building and followed the woman through a foyer and into the waiting room. The cool inside air held the faint scent of lemon and verbena. Classical music played over the sound system, while the end tables held a few more magazines than Dr. Kent had provided, and the same huge glass jar of iced lemon water sat on a sideboard against a far wall. The office furniture, a mix of beachy rattan and oak, gave the room a casual yet elegant feel.

Six women looked up when she and Ms. D&G arrived inside, but only one nodded a hello. The others quickly returned to their reading material. Ellie took a second scan of the room and spotted a large Plexiglas window next to a door that she assumed led to the examining rooms. When Ms. D&G walked to the window, wrote something on a clipboard sitting on the ledge, and took a seat, Ellie figured the receptionist had taken a day off because of the weather.

She sauntered to the window as if she knew the program and clearly printed her name on the patient list. Unfortunately, the names of those who'd signed in before her were impossible to read. These women had either flunked penmanship, or they wrote in a secret code known only to themselves and the doctor.

Hoping to appear unassuming, she sat next to the only woman who'd actually acknowledged her presence when she entered the room. The patient, close to her mother's age, had a remarkably unlined face, courtesy of Botox, she imagined, and seemed friendlier than the others present.

Searching for a conversation starter, Ellie focused on the woman's wrist and immediately recognized her watch. Georgette had given her a similar gift for her college graduation, along with a warning. It was one in a series of special timepieces, each of which cost over twenty-five thousand dollars. The fact that she owned something that rare and expensive so terrified Ellie that the watch was still in its original box on a shelf in her closet.

"Excuse me," she began, eyeing the watch. "Is that a Girard-Perregaux you're wearing? I haven't seen one is a while. It's quite beautiful."

"This old thing?" The woman gave another Botox grin, which meant nothing moved though her eyes did sparkle. "It was my grandmother's. The darling passed away about ten years ago and it's been mine ever since, even though my sisters tried to get it away from me in a battle of, shall we say, wills."

Thinking her answer was a perfect intro to Dr. Kent's death, Ellie said, "Don't you just hate it when people die without a will? I heard that's what's going on because of Martin Kent's murder. Poor Arlene is trying to sort it all out, but it's been difficult."

"You're a friend of Arlene's?" Watch Lady blinked. "What a coincidence. I know her, too."

"Really?" said Ellie, working to keep the inquisition on track. "Then you were with the group that was banned from the prewedding party because of the doctor's demise."

"Well, not exactly," the woman continued. "I've always been a patient of Dr. Bordowski's, but I met Dr. Kent when Sabrina threw a get-together to announce the opening of his new office in Montauk. Arlene was there, of course, and since then I've seen her around." She folded the magazine she'd been reading and inched closer. "I heard that Dr. Kent had his faults, as do most men, but they seemed like a happy couple. I can't believe someone killed him."

"All I know is the family is in shock," Ellie replied, her voice low. "I'm here because I had a little . . . accident . . ." She removed her sunglasses. "And I'm looking for something to take the edge off the pain. I was hoping to get a prescription from Dr. Kent, but that never happened, and I was told Dr. Bordowski could take care of me."

"Oh, dear," said Watch Lady, grimacing when she saw Ellie's face. "That does look nasty. How did you—"

The far door opened and a woman walked out, followed by the doctor, who kissed the patient's cheek, then checked her clipboard. After locating the next name, she walked to one of the waiting patients and whispered a welcome. A moment later, both women disappeared through the door.

"That's the one thing I like so much about Sabrina," said Watch Lady. "Everything she does is private. I've been here when there were twenty women waiting, and no one spoke unless they were drawn into conversation by a friend." She raised her sculpted nose in the air. "If you hadn't asked about Grandma Marion's watch, I doubt we'd have said a word."

Ellie bit her lower lip. "I don't mean to be nosy, but why the secrecy? This is a doctor's office. Why don't these women discuss their ailments?"

The question seemed to set off an alarm in Watch Lady's brain. "I don't believe that's any of your concern," she answered, returning to her magazine.

Well, crap. "Do you know of anyone else who might see me without an appointment? My face really hurts."

Watch Lady thought for so long Ellie was positive she wouldn't answer. Then she said, "Tell me, how did you get that horrendous bruise in the first place?"

Close to whispering a snarky comment, Ellie smiled. It couldn't hurt to gloss over the truth here, since Watch Lady wasn't one of Arlene's friends. "I tripped and fell down a set of stairs that led to the beach. Landed face-first on the bottom step."

"I see a lawsuit in your future. You know, negligence on the part of the homeowner, or are you at the Montauk Manor?"

"A private house," she said, not wanting to get an innocent hotel in trouble. "And yes, I've already consulted an attorney."

"Are you here alone, or was someone with you when it happened?"

"I'm with a friend, but this is my first time 'out east.' As you can see, I'm not familiar with the rules, and I do appreciate you taking the time to fill me in." She figured she was on a roll, so why stop now? "Tell me, have you ever had any trouble getting a prescription for pain from Dr. Bordowski?"

Watch Lady finally cracked a real grin. "Sabrina gives me anything I ask for. Just name your poison and bring the prescription to the drugstore in Montauk. Uncle Mickey will fix you right up."

The front door opened and another woman walked in. At the same time, Sabrina Bordowski escorted her last patient out. Then she walked to Watch Lady and held out her hand. After that, things got complicated.

The doctor glanced at Ellie and flared her nostrils, glaring like a professional female wrestler Ellie had once seen on the TV. Come to think of it, she was built like one, too, nearly six feet tall, with broad shoulders and man-sized hands. "Have we met?"

"I believe we were both at the prewedding party for Dr. Kent and Arlene," Ellie answered.

"Ah, I thought you looked familiar." She scanned Ellie's face with a trained eye. "That looks painful."

"It's the reason I'm here."

"I've been telling her you'll take care of her, Sabrina, so be nice," said Watch Lady.

"Most of the patients I see are here because they've had a personal recommendation," the doctor said.

"Oh—ah—Arlene sent me. She said you and Dr. Kent were in the same type of practice."

"Really?"

"She did."

The doctor nodded. "I'll be with you soon." She waggled a finger and Ellie's new friend, the nameless watch lady, followed Dr. Bordowski through the door.

Ellie settled into a chair in the doctor's office. Ms. D&G had just left the building, marching away in a fit of temper without the usual escort. And that was odd, because every other client had been given a friendly but professional sendoff as they were guided out. But before she had a chance to think on it further, Sabrina took her in hand.

"Rumors travel fast around here, especially in the summer."

Dr. Bordowski trailed her fingers over the bump on Ellie's forehead. "I heard someone broke into Arlene's house a few nights ago and you were the one who stopped the intruder, so I assume that's where you got this beauty of a bruise." She raised an eyebrow as she studied the lump. "I see you didn't need stitches, and I doubt you'll have a scar. Whoever applied the butterfly bandage did a decent job."

"Um, a police officer who came with Detective Wheeling took care of it." Ellie had sat in the waiting room for over an hour, which gave her plenty of time to think of what she would say. There was no way she'd talk about her connection to James Bond and the DEA with Sabrina Bordowski. If she was involved in Dr. Kent's drug ring . . .

"You say you're having a lot of pain. On a scale of one to ten, how bad is it?"

"At least a nine," Ellie lied. "I know people have different pain thresholds, but I'm a sissy. Splinters make me cry, and headaches do me in. Since I was slammed during the burglary, the jackhammer inside my head never seems to stop."

Dr. Bordowski narrowed her blue eyes. "Surely you've been able to borrow something from Arlene."

How many lies can I tell before I get caught?

"Arlene is going through a—a catharsis of sorts. When she found out about the charges the DEA planned to level against her fiancé, she flushed all but a few of her meds. The cops searched her house and her medicine cabinet, and she came up clean. She sent me here," Ellie continued. "Said you and Dr. Kent were in the same—um—line of work."

"Did she, now?" The doctor frowned and ran a finger under Ellie's eye. "It sounds as if the two of you are close."

"I'm a friend of her youngest sister." There was no reason to lie about her connection to Vivian. "She keeps me informed on everything that's happening in the case. And I did have dinner with Arlene last night."

The doctor trailed her fingers from the bridge of Ellie's nose to the tip. "Any pain here?"

"Yes. Especially when I sneeze." That was true.

"So, what have you been using to take the edge off?"

Reaching back in her brain, Ellie recalled the name of the two pills Viv had given her on the night of the attack. "Valium to calm me down and help me sleep and Percocet for the pain. But Arlene's running low. She said she might come to you herself later. Something about her prescriptions running out."

"Hmm. Has she talked to Mickey?" Sabrina cupped Ellie's chin and turned her head to get a side view of the bump. "He'd probably be able to fix her up." She removed her hand, picked up a manila folder she'd started when Ellie came in, and wrote something down. "Did you have an X-ray or MRI?"

"Uh, no." Though she probably should have. "I was flat on my back for a day. Then we had to—to—help Arlene with the memorial details."

After walking to her desk chair and taking a seat, Dr. Bordowski scribbled another notation in the chart. "Have you been dizzy or nauseated? Are you keeping your food down?"

"No problem there," Ellie said, relieved she could give another true answer. "But the headache never seems to go away, even with the Percocet. And it's really hard to fall asleep."

"How long are you staying here?"

"Just a couple more days."

"I could send you for an MRI, though I think you're out of danger. You live in Manhattan?"

"The Upper East Side."

"Do you have a family doctor?"

Only Rudy's vet, Dr. Dave. "Not really. Can I just go to the emergency room?"

"A walk-in clinic might do it, but you'd still need a doctor's prescription, and it would cost you a bundle. Do you have health insurance?"

"A private plan, yes."

She scratched a name on the pad and passed it over. "Lorraine Lewis is a good family practice doc. If the pain is still unbearable in another week, tell her I sent you. She can handle further testing.

"And for now . . ." Dr. Bordowski quickly wrote two prescriptions and passed them across the blotter. "One of these is for the pain and another is a sleeping aid, but they have a little more kick than the Percocet and Valium. Go to Uncle Mickey and he'll take care of you." She stood, signaling the meeting was over.

Ellie collected her slicker and tote bag and followed the doctor to the door. She hadn't said a word about the bill for an office visit, which seemed strange. "Don't you want my insurance information? I'm not sure what my copay is, but I'd be happy to write you a check."

"Consider this visit on the house. I just want to ask one more thing."

"Yes."

"When and where is Marty's memorial service going to be held? I wouldn't miss it for the world."

Ellie left East Hampton, careful to obey all the traffic rules as she drove, just in case Officer O'Brien was still on scouting duty. The sun shining through a thin layer of clouds was a sure sign the storm had passed, but the downed branches and excess water clogging the streets made travel, on foot or by car, a soggy mess.

It was close to three, and she was hungry, but she had to do one more thing before she returned to Arlene's. Staying on the main road instead of turning onto Old Montauk Highway, she rolled into downtown Montauk and pulled up in front of Michael Forrest's drugstore.

Once inside, she took her time wandering the aisles. As on her first visit, the store held the usual mixture of toddler, teen, and adult customers. Several women were talking about the storm while they picked through easy-fold umbrellas and rain slickers. A group of kids inspected the coloring books, crayons, and puzzles displayed in the magazine racks. A trio of adolescent boys thumbed through video rentals, and a couple of teenage girls were giggling in the makeup section while they inspected lipsticks and fingernail polish.

She stopped near the women, hoping to overhear

some bit of conversation about their need for "happy pills," but the talk centered on how to entertain small children in foul weather. Though aware that drug dependency could hit men and women of any age, Ellie had no idea how to start a conversation on the ins and outs of acquiring unprescribed pills to aid with depression, anxiety, or lack of sleep.

After sidling past a group of tweens checking out sunglasses, she arrived at the prescription counter and stood in line behind two women. Uncle Mickey was nowhere to be seen, so she studied the patrons, curious, as she always was, about her fellow man. The moment she got a good look at what the woman directly in front of her wore, she sucked in a "hello." Ms. D&G seemed edgy, crossing her arms, running her fingers through her short dark brown hair, and huffing out sighs like a three-pack-a-day smoker flying on a coast-to-coast flight.

Uncle Mickey came out from the bowels of the drug area, smiling his usual ear-to-ear grin, and passed the first customer a small bag. She handed him a credit card and he took care of the transaction, then sent her on her way with a cheery "Have a nice day."

When Ms. D&G took two awkward steps to the counter, the pharmacist's smile faded. He jerked his chin, as if dismissing the woman, and focused on Ellie. Ms. D&G stepped to the side, her face down, staring at her fidgeting fingers.

"Hey, there. How are you?" he asked, his grin back in place.

Ellie trained her gaze on Uncle Mickey, hoping to sneak a peek at the woman sometime during this encounter. "I'm fine, thank you. I'm here to have a couple of prescriptions filled."

"Well, you've come to the right place."

"Excuse me," Ms. D&G interrupted, "but I'm in a hurry. Mickey. I really need to speak with you."

The pharmacist's expression rolled back to frigid. "We've already had this discussion, Linda. I can't help you."

Linda shuddered a sigh. "Mickey, please. I don't have anywhere else I can go."

Doing her best to ignore Uncle Mickey and his customer, Ellie pretended to check out a display of postcards featuring the bounty and beauty of the Hamptons.

After another minute of arguing, Mickey said, "Come through the side door so we can continue this discussion." He gave Ellie a smile. "I'll be with you in a few minutes. I have to take care of this first."

Once Mickey disappeared, Ellie scrutinized the prescription area, saw that she was alone, and sidled to the door just entered by Ms. D&G. Leaning sideways, she plastered her ear against the door and held her breath. She was terrible at sneaking around, but this was her only chance to get a handle on Uncle Mickey and his business dealings.

"I'm willing to double the price," she heard the woman say. "There's nowhere else I can go."

"If Sabrina wouldn't give you a prescription, I can't help you. Someone's tightened the noose on this end of the island." From the sound of his voice, the cheerful Uncle Mickey had turned into a grump. "Without a current prescription, I'm on hold for a while."

"But I need the Concerta. I've gained four pounds since I sprained my ankle in the last tennis tournament. If I can't exercise, I eat." The woman's last words came out in a sob. "You have friends—connections—in the business. Surely you could send me to someone who would—" Linda's voice dropped to a muffled mix of words.

Ellie remembered Agent Bond's quick diatribe the night he'd accused Arlene of drug abuse. It sounded as if Ms. D&G was a perfect example of the typical user with her need for Schedule II pharmaceuticals.

After a moment, Uncle Mickey said, "Here, this is the best I can do."

Ellie skittered back to her spot and continued her postcard perusal. A moment later Ms. D&G slipped out the door carrying a small white bag, and hurried away without a glance in Ellie's direction. A few seconds later, Uncle Mickey returned to the counter.

"Sorry about that," he said. "Sometimes it takes a while to get through to a customer."

"Is she a regular?" Ellie asked, trying to sound innocent and disinterested.

"A local, at least during the summer. Her husband is some big real estate mogul in the city, and he sticks her in their beach house for four months out of the year. She gets bored and—" He shrugged. "Never mind. How can I help you?"

Mental fingers crossed, Ellie pushed the two prescriptions across the counter. "I heard her mention Dr. Bordowski. That's where I got these."

Mickey collected the sheets of paper and gave them a quick once-over. Then he took a good look at Ellie's face. "That's right. I heard you were the one that burglar bounced around the other night. I'm surprised Arlene didn't fix you up."

"Arlene's downsizing her drug cabinet. Seems she's worried that someone might be looking into Dr. Kent's records."

"Is that so?"

"It's what she said."

Mickey raised an eyebrow. "Hmm."

"You can fill the prescriptions, right? Dr. Bordowski said you were the man to see, but there's another drug-store across the circle. I wouldn't mind going there if you don't have—"

"No, no. We're fine. I have both of these in the back. Just give me a couple of minutes."

He left and Ellie blew out a breath. Then the over-head speaker clicked on and a voice said, "Pickup in pharmacy, Mickey. Pickup in pharmacy."

Aware an incoming call meant she'd have to wait, Ellie took a seat on a metal bench along the wall and let her thoughts roam. The next time she saw Jim Bond, she needed to ask him about Michael Forrest. How involved did the DEA think he was in Dr. Kent's illegal business? Was he under surveillance, too? And what about the women out here who bought the drugs? Were any of them working as a plant for the DEA?

From what she understood, refilling prescriptions too soon, or selling the drugs without a prescription, was against the law. Doctors and nurse practitioners had a national provider identification number, registered with the DEA. The number was used to track sales so overuse of certain drugs didn't occur.

That last idea made plenty of sense to her. Ms. D&G had all the symptoms of a user—at least, all the symp-toms Ellie had heard about. How hard would it be to insert someone who said they were a summer guest and needed relief from any one of a dozen ailments? If they didn't have a prescription, Uncle Mickey might sell them the drugs straight out.

Maybe somehow, he and Martin Kent had figured a way to sell the drugs privately. But something went wrong and they had an argument or . . .

It boggled her mind. She'd learned more about the drug scene than she'd ever thought possible this past week. Any accomplished liar could fake a reason to need more meds.

Drug mixing was another huge problem. Heath Ledger, Anna Nicole Smith, Michael Jackson, and dozens of other stars had taken that route and ended up dead. If it continued unchecked, could it happen to Arlene or Adrianne?

"Ms. Engleman?"

Ellie jumped when she heard her name. Looking to her right, she saw Uncle Mickey's head peering around the counter window.

"Sorry it took some time, but your medication is ready."

She stood and dug through her bag. After finding her wallet, she passed him her credit card.

A minute later, package of drugs in hand, she was sitting in the contrary BMW, shifting and jerking her way back to Arlene's manor.

Chapter 17

"Why the rush?" asked Rudy as Ellie dashed around the bedroom collecting clothes.

"We're late for dinner, and there's a lot to discuss with the McCreadys. I have to find out how Arlene and Viv did with the memorial invitations, see if Detective Wheeling or Jim Bond came nosing around, make sure Rosa and her family are—"

"I listened in on Viv and Arlene makin' those calls, and they did fine."

"You listened in? Since when did that become your job?" Ellie found the sweater she'd been looking for, navy blue with tiny white dots. She planned to wear it over a red T with her white cigarette pants. Dressing as she walked, she finished in the bathroom. "What am I saying? Never mind how you found out, just tell me what you learned."

Rudy parked himself on the plush turquoise rug in front of the shower stall. *"Everybody said yes. People even called here, sayin' they heard about the memorial and wanted to come. In fact, the word spread so fast that Arlene and Rosa decided to call a caterer to be sure they'd have enough food."*

"Good grief, really?"

"Yep. Vivie thinks they're all nosy Nellies. Just want to see if they could pick up more dirt on the doc." He scratched his side with a rear paw, then sighed. *"Ahh, that's better."*

"Leave it to Viv to figure out the real reason people would care about Dr. Sleazeball." Ellie checked her face in the mirror. The bump on her temple was down, the gash was healing, and the bruise had faded. The edges now inched from yellow to green to blue, but the bump itself was still a deep purple. "I look like I'm ready for Halloween," she muttered, wondering if there was anything she could slap on her skin to make the mask disappear.

"You should wear that knot like a badge of courage. Remember, you got it by surprisin' a burglar. If I ever find the guy who did that to you, I'll—"

"You'll do what?" She sat on the commode lid. "The man was big and burly, like a pro football player. He'd chew you up and spit you out in one bite."

"Okay, then, think on it. Who'd you run into in this investigation that fits that description?"

Ellie quirked her lips. How dumb could she be? Rudy was correct, as usual. She hadn't once added the size of the burglar to the equation. Whoever flattened her was strong, just like whoever had pushed Dr. Kent backward hard enough to make him fall. She'd been stupid, worrying about Arlene's and Adrianne's drug use, when she simply should have focused on the clues she'd collected.

Who called Dr. Kent Marty?

Who was in the drug business?

Whose voice did Myron imitate in the threats?

Who was big and powerful enough to mow her down?

Uncle Mickey, she concluded. The answer to all the clues pointed to him like a GPS with extra radar.

"Why are you smilin'?"

Ellie bent and rubbed Rudy's ears. "Because it always pays to listen to you."

"I been tellin' you that since you found me in the big house," he said, flopping to his back.

She gave him one of her best belly rubs, hitting all the good spots as he wriggled and groaned. "Okay, enough until later. We have a dinner to go to, and later tonight I have to talk things over with Viv."

Rudy stood and gave a full body shake. *"Lead the way, Triple E. I'll add color commentary if anyone forgets what the day was like."*

She slipped a pen and her notebook in one pocket, then set her phone on vibrate and tucked it in her other pocket in case Sam called. She and Rudy took the rear stairs down as they talked. "Was T around? Did he pay attention to things?"

"Sort of. I think he was more interested in guarding the back deck. He kept watchin' the guesthouse, growlin' if a car pulled in to read the notice."

"Did Vanessa and Evan show up?"

"Nah. They drove away for lunch and came back later."

"Did you see Adrianne?"

"Nope."

They arrived in the kitchen and Ellie inhaled a wonderful aroma. After quickly mixing Rudy's dinner, she set it on the floor, then scanned the kitchen and spotted several pots bubbling on the stove. Smiling, she walked to the terrace door. Rosa had something special cooking for tonight, and if she was right, it was going to be delicious.

She checked the outdoor seating arrangements before she made her entrance. Vanessa and Evan sat on one side of the table, Viv on the other with Arlene at the far end, while Rosa served some kind of salad. Everyone seemed calm and in a good mood.

Best of all, no Adrianne.

Rudy, a power eater, nudged her calf and they went onto the deck together. When she took her seat, Viv said, "I don't know about the rest of you, but I could eat three or four all by myself." She scooped up a forkful of salad, then looked at Ellie. "Lucky you got here before Rosa served the main course, or you might have left hungry."

"Main course?" said Ellie, playing stupid.

"Lobster." Viv raised her wineglass. "In preparation for tomorrow's unveiling. Rosa found a sale at a local seafood shop. She's celebrating the capture of the real killer, so Tomas will be exonerated."

Ellie stifled a groan. What if she was wrong? What if Uncle Mickey wasn't the killer? What if she let her friend, and Vivian's family, down?

"Um, maybe we're jumping the gun." *Oops. That was a stupid comment.* "I mean, I'm not sure the setup will work here, like it always does for Hercule Poirot. Just remember, he's a model of the perfect detective living in someone's imagination." *To be blunt, the creation of some boring mystery writer looking to be a true-to-life detective.* "Let's not get our hopes up, okay?"

"Awwwk! Hope! I hope you know what you're doin', Marty. Awwwk! Don't try to cheat me. I'll find out. Awwwk!"

Rosa and the rest of the clan paid the African gray no mind. Standing next to Arlene, she said, "Ah, but we believe in you, Miss Ellie. You have done this for other friends, and we know you won't let us down."

"Downtown! Awwwk! Everything's great when you're dooown-town. Awwwk!"

Vanessa gave the bird a look, while Arlene smiled. "Myron's just expressing himself. He has no other way to communicate."

"I hope you don't plan on having him in the middle of the memorial service. Can you imagine the ruckus if he starts to sing?" said Vanessa.

"Awwwk! Sing. Sing a song. Sing it gentle. Awwwk! Sing it all night long. Awwwk!"

Arlene blew the parrot a kiss. "Mommy loves her boy." She stood and dug in her pocket. "Just let me give him an M&M." She kept digging while Myron squawked; then she frowned. "Sorry, baby. Mommy must have left them in the kitchen drawer."

"Awwwk! Good dog. Good boy," Myron continued. Then he began to bark and the three Boston Terriers joined in.

"That's it," Evan said, rising to his feet and tossing his napkin on the table. He stomped to the perch, took it in hand, and disappeared through the door.

"Myron is all I have to remember the last good man in my life by," Arlene said, her voice trembling. "I can't imagine why all those people want to pay their respects to Martin. He was a drug dealer and practically a pedophile. I decided I'm going to hold the main service on the beach and let the tide take him away." Tears filled

Arlene's eyes. "I still can't believe I almost married the man." She sobbed. "Worse, that he slept with my sister."

Evan returned while she was talking and took his seat. "Don't worry, honey. We're straightening it all out. For now, I have a little speech to make. Hear, hear!" he began, tapping his wineglass with his fork. "I know it's a bit premature, but I believe we should toast Ellie for the work she's done for us."

Everyone did as he asked and Ellie inhaled a breath. With Arlene so maudlin, this was not the time to add to her tears. All she could do was mutter a grateful "Thank you."

The family finished their salads while she continued to think of tomorrow and the idea of so many strangers flooding the estate. Somehow, she had to get the extended family into the house alone so she could untangle the strings to get Uncle Mickey arrested.

Viv stood and cleared the plates. "I'm going to help Rosa," she said, heading for the door. "Be back in a second."

Vanessa reached across the table and touched Ellie's hand. "Viv told me you were on a clue hunt today. Did you find anything you can share with us?"

"I can share, but you both have to promise to keep your lips zipped. If I'm correct, revealing the culprit too early could ruin everything."

"Then don't tell us," said Evan. "Vanessa has a hard time keeping a secret and—"

"I do not," Vanessa bit out. "But I can wait. It's almost like watching a movie unfold and waiting until the big moment when the hero unveils the killer."

"Do you really know who killed Martin?" asked Arlene, her voice still quivering.

"I think so, though it wouldn't be smart to alert the murderer ahead of time," she said, hoping she sounded as if she knew what she was doing. "I believe surprise is everything in this type of situation."

"Okay, fine. I can buy that," said Evan. "Besides, if I know ahead of time, I might just whack the guy over the head when he walks through the door." He sipped his wine. "In case you haven't noticed, I tend to get hot under the collar when things get tough."

"I noticed," said Ellie, "and I'm happy you agree to keep the killer under wraps. If I'm wrong, the night could be an utter failure." She glanced around the table. "I noticed that Adrianne is missing. Any news about her?"

Arlene shook her head. "Mom and Dad have her under house arrest."

"She's been ordered to her room," said Vanessa. "Where she will stay until she agrees to apologize to Arlene for her totally inexcusable behavior. She owes an apology to you and Vivian, as well." She crossed her arms on the table. "We're giving her time to think about the damage she's done to this family."

"We're treating her the way we should have when she was a child," added Evan. "Letting her get away with things wasn't just Vanessa's fault. I did it, too."

"I imagine she's not happy about that," said Ellie. Adrianne was in her midthirties and still living off Mom and Pop. If that had turned out to be her, Ellie would have done anything to set herself free.

"Well, I don't care," Vanessa answered after taking a swallow of wine. "Of course, she's not speaking to us. She's been hiding in her room, playing loud music and stomping around. There's food in the kitchen, so she fixes her own meals, and she has a laptop and her painting supplies, so I believe she's all set."

"Has she said anything to you about why she wanted to hurt Arlene?"

"Not a word," said Evan. "And that troubles me. It's almost as if she's planning some type of revenge."

The remark added to Ellie's worries. "Revenge?"

"I have no idea what, but Vanessa and I have already come up with our version of 'tough love.' We told Adrianne she has two choices: She can move out, support herself, and find out how to live in the world on her own, or she can spend a few months in rehab. We'll pay the bill and she can put her priorities and her life in order."

Arlene leaned into the table. "They found a place in upstate New York that handles people with all sorts of problems. Adrianne can paint, eat healthy food, talk to professionals. They even have physical fitness classes, so she can continue her martial arts training." Her expression grew rigid. "If you ask me, that's more like a vacation than a place to reform your life."

"We're asking her for a three-month commitment," Evan continued. "Then we'll welcome her back to the family fold."

"Well, that's—that's some offer." Ellie couldn't believe Adrianne would accept such a challenge. She seemed too used to getting her way after so many years.

Viv took that moment to push through the door, carrying a tray filled with so many gadgets Ellie had to concentrate to name them all. Besides the tools for eating a lobster, there were small stands holding candles, bigger stands with cuts of butter on the top, plates, and more napkins.

Setting down the tray, Viv said to her dad, "How about passing things out and starting up the butter warmers? Rosa has the food, but it's on two more trays."

Two more trays?

Evan separated all the pieces and passed them around. When he was done, he opened the box of matches Viv had supplied and lit the candles under the towers topped with butter. "Good thing each of these warmers has a shield. One gust of wind and the flame would be gone." He took his seat. "Hot butter is the best way to enjoy these babies."

Ellie removed her navy sweater, aware that when most people ate lobster, the fishy liquid usually flew in all directions, and, along with the McCreadys, donned the full-body plastic apron Rosa had supplied.

The kitchen door swung out and Viv appeared, a large platter piled high with steaming ears of corn, a stack of rolls, and lemon wedges in hand. She bumped her butt on the door and held it open for Rosa's grand entrance with a huge tray filled with bright red lobsters.

"Ta-daa," said Viv in an exaggerated tone, setting her tray on one end of the table. "Dad, do you want to do the honors?"

Evan stood and reached for the platter. "I say we all just dig in. One at a time please. Looks like there's plenty for everyone."

"What do you mean 'the painting is gone'?" Ellie asked Viv later, when the McCreadys had left for a movie along with Rosa, Julio, and their daughters.

"Exactly what I said. I took a walk today after Arlene and I made our calls and ended up near the guest cottage. I was going to see if Adrianne would talk to me, but she didn't answer when I knocked on the apartment door, so I wandered into the doc's office."

"And . . ."

"And the wall was empty. I thought maybe Arlene had Julio or Tomas remove the portrait and burn it."

"Burn it?"

"That's what I would have done. I came back here and mentioned it to Arlene, and she said she had no idea where the painting went."

"Was she worried? Did she think someone broke in and stole it? Maybe somebody who was looking for Dr. Kent jimmied the lock, saw it, and took it out."

"Good for them, is all I have to say. I hope the stupid thing ends up on display at the Guggenheim with Adrianne's name plastered over her ass."

Ellie recalled all that had happened on this vacation that would make her best friend so sour. Viv had wanted to come here for some R&R and a little sisterly bonding. Instead, she'd fallen into a family disaster that had yet to end. "I wouldn't have minded if you went to the movies with your parents and Arlene tonight."

Viv emptied the last of the pinot grigio into her glass and took a long drink. "And leave you here to plot out tomorrow night all alone? Not a chance." She stood and brushed off her purple sweater, definitely not from the Ralph Lauren collection. "I'll be right back."

Ellie rested an elbow on the table and placed her chin in her palm. Who could have taken that painting? And what were they planning to do with it?

When Viv returned with a corkscrew and another bottle of wine, Ellie sighed. "Uh, Viv, don't you think you've had enough?"

Vivian shrugged. "Who the hell cares? My family is

falling apart and I can't do a thing to stop it. Now I'm wondering if it's my fault, something that could have been fixed years ago. Maybe I shouldn't have gotten so angry when they forgot my birthday, or Mom took Adrianne to the spa and not me. Maybe I could have—"

Ellie laid a hand on her friend's arm. "No, you couldn't have. They were the ones who left you out in the cold. Look at it this way. Their neglect is one of the reasons we're so close. I don't have a sister, so I adopted you, and you've been the best sister a girl could hope for. You know how to be warm, funny, and supportive. Without you, I'd probably be wearing army fatigues and combat boots. You've turned me into a fashion plate—"

Viv swiped a tear from her cheek. "Let's not go that far. You have a long way to go before you're a fashion plate."

"It might still happen," said Ellie, grinning. "For now, why not forget about the wine and help me finish the plan for tomorrow? I need someone with a clear head, and if you drink any more wine, I'll have to—"

"Talk to me," came a voice from under the table.

"I'll have to talk things over with Rudy."

Viv pushed the wine bottle and corkscrew out of reach. "You're right. Let me hear what you found out so we can finalize things."

Ellie pulled the notebook and pen from her side pocket. "Before I tell you about my day, I want to hear about yours. Arlene hinted that she was expecting a lot of people. Is that true?"

"Oh, please, you wouldn't believe it. We started calling right after you left and by the time we were finished, Arlene's house phone was swamped." Viv narrowed her eyes. "I envision a three-ring circus, complete with the clowns, so when I invited Detective Wheeling I suggested he bring officers for crowd control."

"Wow. That's hard to believe." Ellie pulled the paper napkin out from under her wineglass and began to shred it. "You didn't tell him about our plan to unmask the killer, did you?" She crossed mental fingers. *If we come up with a plan . . .*

Viv cracked a smile. "Of course not. I want to see him grovel when you hand over the murderer. Agent Bond, too."

"Did you actually talk to him?"

"To Double O Seven? No. I left a message on his phone, and he hasn't returned the call."

"I don't expect he will." Ellie shrugged. "My guess is he'll just show up, as usual."

"And how did things go for you?" Viv gazed at the darkening sky and the silver quarter moon hanging over the water. "Wait. It's getting late. How about we go up to bed, and you give me what you have there?"

"Okay, fine," Ellie answered, breathing a sigh of relief. Maybe she'd have an *aha!* moment in the next few minutes, and find the last few pieces of this puzzle.

Viv cleared the leftovers from the table while Ellie led Mr. T and Rudy down the stairs and into a pen. "Last out of the day, boys. Do your business so we can call it a night."

A moment later, Viv joined her at the bottom of the stairs. "I've been thinking. I don't believe we'll ever find out about the painting. If Adrianne took it, well, she's the artist and she's also the person in the portrait. She gave it to Dr. Kent as a gift, and now she's taken it back."

"Arlene should talk to a lawyer. The way I understand it, the doc's brother has signed off on everything, so it's hers. Dr. Kent's two cars are still in the parking lot, his boat is in Sag Harbor, and his clothes are in her house." Ellie opened the gate and let Rudy and Mr. T out. "She said he didn't have a will, so what is she supposed to do with it all?"

"Donate it to a good cause?" Viv grinned. "I bet Martin Kent would have a fit if he knew every nickel of his dirty money went to charity."

They laughed in tandem as the brisk ocean breeze seemed to push them up the stairs. By the time they reached the deck, Ellie was happy she'd slipped her sweater on after dinner. When her cell vibrated as they were opening the rear door, she stopped and checked the number. "Vivie, it's Sam. Can you take the boys up? I'll meet you there in a couple of minutes."

Viv gave her a wave, corralled the dogs, and scooted them through the kitchen.

"Hey, you," Ellie began, greeting her guy.

"Hey, yourself. How are you?" Sam asked, his tone low.

"I'm fine . . . just great." She walked to the fruit bowl as she talked. "How about you?"

"Things are a little slow. I was thinking about taking that ride we talked about."

Choosing an apple, she cut off a chunk and brought it to Myron. When she heard Sam's comment, she swallowed a protest. "Uh, ride? We talked about a ride?"

"We discussed it in our last call. I asked you if there was time for me to come out, and you said something about a memorial service for that friend of Viv's sister. I told you I'd be happy to show up and help you take your mind off things."

"Oh, oh, yeah. That ride. But the service is tomorrow night, and we have a ton of work to do here to prepare.

And I heard there might be another round of storms coming in. That's going to make more trouble. I just don't think it's a convenient time for us to be together."

"More storms? Funny, because I talked to Captain Carmody a little while ago, and he said tomorrow is supposed to be a beautiful day 'out east.' He practically ordered me to take some time off and go see you for a day or two."

"Captain Carmody said that?" *The dirty rat!* She sat at the breakfast table and slumped in the chair. "How sweet of him."

"I thought it was a nice gesture. So, what do you think?"

The knot on her forehead began to throb. She'd already told him what she thought. What else could she say to keep Sam away? Next thing she knew, the cast of *Riverdance* was doing a warm-up drill in her temple.

"The man sees how hard you work. I'm sure he meant it as a reward of sorts, but this just isn't a good time."

"Okay, if you say so, but I really miss you. I've grown used to having someone sleep next to me."

"Lucky for me I still have Rudy."

"Ha-ha. Next thing I know you'll be letting him into bed with us."

"Only when you're not there. He's been very good here. He's still protecting me"—she swallowed—"from—from—things."

"From things?" Sam went into cop mode. "What kind of things?"

If she blurted out one word about the police or the DEA, she was toast. "Uh—stupid stuff. Arlene's three Boston Terriers, her African gray. That sort of thing." The *Riverdance* cast slowed their drill. "That's all." She took a deep breath. "I have to go, Sam. Viv's waiting for me upstairs."

"Planning on a little girl talk?"

"Yep. Girl talk. So I'll say good night. But I'll be home in three more days. That's not so long."

"Nope, not so long. Okay, babe. See you soon. And be careful, whatever you do."

Ellie closed her phone. *Be careful, whatever I do?* What was that all about? She heaved a sigh. Things were going fine until Sam mentioned Captain Carmody, though it didn't sound as if he knew about the conversation the captain had had with Jim Bond or her involvement in Dr. Kent's murder.

Sam always told her to be careful. It was probably nothing.

Putting the phone call behind her, she headed up the back stairs. She still had to fill Viv in on her trip to Dr. Bordowski, and she should probably tell her about the warning she'd received from Officer O'Brien.

They only had about eighteen hours to come up with a workable plan of action for unveiling a murderer, and she still had no idea what to do.

Chapter 18

The next morning, shortly before lunch, Tomas Suarez sat at the terrace table with Ellie and Viv, his shoulders hunched against the gloomy sky. The kid had a funky tattoo on his right arm she guessed was gang related, and another on his left wrist, but his hair was neat, his face free of stubble, and he wore clean but faded jeans and a sparkling white T-shirt. She was certain that Tomas, of medium height with a wiry build, could hold his own in any sort of one-on-one confrontation, especially with a weapon, like the knife the police had found under Dr. Sleazeball's desk.

Though he was polite, his sullen attitude made her again wonder if he was guilty of the doc's murder. But Ellie trusted Rosa and Julio's judgment. Their son swore his innocence with such conviction he'd agreed to go to Mexico with his parents and crawl on his hands and knees up the center aisle of a church, if Ellie could muster her crime-solving skills and prove him blameless.

And since the promise of a *manda* sounded sincere, she also had to assume that, with the help of his parents and sisters, Tomas would find his way back to his loving family. Which meant she had to ignore his punk guy attitude and fill him in on their plans for the beachside service.

"So you're saying you think this *hombre maldito* who killed the doc will be at tonight's memorial?" Tomas asked, raising an eyebrow. "And you're going to out him in front of the whole crowd."

"Not exactly the whole crowd," Ellie admitted. "Because if everyone who called and said they were attending actually showed up, there would be too many people to carry out our plan. We'll have to take the final steps inside the house, probably in the living room, with the smaller group that was at the family party that night."

"And *mi familia* will be allowed in? As guests—not just servants?"

"In order to show a united front, yes."

"Then you only want us there for show, not because we support Arlene or because we're a part of her life?" His smart-ass tone grew stronger. "That figures."

"Hey, Skippy," Viv interrupted, pointing a finger. "Arlene has treated each of the Suarezes like one of her own, including you. There's no way you can pull the race card here."

"What do you know, *hermanita?* I hear you weren't around Arlene enough to act like you cared. You never even met that loco slime-covered joke of a doctor she was so in love with."

Viv tugged her sweater tightly around her and blew out a breath. "Watch what you say, smart guy, or Ellie just might forget to do her thing. If that happens, the cops' case will go through and it'll be *hasta la vista, baby*, for you."

Ever the peacemaker, Ellie tried for a truce. "There's no need for either of you to get snarky. We're all hoping for the same outcome. We want the person who committed the crime to go to jail, and the one who's innocent to go free." She gave Tomas a warning frown. "Understand?"

Shrugging, he sank lower in his chair. "I guess."

Rosa trundled out from the kitchen with a pitcher of iced tea, took one look at her son, and shook her head. "*Basta, Tomas*! *Qué te pasa*? Treat Ellie *con respeto o si no, si no*, and help your father with the yard work, *ahora mismo.*"

"Sí, Madre." He pushed away from the table, his gaze still sullen and unforgiving.

"Tomas." Rosa set the pitcher of tea on the table with such force the liquid splashed out in a puddle.

"*Con su permiso*," he said with a dip of his chin, first toward his mother, then toward Ellie. He sulked off down the stairs and into the garden below.

"*Aye, mi hijo*," Rosa muttered, using a towel to wipe up the spill. "He has, how you say, *mucho rabia*, the chip on his shoulder. But he has promised us he is finished hanging out with bad friends. He will be taking a course this fall, learning how to repair cars. Arlene has offered to pay for the classes, and Julio and I promised her Tomas would pay her back every week, once he finds a job."

"Once this is over, he'll be fine," said Ellie. "Right, Viv?"

"Arlene will keep him on the straight and narrow, Rosa. I'm sure of it."

"Is there anything special you want me to do tonight?" the housekeeper asked, her tone a bit brighter.

"Just try to keep things as normal as possible," Ellie advised. "I've already given Terry and Maria their instructions. We'll want to keep all the guests together."

"Ah, I see." The housekeeper gave a tentative smile. "You know what you are doing, so I am returning to my apartment to put on something warmer. This weather, it is dark and dreary, perfect for an evening funeral."

Ellie and Viv had talked last night, and she still wasn't sure how her "plan" would play out, but she didn't want Rosa to feel defeated. When the housekeeper left, Viv leaned into the table. "Let's go over things again, okay? I don't want to do anything to screw it up."

"You're not the only one," Ellie confessed. "I'm not sure I can pull off my part, either."

"Well, there's a confidence builder," groused Viv. She opened her own spiral pad and surveyed her notes. "I need a timeline, which I trust you and big sis already went over."

Ellie flipped her tablet to the right page. "Arlene and your parents are at the crematorium as we speak, bringing home the doc's ashes in a plain plastic container. Arlene is pissed that he was such a creep and refuses to spend any more money than necessary to see Dr. Sleazeball off. Since his final resting place will be the bottom of the Atlantic, there's no need to buy anything fancy."

Viv stared at the gloomy sky. "Rosa's right about the day being perfect for a funeral, but plastic is too good for the man," said Viv. "If it was me, I'd bring his remains home in a paper cup."

"Me, too, but it's not our decision," Ellie said with a grin. "Next, Rosa is in charge of the caterers. They'll be here at four to set up. They're keeping it simple: canapés, soda, wine, and beer. Terry and Maria will build a child-sized sand castle at low tide, which is scheduled for"—she scrutinized her spiral—"five thirty-seven p.m. They checked the movement of the ocean with the scheduled reports and figure they have about an hour before the water starts to rise and washes the castle out to sea.

"Arlene will hold the short ceremony promptly at six thirty. The entire crowd will then retire to the deck and backyard by seven, where they will enjoy canapés, drinks, and gossip until they get shuttled out by Detective Wheeling's crowd control officers."

"And the immediate family and our suspects?"

This was the tough part. If anyone refused to stay, it could blow the entire plan apart. "Will be corralled by Julio, Terry, and Maria, and led into the living room, because they'll be told Arlene has something personal to share."

"And that will be our big moment. I can hardly wait," said Viv, smiling like a four-year-old at her birthday party.

"Just remember, somber is best in this situation. Don't give anyone a chance to ask what your sister is going to say. If you're cornered, lie your way out of it. I don't mean this the way it sounds, but that should be easy for you."

Viv tapped the tip of her pen on the table. "Because of the situation, it definitely will be." She glanced around the patio, then inched closer, as if she were a spy discussing a secret mission. "Where are we going to practice your act?"

"I thought we'd do it in the same place we'll handle it tonight. I want our prize clue giver to feel comfortable when he does his part."

After setting an elbow on the table, Viv cupped her chin in her hand. "Are you ready to start practicing now?"

Ellie pocketed her tablet and pen. "I think we'd better have lunch first. There's no telling how long this will take."

"Awwwk! None of that Polly want a cracker crap. I want truffles. Awwwk!"

"Oh, Lord, now what?" said Viv, shaking her head. "We've been at this all afternoon and that dopey bird has yet to follow through with one thing we've asked." She dropped into a chair. "Now he's demanding truffles."

"I doubt Arlene's ever given him an actual truffle, so I don't believe he really wants one," said Ellie.

She gritted her teeth and gave Myron a forced smile. She and Viv had eaten lunch, then brought the African gray into the living room and set his stand in the place Ellie thought it might work best. The weather forecasters were now predicting the next twenty-four hours would be cold and gloomy, so a glowing fire might help warm the chilly night. Myron liked it warm, and Arlene had told her he was sensitive to the vibes people threw off. The last thing she needed was a smart-mouthed pseudowitness.

"Ease up on the negativity, please. We're trying for a little cooperation here," she told Viv.

"Well, it doesn't look like we're going to get any," Viv muttered. "We've done everything but stand on our heads, and all that parrot does is yak senseless phrases and oldies tunes. Stupid bird."

"Bird, bird. Awwwk! The bird is the word. Awwwk!"

Frowning, Ellie rolled her eyes. Viv was correct. They'd been at this for so long, she'd forgotten when they started. Myron's seed dish was full, as was his water cup, and she'd fed him bits of raw apple. What more did he want? She cut her eyes to Viv, who was pacing with such determination she was going to wear a groove in Arlene's hardwood floor. "Maybe you should take a break. Go for a walk, see how the caterers and Rosa are doing with the setup, or help your dad with Arlene's speech."

Viv heaved a sigh. "You might be right. We're just not connecting with Myron, and you have more patience than I do. It's frustrating standing here listening to him and his silly antics."

"I thought that hanging-upside-down-by-one-leg thing he did was pretty impressive," said Ellie, giving a tired grin. They both turned at the sound of a police siren. When Ellie grounded herself, she gave Myron the evil eye. "That's not funny, mister. Stop playing games and start working with us."

The African gray cocked his head, raised one leg, and lifted his middle claw.

"I don't believe it," said Viv, her eyes narrowed to slits. "He's flipping you the bird."

Totally defeated, Ellie flopped into a chair. "If he acts like this tonight, I'll look like a fool and the entire exercise will be an embarrassment. James Bond and Detective Wheeling will laugh their heads off and the rest of the guests will think it's the evening's entertainment."

She looked at her watch. "Why don't you find Arlene and see if she's okay?"

Viv gave Myron another once-over. The parrot spread his wings like the American eagle and screeched.

"Okay, that's it! I say there's no way to get that bird to act human and cooperate." Viv stood and aimed for the foyer. "I'll start with Arlene. If she's all right, I'll move to Rosa, then the girls. One of them must need someone with a brain."

When Viv disappeared, Ellie turned to the African gray. He really was beautiful. Close to a foot in length, Myron had light gray feathers cloaking his body, a long red tail, and a black beak with a deadly-looking point at the hooked tip. Whenever she and the parrot locked gazes, she felt as if he was reading her from the inside out, gauging her thoughts and her emotions.

"You're goin' at this the wrong way, Triple E," Rudy quipped. He and T had been curled up sound asleep on a pair of wingback chairs in the living room through the entire ordeal.

"Excuse me?"

"Think on it a minute. Ol' Myron there is an animal. Animals work best for treats. You've given him food, but nothing special, so why should he talk for you?"

Ellie dinged the heel of her hand against her good temple. She was definitely batting zero in this game, while Rudy was batting a thousand.

"Vivie and I have been acting like idiots for the past couple of hours. Why didn't you say something before now?"

"Twink said you had to get it on your own. He was sure Viv would catch on."

"Do me a favor, please. Next time you see that I'm on the wrong track, don't listen to Mr. T. Speak up and set me straight. We wasted an afternoon, and I still don't know if what you're suggesting will work."

Rudy jumped off the chair, gave a full body shake, and parked his bottom on the floor. *"Then I guess you'd better get movin' and make sure it does."*

She opened and closed her mouth. Why argue, when he was right? "I'll be back in a second."

She walked to the kitchen and opened every drawer until she found what she was looking for. After dropping a handful of candies in her pocket, she headed for the living room. If the M&Ms didn't work, she was screwed.

Dressed in sandals, a pair of black linen slacks, a pale yellow T, and a black silk sweater, Ellie was ready to face the blustery evening. Standing on a far side of the crowd, she scanned the hundred or so people gathered to say a final good-bye to Martin Kent.

She still couldn't believe this many folks would be curious enough, or care enough, to pay their respects to an all but convicted criminal, but here they were.

She knew the extended family was attending in support of Arlene, but there had to be a few voyeurs hoping to hear a bit of gossip about the local doctor who had supposedly dealt illegal "happy pills" to people who were their neighbors. Some were probably customers, or women he slept with, sad to see their drug connection get washed away by the tide, while others might actually have known the man when he was a good and honest physician.

As promised, Detective Wheeling brought a cadre of uniformed officers to keep folks in line. The first of the police to arrive had taken over the job of guarding the sand castle so Terry and Maria could change into more presentable clothing. The rest set up a guard line of sorts, directing people straight to the sendoff site.

While in their bedroom getting ready for the event, Ellie and Viv decided to split up and each take a side of the crowd, while Evan had the task of keeping watch over Arlene and Vanessa. Julio became point man, in charge of seeing that the extended family stayed at the house when the service was over, and Tomas avoided the limelight and gave his mother a hand with the caterers.

With everyone now on the shore, it was Evan McCready who would give a short and impersonal good-bye to Martin Kent. First, Arlene opened the plastic box and sprinkled the ashes into the castle where the ocean breeze swirled them up, down, and around on the sand. Then, standing between his wife and daughter, with an arm around each, Evan raised his voice over the crashing of the waves and asked for silence.

"We're gathered here to say good-bye to a member of the community and a part of my daughter's life," he began.

The wind swept in from the ocean, cooling the air and making it difficult for him to be heard. When a voice rose above the sound of the crashing waves, Ellie squinted into the setting sun, surprised to see that the noisy mourner was Ms. D&G, probably crying, thought Ellie, because she'd lost her supplier.

Pulling Vanessa and Arlene closer to him, Evan continued as if he hadn't heard. "Martin Kent was a friend, a neighbor, and a physician who thought he was doing his best to help his fellow man. We say farewell to him now, and ask that you stand silent for a minute while the sea carries him to a better place."

Impressed with Evan's simple words, Ellie waited as the foamy water washed in, inching its way to the sand castle. Several women in the crowd sobbed quietly, while a few clustered to provide commentary. When the first wave touched the monument, she locked gazes with Viv. They were almost ready for the next act.

Detective Wheeling tipped his head to Evan once a minute had passed, and the senior McCready said, "My daughter Arlene would like you all to—"

"If you don't mind," came a voice from the center of the murmuring throng. The mob parted as Michael Forrest, better known as Uncle Mickey, muscled his way to the front. Evan stood strong, his arms still around his wife and daughter, but Uncle Mickey simply placed himself ahead of them.

"Sorry to interrupt the party. I know it wasn't planned that I talk, but Martin Kent was my friend. And he asked me to be the best man at his wedding, so I guess that gives me the right to speak here."

Detective Wheeling took a step nearer the activity, as did Julio, but Ellie and Viv held their ground. If Michael Forrest was planning to out himself as the killer, this was an odd way to do it.

He held up a ham-sized hand, and the crowd fell silent. "I'm here to say good-bye to a man who cared about his friends. In the future, you might hear some things about him that aren't so nice, but I'd like you to forget what you hear and remember him as he was." Uncle Mickey hung his head. "I can't imagine anyone trying to hurt him, but they did, and that was a damned shame, because Marty Kent was a man who did what he could to help his community." He sniffed back a tear. "And I'll miss him."

Then he stepped aside. "Sorry for the interruption, Mr. McCready, but I felt compelled to say my piece."

Viv shrugged, and Ellie knew what she was thinking. The pharmacist had the right to speak, even if he was the one who killed the deceased, but it was a strange thing to do.

Unless it was Uncle Mickey's way of throwing suspicion off himself.

Next came the second part of the evening. Wheeling's officers kept the attendees moving, and didn't allow anyone to veer toward the cottage or parking lot. When they reached the terrace steps, Ellie saw Tomas standing guard at the door leading to the kitchen. The catering staff had set up a bar on both ends of the deck, while a variety of canapés were waiting in trays on the main table.

People could stay on the deck, stand on the steps, or sit at the smaller tables arranged on the grassy area in front of the dog pens. Evan, Vanessa, Arlene, Ellie, and Viv were the last to reach the stairs. Rosa and the caterers were dispensing food up top, while Julio looked on.

"I'm glad this is almost over." Viv landed in a chair facing one of the tables. "This is tough work."

"The toughest is yet to come," Ellie reminded her. Taking a seat, she smiled at the Boston Terriers, Twink and Rudy, lined up behind the fence and staring at her. "Don't drop out on me now. You have to stay sharp and help me see this through to the end."

"How did things go at the service?" Rudy asked, his nose pushing against the screening.

As if she were taking a break, Ellie laid her head on her arm and whispered, "Fine, but Uncle Mickey stuck his three cents in after Evan's eulogy. He shed a tear, and told everyone how much he was going to miss the doc. It was weird."

"Maybe he wants people to feel sorry for him, so he'll look innocent when you put the finger on him?"

"I was thinking the same—"

"Are you talking to yourself again?" asked Viv. "Because trouble is coming our way."

Ellie looked up and saw Wheeling edging toward them with his partner, Detective Levy, at his side. She put on a cheerful grin, hoping to ward off his questions, but, like Myron, there was no guarantee he'd cooperate.

"Okay, ladies. We've done things your way and nothing's happened," he said, stopping at their table. "What are we waiting for?"

"Except for the family members and personal friends who were here at the prewedding party, we're waiting for everyone to leave," Ellie explained, though she'd already given him the drill. "I expect your men to help Julio escort the extra baggage out, say in another fifteen minutes or so. When the last nonguest leaves, we'll go inside, where Tomas is setting up the living room."

"Good thing, because I'm freezing," said Viv. "I can't believe it's the middle of July and there's such a chill in the air."

"How about if you send a couple of your men inside to help Tomas start the fire?" Ellie asked Wheeling. "That will warm things up and give people a reason to stay. We're going to tell the family Arlene has a personal message for them and ask them to remain as a show of respect."

Wheeling tipped his head at Levy, and the detective took off to do, Ellie hoped, what she asked.

"Okay, now what?" Wheeling ground out.

"Jeez, put a lid on it, will you?" ordered Viv. "This isn't going to be easy for any of us. Ellie has a plan, which she's told you about, but there's no guarantee it will work."

"Since it's about the most ridiculous plan I've ever heard, there's definitely no guarantee it will work." The detective loomed over them, his large frame standing firm against the Atlantic wind. "Look, Ms. Engleman. I'm going along with this dog and pony show for one simple reason: because Captain Carmody told Agent Bond you were an okay sort who knew what she was doing. That's the only stamp of approval you have here, and it's fading fast. Let's get a move on, and not waste any more of my force's time."

Ellie smothered a snarky comment and gazed up at the crowd on the terrace, where she saw women hugging their jackets close, while men circled around them as if protecting them from the wind. If they stayed out here any longer, someone was sure to invite themselves inside. When that happened, the entire throng would troop through the door and she'd never get to act three.

"Okay, fine," she said, standing. She opened the gate to the dog pen and released the five dogs. "You guys know what to do," she whispered, bending down to scratch her boy's ears. "Take your places."

The dogs scampered up the steps, moving guests out of the way. Rosa saw the canine commotion and nodded to the caterers, who began clearing trays and dismantling the bar. Julio and Tomas stood in the doorway and refused anyone who wasn't one of the select few to come into the house.

Evan McCready hugged Arlene, then clapped his hands. "We'd like to thank you all for coming. Please follow the police escort down the stairs and around to your cars. The kitchen entrance is for the family only."

People on the deck grumbled a variety of complaints. Some needed to get warm, others wanted a restroom, and a few were just plain rude, but Tomas and Julio held firm and, with the help of the officers, managed to get the nonguests moving in the right direction.

Dr. Bordowski and Uncle Mickey, who'd been huddled near a bar setup, headed toward the stairs, but Terry and Maria blocked their escape. "Ms. Millman wants you both to stay. She considers you family," said Terry.

The doctor and pharmacist appeared confused, but did as they were told and followed almost-aunts Connie and Elsie through the terrace door with Rudy, T, and the Bostons on their heels.

Chapter 19

Ellie followed the group into the living room. Once the dogs had settled into a five-pooch throw rug in front of the fireplace, she gave the nod and the girls blocked the exits with the police close behind.

"I have more men outside making sure the gawkers leave, just like you asked. They'll wait in their cars until something interesting happens," said Wheeling, walking behind her. "And 'interesting' better happen soon."

"Give me a minute," Ellie told him, scanning the room. The impressive fireplace, with its brightly burning gas logs, took up almost one entire wall. Tomas sat on the hearth, guarding Myron, who perched on his stand like a king surveying his subjects. Viv stood on the opposite side of the fireplace, chatting with Mickey and Dr. Bordowski as if they were old friends.

The four R cousins huddled on the sofa, with Aunt Miriam and Aunt Connie sitting across from them on rattan chairs. Uncle Scott, Faith, Christian, and Aunt

Elsie were clustered near the foyer doorway to the right of Ellie and Wheeling. And she found Detective Levy posted in a far corner, taking everything in.

"Excuse me." Cousin Faith, a tall, thin blonde wearing Donna Karan, sneaked up on her from the side. "We really need to be going. What's so important that Arlene can't say it in a phone call or a text message?"

"Give her a chance to gather her thoughts. This won't take long," Ellie assured her.

Aunt Elsie trundled over with Coco in her arms. "Here's my darling," she said, holding the dog to her cheek. "She can't wait to be included in your daily walking schedule."

Cupping the dog's chin, Ellie grinned at the snow-white teacup Poodle. "Coco is a cutie." She spotted Aunt Connie. "But what about Greta?"

"Be thankful Connie left her at home. That dog is a menace. She spent the day jumping on the kitchen counters to look for food." Elsie gave her Poodle a kiss. "Coco was so traumatized she had accidents all day long."

Ellie held back an eye roll. She was going to have her hands full with—

"Ms. Engleman? I believe you have something important to do right now," Wheeling said, breaking into the conversation.

She graced the detective with a frown. "Sorry, Elsie. We'll talk later. Why don't you take a seat and get comfortable? This should be quick." Turning, she said to Wheeling, "Where is Agent Bond? Viv left a message on his cell, telling him to be here."

"He's here. You just don't see him," Wheeling said, his tone snarky. "Now let's get this show on the road."

Ellie scoured the room for Arlene, whom she found standing near the entry to the back hall with Vanessa, Evan, and Rosa. "Wait here, and please don't do anything until I give the signal."

She aimed for the McCreadys with her fingers crossed. "Are you ready to play your part?" she asked Arlene when she reached them.

"I'll do my best." Arlene looked at her parents. "Can you stand nearby for moral support?"

"We'll do whatever you need us to," said Vanessa, taking her daughter's hand. "Come on. Let's get you settled. Then we'll move out of the way."

Ellie heaved a deep breath. Things were taking shape, just as she planned, and her time to act was drawing near. She'd tried to talk Viv into handling this end of it, but couldn't get her to agree. After checking her pocket for M&Ms, she crossed the room with the McCreadys and took her spot next to Myron.

Arlene stood ready on the other side of the parrot's perch and Evan clapped his hands. "Excuse me, everyone, but my daughter would like a few minutes of your time."

Arlene cleared her throat and glanced at the family crowd. Most of the group had closed ranks, while Viv followed the plan and edged Dr. Bordowski and Uncle Mickey to the center of the room.

"I'd like to thank all of you for coming tonight. I know the weather's been lousy and traffic is terrible this time of year, so if anyone wants to stay over, please feel free to do so."

"Elsie and I can't, dear," Aunt Connie announced. "There's no one home to take care of Greta, but thank you for offering."

Arlene tossed her a smile, then said, "I've asked you here because I need your help. I've thought and thought about the night Martin was murdered, and since all of you were here, I assume you've been thinking about it, too. It was an epic event for our family, and when I learned the truth of Martin's business dealings, well, there was no way I could leave things as they were."

"No one here thinks you took part in his illegal activities," said Miriam. "We'd never believe that of you."

Arlene inhaled a breath. "Thanks for the vote of confidence, but there's more. When the police decided the killer was someone at the party, I simply couldn't accept it. Who here would want Martin dead?" She glanced at Detective Wheeling. "The officers gathered evidence as best they could, but when they arrested Tomas, I felt positive they had the wrong man. And that's why I asked for assistance from another source."

She focused on Ellie. "Ms. Engleman has become a friend and a confidante, and she kindly offered to put my mind at ease by performing her own investigation of that night."

"I thought you said she was a dog walker," cousin Christian reminded them. "Now you're saying she works with the police?"

"Not exactly, but she does have investigative experience, and a lot of good ideas about how to find the real killer." She gave a nod. "I'll leave the rest of this talk to her."

Ellie swallowed a nervous chirp. There'd been so many disasters in her life when she performed before a crowd that she'd stopped counting. But just as she'd done for Flora Steinman this past fall, she put her fear aside and came to the aid of a friend.

"Please bear with me while I conduct a little experiment," she began. "Myron—"

"Is a parrot," quipped one of the R people, grinning. The guests broke out in laughter. "Don't tell us you think he was the killer."

"No, but he knows who the murderer is," Ellie shot back.

That seemed to quiet everyone. She locked gazes with Viv, then eyed Dr. Bordowski and Uncle Mickey, who were standing beside her. "As I said a moment ago, please give me a chance to—"

"Awwwk! Let's get this show on the road! Awwwk! Move 'em in, move 'em out! Raaaaw-hiiiide! Awwwk!" Myron squawked the theme song of an ancient Clint Eastwood television show, ending with the exact sound of a cracking whip.

She spun around and held out a candy. If the African gray was ready to cooperate, she didn't want to lose him.

The parrot snatched the M&M in his claw, popped it in his beak, and crunched. *"Aah! That's more like it. Awwwk!"*

She ignored the tittering laughter and wisecracks from the audience and held up a finger. "Myron, remember what we talked about earlier today?" She passed him another M&M. "Marty?"

"Awwwk! Marty, I'm gonna kill you if you steal from me, Marty! Awwwk!"

The guests hushed their comments, looked around the room, and focused on Uncle Mickey. When he saw their questioning eyes, he turned pale. "Hey, that's not me. I'd never hurt my best friend."

"Awwwk! Don't make me hurt you, Marty. Awwwk!"

The family gasped when they heard the phrase, repeated in Uncle Mickey's voice. Ellie passed Myron another candy. As she turned, Mickey shook off Viv's hand and tried to slip past her, but a yell from the hall stopped him.

"Oh, for God's sake, please get this nonsense over with!"

Dressed in red from head to toe and carrying an easel, Adrianne marched into the living room. Pushing past Viv, Mickey, and Dr. Bordowski, she smacked the easel down in front of the cluster of dogs and unveiled her portrait.

"This is what Marty Kent was all about. I was the woman he wanted in his life." Spinning on her four-inch spiked heels, she faced her sister. "And I'm tired of hiding the truth."

"Awwwk! Truth be told, Marty, you're a dead man. Awwwk!"

Ellie passed Myron another M&M, happy to hear he was still on track. As for Adrianne . . . She caught Evan's attention and asked for help.

He rushed to his middle daughter and grabbed her forearm. "Adrianne, stop. You're ruining everything."

She wrenched away from him, the pupils of her eyes dilated to a glassy glare. "Me, ruining everything?" Sneering, she pointed at Tomas. "When that little grease ball killed the man I love?"

Tomas stood, his hands clenched. The canines continued to circle. "Marty was the only man I ever loved," Adrianne shouted again, shoving the dogs aside with her feet. "And he loved this painting."

"Awwwk! Marty loved that self-portrait. Awwwk! It held the secret to his success. Awwwk!"

Ellie gave herself a mental head slap. How could it

have taken her so long to realize what the comment really meant?

Rudy rose on his hind legs and rested his paws on her calf. *"The DEA is lookin' for a record book. And we know where it is."*

"This is too much," said Christian, standing. "You don't need us. You need a television crew to film this circus."

"Darling, really," cooed Miriam. "I'm having such a good time. I've never been to one of those murder-night-at-the-dinner-theater plays before."

"I'm gonna murder you, Marty. Awwwk! Keep on cheatin' me and it's gonna happen. Awwwk!"

The guests stared at Myron, then returned their gazes to Uncle Mickey, who tried to back away. "I didn't kill him, I tell you! It was Sabrina."

His confession brought the entire room alive. The Bostons yowled. Rudy and T jumped against the easel and knocked it to the floor.

Adrianne screamed and dropped to her knees. Myron swooped down from his perch and landed on her head.

Rudy and T darted in and out of the crowd, fighting Adrianne to gain control of the portrait, while the cops broke rank and ordered everyone to calm down.

Ellie held her throbbing temple. It appeared the painting was the key—it had to hold the record book Agent Bond wanted. And had she heard right? Did Uncle Mickey just announce that Sabrina Bordowski killed Martin Kent?

Sam parked a block down from the house he suspected was holding the memorial service. His ride here from downtown Manhattan had taken over three hellish hours. He hoped Ellie would appreciate the trouble he'd gone through when she saw him. Once his boss insisted that he take some vacation time, he couldn't resist making the trip to see her in the Hamptons.

He showed his badge to the cop sitting in the first black-and-white lined up in front of the humongous home. The officer stepped out, checked Sam's credentials, and walked by his side, giving the high sign to the police in three other cars.

Salty air blew in off the Atlantic and he hunched over, assessing the estate in the growing darkness. Ellie said she was staying in a mansion, but he thought she'd been stretching the truth. If this was the kind of money Viv came from, no wonder she had such a kick-ass attitude.

"I thought this was a memorial service. What are you guys doing out here?" he asked them.

"I'm not sure," said his escort. "According to Detective Wheeling—he's the lead on this case—the memorial is a cover for some crazy woman's idea of unmasking the dead guy's real killer. Wheeling is letting her have her way for a while. If nothing happens it was a big waste of time and manpower for the force."

Crazy woman? So Captain Carmody had been right. Ellie was involved in another murder. What the heck did he have to do to get her to follow his rules? Frustrated, he blew out a long breath. He loved her, damn it. How in the hell was he supposed to protect her if she kept getting involved in this stuff?

His escort nodded toward the house. "Looks like something's going on."

Shadows danced in the front windows of the mansion. A racket—barking dogs?—filled the air, and Sam groaned. Didn't it just figure that canines would be involved if Ellie was here?

Inside, a woman shouted and a man yelled in return.

"We're not supposed to go in until Wheeling gives the word," said his escort when they stopped at the bottom of the porch stairs.

Sam heard a loud squawk. Another woman's scream rang out, and he shook his head. "Sounds to me like that's the word."

"I'm not sure—"

"I don't take orders from your boss, so I'll chance a reprimand." He climbed the steps and flung open the door. Edging past a couple of people arguing with the cops, he followed the noise into a huge room rife with screeching civilians, howling dogs, and a shrieking parrot.

He spotted Viv, who saw him and pointed over the head of a woman she was hanging on to like a life preserver. Following the direction of her finger, he spotted a knot of humans and canines scuffling in front of the fireplace.

The closer he got to the mosh pit, the quicker he knew the identity of at least one of the wrestlers. Ellie's back was to him, but her curly copper hair blazed in the firelight. She and the other woman were scrabbling over something on the floor while Rudy, the small mutt Viv owned, and three black-and-white dogs darted in and out between them. To top it all, the downed woman was trying to get a squawking parrot off her head.

Suddenly, the woman Viv had been struggling with broke free and flew into the center of the melee, diving for what appeared to be a painting.

When Ellie stood to let the two women fight it out, he

finally got a good look at her. What the hell had happened to her beautiful face?

Viv's ex-prisoner stood and held up a small notebook, her eyes filled with triumph. Ellie lunged at her, but the woman tossed the book into the fire.

A big burly guy with a face like a bulldog stormed toward the fireplace and Sam followed him.

Ellie yelled, "Tomas, turn off the gas," and the kid standing next to the hearth made for the side of the fireplace.

When the bulldog shoved Ellie, Sam had had enough. Grabbing the man's shoulder, he spun the guy around and clocked him, throwing him to the floor.

It was then Ellie realized he was there. Her eyes filled with tears, she made her way through the mass of mutts and fell into his arms.

He held her tight while a tall cop—Wheeling?—stooped to separate the two women. Then another guy, the one Sam had seen propped against the wall on the other side of the fireplace, stepped in, clamped his hand on the fireplace tongs, and spoke to the kid. Between them, they pulled the charred date book from the dying fire.

When the parrot hopped back on his perch, Wheeling closed in on Viv's girl and hauled her to a stand. Pulling her out of the fray, he began reading the Miranda rights. In only a few minutes the police brought everything under control.

Ellie leaned against him, her breath ragged, her body tense, and he smothered a laugh. "I came here hoping to surprise you, but I don't think there's anything I can do to top this."

Drawing away, she gulped for air. "I was just trying to

help Arlene and Rosa. That's all." She straightened her shoulders. "I had no idea it would turn into—"

"A brawl?"

"What? No! A—"

"Riot?"

Ignoring him, she dropped to her knees, hugged her dog, and patted the others milling around her. "You five were great. You did just what I asked you to do—except for the painting. How did you know what was back there?"

Sam stepped away and waited while Ellie held the same one-sided conversation she usually did with her pooch. She never seemed to mind it when people said she was crazy, so it didn't pay to try to stop her.

He pulled out his shield and walked to the crowd of officials, who were huddled around the beefy guy he'd downed, the younger man who'd rescued the date book, and the woman Wheeling was arresting.

Ellie left the dogs and walked next to him. Loud sobbing made them both turn their heads. The woman in red was still on her knees, hugging the shredded painting and wailing like a banshee.

"What the heck is she crying about?" he asked Ellie.

"I think she just realized she wasn't the love of the dead man's life. He used her precious painting as a hiding place for records of his drug transactions."

"This place is a zoo. Are you all right?"

Stepping closer, she snuggled against his chest. "I am now."

It was then Wheeling sidled over and smiled grimly. "So you're the poor Joe in Ms. Engleman's life." He shook his head. "You have my deepest sympathy."

"You always run a three-ring circus when you wrap up a murder investigation?" Sam asked in return.

Wheeling cocked his head in Ellie's direction. "You can thank your girlfriend for this over-the-top performance. We had nothing to do with it."

"But she helped you nab the right suspects, correct?"

The detective shrugged. "Looks like." He still had a hand on the woman he'd arrested. "But it's going to take a while to sort it all out."

Ellie leaned back in the sofa. For the past hour, the McCready family members had been questioned, one at a time, by the police. Though it wasn't the lengthy grilling they'd received the night Dr. Kent had died, it ate up plenty of time.

With Ellie's encouragement, Viv had spent most of the evening with her sisters and her parents. She imagined their talk would focus on the best place for Adrianne to take her "private vacation" for the next three months. Knowing that if she disagreed she'd be immediately cut loose from her security blanket, Adrianne would take the deal, Ellie figured.

And as much as she disliked the middle sister, she had to admit that Adrianne's idiotic escapade had done some good. Without that painting, Agent Bond might never have found the elusive record book that incriminated Dr. Bordowski and Michael Forrest, as well as a couple of unscrupulous pharmaceutical reps.

Detective Levy and a cadre of cops had taken Dr. Bordowski and Uncle Mickey out with orders to book them both on murder. Now, with the living room in disarray, all five dogs were alongside her on the couch.

Rudy dozed at her thigh, Mr. T was next to him, and the Boston Terriers slept at the end.

Somewhere in the back of the house, a door slammed. A moment later Rosa and her daughters arrived and began putting things to rights. "You were so cool," Maria told her for the tenth time that evening. "What a great way to capture the real killer."

Ellie smiled, but kept mum. She'd tried to explain to the girls, and Rosa and Julio, and Tomas, and anyone else who would listen, that she hadn't planned on Adrianne carting the painting in, and that's what really opened things up.

But no one wanted to hear it. They were positive she was the star of the night, and Viv, too, for corralling the doctor and holding her in place when the brawl broke out.

Viv, of course, took her kudos with a bow, and gave Ellie a cat-who-ate-the-cream smile whenever their eyes met.

Sam, on the other hand, figured out exactly what had happened and razzed her about her big unveiling. He'd gone down the hallway a while ago to lend the local cops a hand, and she hadn't seen him since.

"Ms. Ellie," said Rosa, standing beside her. "How can I thank you for saving my son?" She dabbed a tissue over her damp cheek. "You are an angel."

"You don't owe me a thing." She ruffled Rudy's ears to let him know he was the real hero of the night. "Just take care of Arlene. She's going to need you and Julio in the next couple of months."

"*Sí*, we will. But Ms. Adrianne, she is not so lucky. She is carrying a lot of pain, and she still lets the bad medicine rule her."

"That's why Arlene forgave her. And her parents are going to see to it she gets the help she needs."

Dressed in his usual khakis with a chocolate brown knit shirt, Agent Bond entered the living room from the hallway. He'd been in the background for most of the evening, but he had retrieved Dr. Kent's personal records, exactly what he needed to conclude his investigation.

"I guess you're feeling pretty proud of yourself," he said when he got to the sofa.

"I'm not the kind of person who says 'I told you so' very often, but . . ."

"You were right. About Tomas, at least. Something tells me you were as surprised as everyone else to find that Sabrina Bordowski was the killer."

"Tell him you knew it all along," Rudy whispered, waking from his nap.

She put a hand over his muzzle. "I figured it was either her or Mickey. When he ratted her out, it made things easier."

Jim put his hands in his pockets. "I met your boyfriend. He seems like a nice guy. And a good cop."

"He's a doofus dick, just like you."

Tightening her fingers around her boy's snout, Ellie grinned. "We think so."

"And you're happy living together?"

"Not me. I wanna—"

She clamped her hand tighter and gave Rudy a shake. "So far, so good."

Agent Bond's lips thinned. He pulled out his shield protector, removed a card, and passed it to her. "If that ever changes, call me." Bending down, he kissed the knot on her temple. "And take care of yourself."

He left the room with the same cocky attitude he'd had all week long, and Ellie sighed. *Men!*

A moment later Wheeling and Sam strode into the room.

"Looks like it's all over but the shouting," said Wheeling.

She broke out in a smile. "And everything lines up?"

"I'll leave your friend to give you the report. I'm on a hunt for Ms. Millman." He glanced around the room. "I take it she's upstairs with her family?"

"I think so," said Ellie, jutting her chin toward the foyer. "You know the way."

Wheeling left, and Sam scoured the dog-encrusted sofa. When he snapped his fingers, Mr. T and the Bostons took off after the detective and Rudy jumped on Ellie's thighs. Sam sat and put his arm around her shoulder. "You sure do know how to have a good time on vacation."

Still holding Agent Bond's card in her hand, she nestled into Sam's hard, warm chest. "I could have done without the murder, but everything else was fun."

"We'd have a better end to our vacation if Detective Demento left for home," grumped Rudy. *"The sooner the better."*

She scratched a furrow down her yorkiepoo's back and around to his belly. "Viv says you're spending the night."

"I'd like to."

"She said Arlene's offered us a room upstairs with a big comfy bed, a triple-sized shower, and a great view of the ocean."

"Sounds nice." He pulled back and gazed at her face. "Don't take this the wrong way, but you look like a war mask from some now-defunct African tribe." He touched her temple. "The DEA agent, Jim Bond, told me how it happened. Does it hurt?"

"Not so much. The way I understand it, Michael Forrest was the steam engine that ran me down."

"So Wheeling said. Apparently both Forrest and Dr. Bordowski wanted that book, and each of them argued with Kent the night of the murder. I gathered from listening to Bordowski and Mickey Mouse argue that timing was the key. Dr. Kent had people coming after him one by one." Sam held her hand. "First that Mexican kid, then Forrest, then Bordowski. She's into some martial art and she confessed the killing was an accident. Bordowski broke in on him and Mickey Mouse arguing and gave Kent a shove to break them apart. Kent spun backward and tripped on Mickey's foot. Next thing she knew, he fell and smacked his head, and that was it."

"That part had me confused. Adrianne practiced martial arts, too, Tomas was a street fighter, and Forrest had already mowed me down. The way I first figured it, any one of them was strong enough to push the doc backward and kill him."

He cupped her chin. "I won't repeat this because I know it'll come back to bite me in the ass, but I'm proud of you."

"Hey! What about me?"

"Don't forget Rudy," she said, gulping down a breath. This moment was a high point in their relationship. She wanted to be certain she had it right. "You're really proud of me?"

"Don't get too complacent. There's a lot about this ordeal that has me ticked." He turned her head so they were eye to eye and began counting out her errors.

"One: You didn't tell me there'd been a murder. Two: You decided to investigate it on your own. Three: You put yourself in danger and almost—"

"Viv helped, and so did Rudy."

"Same difference, as far as I see it." He put a finger on her lips when she started to protest. "I don't like it when you put yourself in the line of fire, yet that's where you always manage to end up."

"But Rosa needed my help, and so did Arlene. Viv asked me to get involved. How could I say no to her?"

Sam's lips quirked, but he remained silent.

Rudy raised his head. *"You two gonna talk all night, or can we go to bed?"*

"Did you bring your overnight bag?" Ellie asked. Rudy was correct. It was late, and they were beat.

"It's in the car. Maybe I should go get it?"

She grinned. "Maybe you should."

He leaned back and stared at her, running his thumb along her bump, then following the bruise down her nose to her cheek. "Too bad I didn't know about this when I decked that Mickey Mouse slug. I would have given him what he did to you, only double."

"That was my job, bozo-brain," said Rudy.

When he jerked to a sit and glared at Sam, Ellie set him on the floor, then stood and pulled Sam to his feet. "Get your bag and meet me upstairs. And wait until you see this room . . . this house . . . the beach. It's amazing. Can you stay a few days?"

"The captain said I was free for three. That gives us time to explore the Hamptons." He headed for the foyer. "Just you and me." He gave Rudy a look. "Alone."

"So says the Defective Detective," her boy grumped.

Sam grabbed her and drew her to his chest. "I've

missed you. Since you left, I learned that I don't like being alone."

Dipping his head, he gave her the welcome kiss she'd been hoping for, tender yet demanding. Ellie tingled from her head to her toes. Crushing Jim Bond's card in her hand, she let it fall to the floor. She already had two perfect men in her life; she didn't need a third.

They separated but stood forehead to forehead, breathing in tandem. "You dropped something," he said, his eyes searching the tile.

"It's not important. Rosa or the girls will pick it up." She inhaled a breath. "Go get your bag. It's time for bed."

Sam left and she headed up the stairs with Rudy at her heels. "We're lucky. This room has a king-sized bed."

"Where's Detective Demento supposed to sleep?"

"You're cute when you're cranky." They talked as they walked down the hall. "I'm going to get some stuff from our old room. You can either stay there for the night with Viv and T, or join Sam and me. Arlene has a nice fluffy dog bed nestled in a corner of the new bedroom."

Rudy waited while she opened and closed drawers, gathering her things. When she was finished, she squatted in front of him. "Have you decided where you want to sleep?"

"I can't believe you're askin' me that," he gruffed. *"Where else do I have to be, but with you?"*

Ellie raised her eyes to the ceiling. Her boy always knew the right question and the right answer to everything. The Q-and-A that brought tears to her eyes and tugged at her heart. No matter how things turned out with Sam, Rudy was her fella. The only male she couldn't live without.

Dropping to her knees, she pulled him near and he licked her cheek. *"Are you cryin' again?"*

"Of course I am." She swallowed a sob. "You are my guy, forever and always, and no one can take your place." She kissed the top of his head. "Remember that forever."

"Ahh, that's what I want to hear." He slurped his tongue across her fingers. *"Lead the way to our room. Detective Demento is gonna love that doggie bed."*

Epilogue

It was Labor Day weekend, the end of a long summer of excitement. Ellie and Viv sat outside their usual Joe to Go, enjoying Caramel Bliss coffee and blueberry muffins while Mr. T and Rudy huddled under the table nibbling biscuits from Sara Studebaker's new doggie bakery, the Spoiled Hound, located right next door.

"Look what arrived in yesterday's mail," said Viv, holding up a postcard. "Arlene's in Mexico with Rosa, Julio, and Tomas. The girls stayed home to take care of Myron and the dogs."

She passed the card over and Ellie read the note:

Hi, Vivie,

Let Ellie know that Tomas and Julio fulfilled their *manda* by crawling on their hands and knees up the center aisle of the Catedral Metropolitana as a thank-you for Tomas being cleared of murder charges. Rosa and I cried like babies as we stood and watched. You and Ellie should have been there.

Love,
Arlene

"Sounds intense, doesn't it?" asked Viv, returning the card to her bag.

"It certainly does." Ellie sipped her coffee. "I don't think I told you—Rosa promised me something special for helping to free her son."

"Really? What was that?"

"An entire year of prayers, just for me. I'm covered until next summer." She grinned. "I told Sam and he went ballistic. Said he was the only one who would cover me. Then he told me I couldn't leave the city again unless he was with me."

"And you're going to buy that?"

"Of course not. Wherever I go, Rudy will be with me, and he's all I need for protection."

"You got that right," said a voice from under the table.

"Protection?" Viv rolled her eyes. "Are you planning another murder investigation?"

"Who, me? Absolutely not." She sighed. "Just like I didn't plan this last one."

"I already explained to Sam about a dozen times that you only got involved because Arlene, Rosa, and I begged you." Viv drank the last of her coffee and set her mug on the table. "But I don't think he believed me."

"He did. He just didn't want to hear it." Hoping her smile wasn't too smug, she peeled the paper cup from her muffin. "Arlene sent me something, too."

Viv leaned back in her chair. "How dare you hold out on me?"

"I wasn't holding out, I was waiting. We haven't exactly spent much time together this week."

"I know and I'm sorry. I had to go to that big animal rescue fund-raiser with Dave. Then there was the company emergency meeting. I had to take an important client to dinner, and on and on. There was no way I could miss any of it."

"I understand, and it was fine."

"Enough about me. Let me in on what Arlene sent you."

Ellie dug in her tote bag and pulled out a manila envelope. After opening it, she drew out a few sheets of fine paper and passed the first page to Viv. "Isn't it beautiful?"

Viv held the astrological chart at arm's length. "Wow. Big sis did a great job. You do realize something this involved and intricate takes a couple of days to compile?"

"I do," said Ellie, thrilled that Arlene would spend so much time on her. "She was a doll to do it."

"It's nice to see that she's living up to her promise to change her ways. She's even back to talking to Adrianne."

"How's that going? Has middle sister moved out? Found a job? Got her life in order?"

"In a manner of speaking." Viv returned the chart. "I don't want to talk about Ms. Bossy Boots. Let's hear what Arlene had to say about you."

Ellie held up the first of three more pages. "I'm skipping over the negative stuff, because the way Arlene explains it, I should focus on the positive and do all I can to make it happen."

"I already know your quirks, pal. I'll listen to whatever you want to tell me."

"Okay, here goes." She cleared her throat. "Ambitious, courageous, impulsive, and enterprising, you are a free spirit and you must be first in everything you do. Very self-confident and passionate, you radiate positive energy. Quite gregarious, you enjoy being with people and their animals." She grinned. "How true is that?"

"So far, so good. Continue please."

Wriggling in her seat, she set her elbows on the table and held up the page. "Your mind is curious and inquisitive, always seeking information on a wide variety of topics. You are known for being blunt, honest, and truthful, even if it hurts your best friend."

Viv cocked her head, her smile wide. "You'd never do that to me, would you?"

"I would if it was for your own good."

"Hmm, okay, go on."

"Mmm . . . mmm . . . mmm . . . nothing you need to know," Ellie muttered, moving to the next page. "Oh, yeah, I love this part. Idealistic by nature, you will be in the forefront of humanitarian attempts to help the 'underdog,' whether canine or human. And you are comfortable with the philosophy of improving the lot of those in need of assistance."

"Has Sam heard that one?"

"I read it to him, but I don't think he paid it much attention."

"I can see why. It's exactly what he tells you not to do."

"Too bad for him. He'll just have to get used to it," Ellie said with a shrug. "From here on out, Arlene gets sort of personal: Ellie, with regard to your forecast, you have an array of fortunate configurations during the upcoming year. This promises good karma and protection throughout your life."

There was that word again, Ellie thought. *Karma.* "Good luck will abound, and whatever path you choose will consummate in a well-deserved positive outcome. It is an especially great time for collaborations of any sort, if you relax and go with the flow."

"Collaborate? Are you thinking of writing a book or something?"

"Not that I know of. Now, hush, because there's more." She sat straighter in her chair. "The only caveat is you may feel overwhelmed at times by the unexpected twists and turns. With the planet Uranus transiting your ascendant, while Saturn remains in your seventh house of partnerships, don't be surprised by a few shocking developments. Your life will change, never to be the same, so enjoy the roller-coaster ride."

"That sounds so exciting, I'm jealous," said Viv. "I'm going to phone Arlene as soon as she gets back from Mexico and tell her to hurry up with my chart."

"There's more." She peered at Viv over the page. "You ready?"

"As I'll ever be. Now hurry up and finish."

Ellie heaved a breath. She'd read this bit a hundred times and still wasn't sure if she should take it seriously. "Don't ask questions until I'm finished, okay?" When Viv nodded, she moved on. "Perhaps you should sit down, before reading further—"

"Yikes!"

Ellie raised one eyebrow. "You need to know that I did not read the rest of this to Sam in case he decided to pay attention." She cleared her throat again. "Here's the rest: You just might decide to elope. Yes, I said elope (and wake up in Vegas?). Keep breathing for the next revelation. There is a high probability of some unplanned new 'additions' to your family."

"Oh, my God." Viv pushed away from the table. "You're getting married and you're going to get pregnant?"

"Not if I have anything to say about it."

"Vivian, what did I tell you? Zip it, please. It gets more complicated from here." She blew out another breath. "Indeed, expect the Rudster to enjoy being a wonderful big brother, because there could be the arrival of a little addition to your life."

"Say what?" came a voice from beneath the table again.

Tapping Rudy with the toe of her sneaker, she held up her hand and forged ahead. "This is all Arlene, too: Before you say uh-oh and start hyperventilating while furiously chewing on your lower lip, take comfort in knowing the year promises to be exciting and unforgettable. Far from boring, the next twelve months will be chock-full of startling surprises. Your life will be expanding in many directions, while you remain under the umbrella of Jupiter's protection." Ellie wiped a tear from her eye. "You will find fulfillment and be surrounded by love beyond your wildest imagination."

It was Viv's turn to blow out a breath. "Wow, that is so romantic—all except the part about the baby, I mean."

"She didn't ever say it would be a baby, just an addition to my family."

"Well, who else might it be?"

"Well, it won't be me."

She gave Rudy another poke. “An addition might mean I’ll meet a long-lost cousin, something like that.”

“Only time will tell,” Viv said with a smile. “I’d hang on to that prediction in case you have to refer to it later. Sounds like big things are going to happen.” She glanced at the empty coffee mugs. “How about if I buy the next round?”

“Fine with me,” Ellie said, “and more napkins, please.”

When Viv was safely inside the shop, she felt a paw on her knee. “What can I do for you, big guy?”

“You can tell me that you and the dopey dick are not gettin’ hitched,” Rudy said, his voice a plaintive whine.

She pushed back her chair and he jumped in her lap. “I don’t think that’s going to happen anytime soon, so stop fussing about it.”

He gave her cheek a sloppy lick. *“And what about that addition-to-your-family crack? I’m not exactly a kid-friendly dog, you know.”*

She ran her fingers down his back. “I know, and I don’t think that will happen, either.”

“You and me, we’re already a couple, a duo . . . the Dynamic Duo like Batman and Robin. There’s no room in our lives for anybody else.”

“That isn’t true.” She scratched his favorite spot, the underside of his chin. “You found room in your heart for Sam.”

He gruffed out a laugh. *“So you think. I’m just tolerating him until you get smart and kick him out.”*

“Things are going just fine between me and Sam, so don’t get your hopes up. And if someone else comes along that deserves a place in our hearts and our lives, we’re going to welcome them gladly, you understand?”

When he didn't answer, she tugged at his ear. "Understand?"

"Do I have to?" he grumped.

"You do."

"But I'll still be your number-one guy, right? No one else is gonna take my place . . . ever?"

"No one will ever take your place, I promise." Heaving a sigh, he nuzzled her neck, and she cradled him in her arms. "It's you and me forever, big guy. I love you best."

Read on for a special preview of
another Dog Walker mystery by Judi McCoy

Fashion Faux Paw

Available now from Obsidian.

Ellie hoisted her packed tote bag over her shoulder, keeping Rudy's leash in her left hand. Then she stepped into one of the cavernous rooms that had been prepared to ready the participants for New York City's most glamorous event.

She still couldn't believe she was a part of the grand finale of Fashion Week. The winner of this competition, the one she'd been specially hired for, would capture a one-hundred-thousand-dollar prize and a two-year contract with Nola Morgan Design, a manufacturer of high-end women's ready-to-wear.

Thirty-five hopefuls had submitted their idea of what today's ordinary woman might wear while at work or out on the town. Four finalists were chosen to compete by the CFDA and the contest would be the culmination of Fashion Week.

As one of the models asked to strut the catwalk, Patti Fallgrave, Ellie's client, had an in with the committee, and she'd finagled a great job for her dog walker friend. Ellie was now in charge of the models' canines, and would watch over them while their owners were prepped for the show.

She scanned the mass of people and noted that most of the women appeared to walk, talk, and act untouchable as they went about their business for opening day. Those who were the tallest had to be the models, especially since they were the ones who looked as if they hadn't eaten since the past millennium.

And the rest? She'd bet her last dime that most of the hairstylists, makeup artists, designers, and runners participating in the show were on the same lettuce leaf and one-cracker-a-day diet.

"Geez. Ya think anybody in this crowd knows how to swallow more than one piece of kibble at a sitting?" Rudy asked.

She smiled down at him, her voice low. "We'll talk about it later. For now, let's just find our spot and stay out of trouble."

"Hey, trouble is our middle name. We live for trouble. In fact, we're trouble experts. We—"

She ignored his rambling and jerked on his lead for good measure. After studying the mob of serious fashionistas, Ellie glanced at her work clothes. Her job for the next few days was all dog, so she'd dressed in preparation for poop stains, pee stains, food stains, puke stains, and anything else a furry, four-legged friend might have a paw in creating.

She wore a peach-colored sweater with no designer label, machine washable, and Sketchers Kinetic Response shoes, perfect for walking her usual ten-mile-per-day route. Her special touch for this week-long event was her Calvin Klein ultimate skinny jeans, which she'd found on a half-price mark-down rack. Her friend Viv had insisted it was the least she should wear to work the country's biggest fashion event, and she'd grudgingly agreed.

"'Scuse me," a voice said when someone pushed past her with an overloaded clothing rack.

She darted out of the way and bumped into a girl carrying a stack of shoe boxes. The top box hit the ground and Ellie bent to pick it up. She set the shoe box on top of the pile, and the person behind the cardboard mountain mumbled a "thank you" and stumbled on through the crowd.

"Ellie! Hey, Ellie! I'm over here."

Raising her head, she spotted Patti Fallgrave waving at her from across the room. At six feet tall, the supermodel was easy to find in a normal crowd, but it wasn't so simple locating her in this group of towering pencil-thin figures.

She edged through the busy room, dodging worker-bees with dress racks and half-naked women standing on podiums waiting to be clothed. "I'm exhausted just watching all that's going on," she said when she reached her. "Is it always like this?"

Patti cradled Cheech, one of two Chihuahua brothers Ellie favored, in her left arm and clasped Ellie's elbow in her free hand. "This?" She laughed. "It's nothing compared to showtime. Just be careful of Rudy. Most of the people working this scene love animals, but they're not used to having them underfoot. That's why they hired you."

They dodged another clothes trolley, walked past a group of mirrored tables and chairs and stopped at an open area holding a stretchy metal gate formed into an eight-foot-in-diameter pen. "This is the best I could set up for you," the supermodel said.

After sitting on a chair wedged between a watercooler and a long table filled with fruit, veggies, power bars, and high-energy drinks, she pointed to a corner. "This is just one of several snack tables set up throughout the show. And around that corner is a patch of fake grass, where the dogs can do their business if there's an emergency. Beyond that is a door to the outside, so you can come and go as needed."

Ellie took a seat in a nearby chair and heaved a breath. After resting her tote bag on a knee she peered at the underside of the table, half filled with more food and drinks. "And I guess I can store my stuff down there?"

"Absolutely. Just be aware there's no security guard at this entrance. I'd make sure my cash and credit cards were tucked in my pocket instead of in the bag, because anyone can stop by and start digging. If you ask, they'll tell you they're looking through their bag, but it could be yours."

Ellie shook her head. "They can look in my bag all they want, but the only thing they'll find is canine gear. I brought gourmet biscuits, extra leashes, folding water bowls, a couple of old blankets, and anything else I thought the dogs might need that their owners would forget."

"Perfect. And guess what?" Patti raised an expertly arched brow. "I got you a runner. Kitty's around here somewhere and she can't wait to be your assistant."

Ellie smothered a smile. She had an assistant named Kitty and they were herding a group of dogs? There had to be a joke in there somewhere.

"And the models and their babies?"

"They'll be here soon. The designers are already on site, of course, but they have yet to see the dogs in person. All they know is the breed."

Patti handed her Cheech, checked her watch, and

tucked her own bag under the table. "I have a fitting for a Vena Cava evening gown, so I have to run." She stood. "I guess your first job would be to watch my baby. His travel bed is in my bag. Just get ready to meet some huge personalities while you wait for the models to drop off their dogs. If you're into people-watching, this is the place to be."

When she sauntered away with her shiny dark brown hair swinging down her slender back, there was no doubt in Ellie's mind that her client was a supermodel. Patti commanded attention, even when she was dressed down in a casual top and jeans.

"How about you let me sit up there with you? The less time I gotta spend down here with the hairless wonder, the better."

She patted the chair next to her and trained her eyes on the passersby, while Rudy bolted into position and sat at attention. Just then, a tall attractive man arrived on the scene, followed by two assistants, each carrying a huge box. "I'm Jeffery King," he said, grabbing Ellie's hand. "And I have gifts for the models and designers from Nola Morgan Design." He flashed a bright smile. "And you, too, if you're Ellie Engleman."

"That's me," she said, matching his grin. The assistants began unloading and lining up baskets covered in colored plastic wrap on the table. "And those would be the gifts?"

"They would, and you're in charge until my sister gets here, so watch over them carefully. The swag in each basket adds up to about five thousand retail, and every one is tagged for its owner because the items inside were targeted directly for them." He searched the line and picked up a basket wrapped in pale green plastic. "Patti

Fallgrave hand picked the items in yours, so speak to her if you're not happy with your loot."

Ellie held the basket to her chest. "Thanks, and I'll be sure to take care of it. Will you be around or—"

A tiny woman with blond spiky hair and a huge smile rushed over. "I'm Kitty King, and I'm so sorry I'm late" she said, gasping for breath. "I'm your assistant for the next four days."

Two hours later, Ellie finally had the time to study her runner, who was no more than five feet tall and looked to be just out of high school. So far, the diminutive girl had worked her butt off, welcoming models, collecting their dogs, kowtowing to designers, and running errands for whoever needed her. She'd even held a one-sided commentary with Rudy, who had found an out-of-the-way spot under the table and made it his own.

In short, she'd been a breath of fresh air in the middle of high-fashion chaos.

Because it was near noon, things had quieted down, so Ellie asked Kitty to sit with her next to the water cooler. "You seem to know everyone," she said. "Have you worked in this industry long?"

"I've been an assistant for the past three years while I studied at Parsons School of Design. My brother Jeff—"

"The man who delivered the baskets?"

"Right. When he finally got his big break with NMD, the company sponsoring this event, I got a break, too. He's their new Director of Promotions, so he's my boss."

The information had Ellie recalculating Kitty's age. "Do you mind if I ask you another personal question?"

"You want to know how old I am, right?"

Pleased to see that Kitty was smiling, she said, "Sorry. You must get that a lot."

"At least once a week, and I don't mind." When Rudy crawled out from under the table and jumped in her lap, Kitty ruffled his ears. "I mean, I'll probably be happy that I have this baby face in another twenty years or so." She ran a hand through her blond hair. "I'll be twenty-five on my next birthday."

"Wow, that's amazing. And Rudy seems to like you, too, which is a good sign, considering he doesn't cuddle up to just anyone."

Her yorkiepoo gave a groan of contentment under Kitty's gentle hand. *"This chick is too much."*

Unaware of Rudy's positive comment, Kitty said, "Your boy's a cutie, but I'm into all dogs. What about you?" Then she giggled. "Oh, gosh, that was a totally dumb thing to say. Of course, you are. I mean, you make your living working with dogs, so you must love them, right?"

"Dogs are the center of my life," Ellie answered, hoping her sincerity showed. "When I rescued Rudy he rescued me, and he's become my best four-legged friend. I also walk some of the greatest canines in this city. It's a treat being here with little guys, because they're my favorite size."

"Mine, too," Kitty said, scratching Rudy under his chin. "But my building is a no-go on pets. As soon as my designs make money, I'm going to move to a place that will let me have a dog." She heaved a sigh, leaned back in her chair, and surveyed the people still rushing past. "We may be here all night, even though the designers are supposed to be finished with their first piece by four. The initial runway walk is scheduled to close the day at five, but it'll be a miracle if they make it on time."

Ellie'd been hoping to meet someone besides Patti Fallgrave who had an inside track on the fashion business—

someone who could fill her in on industry gossip—and it sounded as if Kitty would be able to do just that. "I guess you know quite a bit about this contest? What it took for the designers to get here and all?"

Kitty glanced at the industry professionals walking around the pen, stopping at the watercooler, grazing the snack table, and interacting with the dogs. "This business is crazy. You'll meet folks from every walk of life here, all hoping for their big break. Each day is different, and I love it that way."

Ellie moved closer. "But not everyone in the industry is pleasant. There's back-biting and smack talk, plus a lot of design theft." Her eyes filled with tears. "Believe me, I know that first hand."